lie
to me

JESS RYDER

Published by Bookouture
An imprint of StoryFire Ltd.
23 Sussex Road, Ickenham, UB10 8PN
United Kingdom
www.bookouture.com

ISBN: 978-1-78681-189-9
eBook ISBN: 978-1-78681-188-2

This book is a work of fiction. Names, characters, businesses,
organizations, places and events other than those clearly in the
public domain, are either the product of the author's imagination
or are used fictitiously. Any resemblance to actual persons, living or
dead, events or locales is entirely coincidental.

For my family

CHAPTER ONE

Me

I've been in Dad's attic for the last two hours. Aching knees on the hard boards. Blackened fingertips; dry, dusty throat. In the single-bulb gloom, my bent shadow looms large on the sloping wall as I survey the scattered contents of an old box marked *Baby clothes*: over-washed towelling onesies, misshapen little bootees; stiff stained bibs still smelling of mashed banana. *My* baby clothes. I hold a pink knitted jumper against my chest and sigh. What the hell am I supposed to do with all these things? I don't even know if I want kids, and now that it's over with Eliot...

Don't start thinking about all that. Just finish the job.

I grab an armful of items and am about to dump them back in the box when I spot something lurking at the bottom – a hard, black, rectangular shape. An old videotape by the look of it, almost a museum piece these days. I peer in to read the label – *Meredith, July 1990*. I've never seen that looping, egotistical handwriting before, but I instantly know whose it is. *Has* to be hers. I pull back my hand, afraid to touch.

The tape sits there, my name staring up at me. It looks like a bomb, waiting to explode. Smart move, I think, hiding it in a box so innocently labelled, knowing it wouldn't be removed until Dad left the house. Or died. She'd have known he wasn't the type to climb into the loft on a wet Sunday afternoon and have a good old sort-out. Judging by the number of skips we've filled during the last few weeks, I'm starting to wonder whether he's a hoarder. Except hoarders are usually people who are depressed or have psychological disorders. Dad's not like that. He's not the mad one.

Go on, pick it up. It's got your name on it.

The black box feels charged, plugged into my fingers, the current shooting up my arm. I want to play it, right this moment, but there's no VHS machine; I took it to the dump yesterday. Only a DVD player downstairs, so I'll have to wait till I can get it converted. I pass the tape back and forth between my hands, hoping by some magic to reveal its secrets. What's on it? I wonder. Badly filmed images of myself as a toddler, feeding the ducks, playing in the sandpit, reciting nursery rhymes, dancing around naked after a bath? What if there are pictures of *her* on it – dressed up for a party, jumping the waves, the three of us smiling on the beach? Mummy, Daddy and Meredith. Happy days…

I look at the label again and count on my fingers – July 1990: I was four and a half then. It was a few months before Becca (I no longer refer to her as Mother, Mummy, Mum) disappeared from my life. The last time I saw her was in the hospital. So often I've tried to reconstruct that day in my head, but the memory is like an old blanket, frayed at the edges and full of holes. Buildings, objects, other people are easy; it's Becca herself that's never in shot.

It always starts with the journey there. A long ride out of the city, the bus starting full and gradually emptying until Dad and I are the only ones left on the top deck. We get off at a stop on a wide busy road – red flip-up seats in the shelter, crushed diamonds sparkling in the kerb. Cars are whizzing past, neither wanting nor needing to stop, everyone on their way to somewhere else. Daddy takes my hand, leading me down a side turning, more of a country lane, really; tall hedges on either side, crumbling tarmac, no pavements. When there's a gap in the green leaves, all I can see are flat mustardy fields. My arm aches as I hold it aloft. He's so tall I have to crane my neck upwards to see his face. Tired little legs. I ask for a piggyback but he promises me we're nearly there. But Nearly There is nowhere to be seen.

We arrive, eventually, I never remember exactly how. The hospital looks like one of my Lego constructions: shiny white bricks, flat red roof, blue front door. A solid mass of too-bright grass in front like somebody has painted it on, and inside, a large entrance hall with slippery grey tiles covered in black skid marks. We get into the lift and Daddy lets me press the number 3 button. When we come out, I see the staircase has nets strung across the bottom of each floor, like at the circus. I put my chin over the banister and point excitedly, but Daddy scoops me up in his arms and carries me down a long corridor. We pass a room with rows of people watching television in their pyjamas, and an old woman is using the toilet with the door wide open. Daddy tells me not to stare, rushing me past as he looks for the right ward, clutching me even more tightly as he walks in. I press my nose into his scratchy checked shirt – *hairs on his chest where the birds build their nest.*

There are lots of little rooms inside the big one, like my Wendy house in the garden – orange walls, a bed, a cupboard, a chair. On one side, plastic windows scored with nail scratches. No vases of flowers, no Get Well Soon cards. No pictures on the wall. A lady is sitting in the corner of Mummy's little den, knitting in fluffy white wool, knitting without ever looking down at the clicking needles, not speaking, just staring at Mummy, watching her all the time with unblinking eyes. I watch the woman doing the watching. How can she knit so fast without looking? Why does she never stop looking at Mummy?

That's where the memory always falls apart, with the woman on suicide watch. Why can I see the stupid knitter, but never my own mother? Maybe something terrible happened after that, something I've blocked out. All I know is Dad never took me to the hospital again. That was twenty-five years ago. I have no idea where Becca is now, even if she's still alive.

I feel a sudden urge to be in the daylight, fresh air, the here and now. I stand up, nearly banging my head on a cross-beam, and tuck the tape into the belt of my jeans. Walking over to the hatch, I step onto the ladder and lower myself to the soft, carpeted landing.

'Dad? Where are you?' No reply. I scurry downstairs. A cold draught is coming from the kitchen; he's left the back door open by the look of it. 'Dad?'

He's at the bottom of the garden, burning dead leaves. Sweet and sour smoke rises into the air, wizened berries and crackling holly. What's he doing, lighting a bonfire now? Only four days to go until he moves out, and he's nowhere near ready.

'I thought you were supposed to be packing the books.' I walk towards him and he lifts his head, looking at me over his glasses.

'I got bored.' He smiles apologetically. 'What have you got there?'

I hold the tape up for him to see. 'It was in with my baby clothes. Got my name on it. July 1990. Mean anything to you?'

He stops suddenly, throwing his poking stick on the ground. 'Jesus Christ… It's been there all these years?' He flings off his gardening gloves and holds out a hand. 'Give it to me… Now, please.' I frown – it's as if I'm six years old and he's caught me nicking biscuits out of the tin. Only it feels worse than that, like I've done something really bad.

'It's just a home movie or something. You okay, Dad? What's wrong?'

'I mean it, give it to me.' I step back, hovering just out of reach, tightening my hold on the tape. Something tells me that if

I hand it over, he's going to throw it straight onto the fire. I can't let him do that. It's *my* tape. 'Please, Meri, it's for your own good. I know what's on it and you don't want to see it.'

'It can't be that bad, surely? For God's sake, Dad, you're freaking me out. What is it?'

His face has turned pink; even his bald patch is colouring up. Breathing hard and fast, tiny bubbles of sweat popping up on his forehead. He's gone from everyday neutral to super-angry in seconds. Scaring the shit out of me. *Please don't let him have another heart attack.*

'Dad, try to calm down. You know you're not supposed to get in a—'

He lunges at me. 'Give me the sodding tape!' He swats frantically as I dance it high above my head, but this is no game. Both my hands grip the case as he grabs my arm roughly and pulls it down, twisting it into the nook of his curved body.

'Dad! Stop! You're hurting me!' But he carries on wrestling, trying to jerk the tape from my grasp, digging at my fingers until I can fight him off no longer and the tape springs out, falling to the ground. If he gets to it first, he'll put it on the fire. I can't let him – I just can't. He moves towards it and I give him a massive shove. There's a look of hurt surprise on his face as he staggers back several paces, falling comically into the flower bed.

I pick up the tape, shaking off the loose dead grass and shoving it back down the front of my jeans. My body is trembling with the shock of what's just happened. I struck my own father; I pushed him to the ground. I've never, *never* fought with him like that. He was in hospital only three months ago. What was I thinking?

'Sorry, I'm really sorry… I didn't mean… Are you okay?' He nods, but his gaze is glassy, as if he's staring at a stranger. I take several slow steps backwards, my eyes still fixed on him.

'It's something to do with Becca, isn't it? This is her handwriting, she made the video. It's of me and her, right…? Well?' No answer. He just sits there in the flower bed, breathing hard. 'It's up to me, isn't it, if I want to watch it?'

'Don't say I didn't warn you.' He turns sideways onto his knees and heaves himself up, groaning as his bones click.

'I'm grown up, Dad. You can't protect me from everything.'

'No, I never could.' He walks slowly back to his bonfire, defeated.

I want to run into his arms and be his little girl again. I want to say, *I'm sorry, I love you. Whatever this thing is, we'll deal with it; it won't make any difference to us, I promise it'll be all right.* But I can't risk it, I have to stay at a safe distance. If I drop my guard, he could still snatch the tape and commit it to the flames.

He picks up his heavy gloves and puts them back on, then finds the stick and pokes listlessly at the fire. 'Watch it, if you must.' He looks up at me. 'Just don't believe a word you say.'

CHAPTER TWO

Me

I'm a surprisingly beautiful child. Long blonde hair that shines in the sunlight, almost white at the wispy tips. My limbs are rosy chubbiness; I'm barely in control of them as I dance around like a clumsy fairy, laughing at whoever's holding the video camera. Four years old – pink cheeks, pale lemon cotton skirt and a white T-shirt. I'm a bag of marshmallows, all soft and chewy. The kind of child a grown-up would like to eat.

We're in the back garden of a house I don't remember. It's a gorgeous sunny day, warm enough to have the paddling pool out. As the camera follows me, a ring of blue plastic comes fleetingly into frame. Barefoot, I twirl about on the spot and slip on a muddy patch where I've been splashing.

'Look what I can do, Mummy!'

I press pause, freezing the image. As I suspected, it's Becca that's filming. I want to see her. Her face, her hairstyle, the shape of her body. Is she fat or thin? What is she wearing? *Go on, show yourself.* My heart starts to race as I press play again.

In the background, the flower beds are soft-focusing in purple, red and golden yellow. The height of summer. The camera is fixed on its subject, jerking left to right as I dance, or up and down as I collapse on the ground with seeming exhaustion only to bob up again like a cork. There's a furtive urgency about the way she's following me, trying to get whatever it is we're doing done with.

'Meri! Come and sit down.'

Her voice is like a glass bell that's about to shatter. I've heard those ringing tones in my dreams many, many times. She sounds like me when I'm stressed, or rather, I sound like her, and I'm not sure I like it.

'It's time to tell your story.'

I've got hold of the garden hose, making it writhe across the grass. 'Ssss... Sssss... Sssssss.' A trickle of cold water runs out, making me jump aside with a short cry.

'We're going to tell everyone what really happened. Remember? You promised.' Her voice rises by a couple of notes. 'Mummy really needs your help. If we don't tell the truth, the bad man will come and take us away.'

'Look, Mummy, a snake!'

'Please, Meri, please. I need your help. Leave that alone and sit down here.' The camera shakes, then settles as Becca puts it down on the garden table. A thin white arm reaches forward, a beckoning hand, two long fingers weighed down by heavy silver rings. Then the rest of her walks into frame, a gathered skirt in blue and green paisley, a white sleeveless blouse, strands of light brown hair escaping from the loose bun at the nape of her neck. She grabs my chubby little hand and guides me onto a white plastic chair that looks as if it's been placed deliberately for this moment, spotlit by the afternoon sun.

My eyes are fixed on the screen; I'm finding it hard to breathe. *Turn around*, I whisper, *please turn around.* And then, as if she has heard me calling to her across the chasm of the years, she does.

There she is. My mother. I pause the image for a few seconds. Blue eyes, full pink lips and a few freckles scattered over a short blunt nose. She's much thinner than me, almost anorexic-looking, but there's no mistaking we're mother and daughter. I trace my own adult features with a wondering finger. Some part of my brain must recognise this face, as it recognised the voice, but it feels like I'm seeing her for the first time. Becca points at the camera and tells me to look at it when she's talking.

'Tell them who you were before you were Meri,' she prompts. I tuck and untuck my legs and examine a black scuff on the arm of the chair. 'You were someone else, isn't that right? Tell them who you were.'

'Don't know.'

'Yes you do, you do. You told me all about it. You told me you were Cara.' I scrunch up my face. 'Go on. Say it. You were Cara Travers. Nobody believes me, so you've got to tell them. I need you to say it, Meri – say it!'

The sun pops behind a cloud for a moment and suddenly everything looks cold, almost sinister. There's the distant sound of an ice-cream van approaching – a tinkling version of 'Greensleeves' that makes me look up, full of expectation.

'Can I have a lolly?'

'No! First we've got to tell them about Cara and who did the horrible thing to you… Come on, tell them what happened.'

The ice-cream music has stopped, and even at that age I know this means the van has parked outside the house, its noisy engine humming. Other, luckier children are probably lining up, clutching their fifty-pence pieces, elbowing each other to the front, peering over the edge of the counter.

'Can I have stawbelly?' I jump off the chair and go to my sandals.

'Not until you've told everyone the truth. They think I lied, you see, but I didn't. It was the bad man, making me all confused; he made me say the wrong thing. Only you know what really happened. You've got to tell them…'

'I want a lolly.'

'You've got to tell them! Now!' Becca runs back into frame and picks me up. I kick out against her, but she carries me back to the chair and sits. I stiffen and arch my back in protest, but she grips me hard around the waist, pushing my body down, pinning me into her lap. I wriggle and squirm, my little face growing red with effort and fury, but she tightens her hold, forcing me to face the camera.

'Let me go! Let me go!'

'We've got to do this first, before Daddy comes home. This is our secret, remember? Daddy mustn't know. We're going to tell our story and then it will all stop and Mummy will be safe. You want Mummy to be safe, don't you?'

'Want a lolly,' I whimper, tiring of the struggle.

'The bad man knows. If you don't help Mummy, he'll come and get me. He'll come and get you too, and we don't want that, do we?' I shake my head, my bottom lip starting to tremble. 'That's why we have to tell them about Cara. You have to tell them who killed you. Remember?'

'Like this.' I make a stabbing motion with my fist. Up and down, up and down.

'Yes, that's right, but who? Who did it to you?' I stop stabbing and stare back at my mother, my small right arm suspended in the air. 'It was Jay, wasn't it?' Becca whispers. 'Tell them it was Christopher Jay.'

I nod, slowly. 'Yes. Cwister Jay.' 'Greensleeves' starts up again, loud at first, then fades into silence. My clear blue eyes widen with alarm and I start to cry. 'The ice-cream man's gone! You said I could have a lolly!' I wrench myself free of her grasp and jump down, running towards the camera. I sweep it off the table and send it crashing onto the ground.

The screen goes black.

CHAPTER THREE

Me

I slam down the lid of the laptop and jump off my bed. The DVD spins and slows to a stop – I want to stamp on it and break it into pieces, but I know it won't help. I've watched it now, seen Becca in that strange, feverish state, holding me down, making me cry, forcing me to say horrible, crazy things. The image of my tiny self, stabbing the air with an imaginary knife, is lodged in my brain forever. No matter how many times I press delete, I'll never get rid of it.

It's already dark outside. My reflection hovers uneasily in the bedroom window – adult-sized features, weary eyes smudged with the remains of the day's make-up, hair lank with London dirt. I'm worried about the little girl in the video, even though she's tucked away safely inside me, an inner layer of being, like the centre of an onion. I feel I should be doing something – calling Social Services or taking her to a psychiatrist. It's as if her life is still being played out in a parallel universe and she's in sudden danger, reaching out to me through time and space to rescue her from harm.

I rest my forehead on the cool glass, but it doesn't soothe me. My insides are all churned up with emotion, anger for me and pity for Becca. Sadness for Dad because he tried, as ever, to protect me and I refused to listen. Thought I knew better. I was so determined to have my own way, I pushed him to the ground, just a few weeks after he'd had a heart attack. God knows what made me do it. Will he ever forgive me?

I pick up my phone and call his number again. It rings out for several seconds and I imagine him staring at his screen, deciding whether to accept or reject me. I've lost count of the number of times I've tried calling him these past few days – he hasn't picked up once, or replied to any of my texts. The voicemail kicks in and I hesitate, not knowing what to say.

'Dad? It's me. Please, please call me… I'm sorry… Really, really sorry. Please, let's talk.'

The air in the room feels contaminated. I open the window and look down into the back garden – dishevelled flower beds and overgrown trees, last year's dead leaves rotting on the cracked paving stones of the patio. I hate this house. It's dark and damp and I live with two girls I hardly know. When Eliot and I split up, neither of us could afford the flat on our own, so we had to move out. I was in a panic and not in a good place emotionally. I should have moved back home with Dad until I got myself sorted out, but that felt like too much of a defeat. I wanted to be strong, deciding it would be better to live with new people and make a fresh start. But Lizzie is hardly ever here, and I don't really get on with Fay. I can hear her playing music in her room, but I can't go and talk to her – not about something as personal as this. Can't confide in any of my girlfriends either. They don't know about my mad mother. When the subject of parents comes up, I always say she walked out when I was very young and leave it there. That's all I knew for years anyway – it's a half-lie I'm comfortable with telling.

When I was little, I lived very happily with just one parent and rarely thought about my mother. But when puberty struck, I started to miss her, despite the fact that I had so few memories of her and didn't even know what she looked like.

I needed help with agonising period pains and hair sprouting in embarrassing places; I needed someone to explain all these mixed-up emotions I was feeling. In short, I needed a woman in my life. But my mother wasn't around and nobody seemed to know where I could find her. Sometimes I blamed myself for her absence. At other times, I was angry with her for never once getting in touch – not so much as a birthday card or a phone call at Christmas. The feeling of rejection was so painful it was as if she'd only just walked out of the door. Dad refused to talk about what had happened, so I concluded she must have run off with another man. My feelings became even more complicated then; I wanted to find her, but I hated her too. For hurting Dad. I had so many questions going round and round in my head, but another two years passed before I plucked up the courage to ask them.

It was the summer holidays, about eleven o'clock at night, and Dad and I were still in the garden, sitting at a table bathed in candlelight. It must have been a heatwave. Dad was wearing a T-shirt and baggy shorts, flip-flops on his feet, a bottle of beer in his hand. He was a heavy smoker back then, and was showing off his ability to blow rings into the star-filled sky. I was drinking Pepsi, secretly laced with shots of Bacardi that I'd stolen from the drinks cabinet. I'd stuffed my tall tumbler with ice cubes, just like I'd seen in the adverts, and the glass was so slippery I could hardly hold it.

We'd been sitting there since dinner, talking about this and that – how my GCSEs were going, what I might study at university, whether he should apply for an internal promotion or look for a new job elsewhere, how I'd feel about moving house... It was one of our first proper 'grown-up' conversations and I remember feeling pleased that I'd stayed at home for the evening instead of going out with my friends.

I don't know how the subject of Becca came up. Maybe it was the unusual weather, or the secret alcohol running through my veins, but there was a relaxed atmosphere between us I had never experienced with Dad before. We'd reached a natural pause in our conversation and were sitting in easy silence, listening to the night sounds, watching the candle flames flicker in the darkness. Without warning, the words just drifted into my mouth.

'Can we talk about Becca?'

He didn't reply immediately, just took another swig of his beer and gently set the bottle down on the table. 'What is it you want to know?'

'Everything. What happened. Why she left us.'

'She was schizophrenic,' he said. 'Not her fault, but it nearly destroyed all of us.'

I'd vaguely heard of schizophrenia, but I thought it was something to do with having a split personality, like Jekyll and Hyde. Dad explained that it was more of a destroyed personality than a split one. He told me the illness had come on very gradually and taken several years to diagnose. It had probably started when Becca was a teenager, but her family hadn't realised at the time – they just thought she was moody and difficult. Her parents chucked her out and they were estranged. Dad said his relationship with Becca had always been volatile, but he'd thought that was just her personality.

'If only I'd known…' he muttered, blowing smoke rings into the sky as if he were setting the memories free.

I let the ice in my glass melt, not daring to drink in case I broke the spell. Dad had never opened up to me before like this and I didn't want it to stop.

He carried on, speaking without looking at me, as if pretending I wasn't really there.

'We met during teacher training and hit it off immediately, moved in together after a few weeks and got married the following summer. She wasn't the easiest person to live with – we had a few rows, but we had a lot of fun too. Life with Becca was never boring and I liked that. To begin with, anyway… After she qualified, she got a job in a primary school but instantly hated it. Things started to get a bit weird. She became convinced her colleagues were plotting against her, trying to get her sacked.'

'And were they?'

'No, it was all in her head. She was unreliable, didn't turn up for work, or walked out in the middle of lessons. Sometimes she said really odd things to the kids and upset them. There were complaints. She went off on long-term sick leave with stress. Spent all day lying in bed, stayed awake all night. She'd wander the streets in her nightdress and come home at dawn, her feet covered in mud.'

'Didn't she have counselling?' I asked. I'd started to become aware of such things at school. If you had emotional problems, you were supposed to ask for help.

'We tried, but after a couple of sessions she refused to go. The doctor put her on antidepressants, but the drugs weren't right – they seemed to make it worse. At that stage, nobody mentioned the possibility of schizophrenia.' Dad paused to take another drink. His hand was trembling slightly as it held the bottle, and I remember thinking that he was recalling something specific – something too horrible or painful to express.

'We had a very difficult year,' he said finally, 'but then she became pregnant with you and things seemed to improve for a while.' He chose his next words carefully. 'She wanted you very much, but, when you were born, she found it hard to cope. The doctors said it was postnatal depression and it would pass eventually, but…'

'They were wrong.'

'Things went rapidly downhill. She was on her own with you all day and she felt very isolated. She wasn't looking after you properly. Sometimes I'd get home from work and find her asleep on the sofa with you crying in your playpen. I sent you to full-time nursery – she hated me for that, but it was for your own safety. Then the voices started. They told her I was evil and was trying to poison her. She wouldn't eat any meal I prepared and was rapidly losing weight. Every night she woke up screaming, said the house was full of devils and monsters and I was one of them. She was terrified of mirrors and we had to cover them all up. It was crazy stuff. She was self-harming almost daily; her arms and thighs were in shreds. Then she tried to kill herself. I had no choice, Meri. I had to have her taken away. You *do* understand, don't you? I did what I thought was best.'

My mind instantly went back to the last time I had seen her. The visit to the peculiar hospital. The nets in the stairwell and the plastic windows. Finally I understood where I'd been all those years earlier.

'Was that when they finally diagnosed her schizophrenia?' He nodded. 'So what happened next? Where did she go?'

He sighed, leaning back and looking up at the stars. 'I don't know, my darling. After a few months, she escaped from the psychiatric unit and disappeared. My guess is she tried to commit suicide again and succeeded. I'm sorry, it's hard to take, but I think you're old enough to know the truth.'

I picked up my glass and downed the secret Bacardi in a single gulp. 'But you don't know for sure – she could still be alive…'

Dad shook his head. 'I doubt it. Please don't look for her, Meri. She's dead to us – let's leave it that way. For all our sakes.' He stood up, blew out the candles and went indoors. That was the last time we talked about her.

I leave the memory at the window and sit back on the bed, tracing my fingers across the lid of the laptop. Why did Becca make the video? What was she trying to say? Dad never mentioned it that night in the garden, but I have a feeling it was significant. A turning point, perhaps. At the very least, the video is evidence that he was right to have her sectioned. The whole family was suffering. The long-term psychological damage she could have done to me doesn't bear thinking about. But I survived, thanks to him. I was lucky.

I play the tape again, distancing myself this time, watching coolly as if viewing a documentary, listening carefully as I try to work out what's really going on. Some of what Becca says has no grip on reality – *tell them who you were before you were Meri… if we don't tell the truth, the bad man will come and take us away.* But other bits are very specific. Names are mentioned – Cara Travers, Christopher Jay. Did she make them up, or were they people she knew? Perhaps there was an actual murder. I type the names into my phone and wait for the search engine to do its stuff, but the results are inconclusive. There are such people in existence, several in fact, but nothing linking them together. Of course there's nothing. I click out of Google and slam my phone down on the bed. Why am I taking this at all seriously? There's nothing to investigate here; it's just a load of pitiful, insane rambling – a random chapter in the life of my poor schizophrenic mother, that's all. It has nothing to do with the real world, or with my life now. And yet…

I lie back and gaze up at the cracked grey ceiling. A cold shiver runs through me and I reach for the duvet, pulling it across my body. I want to forget I ever saw the video, put it on the top shelf and leave it to gather dust. But I know I won't be able to. Something inside me has changed. A light has been turned on; a door to a forgotten room has been opened.

CHAPTER FOUR

Cara
January 1984

It was gone eleven by the time they got to the house, taking it in turns to carry Cara's huge suitcase from the bus stop at the top of Darkwater Lane, the weight of it propelling them down the hill towards the pond.

'It's known as a pool – not that you can swim in it,' Isobel explained, stopping to catch her breath. Cara looked at the flat black expanse of water, its surface lit by a couple of street lamps, and shivered at the mere thought of anyone jumping in.

'What's that?' she said, pointing to the dark shape of a building at the far side.

'The old boathouse. You used to be able to hire these sweet little rowing boats. I've got a very dim memory of Grandpa taking me out and the ducks following us around.' Isobel laughed softly. 'Our garden backs onto the footpath that goes round the pool – there's a gate in the fence. I'll show you properly tomorrow.'

Cara peered around her in the darkness, impatient to understand the geography of her new surroundings. Tall silhouettes of houses curved in a gracious arc around three-quarters of the pool; that must be Darkwater Terrace. They were standing on the open side, by the road. Two wooden benches overlooked the water and there was a gate in the low brick wall – leading, she presumed, to the footpath, hidden by the trees and bushes lining the banks. It was very secluded. They were only a couple of miles from the city centre, but it felt almost rural.

Isobel picked up the suitcase again. 'Come on. Nearly there.' They took the first road on the left and walked along until they reached number 31 – a large brick terraced house, bay-fronted on both floors with a small pointed attic window in the roof.

'This is it,' she announced, heaving the case up the path and resting it on the tiled step while she searched for her door key. 'Welcome!'

Cara felt again the surge of joy she'd had after Isobel's phone call a week ago. In the six months since they'd graduated, her life had virtually ground to a halt; more accurately, it had gone back to how it had been before, as if the last three years had never happened. With no job to go to, there'd been no alternative but to return home. She'd written dozens of letters to agents and rep theatres, but nobody had shown the slightest bit of interest and her parents had more or less told her to give up the idea of acting. Her mother wanted her to do teacher-training, whereas her father – who disapproved of teachers almost as much as he disapproved of actors – thought she would do better in personnel. The one thing they were both agreed on was that she should start paying her way, so she'd signed up with a temping agency – photocopying and filing mostly, as she couldn't type. She'd spent the last few months shuffling between construction companies, accountants, conveyancing solicitors and the local council, feeling more and more depressed. Then, last Monday evening, the phone rang.

'It's a beautiful house and it'll make the perfect base for our theatre company,' Isobel said. Her grandmother had died nearly a year ago, leaving her entire estate – including 31 Darkwater Terrace – to her only grandchild. The will had been contested and the whole business had caused an unpleasant rift between Isobel and her mother's side of the family.

'You *will* come, won't you?' Isobel had pleaded. 'I couldn't possibly do it without you.' It had taken less than a second for Cara to make up her mind.

Isobel was right – the house *was* beautiful. It was like wandering through an antiques shop, with ornaments and silverware crowding every surface, oil paintings of hunting scenes and sea storms and delicate Victorian watercolour landscapes on the walls. The contents alone must be worth a fortune, thought Cara, gasping at the sitting room with its enormous carved wooden mantelpiece, the large, graceful settee and small velvet armchair. She admired the contents of the half-moon display cabinet and the faded Turkish carpet on the floor. In the dining room she was suitably impressed by the huge polished table and its twelve matching chairs, and easily agreed that the long, thin kitchen, where the units looked like something out of the 1950s, was 'perfect'. But her favourite room was the ancient conservatory, bursting with rickety bamboo furniture and overgrown cacti.

'I want to use Gran's old bedroom for rehearsals,' said Isobel, leading the way upstairs. 'So I'm in the attic – it's where I used to sleep when I was a child – and I've put you in the back bedroom. It's got a lovely view of the garden.' She pushed open the door to reveal a rectangular room full of red mahogany furniture – a double bed with a high headboard, a small matching wardrobe and a dressing table decked with three hinged mirrors. Cara threw her bag onto the bed and walked straight over to the window, but it was too dark to see the garden below.

'You'll love it,' said Isobel, standing behind her and folding her arms around Cara's waist. 'It was Gran's pride and joy, so we've got to look after it.'

'Yes, we must,' Cara murmured, thinking that she didn't know a thing about gardening.

'Anyway, you must be worn out,' Isobel said, releasing her with a final squeeze and moving back to the doorway. 'Get some sleep and we'll start work in the morning. I've already made a frighteningly long list of jobs, but now there's the two of us...'

'Can't wait.' Cara sat down on the mattress, feeling the ancient springs twang. 'Have you had any thoughts about what we should call the company?' She'd always liked naming things – dolls, pets, imaginary children...

'Oh, didn't I tell you?' Isobel pulled a mock-guilty face. 'It just came to me the other night.' She gestured at her purple dress, mauve patterned scarf and woollen tights the colour of aubergine; as if Cara wasn't already aware of her best friend's obsession with the colour. 'Purple Blaze. What do you think?'

Cara thought it sounded more like a name for a cocktail than a left-wing touring theatre company – but before she had time to voice her opinion, Isobel told her she'd already designed the logo and had some letterhead printed. It was the inheritance money that was paying for all this, so it was right, Cara supposed, that Isobel made the main decisions, although in the past, she'd talked a lot about wanting to start a cooperative (or was it a collective? Cara didn't really know the difference) in which everything would be agreed unanimously. What did it matter, anyway? Of the two of them, Isobel always had the best ideas, and it would be churlish to start raising objections. Her friend had thrown her a lifeline – not for the first time – and Cara had no intention of letting it go.

She went to fetch her suitcase, dragging it upstairs and laying it on her bedroom floor. She unzipped the lid and took out her pyjamas. The radiator was stone cold and there was a nasty draught coming through the window, so she drew the curtains. Then she undressed, slipped on her pyjamas and got into bed, keeping her socks on. The mattress was very soft and dipped in the middle, so it took a while to find a comfortable position. She switched off the bedside lamp and lay in the darkness, her eyes still wide open. Her head felt too buzzy to sleep, her thoughts drifting further and further back to when it had all begun.

It was almost painful to remember how she'd been when she arrived at university, that first bewildering week away from home. Mouse-haired and mouse-timid Cara Jane Travers, sitting primly on the only chair outside the admin secretary's office, clutching her neatly filled-in forms, looking and feeling anything but the bohemian drama student. Everyone else was chatting to each other like old friends even though they'd only just met – boasting about their exotic gap years (she hadn't been allowed to take one), rubbishing the importance of A-level results (she had three A's) or comparing notes on the latest production at the Royal Court (she hadn't even heard of the place). And they were all dressed the same, as if there was a uniform but nobody had sent her the list of requirements. The girls were wearing scruffy jeans, sweatshirts, coloured berets, oversized blazers with turned-up shiny lining cuffs, and big laced boots. Their hair was universally dyed with henna in varying intensities of red, and nobody wore make-up – all blemishes defiantly on display. They sat on the hard floor with legs outstretched, unaware or uncaring that people had to step over them to get past, leaning intimately on strangers' shoulders, begging tobacco and rolling up their Rizlas with the expertise of workmen on a building site.

The boys were no less self-styled, their skin, hair and clothes deliberately unwashed, dressed like would-be farmers or fishermen – flat tweedy caps, knotted neckerchiefs, hand-knitted Fair Isle tank tops, corduroy trousers and crumpled collarless shirts. They stood in earnest, competitive clusters, canvas bags covered in badges advertising various political causes lurching off their shoulders, and one of them was even waving the *Morning Star*.

CHAPTER FIVE

Me

It's half past one, and as usual, Eliot is late. What will the excuse be this time? This restaurant used to be one of our favourite haunts, ten minutes' walk from the old flat, so he can't pretend he got lost. I like Echo Beach, it reminds me of the old days, when things were easy between us and it never occurred to me that we wouldn't be together forever. The name must come from the song – it was on an album of eighties hits Dad used to play in the car. *Echo Beach, faraway in time, Echo Beach, faraway in time...* Eliot and I discovered the place early on, before *Time Out* ranked it third out of the ten best restaurants in south London for weekend brunch. Now every Sunday people queue all the way up the street for their deep-fried duck egg and baba ganoush. Evenings are big too, with live music and a DJ on Fridays. But it's relatively quiet at lunchtime so you can usually hear yourself talk. Not that I've got anyone to talk to yet. *Where the hell is he?*

In a way, I find it comforting that Eliot is behaving just as he used to when we were together. I don't like the idea of him improving under somebody else's tutelage. Not that there seems to be a somebody else. Not judging from Facebook, anyway. I stab a Kalamata olive with a toothpick and suck it into my mouth – I'm proud to say that until yesterday, I hadn't looked at his page for months.

We met in the local pub, the summer after I graduated, and lived together like a proper grown-up couple for four and a half years, so understandably it took a while to get used to being single again – living in an all-girl house-share, having to plan things in advance so I don't end up on my own on Saturday nights. But we did the right thing, splitting up; I couldn't take any more of that stressful life. I thought it might be painful coming back here, but actually it's fine. I'm over him. Really, I am. Anyway, it's good we're still officially friends, because I need his help.

I keep replaying the DVD. It's like watching a human puppet show: Becca pulling invisible strings, raising Meri's little clenched fist, holding an imaginary knife and bringing it down, up and down. I can't leave it alone. Can't stop looking at Becca either. I put the laptop on my chest of drawers and freeze on the shots of her – stare in the mirror on the wall above and compare our features. Sometimes I look so much like her, I forget I'm the child in the scene. I'm both people – victim and abuser – and yet Becca's a victim too. She didn't choose to have a mental illness, she didn't mean me any harm. I don't know what to think. I'm dreaming about her at night and waking up in a sweat. Stuff that's lain dormant for years has suddenly been activated and I can't put it back to sleep. There are so many questions I need to ask and only one person who can answer them: Dad.

Suddenly Eliot's standing next to me saying, 'Sorry, sorry, sorry, couldn't get away, I had to finish this interview and it took way longer than I'd expected and now I've only got twenty minutes…' I stand up and we hug, holding on a few seconds longer than friends do, catching the memory of each other. He sits down and removes his light silk scarf, sticking it in his jacket pocket. One of the first presents I ever bought him; I wonder if he remembers, if he chose it deliberately today.

'The waiter was pushing so I had to order,' I say. 'Hope you still like ham hock croquettes.'

'Of course. You're having the Burmese chicken salad, yes?'

'Of course,' I echo.

'So predictable, aren't we?' He laughs and beckons the waiter over to order sparkling water, refusing to join me in my bottle of Rioja – he has a meeting at two sharp and then a load of paperwork to get through this afternoon. Still on the twelve-hour shifts, he explains ruefully. As the waiter tops up my glass, I have a brief flashback to those solitary evenings on the sofa wading through endless box sets, my legs stretched out into the space where Eliot should have been sitting, persuading myself that his absence meant I could watch girlie stuff but actually bored out of my skull. If I succumbed to wine and waited up, I was leery by the time he got home, spoiling for a row. Then he'd tell me what he'd just seen – a woman with an eyeball hanging out of its socket, jaw caved right in, teeth scattered across the carpet like a broken string of beads. I never could compete with that.

'This is nice,' he says, leaning back in his chair. 'How are you doing?'

'I'm good, thanks.'

'I'm really pleased to hear that…' He pauses. 'Cos I heard you'd been through a bit of a rough patch, you know, after we ended…'

'Really?' I try to look as if I've no idea what he means. One of our mutual friends has clearly been gossiping. There's female loyalty for you. 'No,' I reply airily. 'I'm absolutely fine, thanks.'

We hold a smile for each other. He's wearing a shirt I don't recognise and his wiry black curls have been cropped tight against his skull, much smarter than the old Afro. Same Eliot, though. I can still remember what he looks like naked. Long brown legs, muscular arms, a spray of dark freckles across his back, birthmark on his right – no, left – thigh. Has somebody else discovered that fluff collects in his belly button? I pull my thoughts up short and reach for my wine glass.

'How's your dad?' He moves aside his cutlery and places his elbows on the table, resting his hands on his chin. 'Someone told me he had a heart attack.'

'He's okay, pretty much fixed. Horrible when it happened, though. Got two stents, on medication for the rest of his life. Did you know he retired? He's just moved to Suffolk.'

'Good for him, sounds like he needs the rest.' He catches my expression. 'How do you feel about it?'

'Well…' I say, about to embark on my story, but the waiter arrives with our food and the intimacy of the moment is lost.

As we eat, Eliot asks me how my work's going. I wave it aside, telling him it's the 'same old, same old', that I've had enough of online marketing but can't think of what to do instead. Eliot's the opposite: he's always wanted to be a policeman and one day he'll be a chief superintendent or a commissioner or something, but for now he's a detective constable in Lambeth's Domestic Violence Unit. He spends a few minutes moaning about the CPS blocking their investigations at every turn, refusing to let cases go to court unless they're a hundred per cent watertight; tells me how bad he feels for the poor women he's encouraged to speak out, only to leave them at the mercy of their husbands/boyfriends/exes. I've heard it all before, several times over.

'It's time I moved on,' he says, leaning across the table to steal a sip of my wine.

'I was sure you'd be a sergeant by now. Didn't you sail through your OSPRE?'

He shrugs modestly. 'I'm just waiting for the promotion.'

'They'll give you something really juicy; isn't that what the High Potential Development Scheme is all about?'

'Supposed to be.' He takes a sneaky glance at his watch. 'What I'd really like is murder.' I've heard that before too. I have to cut this subject short or my twenty minutes will be up and I'll have got nowhere.

'I need to talk to you about something.'

'Yes, sorry, you said on the phone. Didn't mean to bang on.'

So I tell him about the videotape. Becca's paranoid fantasies about the bad man, Meri stabbing with her little fists, the accusation, all of it, right down to the strawberry lolly. His generous brown eyes widen, and at one point he puts his fork down and murmurs, 'What a thing... what a thing.' When I finish, he reaches out and lays his hand gently on my arm. 'I'm so sorry, Meredith. I knew your mother had mental health issues, but that's appalling.' Eliot is the only boyfriend I've ever told about Becca. 'So what does Graeme say? Did he know the tape existed?'

'Oh yes, he knew. When I showed it to him he got himself in one hell of a state.' I tell Eliot about our ugly fight. 'Now he's behaving like I've betrayed him. He won't answer any of my calls. He was supposed to be moving yesterday. I'm guessing it all went through. He didn't even let me say my last goodbyes to the place. I mean, that was my childhood home.'

'He's trying to punish you,' says Eliot. 'Don't worry, he won't be able to keep it up. Give it a few more days and he'll be texting you every other minute again.' Every other minute is an exaggeration, but Dad usually texts me morning and evening; it's a ritual he's been performing since I left home: '*Hope the meeting goes well xxx*'... '*Rain's expected, don't forget your umbrella xxx*'... '*How's the cough? Thinking of you xxx*'. The caring but slightly bossy messages used to get on my nerves a bit, but now I miss them. Dad will hate the fact that I've turned to Eliot for help, but he's left me with no choice.

I take a DVD from my bag and push it across the table. 'I burnt you a copy. Tell me what you think.'

He picks up the disc and spins it between his fingers. 'About what? Sorry, I don't understand.'

'On the tape Becca mentions two names – Cara Travers and Christopher Jay. I need to know if they're real people, if there was an actual murder.'

Eliot screws up his face. 'Why? What difference does it make?'

'I just need to know.'

'You've googled them?'

'Honestly, El, I'm not a complete idiot. Nothing comes up, but it was a long time ago, so maybe…' I hesitate. 'I mean, not *everything*'s on the internet. And if there was a murder, I thought you might be able—'

'So that's why you asked me to lunch. You want me to look at police records.'

'Could you?' I lean forward.

He puffs out a sigh. 'You were four when the video was made, right? That's twenty-five years ago. So if there *was* a murder, it would have been before we were fully computerised and the HOLMES database was created. It could have taken place any-where in the country – nothing was joined up back then…'

'I'm not asking for a full investigation. Just have a quick peek. Please?'

Eliot gives me a pitying look. 'Okay, but I'm not sure what it is you're hoping to find.'

'Nor am I. But thanks, it would mean a lot.'

He looks at his watch again. 'Gotta go.' He takes out his wal-let and searches for a note.

'Don't worry, I'll get it,' I say. 'Just call me as soon as you find out anything.'

'Promise.' He swoops the scarf – my scarf – around his neck. 'So good to see you… I miss you, you know.'

'Yeah, yeah.' I opt for mock-dismissive. 'Now piss off and do some detecting for me, Sherlock!'

I watch him go – weaving his way to the door, spinning through and hanging left, leaving the frame without once looking back, without so much as a wave. I turn my gaze to his empty chair, soaking up the memory of his eager, restless face, the soft, broad nose and high cheekbones, the trusting brown eyes. How long is it since I've had sex? *Don't go there, Meri.*

I return to the office feeling strangely elated. The lunch went well, considering. Being friends with an ex is hard, even when you no longer have feelings, as they say. Neither of us asked if we were seeing new people – I wonder if that's significant. Does it suggest that we don't want to think of each other with new partners, or did it just not come up in the conversation? We had other, more urgent things to discuss, so maybe he just didn't get around to it. Maybe I just didn't get around to it. No, that's not true. I wanted to know, but I couldn't bear to ask, because… because? …

Only a few emails have come in since I left my desk. It's Friday afternoon; everything's winding down for the weekend, there's nothing urgent or interesting. I compose an email from self to self, with no message, just a heading: *Stop analysing everything.*

But as the afternoon makes its slow, weary way to 5 p.m. – the earliest we can all leave for the pub – my thoughts wander back to Eliot. Vague, Rioja-fuelled feelings of lust rise within me, making me hot and restless. I try to imagine him having sex with someone else to test my lack of desire, but it keeps turning into memories of being with him. It was good, I remember. The sex. It was always good, from our very first night together.

We fell in love really quickly, moved in together after only three months; found a tiny one-bedroomed flat above a green-grocer's, damp and dark in the winter, stinking of rotting veg-etables in the summer and outrageously expensive all year round. We went to IKEA and bought throws and blinds and lamps, car-ried home flat-packed bookshelves on the bus. Dad gave me his old dining table, Eliot's parents a set of wine glasses and a fancy grater for Parmesan cheese. He was working on the PC Response Team then – 999 calls all hours of the day and night, burglaries, robberies, car crime; it was exhausting. But we still made love several times a week and all through the weekend. For the first six months or so, anyway.

Inevitably, things slowed down – that didn't worry me; I mean, nobody can keep up that kind of pace. The sex was never the problem. It was Eliot's job. The long, awkward shifts, the can-celled leave, the lack of social life, the physical and emotional strain. Eliot brought his work home every night – and not only in his briefcase. He couldn't stop talking about the victims, as if he felt responsible for them. I know it was stupid, but I started to feel jealous. And I wasn't allowed to complain about my work or our relationship – or *anything* – because there were all these poor women out there who were *really* suffering. And that just made me feel worse. Selfish. Guilty. Resentful. He was off-loading all his stress onto me and then criticising me for not coping. It started off as lightweight bickering, with the occasional row. Then we started screaming at each other. We weren't special, we were disappointingly normal. The divorce rate amongst police officers is extremely high, but we never even made it down the aisle.

Looking back, it was amazing that we stuck it out for four years. We loved each other, that's why. I didn't want us to split up, but I also knew I couldn't be a policeman's wife. And there was no way he would give up his career. I remember those last months when the relationship was dying – all that talking, talking, talking through the midnight hours, lying in bed in the darkness, him exhausted and me refusing to let him sleep, going on and on about how I didn't know what I felt any more, not just about our relationship but my whole life. I know I wore him out. But even after awful, no-going-back things were said and we'd both wept and begged forgiveness, we still made love; a desperate, clinging kind of sex, both thinking maybe this was the last time, maybe we'd never do it again, not with each other, not with anyone.

Then one lazy Saturday morning we had an early-morning cuddle that turned into something more, desire creeping up on us unawares. Warm, affectionate lovemaking, not like those mad, sad fucks of previous weeks, and I remember feeling that we'd turned a corner. Afterwards I got up and made tea and Scotch pancakes to have in bed, but when I got back he was already dressed, told me he was moving out, that he couldn't go on like this. I'll never forgive him for making love to me without telling me it was the last time.

My mobile rings and his photo comes up on the screen, making me jump, as if he's been eavesdropping on my thoughts. I take a deep breath and answer as casually as I can.

'Eliot! How's it going?'

'Fine… Can you talk?'

'Hang on,' I say, getting up from my desk and going into the corridor. My hands feel clammy around the phone. *He's found something. He wouldn't have rung if he hadn't found something.* 'So? Any luck?'

'Sort of… You were born in Birmingham, right?'

'Yeah.' Trust him to remember. 'We moved to Essex when I was about six.'

'Hmm, that makes sense. Local murder case, lots of stuff on the news.' He sounds pleased with himself.

'So there *was* an actual murder?'

'Cara Travers was a young actress, stabbed to death at a local beauty spot in August 1984. The case was never solved.'

'She was a real person…' I feel a shiver run right through me. 'And what about the other one? Christopher Jay?'

'Don't know. It was before computerisation, so there's no detail on the original case on HOLMES, just a couple of case reviews that got nowhere.'

'And this was in Birmingham?'

'Yup. It was known as the Darkwater Murder. As it happens, my boss used to work at Heartlands – DI Gerrard, remember her?' Of course I remember Siobhan Gerrard; I used to be jealous of her. An Irish Brummie with flaming-red hair and a large bosom, brain the size of a department store, ten years older than Eliot and happily married, but otherwise a perfect match for him – another cop, someone who understood the life.

'Did she work on it, then?' I say.

'No,' he laughs, 'way before her time. But *her* boss back then worked on the case as a young DC, so she knew a bit about it. Anyway, I showed her the DVD – hope you don't mind – and she immediately sent it on to this guy in Birmingham.' He lowers his voice conspiratorially. 'Turns out he's now the chief constable! How crazy is that?'

He showed her the video. Why did he do that? 'It's not a public document, Eliot,' I say, stiffly. 'It's not like I put it on Facebook.'

'I thought you wanted me to investigate.'

'I did, but…'

'Chief Constable Durley came straight back to Siobhan, really interested. He wants to talk to you about it. Off the record.'

'What? But I don't know anything.'

'He wants to see us both tomorrow afternoon, at his place. It sounds important.'

'We've got to go all the way to Birmingham?'

'It's not that far; there are loads of trains.'

'But why? I don't understand. Anyway, I don't think I'm free… I… I'm,' I stammer, desperately trying to think of a reason to get out of it.

'Look, Meri. When a chief constable asks to see you, you jump. We can't refuse to go.'

'But why does it have to be off the record?'

'I don't know… I guess we'll find out.'

CHAPTER SIX

Cara
February 1984

Isobel's list of things to do was extensive, with actions grouped into headings – Creative, Admin, Transport, Finance, Publicity, Miscellaneous – and a separate column denoting who was going to take responsibility for what. As Cara had recent clerical experience, her initials featured strongly in the Admin and Finance sections, while Isobel put herself down for Transport and Publicity. Tasks under Creative were allotted to both of them jointly – this was, after all, what Purple Blaze was all about.

After hours of animated discussion, it was unanimously decided that their first production would be a one-hour original play, devised through improvisation and then scripted by Isobel, which would be toured to community venues in the Midlands area. As for what the play would be about, they didn't yet know. The nuclear threat, Margaret Thatcher, whales and glue-sniffing were themes under consideration, but so far no clear front-runner had emerged. Until they knew what their first show was about, there was little they could do on any other front, but Isobel would not be rushed into creative decisions. It was all very well for her, thought Cara, she had her inheritance money to live off, some ten thousand pounds. In contrast, Cara had used up her meagre savings and was signing on.

While waiting for creative inspiration to strike, Cara busied herself organising the dining room as the company admin office. With Isobel's money, they bought a grey metal filing cabinet from the junk shop in Redborne High Street and dragged it all the way down the hill. At the moment, all it housed were two reams of Purple Blaze letterhead and a hundred matching envelopes, but there was enormous potential for alphabetically ordered suspension files and colour-coded labels.

A month had quickly passed and Cara was sticking the calendar to the chimney breast with Blu-Tack when she heard a loud beeping sound outside. Somebody was clearly trying to attract attention. She ignored it at first, thinking it must be a taxi for one of the neighbours, but when it didn't stop, she finally went to look out of the living-room window.

The sound was coming from a battered old Bedford van, parked right outside the house, and Isobel was sitting in the driver's seat. Cara ran into the hallway, threw open the front door and rushed out.

Isobel wound down the window and the strains of a pop song wafted out. 'Fifty quid! And it's taxed and MOT'd for nine months.' She waited for Cara to respond. 'Well, what do you think?'

The first phrase that came into Cara's head was one of her father's favourites – 'throwing good money after bad' – but Isobel's face was shining so brightly, she didn't dare say it. Instead, she laughed and said, 'Well, I guess that's Transport ticked.'

The van had been resprayed but the name of its previous owner – the *Birmingham Evening Mail* – was still visible under the patchy white paint. Isobel slid open the door and then moved across so that Cara could climb inside and sit on the torn mustard leatherette seat. The cab stank of stale tobacco and male sweat, and Cara immediately imagined the ghosts of two overweight men with cheerful Brummie accents hauling bundles of papers onto damp pavements, dodging through the rush-hour traffic, parking up on kerbs, reversing into bollards.

'Let's call her Bertha,' said Isobel. 'Bertha the Bedford.' She slapped her hand on the dashboard and the cover of the glove compartment fell off. 'Only sixty thousand miles; amazing, eh?'

'Hmm…' Cara frowned. 'It must have gone round the clock. At least once.'

'Oh, don't be so negative! What do you expect for fifty quid?'

'We should have it – I mean *her* – sprayed purple, with the company logo on the side,' replied Cara, trying to make up for the previous remark.

'That's a brilliant idea… Come on, out you get.' Cara climbed out, then Isobel heaved the door shut and locked it, dropping the keys into the front pocket of her skirt. 'Let's go inside and celebrate – I've got teacakes.'

Teacakes. Cara knew what that meant: Isobel had been worried about her purchase, so she'd bought a peace offering in advance. Teacakes were special; they played an important, symbolic role in their friendship. It had begun shortly after Cara left her student accommodation and moved in to share with Isobel. About ten people lived in the house – allegedly; the landlord rented by the room, each secured with its own padlock. The two girls were never really sure who their housemates were, rarely meeting the same person twice on their way to the grimy shared bathroom. There was a hole in the roof so large that when it snowed just before Christmas, a shaft of snowflakes fell spectacularly onto the upstairs landing, and the very top bedroom had been taken over by pigeons. The oven didn't work and they'd found mice in the cutlery drawer, so they only ever ventured into the tiny galley kitchen to fill the kettle. Cooking was impossible, but Isobel discovered that if you sliced a teacake down the middle you could just about shove the two halves into the rusty old toaster they kept in their room. Cara would watch anxiously as Isobel poked about with a knife, saying, 'Turn it off at the socket, you'll electrocute yourself!' and Isobel would laugh and tell her she liked living dangerously.

Now Cara followed Isobel into the house and put the kettle on. The teacakes were sliced and placed in the toaster and soon the kitchen was smelling sweetly of melted butter and burnt raisins.

'Now we've got the transport sorted, I suppose we can start hiring actors,' said Isobel casually, as she poured the tea.

'It's too early, isn't it? I mean, we don't know what the show's about yet.' Cara felt instantly miffed. She was enjoying their life here, just the two of them, buying stationery and rearranging furniture – playing at theatre companies as she'd once played schools or hospitals with her dolls.

'Plays with only two people in are so dull.' Isobel bit into a teacake, letting the melted butter dribble down her chin. 'And it would be better if I just directed.'

'But actors will need paying.' Cara heard her voice rising with desperation. 'I don't want you spending any more of your inheritance, it's not fair.'

'We'll do it as a profit share. I've already written the advert and sent it to *The Stage*. It'll be in this Thursday.' Isobel leaned across and planted a kiss on Cara's head. 'It's all sorted,' she said.

'We ought to go through all these CVs,' said Isobel, a week later. They were sitting on the rug in the beautiful sitting room, trays of Chinese takeaway littering the highly polished coffee table. *My treat*, Isobel had insisted. 'Decide on a shortlist, then we can run auditions next week. Sooner the better really. Don't want the good ones getting other jobs.'

'They won't…' Cara stabbed a piece of fried chicken with a plastic chopstick. She felt strangely aggressive towards the torrent of applications that had poured through the letter box over the past few days. They were piled on the dining table in the office, reeking of desperation. It wasn't a nice feeling, being on the other side of the process – suddenly an employer instead of an applicant – and she felt like a fraud. Actors, it seemed, were easily duped. All you needed was a logo, a company name and an advert the size of a postage stamp.

'We've got to get them down to a manageable number.' Isobel slurped up her last noodle noisily. 'What do you reckon? Twenty?'

'Okay.'

'Great. Do you want to fetch them while I clear the decks?' No, Cara didn't want to fetch them. She wanted to put them in the bin and forget they'd ever arrived.

Isobel climbed onto the tiny sofa and patted the cushion for Cara to join her. They spent the next hour reading through what turned out to be nearly two hundred submissions of varying quality, sharing dreadful photos of young would-be actors posing with their chin resting on a single pensive finger, or sitting glumly in a Woolworth's Photo-Me booth because they couldn't afford to pay for a professional photographer. Anyone not obviously left-wing went into the reject pile straight away. Nor was Isobel interested in anyone who said they loved musicals.

'It's so hard,' said Cara, thinking of all the failed applications she'd made over the past months. 'Who are we to judge?'

Isobel sat up straight. 'Have they started their own theatre company? Have they had the vision, the passion – the ambition to do something for themselves?'

'Have they got a Bertha the Bedford?' Cara parried, trying to warm things up with a touch of self-irony. There was a pause, then Isobel threw back her head and laughed. After that, she treated the submissions with more kindness. They discussed the candidates one by one, finally making a small pile of auditionees, who would be rung the next day and invited to attend 'an informal devising workshop'.

It was happening, whether Cara liked it or not.

CHAPTER SEVEN

Me

'You okay?' asks Eliot as the black cab pulls up outside Chief Constable Durley's house.

'Think so...' A shiny black Mercedes is parked on the huge block-paved driveway. 'Just not sure why I'm here. It all feels a bit too... official.'

'You were the one who wanted to find out more.' He gives me a reassuring smile.

Durley must have heard the taxi because he opens the front door before we ring the bell. He's tall and slim, a good head of salt-and-pepper hair cut square and short, clean-shaven, thick eyebrows plucked and trimmed, a pair of steel-rimmed glasses resting on his long, straight nose, his face set in a professional smile. He looks like one of those men who don't do casual, not even when they're gardening or mucking out the garage; I imagine him still wearing his uniform underneath the brown cords and green checked shirt and I want to giggle.

'Thanks for coming,' he says. 'Good journey?'

Both men do the niceties so well. Durley talks to Eliot mainly, asking after Siobhan Gerrard, whom he calls a smart cookie, reporting that he's heard what a bright young thing Eliot is, a glittering future ahead of him and all that guff.

'The country's short of talented detectives, a lot of young people can't hack it, aren't prepared to put in the hours.' He takes our coats and hangs them on a set of brass hooks. 'The force needs to hold on to people like you.'

The house is imposing and a little chilly – high decorative ceilings, a large tiled hallway with several heavy doors no doubt leading to well-proportioned reception rooms. Durley opens one, and sure enough, we're in a large lounge overlooking a beautifully kept garden. My eyes wander over the pale pink three-piece-suite, the dark polished furniture, family portraits in silver frames jockeying for position on the sideboard, a modest-sized television in one alcove, a small bookcase in the other, an immaculate cream carpet protected by a large Chinese rug. The chief constable asks us about milk and sugar and then bustles off to make tea.

There's a large framed photo on the wall above the mantelpiece: Durley and a thin, frail woman, smiling from her wheelchair as she hands a bunch of flowers to the queen. 'Is that his wife?' I whisper, afraid to say anything out loud, as if the place might be bugged.

'Think so. She died last year – bowel cancer. Durley does a lot of fund-raising for Macmillan Nurses, ran a marathon the other week.'

I choose the middle seat of the sofa and sit down. 'Impressive.'

'Yup, he's impressive all right…' Eliot walks over to the large French windows and stares out at the patio with ornamental pond, a long green rectangle of lawn, neat shrubs and well-weeded flower beds. 'Joined the local Heartlands force under the fast-track graduate scheme and made it to inspector in record time. Went to Mercia as assistant chief at forty, back at Heartlands as the dep at fifty, chief since 2008, honorary fellow of King's College, Queen's Police Medal, OBE, retiring at the end of the year.'

'Done your research then,' I say, teasing.

The tea-making's taking forever and I'm thinking of going to offer help, when the great man comes back in, carrying a tray laden with a floral china tea set and a plate of chocolate biscuits.

'Sorry for the delay. I was stupid enough to check my emails while I was waiting for it to brew... Do sit down, Eliot. We don't stand on ceremony here.' Durley pours and hands out the cups and saucers, pulling out two small tables from a nest and positioning them precisely at our right-hand sides. He finds coasters in the side-board drawer, glancing up at the photo of his wife as he fusses, then sits in the big armchair. 'Yes, very good of you to come.' He takes a tentative slurp. 'Difficult to have this kind of conversation over the phone. And probably better if it's off the record at this stage.'

'No problem, sir.'

'Do have a biscuit.' Eliot leaps up and passes me the plate, but I'm too excited to eat. Durley takes one, dunking it briefly in his cup before sliding it into his mouth. He crunches away slowly, staring at me like I'm an object of some considerable interest. 'How much do you know about the Darkwater Murder?' he says eventually.

'Nothing really,' Eliot replies on my behalf. 'There wasn't much on HOLMES so I asked Gerrard – she said you worked on it.'

Durley nods. 'Cara Travers, a twenty-two-year-old drama graduate – pretty girl as it happens – stabbed in the chest with a kitchen knife. I was exhibits officer on the case.' He turns to me. 'Bagging and labelling, establishing the chain of evidence. My first murder, that's why I've never forgotten it.' He puts his mug down. 'You know, you *do* look incredibly like your mother.'

My heart falls into my stomach. 'You *knew* her?' I pull a face at Eliot, but his expression doesn't shift.

'Well, I met her a few times, if that's what you mean,' Durley replies. 'Bit of a hippy, if I remember rightly.'

'I'm sorry, I don't understand. Are you saying my mother had something to do with the murder?'

'She found the body.' He registers our astonished expressions. 'I beg your pardon, I assumed you knew.'

My heart starts to race as the chief rises and walks over to the sideboard.

'My wife kept scrapbooks of every major case I was involved in. It was her way of being involved, bless her. God only knows, she spent enough time by herself. Barbara loved following the trials, read all the papers, even sat in the public gallery sometimes. She missed it when I went into management.' He glances towards her photo on the chimney breast. 'Anyway... I had a rummage this morning and found this.' He gestures for us to come over.

It's the kind of old-fashioned scrapbook Dad used to buy me when I was a child, so we could make a record of our holidays. The same coloured sugar paper, pink, purple, acid yellow and sludge green, faded and bitten at the edges. We used to stick in postcards and publicity leaflets, tickets for boat rides and museums, drawings I'd made on rainy days. And later, when we got home, we'd add photos he'd taken of me proudly standing next to a sandcastle, or lying on my surfboard, triumphant after a good ride to the shore. I suppose kids nowadays do it all with an iPad... I don't know why I'm thinking about that now. Maybe it's because I can't take all this other stuff in. Maybe I don't want to know the truth about what Becca did.

'Here you go. This is Cara Travers.' He points to a grainy black-and-white head shot of a young woman with even features and long straight hair; blonde or perhaps mousy, it's hard to tell. She's all smiles and innocence, her expression hopeful and eager, as if contemplating a long, happy life stretching before her. Girl-next-door pretty. The perfect murder-victim photo. I turn a few pages, casting my eyes over the yellowing newspaper cuttings. The press used the same photo again and again, fixing her personality, defining her in death. 'Cara Travers, young actress', 'Cara Travers, victim', 'Cara, aged 22'.

'It should have been one of the simplest cases the team ever put together,' Durley says. 'There was only one suspect – her ex-boyfriend, Christopher Jay. He was a nasty piece of work, pot-head, thief, violent bully. Cara had been brave enough to finish the relationship, but he wouldn't accept it. It was a classic case of "if I can't have you, nobody else will".'

Christopher Jay. In my mind, I can hear my tiny voice struggling to pronounce his name.

'So what was the case against him?' asks Eliot.

'It was made up of lots of little things; when you put them together, they added up. For a start, there were no signs of forced entry, which meant Cara probably knew her killer. She hadn't been living in Birmingham long and hadn't made any friends outside of their little theatre company. The other actors had left weeks earlier and had cast-iron alibis, and – importantly – no motive. Jay was the last man standing. Cara had recently done a big clean-up of the house, but his fingerprints were all over the kitchen and there were signs of a struggle. Nothing on him, unfortunately, but he had plenty of time to dispose of any bloody clothing, along with the murder weapon, which we never found, although a large knife was missing from the block. Jay admitted going to the house that day. A neighbour saw him arriving in the afternoon, but nobody saw him leave, suggesting he remained there until the time of the murder. And Cara's friends testified that he'd been violent towards her during and after the relationship. Motive, opportunity and no alibi for time of death – it was all there. So we took it to trial and…' He pauses, as if it's too painful for him to continue, walking away from us towards the window, where he stands, gazing at the large, empty lawn.

I exchange a curious look with Eliot. 'So what happened?' I say, after a pause. 'Did something go wrong?'

Durley turns round to face me, a look of cold hostility in his eyes. 'Your mother, that's what went wrong.'

My stomach turns over. 'My mother? What do you mean?'

'The statement she gave the morning after the murder was consistent with the timeline. She claimed she'd had an argument with her husband and left the house in the middle of the night to get some fresh air. She went for a walk around Darkwater Pool and came across Cara's body, ran to the nearest phone box and called 999. When the duty officers turned up ten minutes later, they found her weeping hysterically and covered in the victim's blood.'

Eliot raises his eyebrows. 'But she wasn't a suspect?'

'No,' replies Durley firmly. 'There was nothing to link her to Cara Travers.'

'So what did she do? Move the body? Compromise the forensics?'

'It was much worse than that.' Durley turns around and goes back to his armchair, sitting down heavily. 'When Rebecca Banks took the witness stand, she gave a different version of events, said the victim was still alive when she found her. She even claimed Cara spoke to her, asked her to stay with her until she died. It was a complete shock to us – my DI was absolutely furious. She'd been called as a witness for the prosecution and suddenly she'd switched sides.'

'Switched sides?' I echo. 'Surely she wouldn't have done that deliberately.' I don't get what he's talking about, but the disgusted look on Durley's face is making me feel defensive.

'If you let me explain,' Durley replies, his tone a little patronising. 'The pathologist put the time of death at between 9 and 11 p.m., but Rebecca Banks dialled 999 at 12.42. If Cara was still alive, with her injuries giving her a twenty-minute bleed-out at most, it put the time of the attack at around midnight. Which meant Christopher Jay couldn't have killed her, because at that time he was conveniently getting chucked out of the Punjabi Paradise restaurant six miles away, and there were half a dozen people prepared to swear to it.'

'How annoying,' says Eliot, creasing his forehead into a sympathetic frown. 'Why do you think she suddenly changed her mind?'

Durley shrugs. 'I think she just got a bit carried away by the drama of the occasion, didn't realise the implications of what she was saying. The prosecution gave her a really hard time, but she wouldn't budge – said she'd forgotten to mention it when she made her original statement because she was in a state of shock or some such bullshit. It was a gift to the defence. They made the most of it and suddenly our case didn't seem so watertight.' Durley sighs with irritation.

Eliot walks over to him. 'Didn't the judge advise the jury in her summing-up? Surely she told them to put science above faulty witness testimony?' I bristle at the word 'faulty' and turn back to the scrapbook, searching for a mention of Becca's name.

'Yes, but instead of clarifying things, she made it worse. She reminded them that the pathologist had admitted it was more difficult to accurately determine time of death in very hot weather. It was supposed to help, but it undermined the pathologist's expertise and confused the jury even more. After six hours they delivered a not-guilty verdict. Christopher Jay is still running around free as a bird, might even have gone on to kill more women, who knows?'

I turn over another page and see a photo of a man who must be Christopher Jay leaving the court. He's flanked by what looks like his lawyer and an older woman, probably his mother. Journalists are crowding around him, thrusting microphones at his chest. In the background, standing on the steps of the building, I see a face I vaguely recognise. Not Becca, though. A young woman with jet-black hair and a short fringe. Her mouth is wide open; she looks as if she's screaming at Jay. Who is she? She doesn't look like Cara's sister. A friend, perhaps?

'The video is very confused, but it gives us one very important piece of information,' says Durley. 'Rebecca Banks realised she'd made a terrible mistake and wanted to tell the truth.'

'But given her state of mind, sir, surely we can't trust the video any more than what she said in court.'

'My mother was – *is* – schizophrenic,' I add, looking up from the scrapbook. 'She wasn't diagnosed until after I was born. Apparently there were earlier symptoms, but nobody put two and two together.'

Durley nods sagely to himself. 'I remember she was off work with depression at the time of the murder. If we'd known it was schizophrenia, she could have been declared mentally unfit to give evidence and Christopher Jay would have gone down for life.' He turns to me. 'It could still be useful to us. How is your mother? Can she function?'

'I've no idea,' I say, as I reach the end of the cuttings and close the book.' She escaped from the psychiatric unit in 1991 and nobody's seen or heard from her since.'

'But she could still be alive.'

'We don't know that she *isn't*, but—'

'Thank you for bringing this matter to my attention,' Durley interrupts, standing up and putting on a formal voice. But it's obvious he's excited: his trimmed eyebrows are raised and he's trying to curb a smile. 'The timing couldn't be more perfect; we've just launched Operation Honeysuckle, a major review into high-profile unsolved cases from the 1980s. Recent advances in DNA recovery and blood detection makes it worth us revisiting these cold cases one more time. They've had a lot of success in other forces, which is great for the victim's families and, to be frank, good for PR. Now it's time for Heartlands to step up to the plate.'

'So the case is already under review?' Eliot asks.

'No, but it's on the list. I'm boosting the cold-case team – they need a kick up the arse, to be frank – so I've allocated funds for a temporary promotional secondment and we're about to advertise. You're just the kind of chap we need – on the High Potential Development Scheme, passed your OSPRE, ready for your next challenge. If you were to apply, I'm sure you'd be an excellent candidate…' He lets the words dangle enticingly in the air.

Eliot almost jumps to attention. 'God! I don't know, sir, I mean, that sounds really interesting, but…'

Durley smiles. 'You'd be a DS, and once you've got a couple of high-profile convictions under your belt, who's to say where it might lead?'

'Well, it's really good of you to think of me, sir.'

'Strictly speaking you shouldn't work on the case because of your connection to a chief witness, but it was a long time ago, Meredith's estranged from her mother and it's not like the two of you are in a relationship.' He pauses. 'You're not, are you?'

'No,' we both say hurriedly.

'Good.' A chirruping sound comes from Durley's trouser pocket and he takes out his phone. 'Sorry, got to read this.' He frowns at the screen.

'Well, sir, we won't take up any more of your valuable time.'

'I was supposed to be going for a run,' he says, quickly texting his reply, 'but I've got to go into the office now. Such is life.' He leads us back into the hallway. 'The Cara Travers acquittal has bugged me for years so I'd like to help all I can. Make the most of this opportunity – you'll learn a lot.'

'For sure. I'll definitely think about applying.'

'Don't think. Do.' Durley gallantly helps me on with my coat. 'If we can finally nail Christopher Jay, it'll make the perfect retirement present.'

'Pub?' says Eliot as soon as we reach the end of the driveway.

There's no sign of one in any direction so we decide to carry on up the hill, following the diminishing size of the houses. We don't say much. The conversation is too big to have on the street. Eliot's long legs stride out and I remember how I always had to walk twice as fast to keep up with him; how he made me feel like a kid, especially when he held my hand and dragged me along at his pace. He's so used to being in a rush that he can't walk slowly any more, and it puzzles me how he's not early for everything instead of late.

After five minutes, we reach a small village green, with a post office, a couple of hairdressers, a newsagent and a curry house. At the far point of the triangle of neatly trimmed grass is The Saracen, whitewashed with black beams in the same style as Durley's house. The pub is almost empty and deathly quiet. The afternoon sun is streaming dustily through the leaded windows and everything – the walls, the patterned carpet, the upholstery on the seats – is the colour of dried blood. Eliot buys us a couple of Beck's and a packet of cheese and onion crisps and leads us to a table in a dingy corner.

'Well…' he says. 'What do you make of that?'

'I don't know, I can't take it all in.' I open the crisp bag and the pungent smell of old socks wafts out. 'Do you think she made the video to show to the police?'

'Yeah, that would figure.'

'I wonder why she didn't go through with it.'

'Maybe your dad stopped her.'

'But why? If she realised she'd made a mistake with the evidence… I don't think she lied deliberately; she was just ill.'

'Your dad was probably trying to protect her.'

'But they could have had a retrial…'

'Not back then. There was double indemnity; you couldn't be tried for the same crime twice.'

'But you can now?'

'For murder and very serious offences, yes.'

We sit in silence for a few moments, drinking our beers and thinking our own thoughts.

'So does that mean you're going to take the job?' I say eventually.

'I've not been offered it yet.'

'As good as…'

'Hmm,' he says. 'There are procedures these days, equal opportunities…'

'But he's the chief constable; if he wants you then he'll make it happen. He'll be like your sponsor, he'll mentor you.'

'I'll be his bitch, you mean.' He laughs. 'Anyway, I'm not sure I want to spend six months in Birmingham.'

'It'll be okay. And you'll be a sergeant, you'll be working on a murder; that's what you want, isn't it?' I persist.

'It's a cold case, Meri, it's not the same. It'll be mostly paperwork – reading endless statements, chasing up forensics …'

'Well, I think it's a great opportunity and you should take it. You'll regret it if you don't.'

'You just want me to find your mother.' He lifts the bottle to his mouth.

'No, I don't,' I bite back instantly. Too instantly.

'You do. That's what all this is about.'

'No, it's not. I've never had any interest in finding Becca.'

'Not even now?'

'Especially not now.'

'Not true, Meri.' He takes my hand. 'You forget how well I know you.'

I snatch my fingers away and grip the edge of the table. 'Well, you're wrong. I wanted to know why she made the video and now that bit makes sense, kind of… But I don't want to *meet* her, I don't want a reunion. Anyway, Dad would have a fit.'

'Okay, okay, I'm sorry.' Eliot takes my hand again. 'It's just that… well, you do realise, whoever's investigating will want to interview her.'

'They'll have a problem,' I say, looking into my lap. 'She's dead. Killed herself. That's what Dad thinks, anyway.'

'And what if she's not dead?' Eliot presses. 'What if we discover she's still alive… where she lives… what then? Do you want to know?'

Do I? I wish I could say I didn't. I wish I didn't care, that I could walk away, leave the police to get on with it. But it's too late now. The genie's out of the bottle.

CHAPTER EIGHT

Cara
March 1984

At last the front bedroom had been transformed into a studio space and was ready for the auditions.

'I'll lead the workshop while you observe and take notes,' Isobel said as they ate an early breakfast.

Cara's face fell. 'Oh… I thought we'd be doing it together.'

'Somebody's got to do the paperwork, and you're so good at that kind of thing.' Isobel paused her toast-buttering to check her friend's expression. 'And I'm going to be directing the show, so it makes sense for me to cast.'

'You want to direct? But I thought it was going to be group-devised.'

'Come on, we all know that never works in reality.'

Cara knew she'd been outmanoeuvred, but there was nothing she could do about it. In truth, she *was* good at the paperwork and Isobel had directed shows for Drama Soc at university. It made sense to share out the responsibilities in this way. She just wished they could have had a proper discussion about it and reached a joint decision. She tried to put the matter to the back of her head. The auditions were more important and she couldn't bear even the thought of falling out with Isobel. In all the years of their friendship they hadn't had a single disagreement about anything – something they were both very proud of.

To their surprise, only half the number of actors they'd called to the first session actually turned up.

'I don't care,' said Isobel. 'I'd rather have people with commitment.'

She had forbidden any discussion of the candidates until everyone had been seen, but Cara thought she'd already worked out who were her favourites: a young man called Toby, who campaigned regularly with CND; and an older woman from Manchester called Gina, who clearly knew a lot about the Arts Council and getting funding from charities. Ideally, Isobel wanted to recruit three people, making five of them altogether. She liked odd numbers because it meant the group couldn't split down the middle.

'Let's hope there's somebody good in the last session,' said Cara, turning over a new page on her notepad.

They had a full turnout for the final workshop of the day, and soon Isobel was putting them through their warm-up stretches and vocal exercises. Cara, installed behind the card table in the corner, pen poised over the paper, tried to think of something insightful to write about each candidate. But so far, she'd found herself only looking at one person.

You couldn't call him handsome, not even fashionably so, but he was ugly-beautiful: thick, unkempt black hair, pale, almost transparent skin, and a slightly broken nose. Cara caught glimpses of him darting like an insect between a forest of bodies – bare, skinny arms and bony legs wrapped tightly in black jeans. He was tall and slightly built, with the haunted look of somebody who didn't eat properly and spent a lot of time in darkened rooms.

If I put my arms around him I would be able to feel his ribs, thought Cara, and immediately blushed inside. He looked a couple of years younger than her and wasn't even her type; how could she be thinking about touching him? Nothing about this boy invited intimacy. He was wearing a grubby sleeveless T-shirt featuring a stick-man hanging from a gallows. She wondered whether he'd worn it deliberately or whether it had been the only clean thing available, and found herself wanting to know, because either way, it would reveal something about his character.

Isobel sat everyone down in a circle and gave them her well-rehearsed spiel about Purple Blaze taking provocative new work to people and places up to now ignored by the theatrical establishment. She kept saying 'I' instead of 'we' and if Cara hadn't been so distracted she would have felt hurt by the exclusion. She surreptitiously read the boy's application again. His name was Jay. Whether that was his first or last name, he wasn't prepared to divulge. He'd left school with only two O levels, was currently unemployed and lived in a part of Birmingham Cara hadn't heard of – in other words, he was their target audience, the disenfranchised proletariat, supposedly hungry for culture but until now unable to access or afford it. He'd sent them a short hand-written letter with no photo or CV attached, the facts unembroidered, the tone cool with not a hint of begging. Cara had initially rejected him for being too young and inexperienced, but Isobel had thrown him back onto the pile because he was local and 'real'.

As the session wore on, Cara dutifully jotted down comments against every name on the list – 'stiff and physically bound', 'probably not a team player', 'definite maybe', 'sorry, just don't like her'. She didn't write a thing next to the boy's name, just drew a big hairy asterisk and doodled around it until she'd covered the page.

And then the workshop was over and all the auditionees were leaving, congratulating Isobel on the amazing session she'd run, and reaffirming their commitment to coming to live in Birmingham and working for nothing for as long as it took to get Purple Blaze off the ground. Only Jay left without making a final gushing plea, putting on his heavy black boots and tying the laces in silence, looking up only once to meet Cara's insistent gaze – as if he'd known she'd been staring at him all afternoon.

'I think Jay's definitely a possibility,' Cara declared later, trying not to betray her keenness.

'Yes, he was by far the best,' Isobel agreed, opening a bottle of wine to celebrate. 'Goes by gut instinct, doesn't over-think everything. You can spot the university graduates a mile off. Too intellectual, too competitive. And the drama school ones can't improvise. I like his vulnerability – it's attractive don't you think? He might not hack it, but he's worth a try. He's got it, that thing. He's watchable.'

'So you think we should offer him the job? I know it's not actually a job, but you know what I mean…'

'Definitely. He'll still be on his way home, but we can ring him later.' Isobel put down her glass and smiled. 'Actually, why don't *you* ring him? It'll sound more official coming from you.'

'Okay.' Cara felt a thrill course through her body, like she'd just stepped onto a fairground ride. Excited and afraid. She couldn't explain it, daft really…

CHAPTER NINE

Jay
Now

He blinks at the dance of fuzzy coloured lights from cars and shops and street lamps as the day cross-dissolves into evening. He hates driving the minibus, especially in Camden, and especially when it's full of rowdy students, joking and arguing with each other, behaving like kids on their way to the seaside. Time's running out, so he drops the students off at the front door of the theatre and goes to find a place to park.

'Jesus Christ!' He beeps the horn as a young man appears from behind a parked car and saunters across the road right in front of him, hands in pockets, head down, not even looking up once to check that it's safe. Yet whose fault would it be if he got knocked over? Nobody takes responsibility any more. If they scrape your car in a car park they just drive away, don't leave a note or anything. That's why he's given up his Fiesta – the insurance was crazy, he could never park outside his front door and he lost count of the number of times the wing mirror was knocked off. You didn't need a car in London anyway.

A small van suddenly pulls out of a space a few cars ahead of him and his stomach knots. Will someone else get there first? Will the space be big enough for the twelve-seater? He flicks on the left indicator and stops just beyond the space, but the guy in the car behind either isn't concentrating or doesn't care and drives right up to his back bumper, leaving him no room to reverse.

'Bastard!' He peers into his rear mirror; he can't make out the driver in the growing darkness, but he'd like to get out and punch him. He looks at the clock – how can it already be five past seven? Cars behind start sounding their horns. Nobody's prepared to back up; he has no choice but to move on.

He turns into the next side street and finds a nice juicy space a hundred yards further down. Maybe he'll make it after all. He locks up the minibus and starts retracing his route with long, impatient strides. He's sweating under his overcoat, the cold wind snatching at his breath, but he quickens his pace all the same, turning onto the main road. Commuters are emerging from the tube, slowing him down as they pause to check their phones. He shoves his way past, sidestepping like a rugby player with his eye on the try line. Squints at his watch. Seven fourteen; there's still time. Just.

Why did he wait for the latecomers? Why didn't he take the students on public transport instead? Or better still, tell them to make their own way? They're all seventeen or eighteen, for Christ's sake, they're not babies, but you have to wipe their arses or they won't do anything. He might have known that their appalling punctuality would conspire to fuck it up, although they had no idea how important tonight was for him. They thought they were just seeing the opening performance of a new play directed by someone they'd never heard of. How he'd enjoyed their vacant shrugs at the mention of her name; their ignorance had comforted him. And God bless the Arts Theatre for 'reaching out' to the community with free tickets for local college students and a first-night drinks reception for heads of department. Not that he *was* a head of department – Isatu had been busy tonight and asked him if he wouldn't mind stepping in. Wouldn't mind?!

He'd nearly kissed her. For once in his life all the stars had lined up in his favour. He'd had his hair cut and nostrils trimmed; spent days planning what to wear, what he was going to say, how he was going to do it. This was the best opportunity he'd had in years to get to her.

Isobel Dalliday.

She'd always been there, lurking in the shadowy corners of his mind. When they parted company over thirty years ago, he knew they hadn't quite done with each other. He heard that she'd sold the house (well, who wouldn't after what happened?) and moved to London, no doubt in search of the fame and fortune she'd always believed was rightfully hers. He'd had to get out of Birmingham, choosing London for opposite reasons, seeking anonymity and finding it easily enough. He gave up his non-existent acting career and went to college to get some qualifications; stopped insisting everyone only called him by his cool, monosyllabic surname and returned to his first name, Christopher, shortening it to Chris. He started behaving like he thought a guy called Chris should: quiet, calm, private but not unsociable. Unthreatening. Normal. Forgettable. He grew into the part; sometimes even playing 'Chris' when he was on his own. It really helped with the anger management. So much so that there were days when he hardly clenched his fists, when he only thought about *it* a few times; in his solitary moments, when he was on his way to work, or trying to get to sleep.

For seventeen years he heard nothing of Isobel Dalliday, which, to be honest, surprised him. He started to wonder whether she'd gone abroad, or got cancer, or been killed in a car accident. As much as he liked the idea of Isobel being dead, he preferred the explanation that she'd left the theatre and was stuck in some mind-numbingly boring job. His fantasies spurred him on. In those seventeen almost-happy years, he put himself through teacher training, got a job in further education, saved up a deposit and bought a small flat. He dared to think that maybe, just maybe, Chris Jay had turned out to be the success and Isobel Dalliday the failure.

Then everything came crashing down – in an instant, when he was totally unprepared. He'll never forget how it happened, every single detail branded into his memory. He was in the staffroom, moaning about how hard it was to find material that was relevant to a group of mostly BAME students, when a colleague suggested a play she'd recently seen at the Royal Court and handed him a copy of the script. He started flicking through the pages, idly, just to get a feel for the dialogue. It looked promising, so he checked the cast list to see how many actors were needed and her name shot out from the page, stabbing him in the eyes.

Isobel Dalliday had directed the first production. Or, as he'd come to refer to her in his thoughts, Isobel Fucking Dalliday. It *had* to be her, it couldn't be anyone else with the same sunny, irrepressible name. Isobel Fucking Dalliday had become an associate director at one of the most dynamic, cutting-edge, highly regarded theatres in the whole country, maybe even the world.

He'd been living in a state of permanent envy and hatred ever since, watching her career rise to ever greater heights, with her Evening Standard Theatre Awards, her thousands of Twitter followers and her much-appreciated support for popular causes like climate change and female genital mutilation. Not only that, she'd become a celebrity dyke – she and her girlfriend Alice Anderson among the first to have a civil partnership and then to get married.

Oh yes, everyone loved Isobel Dalliday, even more so now that she was 'giving back'. She'd spurned the National Theatre and the RSC. Now she was only interested in doing creative work with London's disenfranchised 'youff' – the more multicultural, poverty- stricken and inner-city the better. That was when it all got too much. Because it was exactly what *he'd* been doing for the last twenty-odd years, although nobody gave a shit about that; nobody even knew. Only clever, talented, beautiful people like Isobel Dalliday could make the world a better place. Now she was going to single-handedly stem the flow of Islamic radicalisation by founding a citywide festival of young people's theatre, including a playwriting competition for under-25s. Yup. Isobel Dalliday (OBE for services to theatre) had even stooped to direct the winning play, written by a Muslim teenage girl and performed by young, local amateurs. There'd been an item on the local news, articles in the *Guardian*; the London glitterati were wetting their pants with right-mindedness. Tonight is the big opening night, with champagne and samosas and journalists from all the quality broadsheets. And he's going to piss all over it.

Jay pauses outside the theatre to compose himself. When he's nervous, his voice squeaks, and he wants to make sure that doesn't happen tonight. He clears his throat and makes his entrance. To his surprise, the foyer is empty save for a few stragglers. How come? He glances at his watch: it's only twenty past, ten minutes to go until curtain-up. Maybe the audience are so eager they've already gone in to take their seats.

He looks about for the VIP drinks reception. It'll be in some discreet corner, roped off from the public – it's probably taking place in the upper foyer, he thinks, reaching into his breast pocket for his invitation and bounding up the stairs. His heart is thumping. Isobel will still be there, holding court, waiting to be escorted into the auditorium at the last moment like the queen. He reaches the top step and halts. He can see the white-clothed tables, the red rope cordon. But the only person there is a waiter, stacking empty wine glasses and bowls of peanut dust onto a tray.

Jay marches up aggressively. 'Where is everyone?'

'Watching the show, of course,' says the waiter. Jay stands there, his brain whirring. *But they can't be. They can't be.* 'It's press night. We always start at seven on press night.'

'But it says seven thirty on the ticket! I'm sure it does!' He takes out his ticket and stares at it. Fuck. How could he have been so stupid?

'If you ask the steward, she'll let you in when there's a—'

'I don't care about the fucking play. I haven't come for the fucking play.'

'Members of staff should not be subjected to verbal or physical abuse,' the young man recites, adding, 'and I'm not even paid. I'm a volunteer.' He points to the large white V on his purple T-shirt.

'Fuck!' Jay picks up a bottle and pours wine into a glass with the remains of red lipstick around the rim. The volunteer opens his mouth to protest, then seems to think better of it, shuffling off down the stairs with the loaded tray.

Jay swallows the wine quickly and then drains the bottle. After all the build-up, the planning and preparation, the hours spent going over his lines only to be let down so cruelly – fuck it, he deserves a drink. He looks towards the auditorium door. At least he knows where the enemy is: no more than a few yards away, sitting in the darkness with no idea that he's on the other side of the wall. He has her trapped; all he has to do is wait for the interval. Impossible that she could come out of the auditorium without seeing him. But... there'll be hundreds of people milling around, the great and good of Camden pressing around her; he'll have to barge his way through the crowd and get her attention above the chattering teenage throng. It won't work, or even worse, it'll go off at half-cock. She might not recognise him immediately; she might not hear what he's saying. If he's going to do it, he's going to do it properly. She has to know it's him and she has to be terrified.

Another chance will come. He just has to be patient.

CHAPTER TEN

Me

It's a beautiful day, the air so clean and sharp it sticks to my tongue as I come out of the railway station. There's a small taxi rank and I only have to wait a few minutes before a white mini-cab pulls up. I climb into the back and ask the driver to take me to Berryfield.

I spoke to Eliot last night. He got the job at Heartlands and has been promoted to detective sergeant on Cold Case Review. He called me from his new one-bed flat in Birmingham, his voice echoing as he walked around, his shoes clipping the laminate flooring like some out-of-time tap dance.

'What's the place like?' I asked, thinking it sounded empty and dismal.

'It's fine. Half the rent I'd pay in London and I can walk to work.'

'Let me have your new address and I'll send you a congratulations card.'

'No need, it's only a promotional secondment,' he said, but he gave it to me all the same. There was a long pause, then he said, 'How are things with your dad?'

'He's still ignoring me. Why?'

'It's just that… well, I'm going to need to talk to him about the Cara Travers case.'

'But he had nothing to do with it.'

'He made a witness statement at the time that needs checking. And I need to ask him if he knows where Becca is now.'

'He doesn't.'

'He's still legally her husband, so I have to ask.'

I started to feel panicky. 'Please, El, can't you keep him out of it? For my sake?'

'I'm sorry,' he said. 'I just wanted to give you the heads-up – thought you might want to have a word with him first, you know, smooth the way… I know he hates my guts.'

I didn't bother to deny it. Dad liked Eliot at first and was really impressed when he was selected for the High Potential Development Scheme – only sixty a year out of the whole country, he kept telling people, like a proud parent. But when things fell apart, he naturally took my side. He couldn't bear to see me hurting – wanted to make it all better, to pick me up, sit me on his knee and rub the pain away like he used to do when I fell off my bike. He'll loathe being questioned by Eliot, but it can't be helped. As I started this whole business, the least I can do is warn him first.

As the taxi scoots around the twisting lanes, barely braking for the bends, I fix my gaze on the landscape. Billowy clouds hang over the undulating fields, the pale blue sky streaked with liquid morning gold, like a Turner painting. I'm glad now that Dad didn't take any notice when I tried to dissuade him from moving to Suffolk. His heart was set on it, and it's his heart that calls the shots these days. After twenty years teaching maths to the unteachable – stressed, overweight, with dangerously high cholesterol – he was a cardiac arrest waiting to happen. Now, at fifty-eight, he's the relieved owner of two drug-eluting stents, has lost two stone and swallows a daily cocktail of beta blockers, aspirin and statins. Dad was offered early-retirement and he decided enough was enough.

I thought he was mad at the time, but now I understand. This is the perfect place for him – he can eat healthily, go for long walks, buy his newspaper and his semi-skimmed milk from the village shop, be part of the local community, meet new people, 'for friendship, maybe love'. The last thing I want to do is disturb his new-found peace, but it's going to be disturbed anyway, so I've no choice.

We pass under a railway bridge and turn sharp right onto Berryfield High Street. 'What number?' the driver asks.

'It's just called North End Cottage. I think it's at the end, on the left.'

I've only been to Dad's new home once before, when it still belonged to someone else. We went up to Suffolk for a few days for viewings and blitzed the area, seeing every two- or three-bedroom cottage for sale within a ten-mile radius of Ipswich. That was months ago now, the tail end of summer, and I remember it rained constantly, so much empty grey sky, like a band of depression round my head, that it made me long for the crowded London horizon.

'That's the one,' I say, leaning forward. 'With the blue front door.'

I ring the bell and Dad opens almost straight away, as if he was expecting a parcel. His face flushes when he sees me.

'Meri! What is it? What's the matter?'

'I'm sorry,' I blurt out. He holds out his arms and I fall into them, instantly warmed by his body.

'It's okay, love, it's okay,' he murmurs, stroking my back a couple of times before pulling away. 'You should have told me you were coming.' He removes his glasses and cleans them with the corner of his shirt. 'You haven't lost your job, have you?'

'No, no… I just had to see you.' We go through the tiny hallway and into the living room. He nods at me to sit down.

'I'll make some tea. Are you hungry? I bet you didn't have breakfast this morning.'

'I did, actually. On the train. But I wouldn't mind a biscuit,' I call out as he shuffles off to the kitchen in his old man's sheepskin slippers.

I look around at the familiar furniture, strangely revived by its new surroundings. His books are already on the shelves, his pictures on the walls, and a wood-burning stove is glowing in the fireplace. I take a couple of small logs from the wicker basket, open the door and shove them in, not because it's cold, just for the pleasure of seeing them flame. Dad loves his fires. All those Sunday afternoons in the old garden, the dead leaves crackling, the choking smoke. Saving up bits of wood and cardboard for Bonfire Night, inviting my friends round for hot dogs and his humble firework display. He was burning things the last time I saw him. An image of him sprawled among dead flowers instantly pops up before my inner eye, and I will it to pop down again.

'What do you think?' he asks from the kitchen.

'It's great. You've made it really homely, Dad.' I stand up, restless, and hover in the kitchen doorway. 'I wish you'd let me help, though. It was silly, doing the move all on your own.'

'I thought you didn't want anything to do with me.'

'You know that's not true. I left loads of messages. It was more like the other way round.'

'Well, let's forget about all that now,' he says, giving me a warning smile. I wish I could forget about it, but I can't. It's out of my control. Eliot's sitting in some Birmingham police station reading through statements, studying grisly photos of the murder victim and booking witness interviews; the past is alive and kicking and it's about to come and grab Dad by the throat.

Walking past me with a laden tray, he puts it down on the coffee table we used to have in the old lounge and hands me a mug I've not seen before. It's from a National Trust property – a good sign that he's getting out and about. He flops into his armchair and reaches over for his own mug, dunking his ginger nut into his tea and lifting it, dripping, into his mouth. Every sound seems amplified by our silence. The seconds are passing. If I don't say something now, I never will.

'So to what do I owe this unexpected pleasure?' he asks, searching my face for clues.

I take a long, deep breath. 'I watched the tape.'

No reply.

'You obviously know what's on it,' I continue. 'I mean, I understand completely why you didn't want me to see it, but… well, I have now, so we need to talk about it.' I try to catch his eye. 'Don't we?'

'She told me she'd destroyed it.' He looks past me, staring into the middle distance. 'I shouldn't have believed her; I should have stood and watched while she did it.'

'Well, maybe, but the thing is, I've watched it now. I did a bit of research… I know who Cara Travers was, I know Becca was a witness. I know what happened at the trial.'

'I see…' There's a long, heavy pause.

'And now I'd like to hear your side of the story.'

He sighs deeply, putting down his mug. 'There's not much to say. Your mother was a very sick woman when she made that tape. I'm sorry you watched it, but now you understand the hell we went through – why I had to get her away from you. My advice is to try to forget about it and move on.'

Okay, this is it. This. Is. It.

'The thing is, Dad, we can't forget about it. The tape undermines Becca's original evidence at the trial. The case has never been closed, you see, and now there's this review called Operation—'

He lets his mouth fall open. 'What? You mean you took the tape to the police? For God's sake, Meri! I can't believe…' He gets up and walks towards the conservatory doors, turning around to face me, his body tensing with anger. 'You idiot… you stupid, stupid girl! I *told* you not to watch it. Why didn't you let me put it on the fire where it belonged?'

'I know, I know, I'm sorry, I was just trying to find out some background. But it's not only because of the tape. The case was being reviewed anyway, as part of Operation Honeysuckle. Forces all over the country are looking at pre-DNA cases now they've got this new technology, Eliot says a lot of—'

'Eliot?' He presses his fingers against his chest and winces. I redden, cursing myself inwardly. I was supposed to lead in gently to Eliot, once I'd explained everything else. That's how I rehearsed it on the train this morning, but my plan has totally fallen apart. Dad is behaving really oddly, screwing up his eyes and breathing in rapidly through his nose. Is it anger or is something wrong?

'Why are you still in touch with Eliot? I thought it was… all over with that… bastard…'

'It is. We're just friends now. Dad, calm down!'

'Friends? After he gave you a nervous breakdown?'

'It wasn't a breakdown. Are you okay?'

'Why couldn't you… leave well… alone?' he says, gasping as he reaches out to steady himself on the back of a dining chair. 'Raking up the past… I'm warning you… you'll be sorry. No good… will come of it.'

'But if the police can finally convict Christopher Jay…'

'I don't care about that little shit,' he mutters. 'It's you I'm worried about. Us!'

'Dad – you look awful. Please sit down.' I try to take his arm, but he bats me off.

'I've always tried... my best... to give you what you needed... but it's never enough for you, is it? Never... enough...' He lets out a small cry and starts to crumple.

'Dad!' I leap forward. 'What is it?'

'My chest. Pain. Can't breathe...' I catch him as he sinks down, breaking his fall. Oh God, what's going on? He rolls sideways onto the rug, folding in on himself. His skin has gone grey and when I touch his forehead it feels cold and clammy, like a rubber toy.

'What is it? A heart attack? Dad? Talk to me! Are you having a heart attack?'

'Don't know,' he murmurs. 'Can't breathe.'

'Should I call an ambulance?'

He nods.

I grab the house phone and dial 999. 'What's the postcode?' the operator asks patiently. I look across the room to Dad, his eyes closed, hand pressed against his chest, as if feeling for his own heartbeat. 'No idea. All I know is North End Cottage, High Street, Berryfield... It's at the end of the village, there's no number.'

I run to the front door and look out onto the street, half expecting to see the ambulance already careering towards us, siren blaring, blue light flashing. But the road is empty and quiet. I don't know where the nearest doctor's surgery is; I don't know anything about this place. I prop the door open with one of Dad's walking boots, then rush back to his side.

'They're coming as fast as they can, Dad. Can I get you anything?'

'Blanket...' he whispers faintly. I hurtle up the stairs and drag the duvet off his bed, putting it over my shoulder and bounding down again. He's looking greyer and clammier than ever, but opens his eyes and smiles when I cover him up. It's a weak smile, the corners of his mouth only lifting slightly, but it's something.

I hold his damp, limp hand and tell him I love him; that everything's going to be all right. What else can I say? I can't bear the thought that we might have had our last proper conversation.

The ambulance arrives within ten minutes. Two jolly paramedics, one fat and chatty, one thin and quiet, swathed in bright green overalls and padded vests, run into the room and almost push me out of the way.

'Hello, I'm Mark,' the fat one says. 'What's your name, sir?'

'Graeme Banks,' I reply, but he ignores me. 'Who am I talking to, sir?' *What does it matter? Just take him to the hospital!* 'Where's the pain worst? In your arm?' He shakes his head. 'Not in your arm. Where, sir? In your chest?'

'It's not so bad now… I just feel so cold.'

'Okay, I'm just going to take your blood pressure.' He takes out the machine and nods at the result. 'Yes, it's extremely low.' He turns to me. 'I don't think it's a heart attack, but we'll get him in the ambulance and do some tests, just to be on the safe side.'

'Not a heart attack? Are you sure?'

'Most likely just a vasovagal episode.'

'A what?'

'It's a posh word for fainting, basically. What some people call a funny turn.' He sends the thin paramedic back to the ambulance, who then returns with a small chair on wheels.

'So nothing to do with his heart problems?'

'Not as such. Vasovagal episodes can be brought on by severe stress or a traumatic incident. His chest started tightening and he panicked; that's what I suspect happened. He'll be fine, honest.' Mark lowers his voice. 'Do you know what brought the attack on?'

'Not really,' I lie. I can't go into all that now, not with these people.

'Strange… It was quite a bad one.'

The paramedics help Dad to his feet, removing the cumbersome duvet and putting a thin hospital blanket around his shoulders instead. They lower him into the little chair and trundle him out of the house. He's speaking more clearly now, apologising for putting them to so much bother, making self-deprecating jokes. This is what he does when he's embarrassed. I watch as they load him into the back of the ambulance.

'We're going to do an ECG. Saves him sitting in A & E for four hours. You can sit in with him, if you like.'

'No, it's okay.' I can't sit there being all matey. I have to think.

I walk into the kitchen and fill the kettle for another cup of tea. *Funny turn.* I feel vaguely offended on Dad's behalf. I can't remember what the paramedic called it – vaso something. A posh word for fainting? I nearly fainted when I had my ears pierced, and it was nothing like that. Was it panic, because I mentioned the police? Or did he do it deliberately, so that I'd stop asking him questions? I don't understand why this news has upset him so much.

The kettle comes to the boil, but I leave it. I go into the conservatory and sit on the sofa, its cushions slightly damp. Beyond the tiny garden and the small chicken-wire fence a large muddy field stretches all the way to the horizon, a mass of sticky brown clay squatting under the huge cornflower sky.

What's he hiding? I wonder.

CHAPTER ELEVEN

Me

It's a relief to be back in the city: navigating my way through irritable commuters, tired mothers pushing laden buggies and people shouting down their phones in languages I can't recognise, let alone understand. As I wait on the underground platform, looking over dozens of expectant shoulders towards the tunnel, I am comforted by the lack of interest in my existence. It means I can concentrate on reorganising my universe.

There's been a seismic shift in my relationship with Dad. On the surface, the changes are barely discernible, small enough to ignore. But deep down at the core, we no longer trust each other.

When the paramedics left, he shuffled back indoors, sank into his favourite armchair, pointing the remote control at the telly and switching on *Cash in the Attic*, as casual as you like, and started telling me some humorous story about next door's dog. It was as if the paramedics had wiped his memory banks inside the ambulance, only we both knew full well they hadn't. Whenever he thought I was about to speak, he put his hand against his chest in a protective gesture – subtly warning me of the risk I'd be taking if I brought up the subject again. I glared at the television, silently fuming. Then he announced he was hungry and sent me to the kitchen with an order for cheese sandwiches and tomato soup.

'Thanks, love,' he said, picking up his spoon immediately and slurping the too-hot soup into his mouth. I put my own tray on the coffee table and knelt on the floor. We ate in silence, our spoons clinking the sides of the bowls, an unsteady metronome. Once he'd finished and I'd made another cup of tea, I called a taxi to take me back to the station. He tried to guilt-trip me into staying overnight, saying he was worried he might have another attack and would need me to call 999. I told him I had to get back to work tomorrow. Not true. I've actually booked three days off.

So here I am. Back home. If you can call this shabby room in a crappy shared house with damp home. I can smell it as soon as I walk into the kitchen; I'm sure it's getting worse. God, I miss our flat above the greengrocer's: just me and Eliot, with only *our* food in the fridge, *our* books on the shelves, *our* discarded socks in the sitting room. Growing pots of parsley and coriander on the kitchen windowsill, inviting friends round for Sunday brunch, talking about saving for a deposit. That was a grown-up kind of life. And although I moaned about Eliot's shifts, and worried that he might be shot or stabbed, I realise I was happy then. Happier than I am now, anyway. I hate this single girlie sharing, this throwback to my student days. I should not have to live with someone who puts Post-it notes on their food, or texts me from their bedroom to complain that their bottle of wine has 'mysteriously gone down'. I'm flailing about in the pit of post-long-term-relationship hell. I'm nearly thirty; I need to sort myself out.

But there's no way I can do the sorting – get a new job, meet a new guy, find somewhere decent to live – while all this stuff is going on with Becca. Something is wrong. I can't believe Dad is *lying* to me, but I don't think he's telling the whole truth. The truth about what, though? Becca's disappearance, the murder, or both? The more I think about it, the more the two events seem to be linked, even though they took place several years apart. Yet if Dad had had his way, I would never have known. He wrote the official narrative of her life, and for all those years I believed it without question. Until now, that is.

It's evening when Eliot calls me from his flat. 'Did you manage to speak to Graeme?' he asks, cheerfully, as if it's no big deal. I tell him about Dad's 'funny turn'.

'You think he faked it?'

'I wouldn't go that far. But he panicked, that's for sure. I've no idea why. I think he's hiding something from me.'

'Hmm… I definitely need to speak to him.' He starts stacking plates noisily into the dishwasher.

'Best of luck with that,' I say. 'If he's managed to keep a secret for over thirty years, he's not going to talk now.'

'You never know. Sometimes people want to get things off their chest, especially as they get older.'

I hear the dishwasher door slamming shut, the rush of water as the machine whirrs into life. We never had such a luxury at the flat above the greengrocer's. Whoever didn't cook did the washing-up; an unspoken rule in the easy ebb and flow of our existence. I think of the full greasy sink downstairs and shudder.

'So what have you been doing? Found out anything interesting?' I say, picking up my pen and adjusting the phone under my chin.

'Well, yes, actually,' he says. 'I've been going through the evidence boxes – fascinating stuff. Guess what? Cara's best friend, who gave evidence against Jay at the trial, happens to be none other than Isobel Dalliday – *the* Isobel Dalliday.'

'The director?'

'Yup. Amazing, eh? Hopefully I'll get to meet her,' he carries on. 'Unfortunately, my boss isn't too keen, because she's a celebrity. In the theatre world, anyway.' I can hear him drawing the curtains, a soft thud as he sits on the sofa. He's probably got the television on, muted, and is hopping through the channels to see what's on after the news. 'My DI hadn't actually heard of her, but then I showed him her Twitter feed… all the political stuff. Stupid of me. I shouldn't have mentioned it.'

Is this why he called? To tell me about Isobel Dalliday? I know he's long been a fan. We've seen several of her productions, at the National and in the West End. *And* she's a lifelong member of the Labour Party, part of the arty left. Then it clicks: *that's* who I recognised in the press photo taken after the trial. It was *her* face, framed by a sharp black bob, her mouth screaming abuse at Christopher Jay. Interesting, yes. But not the person I want to hear about.

'So why have you called?'

'Well… we've spent the past week trying to track down the original witnesses,' he says, 'but we're not having much luck – with some people, anyway…' His voice tails off.

'With Becca,' I say, after a pause.

'Yes.'

'Meaning?'

'Meaning nothing yet. There's no record of her death, so we're working on the basis that's she's still alive.'

'Oh.' My heart skips an infinitesimally small beat, and in that microsecond I realise that I want him to find her.

Eliot breezes on, oblivious to the slight change of atmosphere. 'We've called up the exhibits and forensic evidence and they're going to be tested for DNA traces. It occurred to me that if you gave a DNA sample, it could help with eliminations. You know, in the event that we can't trace Becca.'

There it is. The intimate connection between us confirmed in a spit of saliva.

'Okay, fine,' I say, trying to sound as if it means nothing. 'What do I have to do?'

'Siobhan Gerrard says she'll take your sample for me.'

'Why don't I come up to Birmingham, then you can do it in person?'

'No need. Just give Siobhan a call and arrange a time. Have you still got my old office number?'

'Er… dunno… probably. I just thought…' I tail off. Should I tell him I'm already coming up to Birmingham tomorrow, to visit the newspaper archives? That I want to find out everything I can about the murder and Becca's part in the trial; that I want to make my own scrapbook, like Chief Constable Durley's?

No, not yet.

DI Siobhan Gerrard shows me into a small interview room, flooded with morning light. The atmosphere is cheery, with IKEA-style furniture and no sign of the ubiquitous one-way mirrors you see in crime dramas.

'I was sorry to hear about you and Eliot splitting up,' she says, as I unzip my jacket. 'I thought you two were for keeps.'

'Well, these things don't always work out.' I look around for a hook, then drape it over the back of my chair. 'I think we both feel we made the right decision.'

'Sure.' She smiles. I sit down and tuck my legs behind me. I don't know what to do with my arms – elbows on the table, hands clasped together in my lap? I mustn't touch my lips or she'll think I'm lying. How come being in a police station instantly makes me feel guilty? Siobhan pulls her chair alongside me. Before she can take my DNA, she explains, there are forms to be filled in, and she's obliged to tell me my rights.

'As this is a voluntary sample, it can only be analysed in connection with the Cara Travers case,' she tells me, passing over a chewed black biro. 'It will be destroyed as soon as the investigation is concluded and your profile won't be added to the national DNA database unless you specifically request it.'

'Why would I request it?' I say, signing the form at the bottom. Siobhan snaps on a pair of blue disposable gloves and tears at a plastic bag.

'Your mother is long-term missing, yes?'

I nod. 'She was suicidal, so…'

'One assumes…' She removes what looks like a giant earbud from the packet. 'So there's a chance that her body was found but not identified. If she died a long time ago, we won't have the records, but these days DNA and fingerprints are taken as standard procedure. You never know, there might be a match. If not now, maybe in the future.'

'Right… I see. Well…'

'Scrape this gently across the inside of your mouth, please.' Siobhan hands me the swab and then watches to make sure I'm doing it properly.

'Is that enough?' She nods. I give her the swab and she pops it back into a transparent tube. 'I'll go on the DNA database – I've got nothing to hide.'

'No past crimes?' Her tone is joking, but her gaze is serious.

'Not that I can remember.'

'I'm obliged to tell you that once your profile is added to the NDNAD, it can't be removed. So if in the future—'

'I'm not planning any murders!' I laugh. 'And if my mother *has* already been found, it would be good to know once and for all. So let's do it.'

She reseals the kit and writes my name on the label. 'Okay, but I'll have to fetch another form.'

It's gone eleven by the time I get out of the police station. I take the Northern Line to Euston, buy a packet of sandwiches, a Diet Coke and a supersaver day return to Birmingham New Street. The train leaves in fifteen minutes, giving me enough time to go to Smith's and get a load of new stationery. If I'm going to research this murder case, I'm going to do it properly.

The train is quiet and I easily find a seat with a table, spreading out my purchases to claim my territory. As I struggle to extricate the pen from its high-security packaging, my fingers tingle excitedly. I'm breaking free – from Dad, from Eliot. Doing what *I* want to do, taking control. About time, too.

On the journey, I write down the few facts I already know about the murder case on my new A4 pad. Names, locations, a couple of dates. Hopefully the library will have back copies of local newspapers I can look at. I turn over the page and write 'Rebecca Banks' in large letters at the top, adding her maiden name underneath in brackets and making a note to remind myself to tell Eliot he could try searching for her as Rebecca Harwood instead. Then I immediately cross it out. The police will already be doing that, surely.

How old was she in August 1984, when the murder took place? I've always assumed Becca was about the same age as Dad, so… twenty-six. But she could have been younger or older. I put down my pen and look out of the window as green fields dotted with small villages and distant church spires flash past, suddenly hit with a wave of sadness. I don't even know my mother's birthday, or where she was born. I make a note to search for a reference to her age in the press reports; failing that, I suppose I could ask Eliot. I'd rather not, but if I can find out some basic information, I can send off for her birth certificate.

My mind starts to race on another course. What happened to Becca's personal documents after she disappeared? Birth and marriage certificates, driving licence, passport… I wonder how long Dad held onto them, hoping or fearing that she might return; how long before he emptied her wardrobe and removed her underwear from the chest of drawers. Weeks, months, years? I don't remember seeing anything of hers around the house, so he can't have waited long. If I'd carried on searching through the attic that day, would I have found her belongings, cold and slightly damp, stuffed into dusty bin liners? No. Knowing him, he burnt everything.

I carry on staring out of the window, stacking up the consequences as fields give way to the backs of terraced houses – gardens festooned with trampolines, barbecues, plastic chairs and tables, the essential equipment of outdoor family life. It seems strange to destroy somebody's possessions when you don't know for certain that they're dead, even if you hate them and want to forget they ever existed. Maybe I'm doing Dad a disservice. He probably waited a couple of years and then passed Becca's stuff on to a member of her family. That would have been the right thing to do. I return to the A4 pad and write myself a note. *Brothers and sisters? Names, addresses? Do they have her things? WHERE ARE HER THINGS?*

The train pulls into Birmingham sooner than I expected, and I have to hurry to pack up. This is where it all happened, I think to myself as I follow the signs to the exit. And not just the murder; this is where my parents met on a teacher-training course. Dad came from Essex, but I haven't a clue about Becca. She could have come from anywhere in the country, or she could have been a local girl. All I know is that by 1984 they were living within walking distance of Darkwater Pool. I've looked it up on the map – a small splodge of blue in an area called Redborne. It's near the university, to the southwest of the city. You can get there on the number 23 bus. But bare facts are of little use. They don't tell a story.

I emerge from the station and follow the signs up a long pedestrianised street, my carrier bag of stationery banging against my legs. The new library is beautiful – an enormous shiny silver-

and-gold box, gift-wrapped in barbed wire – an architectural present to the people of Birmingham. It glints invitingly in the sun, promising knowledge. Inside, I step into the sleek, silent escalator and take the stairway to heaven, alighting at the fifth floor.

The newspaper archive is kept on old-fashioned microfiche – I find the box for the *Post and Mail*, 1984, load the spool and start scrolling. The print blurs as it rushes past, my eyes ready to pounce on likely words. Murder. Darkwater. Cara Travers. Then, at the very end of August, I find the first mention of Becca. *In the early hours of yesterday morning, police were called to Darkwater Pool after a local teacher discovered the body of a young woman.*

Local teacher. How respectable that sounds. Two weeks pass before the police announce that 'a twenty-year-old man is helping with enquiries'. The following day he's charged. Then there's nothing in the papers until the trial, four months later.

Christopher Jay was evidently violent and jealous. During the trial, Isobel Dalliday spoke of seeing Cara's bruises, and said she'd urged her friend several times to report him to the police. After the acquittal, the detective in charge of the investigation made a brief, bitter statement saying that while the case remained open, they were not looking for new suspects. In other words, thanks to my mother changing her evidence, a murderer walked free.

Did somebody persuade her to lie on the witness stand? And years later, was she trying to shake free of their grasp? I think back to her frightened words on the videotape: *The bad man knows. If you don't help Mummy, he'll come and get me.* Is that why she disappeared?

CHAPTER TWELVE

Cara
April 1984

To Cara's surprise, Toby, Gina and Jay all accepted the non-existent jobs and started work at 31 Darkwater Terrace the following week. But the first bit of drama had nothing to do with the play about nuclear disarmament. Cara had sensed that Gina would be trouble, even from the auditions, but Isobel had liked her feisty spirit and thought her knowledge of arts funding would be useful. Gina was always the first to offer her opinions in company discussions, whether it be about what time they should start rehearsals, whether the main character in their new play should be male or female, or whether people should contribute to the tea and coffee fund or 'the company' (i.e. Isobel) should pay. She also had the irritating habit of ending every sentence with 'you know what I mean?' Isobel and Cara had both picked up on it, and imitated her strong Manchester accent when the others had gone home.

The big row happened three weeks into rehearsals. Cara couldn't remember exactly how it had started, but it was something to do with Isobel wanting to cut a scene in which Gina had a long, passionate speech about her daughter dying from radiation poisoning (the play imagined Britain under nuclear attack).

'You can't just cut it,' Gina protested. 'The show's group-devised, you know what I mean?'

'Yes, group-devised, not group-*directed*,' replied Isobel, giving her what could only be described as a superior look. 'Somebody has to be in charge or it'll be crap.'

'Are you saying I'm crap?' Gina demanded, squaring her jaw.

'No, I'm saying the scene is crap.'

At that point, all hell broke loose. Gina launched into a diatribe against Isobel, whom she accused of being a capitalist dictator, no better than Maggie Thatcher, using the rest of them as slaves to make money and promote her own career. Toby pointed out that nobody had forced Gina to join Purple Blaze, and that as she'd agreed to work on a profit-share basis she was just as much a capitalist as Isobel. Gina countered that this couldn't be the case, as unlike Isobel she didn't own a 'fucking big house', and then threw a chair at the offending wall to emphasise her point.

'Oh dear, jealous, are we?' sneered Isobel. This accusation seemed to drive Gina into even more of a rage, and the whole thing degenerated into a horrible shouting match, inflamed by Toby telling the women to calm down. Cara shrank into the corner with her hands over her ears, chanting, 'Stop it, please stop it!' and Jay, who'd not said a word, left the room and went downstairs to make himself a cup of tea. Cara found him in the conservatory fifteen minutes later, sitting with his legs over the arm of a bamboo chair, smoking a roll-up as he stared vacantly at the garden.

'Gina's been given the sack,' she informed him. 'Isobel told her to get out and never come back.'

'And there's me thinking we were a cooperative.'

'We are.'

'Yeah, right...' He pulled deeply on his cigarette.

'Gina had to go, surely you'd agree. She was so horrible to Isobel, after all she's done for the company. Some people are so ungrateful.'

He turned his head towards her. 'You don't see it, do you?'

'See what?'

Jay drew on his cigarette and then slowly puffed out the smoke.

'It doesn't matter.'

'Are you saying you're on Gina's side, then? Do you think you're a slave too?' Cara felt herself prickling with indignation.

'No, I don't. But…' He paused, swinging his legs back in front of him and standing up. 'Isobel's a bully; she's got you right where she wants you. But she doesn't own you,' he added quietly. 'Or me. She doesn't own any of us.' He was standing very close to her, and she could smell the tobacco on his breath. It revolted and attracted her at the same time. Their eyes connected and she thought for a second that he was going to kiss her, or even slap her round the face. But then he pulled away and went back upstairs, leaving her stranded in the conservatory, angry and confused.

Gina's departure turned out to be a relief rather than a loss, and over the next weeks everyone made an extra effort to be jolly and cooperative. The play was reworked and it was agreed that it was more punchy and dramatic for it. Toby brought chocolate biscuits and Jelly Babies in, and even Jay started to make a few jokes. One Friday, after a particularly creative day, they went out for a curry together, which Isobel insisted on paying for, despite everyone's protests. She made a tearful, drunken speech about being grateful for all their support, and declared that Purple Blaze was going to 'set the world on fire', which even Cara thought was going a bit too far.

The Gina incident had another surprising effect on Isobel: she decided she wanted to try to be reconciled with her parents, or, to be more accurate, her angry, disinherited mother. 'I've realised that I can't bear people hating me,' she told Cara, as she packed a bag for the weekend. 'I can't do anything about Gina, but I should be able to sort things out with the folks.'

'Best of luck,' said Cara, thinking that the only way to sort things out was to share the inheritance, which she knew Isobel would never do.

'Will you be all right on your own in the house?'

'Yes. I might try to tackle the garden – you know, mow the lawn or something.'

'That would be wonderful, if you could,' said Isobel, giving her a tight hug, which went on so long it started to hurt Cara's chest. 'You're a darling,' she whispered, kissing her cheek. Cara felt herself colouring up, but couldn't understand why.

When she woke on Saturday morning, the sun was shining and the sharp wind that had chilled the air all week seemed to have subsided. She couldn't think of a single good excuse for not getting up and going outside, although what she really wanted to do was stay in bed and luxuriate. It had long been a Saturday-morning ritual (a bit like the teacakes) for Isobel to bring her a cup of tea and sometimes peanut butter on toast. She'd jump into Cara's bed and they'd have a girlie gossip under the duvet. Recently, some of those chats had felt awkward, because Isobel had made a few bitchy remarks about Jay, saying he couldn't re-spond to direction and wasn't as talented as she'd first thought. Cara had wondered whether Isobel was saying things deliberately to test her, or whether it was just a coincidence. She was glad to have a weekend off from thinking about it.

She got out of bed and dressed in the worst clothes she could find, in case she had to sacrifice them to the gardening. Footwear was a problem, but there was a pair of wellington boots in the conservatory – belonging to the dead grandmother, she presumed – and she tried them on. They were a size too big but comfortable enough. Outside, the grass looked like a tatty shag-pile carpet, and weeds were already sprouting in the flower beds. The garden shed was padlocked, but she found the key in one of the kitchen drawers and managed to get the door open. As she stared at the torn compost bags, towers of empty flowerpots, watering cans, sieves, odd bits of chicken wire and the jumble of spades, forks, shovels, hoes, rakes and trowels, she was suddenly overcome with apathy. She shut the door and snapped the padlock back on.

As soon as she went back into the house, she knew she wasn't alone, even though she couldn't hear anybody moving about. The atmosphere had changed.

'Hello?' She walked through the kitchen and stood in the hallway.

Jay came out of the rechristened dining room, his door keys still in his hand. Isobel had had copies cut for him and Toby so they didn't have to ring the bell every morning, but there was an unwritten rule that they didn't use their keys outside office hours.

'I rang first, but there was no answer,' he said, as if reading her mind.

He'd come bearing gifts – a bottle of cheap vodka and some dope. Cara didn't usually indulge in either, but she let him pour her a glass and had several puffs of the first, tightly rolled joint.

'I picked this up at the market,' he said, taking a tape out of his pocket and slotting it into Isobel's radio cassette player. It was an album by Siouxsie and the Banshees – not Cara's usual taste, but she didn't object. She made some cheese on toast and they sat in the conservatory, squeezed onto the small sofa, hips touching, their feet resting on the coffee table. The closeness of Jay made her feel dizzy. Or maybe it was the marijuana. She took another drag and let Siouxsie Sioux's ethereal whining reverberate through her body.

'I've been wanting to get you on your own for a while,' Jay said, when the track came to an end. So, thought Cara, he knows…

They carried on drinking and smoking through the afternoon, stopping briefly for a game of chess, which descended into chaotic giggles as neither of them knew how to play. Then Jay declared he was starving and needed more food. They staggered to the corner shop and came back with beer, crisps, chocolate bars and several packets of Mr Kipling cakes, which turned out to be past their sell-by date, but they ate them all the same. Cara was so pissed she could barely put one foot in front of the other, all the time wondering why Jay hadn't yet made a pass at her. Had she misunderstood? Had he just popped round to give her some company? She desperately wanted to kiss him, but didn't dare make the first move.

'Let's play hide and seek,' he said. 'I'll hide, you count to a hundred, then come and find me.' She closed her eyes and listened to him climbing the stairs, the floorboards creaking above her. Then the noises stopped. He was in her room.

She opened her eyes immediately and went upstairs. Jay had taken all his clothes off and was lying in her bed with his hands clasped behind his head and a cheeky grin on his face.

'That was nowhere near a hundred,' he said. 'Tut, tut. Couldn't you wait?'

Cara smiled and started to undo her shirt.

CHAPTER THIRTEEN

Me

After three hours in the library, glued to the microfiche reader, my head is swimming. I go down to the café and buy a cup of tea and a huge chocolate muffin. It's half past five. Eliot's bound to still be at work, although he did say Cold Case Review was much more of a nine-to-five job. No weekend shifts. Proper lunch breaks. I call up his new address on my contacts list and check the location of his flat. It's only five minutes' walk away. It would be churlish to be so close and not to visit. Dare I just turn up? I peel the wrapper off the muffin and take a large, hungry bite, feeling the sugar rush instantly through my veins. If I call ahead, he can easily put me off. Then again, maybe he'd like a visitor. He's up here on his own; he doesn't know anyone in Birmingham. Why wouldn't he be pleased to see me?

I hang around in the café for as long as I can, reading through my notes and the photocopied articles, checking the time every few minutes. Finally I leave and head for the International Convention Centre, stopping to read every concert poster and taking a detour around the gift shop. Canals seem to head off in every direction, lined with bars and restaurants and connected by pretty brick bridges. It's gone half past six before I find Eliot's apartment block on a side street that backs onto a mooring site for narrowboats. I position myself in front of the security camera, fixing a friendly smile on my face. Here goes… I punch in his apartment number.

'Hello?' His voice sounds uncertain. I imagine him peering at the little screen on the entryphone. 'Meri, is that you?' I tell him it is. 'What the hell are you doing here?'

'If you let me in, I'll explain.'

His tiny flat – one bedroom, kitchen/living area and bathroom – is on the second floor, overlooking the gated private car park.

'Pity you haven't got a canal-side view,' I say, trying to sound casual and cheerful, as if I'm always popping round on the off-chance.

Eliot's not pleased to see me. He's obviously only just got in and is unpacking his shopping, trying to make as much noise about it as possible – banging cupboards, plonking jars down on the worktop, slamming the fridge door so the beer bottles jangle. I pretend not to notice, studying the bare white walls, the neutral beige curtains, the glass coffee table, the empty bookshelves, thinking about how homely I could make it with a few pictures and cushions, a warm colourful rug on the cold laminate floor. I want to feel welcome. I want Eliot to offer me a beer, stick a couple of those pizzas he's just bought in the oven. I want him to sit down and pull his shirt out of his trousers, put his feet up on the sofa, point the remote at the telly and ask me if there's anything worth watching tonight.

'I got my DNA done,' I say.

He tries to slash open the cellophane wrapping on a box of tea bags. 'You can't just turn up like this, out of the blue. You should have called. I'm… I'm *busy.*' He waves his knife in the direction of his work satchel. 'You wouldn't believe how much reading I've got to do. And we're not supposed to be in contact, remember – my boss is already making remarks about me and Durley; if anyone finds out you're here…'

'They won't, though. Unless they've installed secret cameras.' I force a laugh.

He liberates the tea bags and then imprisons them again in a shiny white canister. 'Are you going to tell me why you're here or what?'

'I've been doing some research.' I hold up my plastic carrier bag by way of explanation.

'What sort of research?'

'You know, into the murder case. Local newspapers, mainly. Everything else has restricted access.'

He raises his eyebrows. 'But why?'

'Why do you think?'

'Okay!' he says, raising his hands in a not-guilty gesture. 'No need to snap.'

At last his shopping is all unpacked and tidied out of sight. The beers stay in the fridge, but he makes me a cup of tea and offers me a biscuit. Things are looking up. He finally sits down too, but on the white wicker chair opposite the sofa, at a safe distance. There are a few moments of heavy silence. Then he leans back into his seat and folds his arms.

'I understand why you want to know more about Becca's part in the case. But I don't see how it's going to help you come to terms with what's on the tape. Counselling maybe, but…'

Fuck counselling, I think, but instead I say, 'I have a feeling her disappearance had something to do with the murder case.'

He almost laughs. 'But they happened several years apart.'

'Yes, but the videotape was made only a few months before she disappeared. In it, she says, "The bad man knows. If you don't help Mummy, he'll come and get me." She's got to be talking about Jay. What if he *did* come and get her?'

Eliot wrinkles his nose as he considers the possibility. 'Unlikely. He'd moved to London by then. Still there, actually, teaching at some FE college. I've got to go and see him next week.'

'Did she feel guilty about lying at the trial and tell him she was going to tell the police?'

'Why would she? It doesn't make sense. Anyway, they didn't know each other, there was no connection between them.' He runs his hands wearily over his new haircut, and I think how hard and distant it makes him look. Detective Sergeant Myles – leading light of the High Potential Development Scheme. Is this what happens when you get promoted? I want the old Eliot back, with the semi-Afro, soft and fuzzy and smelling of almond oil. The old Eliot who listened to me and took my ideas seriously; who liked having me around.

'It's obvious, isn't it?' I say. 'The answer's been staring us in the face. We know Jay killed one woman. Maybe he killed two.'

He twists his mouth. 'That's a bit of a leap.'

'He needed to shut Becca up.'

'That's pure speculation.'

'She's a missing person.'

'Not exactly.'

'That's what Siobhan Gerrard called her. There's no record of her death, and no record of her being alive.'

He gives me one of his wry, patronising smiles. 'So, where do you suggest we start digging for a body?'

'I'm serious. It needs investigating!'

Eliot stands up and stretches his arms. 'I'm sorry, Meri, but nobody's going to allocate resources when there's no evidence. Particularly not when there's a history of suicide attempts.'

'You can't discount murder because the victim's got a mental illness. That's discrimination.'

'No, it's not. It's making a realistic assessment of the situation.'

'That's just bullshit and you know it.' I feel myself heating up. 'Okay. Fine. If you can't be bothered to find out what happened to your key witness, I'll do it myself.'

'Oh yes? Like how? You think you can do better than a team of detectives?' I'm about to release a torrent of invective at him when his phone rings. He fishes it out of his trouser pocket and glances briefly at the screen. 'Got to take this.' He walks out of the room and into the bedroom, slamming the door behind him.

Waves of anger start to build in the pit of my stomach. He's trying to make me feel small – a bungling amateur with silly far-fetched theories. But I have this feeling that Becca didn't abandon me voluntarily, that she would have come back eventually if she'd been able. Only somebody stopped her. Christopher Jay stopped her.

I can hear Eliot's muffled voice through the thin partition wall. He's not saying much, but I can tell from the tone that he's pleased to be talking to whoever's on the other end of the phone. His mother? A new girl? There's a sudden burst of easy laughter, as if everything's fine and our row hasn't just happened. As if I'm not even here.

I suddenly feel a strong urge to do something. Nothing violent; I'm not going to start throwing crockery at the walls or put his laptop in the washing-up bowl, as tempting as that is. But I can't just walk meekly away. I'm going to stand my ground and make him take me seriously.

His old leather satchel is standing upright on the dining table. Eliot has always brought work home. There will be case documents in there: witness statements, notes, plans, photos. I stand up and go over to it, glancing back into the hallway at the closed bedroom door. Eliot's still in mid-conversation, chuckling away. I unbuckle the straps and push over the flap. The satchel smells deliciously of secrets. I walk my fingers through the files and remove a brown card folder.

Inside are photographs taken at the scene of the crime. Cara is barely recognisable from the smiling press shot. She's lying on her back, legs twisted to one side, arms splayed. Dirty bare feet, scratched with running. Her pretty summer dress – sunflower yellow, patterned with large pink roses – is crumpled above her knees, the flimsy straps fallen from her shoulders, her face pale, eyes glassy and staring up at the sky. And blood. So much blood. On her clothes, her arms, her hands; it pools around her torso, dark and sticky. I run a finger across her face. Poor, poor Cara. She didn't deserve to end up like this.

I'm so absorbed, I don't hear Eliot coming back into the room.

'What the hell do you think you're doing?' he says, marching forward. He looms over me, holding out his hand, palm upwards, like a teacher about to confiscate some contraband. 'Give them back, Meri. Now.'

'Don't talk to me like that!' I reply, hugging the photos instinctively to my chest. 'I wasn't doing any harm.'

'They're police property, not for public consumption.'

'I'm hardly the public!'

'You've no right to go snooping about in my briefcase.'

'I wasn't snooping, don't be ridiculous. You were on the phone and... Look, I'm actually trying to help.'

'I don't need your help... I don't *want* your help – you'll just get in the way. This is a police investigation, not some family fucking history project. The Cara Travers murder has nothing to do with you. Nothing! And nothing to do with your mother's disappearance. You need to accept that, or you're going to end up like her.' He holds out his hand again. 'Now give me back the photos.'

I stand up and fling them to the floor. 'Fuck you, Eliot,' I say, pushing past him. I grab my things and storm out of the flat, marching indignantly along the corridor and down the stairs and landing furiously on the street. I seem to have emerged on a different side of the block and I can't orientate myself, but I'm so angry I just set off regardless. I don't care where I'm going. All I know is I've got to put as much distance as I can between the two of us.

After a few hundred yards I glance over my shoulder, imagining Eliot chasing after me, shouting apologies, but there's nobody there. In fact, the street is strangely quiet. I can't see any other pedestrians, and only a couple of cars drive past. I know I should probably turn back, but I can't. I'm still too angry, and more to the point, it would look like a retreat.

I walk on, ending up on a badly lit towpath – cold black water on one side and a high brick wall on the other. The bars and restaurants have petered out and all I can see is what looks like a derelict factory. I bend my head to walk under a bridge and am nearly knocked into the canal by a cyclist coming in the opposite direction. This is getting stupid. I need a taxi rank. I climb some uneven steps and find myself on another dismal side street. I seem to have overshot the main road, so I turn around and walk back towards the lights of the city centre.

There are plenty of empty black cabs cruising past and I flag one down almost immediately. 'Where do you want to go?' asks the driver. I start to say 'New Street station', but then I have another idea. It's as if someone's just dropped the words into my head, calling me there.

'Darkwater Pool. Do you know it?' Fortunately – or unfortunately – he does.

CHAPTER FOURTEEN

Me

The cab hangs a sharp right at the roundabout and we join fast-moving traffic out of the city, past large houses turned into cheap, miserable hotels and characterless blocks of flats. Asian music hums in the background, its delicate, summery tones at odds with the view out of the window, or indeed my mood. I try to concentrate on the dull urban scenery, but my heart is fluttering like a moth trapped behind a curtain. I don't know why I'm doing this. Only that I have no choice.

We reach a junction and the driver turns left. The area starts to look more residential – nondescript semis interspersed with short drags of small shops. We could be anywhere. We could still have miles to go, but something tells me we're getting close to the scene of the crime. I imagine a square white tent, red tape, and a body bag being stowed in a hearse. It feels like the murder's only just happened; that I'm going to turn up and see the place swarming with detectives and uniformed officers, pathologists in paper suits, police divers searching for the weapon, journalists, nosy neighbours…

The driver turns right and the street sign flickers past, my eyes catching the word 'Darkwater'. My pulse quickens. I try to picture the map I printed out for my files. This must be Darkwater Lane. Darkwater Terrace, where Cara lived, runs off this road in a semicircle around the pool, the rear gardens of the houses backing onto a path. I lean forward and peer out of the window. Maybe it's because I've seen the photos, but the place feels familiar.

'It's the actual pool you're wanting, yes?' the driver says, slowing down as we reach the bottom of the hill.

'Please. If you could just pull over in front of it…' The car splashes through a large puddle in the middle of the road and parks up.

I stare out, arrested by the view. The pool is smaller than I was expecting, more of a large pond really, eerily lit by the two street lamps on the pavement in front of it and a few lights shining in the back windows of the surrounding houses. I wish I knew which one Cara lived in. Eliot will know, but I can't ask him, not any more. From now on, I'm on my own. But I don't want to think about Eliot, don't want to think about myself either. I want to see the pool as Becca saw it, back on that hot August night in 1984.

'Are you getting out or what?' The driver's voice makes me jolt. I don't answer him straight away. I'm thinking. *Am I getting out?*

'Er, yes, just for a few minutes. Would you mind waiting?' He makes a tutting sound, like he doesn't believe me. 'Please. I need to go back to New Street station, I've got a train to catch.'

'Okay, but I'll have to keep the meter running,' he says. I open the door and step onto the pavement, heaving my bag onto my shoulder. God knows what he thinks I'm doing. *What am I doing?*

Skimpy silver birches list perilously over the water, the banks edged with clumps of dank brown reeds. To my left is the path that embraces the pool, where Cara's body was found. I shiver as I walk towards it, my stomach gurgling with fear. It looks narrow and dark, hidden from the road, fencing on one side and scrappy trees and bushes on the other. I take my phone out of my pocket and activate the torch app. There's a free-standing noticeboard sponsored by a local estate agent; laminated posters telling me about the history of the place and the wildlife I might expect to find. I'm invited to enjoy the natural surroundings and reminded not to drop litter, but as I step onto the path and start to make my way around, it seems like nobody's been taking much notice. I shine the torch over beer cans, polystyrene chip cartons, wet newspaper and unidentifiable packaging bleached by the wind and rain. My shoes crunch on shards of broken glass. The tarmac bulges with invading tree roots and tufty weeds sprout through the cracks. The past is lurking just beneath the surface, looking for places to reassert itself.

I wave the beam across the garden fences, of various heights and colours, with strong wooden gates no doubt padlocked on the other side. A few brown wheelie bins, numbered roughly in white paint, are hanging around like bored teenagers. I stare up at the back windows – bedrooms and bathrooms, some dark, some illuminated – hoping that one of them will speak to me, but they stare back blankly. Which gate did she unbolt? Which direction did she run in? Where *exactly* did she fall?

I wish I'd taken Eliot's briefcase. I need to look at the photos again, examine the maps and the ground plans, I want to know where X marked the spot. But I've only got my instinct to go on. I stop moving and listen. I can just about hear the black cab purring in the distance – thank God he's still waiting for me. A car drives past. The undergrowth moves and I jump back. My heart's galloping like a runaway horse and I press on my chest to soothe it.

I try to take myself back in time. It was a hot night, the middle of a heatwave. Becca had a row with Dad and left the house to get some fresh air. So they must have lived nearby. Why choose such a creepy place, though? Perhaps it wasn't so overgrown back then. There was a boathouse – I've seen it in photos – a large wooden shed painted dark green with small white-framed windows and a pitched roof. No sign of it now, but I think it was on the far side of the pond, a dead end, hidden by bushes and trees. That was where Jay cornered Cara; where Becca found her.

I step over more broken glass, following the path around the water to where the building must have been. The overgrown, leafless trees form a spiky archway above me, glimmers of the polluted grey-orange sky peeping through. A few yards further on, I find a large square of concrete, crumbling in patches, stained with the charred remains of old bonfires, littered with empty beer cans and cheap vodka bottles. The boathouse foundations. A wooden bench, covered in bird shit and graffiti, lies on its side, and the torch beam catches something shiny on the back of the seat – a small brass plaque. I hover the light over the words and whisper the inscription:

In memory of
Cara Jane Travers 1960–1984
Love you forever,
Isobel

Something stirs close by. A fox? My grip tightens on my phone as I beam the light into the corners. There's a dark mound on the ground. The shape of a human body. My heart jumps out of my chest and the past and present instantly collide in my brain. I see Cara lying there, covered by a blanket, her limbs sticking out awkwardly. She moves slightly, withdrawing her arm, tucking back her legs. She's breathing, still alive… I creep forward, the phone outstretched, my hand trembling, my whole arm shaking. She moves again, this time twisting to one side and rising to her knees. Her head jerks up and the light finds the curves and edges of her face.

'Who told you I was here?' She hurriedly gets to her feet and sticks her hands on her hips. I step back, confused. This isn't Cara. Her hair is dark and her features are sharp and rat-like; black jeans slashed at the knees, a dark bomber jacket, and three or four scarves wound around her neck. She walks towards me, jerking her head. 'You come to pick up?'

'No – I... er, sorry... I didn't realise...'

'Then fuck off.' Two loud beeps pierce the air and she flinches. 'I said. Fuck. Off.'

I turn and run, back along the path, skirting the water's muddy banks, stumbling over the roots and broken glass, scratching my face and hands on the brambles. I run and run, back to the road, the pavements, street lamps, houses, parked cars... The taxi's still there, humming impatiently, its headlamps glowing warmly in the darkness. I fling open the door, hurling myself onto the back seat.

The driver tuts again, then does a three-point turn, and we head back the way we came, away from Darkwater and back to the light.

CHAPTER FIFTEEN

Jay

Jay fixes the Waterstones publicity leaflet to the wall with four small pieces of sticky tape. Isobel's face grins out at him and he has a sudden impulse to blacken her teeth with a biro, but he leaves her be, noting with some satisfaction that she looks old enough without his childish embellishments. Compared to the photo next to it, taken from the programme of a play she directed ten years ago, she's looking positively ropy. No amount of make-up can fill in the heavy wrinkles around her eyes – crow's feet, his mother used to call them. She looks like an old hag, even more so with that bottle-black hair.

He trolleys back in his office chair to get a better view of the whole piece. Creepy, yes. But strangely beautiful. A work of art. Such a pity he can't invite anyone around to see it. They wouldn't understand. They might think it's a shrine, and it's definitely not a shrine. It's the opposite of a shrine, if there is such a thing.

He leans back and laughs to himself. Pretentious tosspots would probably call it an installation, implying that Christopher Jay, the artist, was making some kind of statement about the cult of celebrity. They might also think that the materials – sorry, the *exhibits* – had been chosen and assembled deliberately, *curated*, in fact, to make some kind of sociopolitical point. But they'd be so very wrong. It started out as a dartboard, expanded a bit, and then kind of took on a life of its own. He can't control it any more; it's like a monstrous alien that has to be fed human flesh.

The original image still occupies a central position, from which everything else radiates. Randomly. It's still his favourite: a black-and-white photo of Isobel from *The Stage* that he enlarged on the department photocopier and then pinned to the cork noticeboard, in between his teaching timetable and takeaway menus. Those were the days… when he used to sit at this cheap old desk in the box room, marking coursework and preparing lessons, rising every so often to stretch his legs and throw a few arrows. You can still see the pricks on her face, like intense acne. But he doesn't work in this room any more. One, because he doesn't prepare or mark unless he can help it. And two, because the installation, or whatever you want to call it, has taken over. The room *is* the installation now.

It's taken several years to amass all this material: photos snipped from newspapers, programmes, theatre reviews, billings in the *Radio Times*. Anything that mentions her name, in fact, which he usually underlines in red felt pen. Now that she's become a middle-class celebrity, features constantly appear in the quality Sundays and those tedious lifestyle magazines – 'A Day in the Life of', 'My Book at Bedtime', 'Holiday Hideaways', 'How We Do Christmas'. There's very little he doesn't know about where she lives and what she likes to do. It makes him feel sick, reading about her charmed, privileged existence, but he resolutely tears out the pages and sticks them up. Got to feed the monster.

The corkboard has long since disappeared from view, but it's still there somewhere beneath the vast ocean of paper. It quickly filled up, so he had to spread out, attaching each piece of paper to the next to make an enormous collage. Now it takes up the entire side of the box room and is threatening to colonise the adjoining wall. It seems to breathe. If you open the door too quickly, the draught from the corridor makes the whole thing shiver like a giant jellyfish. Sometimes he dreams that all the images of Isobel come to life and chase him around the flat, or that every surface – walls, floors and ceilings – is covered in her grinning, self-satisfied mug, like a plague of cockroaches. He's thought about taking the installation down, cutting up the images and burning them ceremoniously in the bath. That would be the sane thing to do. But instead he keeps adding to it.

He looks at his watch. It's gone eight o'clock; he can't put it off any longer. If he doesn't leave for work now, he'll be late. Again. He still hasn't forgiven his students for the mess-up at the theatre – if they hadn't turned up late for the minibus, he would have made it to the drinks reception. Even they seem to be on Isobel's side – her unwitting guardian angels, protecting her from harm. He hates the lot of them.

The bus trundles down the Camden Road, lurching forward a few yards at a time, so slowly he has half a mind to get off and face the rain. How many years has he been doing this journey? He's considered buying a bike, but he's frightened of being run over, his epitaph a bunch of dead flowers tied to a lamp post. Not that he has any friends who'd care enough to pop to Tesco for a £5 bouquet. They seem to have drifted away over the years.

The same irritating voice announces the stops, as if everyone didn't already know. 'Her Majesty's Prison, Holloway,' it says in its clipped RP, taunting him. Why does his journey to work have to involve passing a prison? Is God trying to make some joke? A reminder, a little dig? He watches a few people getting on and off at the stop and wonders whether they work there. It's too early in the day for visiting. Mum was the only person that visited him while he was in Winson Green – only on remand, but that was bad enough. He loved her for that, God rest her soul. Four months he was there awaiting trial; it was a revolting place. He would never have survived a life sentence.

Jay has never been inside Holloway, but he's got a pretty good idea what it's like. Some nasty types in there, that's for sure; really rough women. Drugs. Violence. That's where Isobel should be, making up for lost time. He checks himself. Got to stop thinking about her or he'll go insane. It's like being madly in love, except the feelings are the opposite. Negative instead of positive. He keeps thinking about seeing her, planning what he'll say, what he'll do. Plotting ways he could harm her and get away with it. Piccadilly Waterstones is his next chance, although that's not for a while. Isobel's launching her latest book on directing there. It's a public event, anyone can attend, and this time he's not going to cock it up.

The college sits at the fork of three roads, a few stops further down. Jay cuts through a side street and crosses over. It's a large glass-walled building with concrete steps and a wide pavement, where the students regularly hang out, smoking, talking, eating crisps or takeaway chips, absorbed in their phones. There are often more standing outside than there are in the building. They do a lot of gesticulating and shouting at each other; it sounds like they're arguing, but Jay's come to learn that it's just the way they are – they shout because they're anxious that nobody is listening. They feel invisible and it scares the shit out of them. It's Monday, but some of them have already got that Friday look – tired and jumpy, like shaken bottles of fizzy pop ready to explode.

He used to think of them as kindred spirits; that's what drew him here. He was brought up on a miserable council estate himself, never knew his father, was bullied by his classmates and then by his alcoholic nan who babysat while his mum worked as a night cleaner at the Longbridge car factory. He knew what it was like to fail at school, to have low expectations. Only his drama teacher, Mr Nellis, had time for him. He recognised his talent, encouraged him to join a youth theatre. There was no way he could afford to go to drama school – you couldn't get grants for places like RADA in those days; you had to be rich. So when he left school, aged sixteen, with a couple of unimpressive O levels, he took a job at the large Woolworth's in the Bull Ring. Youth theatre on Wednesday nights was the only thing that kept him going; it broke his heart when he turned eighteen and had to leave.

Mr Nellis kept in touch; looking back, Jay realised the man probably fancied him, but, all credit to him, he never made a move. They'd meet up for a drink every now and then, in the pub behind the Alex Theatre, where the actors went after the show; necking pints before last orders. Jay and Mr Nellis loved to watch them laughing in their rich fruity voices, charming the bar staff and taking the merry piss out of each other. It was a performance in itself. Mr Nellis always brought *The Stage* with him so that Jay could scour the small ads for vacancies. The job had to be in Birmingham, because he couldn't afford digs. He couldn't play an instrument or sing, so pantos and musicals were out. He wasn't abnormally tall or short, horribly ugly or stunningly good-looking. Most proper jobs were beyond his reach, because he didn't have an Equity card and no hope of getting one. The union was all-powerful then; it was a closed shop. So when he saw the advert for Purple Blaze, his heart danced in his chest. *Small new experimental theatre company needs brave, exciting actors for profit-share Birmingham tour.*

'That's the one for you,' said Mr Nellis, taking his red pen out of his inside jacket pocket and circling the advert. 'Got your name on it.'

Jay enters the college and nods a grudging hello to Saf on reception as he swipes his ID card through the barrier. His first class of the day starts in two minutes, but there's no need to rush; it's not as if the students will be lined up eagerly outside the drama studio. As he walks down the corridor – white breeze-block walls covered in framed photos of past productions – only two students are waiting. Another couple emerge from the shadows as he unlocks the door and turns on the lights. The studio – your typical black box with no windows – is cold after a weekend of inactivity, but it still smells faintly of bare feet. He walks in, taking his coat off and hanging it over a grey plastic chair to dry. Over the next few minutes, five more students wander in, talking to each other or preoccupied with their phones. Nobody so much as acknowledges him.

'So where is everyone?' Jay looks around accusingly at the assembled throng, as if they've captured the others and disposed of their bodies. Silence. 'Okay, we'll give it another five minutes…' He sits back in his chair and crosses his leg, his thigh twitching nervously. Then Santianna Makepeace, a large black girl with super-long painted fingernails, enters the room and walks straight up to him, a purposeful look on her face.

'That play was banging! You know what one I'm on about, dat play you took us to?' She looms over him, flinging a lump of backcombed hair over her hefty shoulder. 'It was like, real, you get me? Real life, like it was me up there! So I'm thinking, maybe I could do an audition piece from that. There's a character in it I could act so good. Is that bless? Be so much easier than this Chekhov shit. No one cares what he's on about anyway, man. So I was thinking, yeah, would it be cool if you asked them? You know that director woman who made that looong speech for tiiime? You could try get a photocopy off her or suttin'?'

That. Director. Woman.

'I don't want to hear another mention of that fucking bitch,' he says, forgetting he's not supposed to swear in class.

'Wagwan with you, sir?' Santianna puts her hands on her hips. 'Why you swearin' at me? I'm a bitch, yeah?' She turns to the others. 'Did you lot hear dat? He's a teacher man, he can't call me a fucking bitch.'

'Not *you*,' he says irritably. 'I didn't mean *you*.'

'Who the fuck then? You was talking to me!'

'I wasn't, Santianna. Not everything's about you, okay? I was talking about the director woman.' God, he can't take much more of this. He stands up, hands in pockets, and walks into the centre of the room. 'Isobel Dalliday is a fake. She doesn't give a shit about you lot. All she cares about is herself. Oh, she'll throw a few free tickets your way on press night to make it look like "lovely black people" go to the theatre. She might even let you ponce about on the stage once in a while, as long as you're do-ing a show about racism or gangs or drug abuse. People like the great, wonderful, award-winning Isobel Dalliday, they do it for themselves, not you. It's all an act. Believe me, I *know*. I know the truth about Isobel Dalliday.'

Santianna raises her thick black inked-on eyebrows. 'Oh my daiz, you *know* Isobel Dalliday?'

'Jesus Christ – do you ever listen to a word I say?' He charges back to his chair, scooping up his coat and grabbing his bag, nearly spilling papers onto the floor.

A couple of the students exchange a glance but most of them look down at their feet, embarrassed, trying to suppress their laughter. He knows he's making a fool of himself, but he doesn't care. He shoves his way past them, banging open the heavy black doors and stomping down the corridor.

An hour later and he's been summoned to see Isatu Clarkson – their new head of department. She got the job over three internal candidates, including him, although that's not why he resents her. He never really wanted to be HoD, just fancied the status and the pay rise. Isatu is young, mid-thirties at most, and dresses like she works in the City; wears her hair in thick oily plaits coiled at the back of her head like venomous snakes ready to rise up and bite anyone who dares to contradict their mistress. Too smart, too ambitious, too full of PC jargon. And she's on to him. Not that his disaffection is a big secret. She was probably warned about him by the previous incumbent – 'Watch Chris Jay, he's on a knife edge. Washed up, burnt out and any other cliché you can think of… If you get a chance to get rid of him, take it.'

'So you're not denying you lost your temper with the students?' Isatu says, her pen poised to write a note on some form.

'That wasn't me losing my temper,' he replies. Not by a long way, he thinks. You have no idea what happens when I'm really angry.

'It was inappropriate behaviour at the very least. And you can't just walk out of a lesson because you've lost control. You're supposed to set an example, be a role model. These young people have enough violence and bad language at home to deal with; they don't need it when they come here.'

He shrugs. 'It's just bullshit. All this – it's bullshit.'

'What do you mean, exactly?'

'Pretending they can make something of their lives, that they can escape, be actors. It's all total bullshit.'

'I'm sorry to hear you don't believe in our students.'

'Oh, give me a break…' He can't stand the word 'believe'. Or 'dream', for that matter. In his view, the phrase 'believe in your dreams' should be universally banned, punishable by death.

'You seem to be under a lot of stress at the moment,' she continues. 'I don't want to intrude, but is there something going on in your private life? Obviously, I'm sympathetic, but I can't have your problems impacting negatively on the students.'

'There's nothing *going on*,' he mumbles.

'Maybe you should see your GP, take some time off sick. Have you thought about counselling? Or Cognitive Behavioural Therapy? I've heard that can be very helpful.'

'I'm fine. It's the job that's shit.'

'Hmm…' She puts down her pen and sits back in her chair. The snakes on her head shift slightly, as if waking up. 'I'm afraid I'm going to have to issue you with a verbal warning.'

'Whatever…'

'Don't come in tomorrow, Chris. Stay at home and reflect on what's happened today. See a doctor. Think about what's really bugging you, and what you can do about it. Okay?' She nods towards the door, dismissing him.

CHAPTER SIXTEEN

Me

It's Cake Club day. Every week, eight of us in the communications department – seven girls and a token man – take it in turns to bring in home-made calorie fests. Sponges, brownies, muffins, tartlets, tray bakes... Work stops promptly at twelve for the tasting, which eases nicely into lunch. They're at it now, my fellow Cake Clubbers, gathered around the design assistant's desk, picking crumbs off their lips, slurping at their fingers and saying, 'I mean, like YUM, Amy!' – agreeing that just one bite of her chocolate hazelnut torte is better than sex, which for a couple of them is probably true.

'Come on, Meri, you're missing out.' Amy holds up a slice of torte, balanced precariously on a piece of kitchen towel. I smile and shake my head. It was my turn to bake this week but I managed to swap with her, thank God. I've got enough on my plate without making cupcakes.

I retreat to my computer screen, deleting the non-urgent or copied-in emails that have been pinging their way into my inbox over the last few days; deleting, filing or fraudulently marking them as read. Clicking and dumping, clicking and dumping. My body's here but my mind's gone AWOL; for all the use I am, I might as well have stayed at home. I've never felt so tired in my life.

I can't sleep – keep having these really horrible dreams. Sometimes I'm wandering about, in a field or down a busy street, or even a shopping mall, searching for somebody, always searching. I don't know who I'm looking for, because I never find them. In other dreams, I'm being chased. The locations change; sometimes I'm deep underground, or in a labyrinth with high walls, but usually I'm at Darkwater Pool. The sense of dread is overwhelming. I mean, absolutely terrifying. Somebody wants to hurt me, really badly. My life is at stake and I have to run. But I don't know which way to go, can't see a way out. I have to force myself to walk into the blackness, edging forward like a blind girl with my hands outstretched. I know I should just run, run as fast as I can, but I can't see where I'm going. My steps shorten, then slow down, then stop... I've reached a dead end. My attacker is behind me. I can hear their footsteps, their heavy breath on the back of my neck. I want to see their face, keep trying to turn around, but it's as if I've been paralysed, my feet welded to the ground. Then a dull pain hits me between my ribs and I fall to the ground, screaming. Last night my screams were so loud they woke Fay. She thought I was being raped in my bed and nearly called the police.

'For God's sake, don't *do* that!' she yelled from my bedroom doorway. 'You scared the life out of me.'

'Sorry,' I mumbled. 'Nightmare...'

She rolled her eyes at me. 'It's the third time this week. *How old* are you?' This from a woman wearing a nightie appliquéd with a teddy hugging a pink heart.

I nearly told her, but it was obvious she wasn't in the mood for a deep midnight chat. Fay doesn't know about the videotape, or the murder case. I've been acting pretty strangely these past couple of months but she hasn't once asked if I'm okay. That's fair enough, I guess. We're flatmates, not friends. Fay and Lizzie advertised my room when their other 'bezzie' went travelling. I think they were hoping I'd replace her, but for some reason –

probably my fault – we haven't bonded. Now that Lizzie's virtually moved in with her boyfriend, Fay's feeling pissed off and is taking it out on me.

It's almost a week since I went to Birmingham, and there's been no word from Eliot. I'm still feeling angry about the way he behaved. I know I shouldn't have raided his briefcase, but he was being so pompous and patronising. Anyway, I'm not going to apologise for that unless he apologises to me first. And I can't just give up on my search for Becca. I *know* her disappearance is connected to the murder case, I just haven't worked out how yet. First I need to find out more about what happened all those years ago.

There is somebody I could talk to about it – somebody who knows almost more than anyone. Eliot would tell me to keep well away, but the longer the silence between us, the more inclined I am to risk it. I could do it today. This lunchtime, in fact. She's only fifteen minutes' walk away, been there all week, at the Scottish church, just behind Tottenham Court Road, rehearsing for her latest production – a radical adaptation of *Jane Eyre*.

Isobel Dalliday. Judging by her Twitter feed, she takes lunch between one and two, so if I'm going to do it today, I've got to leave within the next ten minutes. Why shouldn't I? She can hardly blame me for accosting her, not when she announces her every movement to the entire world. She obviously thinks people are interested. I started following her after I saw the inscription on the bench at Darkwater Pool. *Love you forever, Isobel.* A very public declaration. But that's what she's like. She blogs and tweets continuously, turns up at loads of public events, and is an outspoken supporter of left-wing causes. I don't have a problem with that; she just seems a bit too good to be true. But she was Cara's best friend, she owned the house in Darkwater Terrace, knew Christopher Jay. She may even have known Becca.

'Meeting a friend for lunch,' I tell Amy and the girls, applying a quick swipe of lipstick and picking up my coat. 'If I'm not back by two, say I've gone to a meeting, will you?'

I walk through Chinatown, cutting across Soho Square and emerging at the grubbier end of Oxford Street. It feels good, darting through the trudging tourists and hurrying shoppers, moving in the slipstream of the city's energy. I weave through foreign students smoking outside a language school, get shouted at by a rickshaw driver as I cross and take one of the quiet fashionable side streets that run parallel to Tottenham Court Road. My pace is urgent, eyes on the target, my flat black pumps skimming the pavement. Every nerve is tingling as I take the dog-leg turn, then a small right, skip straight over at the junction, hang right again and finally double back. A smile twitches as I arrive in the windswept, littered square. I find the annexe at the back of the church and check the time: Isobel should be out in about ten minutes, assuming they stick to schedule. I sit on the cold concrete steps and run a silent rehearsal of my own – *got to get the opening words right.*

Virtually bang on one, the doors swing open and half a dozen scruffily dressed actors spill onto the steps, pulling on jackets and odd hats, all rapidly talking at once. Isobel isn't among them. I stand up quickly, hoping to slip inside before the door closes, but I'm too late. I press my forehead to the window. What if she doesn't go out for lunch? What if I've already missed her? The actors are ambling across the square in the direction of the pub. I think about running after them to ask if they know where she is. I don't know what to do. My confidence is ebbing away and I'm about to give up when I see her walking into the foyer. She stands there in close conversation with an overweight guy in baggy, unseasonal shorts – the stage manager perhaps? His phone rings and he holds up a hand in apology, turns and steps into a room to take the call, leaving Isobel on her own. *Please come out now*, I whisper, moving back onto the pavement.

Isobel puts on a long, beautiful cardigan – hand-knitted in heathery colours – and hitches a large leather bag onto her shoulder. She presses a button and pushes against the entrance door. As soon as she's outside, she pauses, pulling out a packet of cigarettes and a lighter. I stand there, blocking her way. She lights up and takes a long drag, looking at me suspiciously.

'Excuse me, Ms Dalliday. I was wondering if… I mean, do you mind if… You see, I…' I stall, feeling my cheeks turning pink. That's not how I'd planned to start.

'Please don't ask for my autograph.' Isobel signals at me to move out of her way. 'It's so naff.'

'No, no, it's not that. I was wondering if I could talk to you. It's a personal matter.'

Isobel halts, pulling on her cigarette. 'Oh dear,' she sighs, exhaling a large white puff of smoke. 'If you're an actor, this is a really bad way to get my attention.'

I take a big breath, casting my line out far and deep. 'I'm not an actor. I'm Rebecca Banks's daughter.'

We sit in a little Italian café on a side street and I buy the coffees. As I carry them to the table, Isobel finishes sending a text and puts her phone away.

'Okay, so what's this about?' Her deep blue eyes peer inquisitively from beneath her shiny black hair, expensively cut into a bob.

'It's a bit complicated to explain…'

She stirs the chocolate sprinkles into her cappuccino. 'Well, I've only got forty-five minutes.'

So I tell her my story. It's hard to know how and where to begin, hard to push the emotion to one side to let the facts – or fictions – speak for themselves. Isobel listens intently, her gaze never breaking away from mine. She doesn't interrupt. Neither of us drinks our coffee. The words start to flow and I find myself going much further and much deeper than I intended: my childhood, Becca's illness, the suicide attempts, the hospital visit, the disappearance… I tell her how Dad tried to make up for the loss, tried to wipe my mother's memory from my mind, and almost succeeded. Then the videotape turned up. Now everything's been turned upside down and I don't know who's telling the truth. Isobel keeps nodding like she completely understands.

'I'd love to see the video,' she says. 'Can you email me a copy?'

'Well, yes, but… why?'

'Isn't it obvious? Because I want to see the moment you reveal you're the reincarnation of Cara.'

I stare at her, stupefied. *What?* This is not the reaction I was expecting and absolutely not why I wanted to see her. 'No… no – you don't understand,' I stammer. 'I'm not saying I'm the reincarnation of Cara, not at all.'

'Don't just dismiss it out of hand,' Isobel says, her tone slightly reproving. 'A lot of people believe in reincarnation. Buddhists for a start.'

'I know, but… My mother was psychotic, she'd lost all grip on reality…'

'Honestly, I've read several books about it,' she carries on, pausing briefly to sip her cold coffee. 'There are thousands of cases of children with past lives; there's even been proper academic research. Okay, so it's in the States, but they're not all idiots. And these families, they can't all be telling lies.'

'I still don't think, in this particular case—'

'I've always been fascinated by reincarnation.' Isobel leans forward, beautifully aligned white teeth framed by scarlet lips. 'I directed a play about it once, based on an incident in India. There was this boy who claimed he was a murdered shopkeeper; knew his name and everything, all about his wife and kids. He was six years old! He took his parents to a town a hundred miles away, knew exactly where to find the shop, and it was all true. Of course, then he was torn between the two families, it was agony for him. The play wasn't great, if I'm honest, but it was an amazing story.'

I don't know what to say.

She reaches out and grabs my arm. 'Please, let me watch the video. I'll tell you if it's genuine or not. It's virtually impossible to coach a four-year-old like that – I should know, I've worked with child actors.' She lets out a short laugh. 'Your mother wouldn't make such a thing up, even if she was ill. You were her little girl. She *loved* you.'

You haven't a clue about how this illness works, I think, but I don't argue. Isobel's clearly a bit bonkers, but at least I've got her interest and hopefully she can tell me more about what happened. 'Okay,' I say. 'If you want. But please don't show it to anyone else.' I give her my mobile number and she gives me her business card. I promise to email her the footage by the end of the day.

'We'll have a nice long lunch at my club next week and talk about it properly,' Isobel says. 'I'll look at my diary and ping you a date.' We stand up and she puts on her cardigan. 'I can't tell you how glad I am that we've met.' She holds out her arms and hugs me into her soft, heaving bosom. I feel like a small animal about to be crushed with love. As I briefly suffocate against her woolly chest I decide I like Isobel Dalliday. She may have some way-out beliefs, but she's the only one who understands how I feel.

'I still miss Cara,' she says softly in my ear. 'I think about her every single day.' As she pulls away, I see tears in her eyes. 'Right,' she sniffs. 'Better get back to rehearsals.' She swings her bag over her shoulder. 'Send me the tape. Promise?'

'Promise.'

CHAPTER SEVENTEEN

Cara
May 1984

The weather had recently taken a turn for the better and they were holding their weekly company meeting in the garden, flattening the overgrown grass as they sat in a circle, their legs stretched towards the centre like the spokes of a wheel. Isobel was holding forth about everyone needing to get more involved in the marketing side of Purple Blaze – disappointingly, they still had no bookings for their show and it was virtually ready for performance. Cara was feeling hot and bothered. Jay had deliberately sat next to her and was lying back at an angle supported by his outstretched arms, his left hand so close to hers she could feel a current passing between their fingertips. He'd been in this mischievous mood all morning. The rules were no touching and no secret glances, rules she'd insisted on, but God, was he testing her resolve. She tried to focus on what Isobel was saying – something about publicity leaflets – but all she could think about was the night before and the night to come.

She felt as if she'd given birth to a new version of herself – a brave, daring, almost reckless Cara, whom she admired almost as much as she loved Jay. Their affair had been going on for three weeks now, and they were sure the others didn't have a clue. Although the sex was amazing – nothing before had even come close – it was the secrecy that thrilled her most. It was like hav-

ing a sixteen-hour-day acting job playing the old Cara – compliant, cautious, conventional – in front of Isobel and Toby, then
reverting to her new, true self at night. Like being a vampire, she
thought, trying not to grin. Sex with Jay was a bit on the rough
side, but there hadn't been any biting. Not yet. But who knew?
In her current febrile state, she'd probably let him do anything.

That first weekend they'd done all their lovemaking in Cara's
bed, but it had proved impossible now that Isobel was there all
the time. She rarely left the house, other than to go to the local
shops, and appeared content to spend each evening alone with
Cara, chatting about the day's work and listening to music. They
couldn't go to Jay's place because he lived with his mum, and,
anyway, it would look very odd if Cara suddenly started disappearing for the evening. So they'd been meeting at the pool, late
at night, after Isobel had gone to bed.

It was hours and hours till then; Cara didn't think she could
bear the wait. If only she could manufacture a reason for getting
Jay indoors for a few minutes, so they could kiss and touch. *I'll
make some more tea – Jay, would you mind helping?* Could she say
it without the edges of her mouth curving into a lustful smile?
The mood Jay was in today, he might even refuse just to torment
her. No, they had to stick to the rules, something that up to a
few weeks ago had been second nature to her, but that didn't suit
the new Cara one bit. It was very confusing. All the elements
of her personality had been thrown into the air and had landed
awkwardly in a different place.

Cara drew her feet under her knees, hugging herself protec-
tively. Toby was talking now and she turned her attention to him
as he said, 'I think we should forget theatre venues and take the
show to the Yorkshire picket lines.'

'But there's so much violence going on, we might be arrested,'
said old Cara (compliant, cautious, conventional).

Jay rolled his eyes. 'Who cares?' he said. Good move, she thought. If they openly disagreed with each other, it would help to put Isobel off the scent. And it was Isobel that Cara was most concerned about.

'We've got to show our support for the miners somehow.' Toby looked around the group earnestly. 'Perhaps we should do a play about the strike instead.'

'That's a great idea, but it's too late to change now,' said Isobel, 'I'd love to do free shows for the community, but we can only do that if we've got proper funding.' She turned to Cara, who gave her the expected nod of support. 'As you know – and I really, really hate mentioning this – I'm subsidising the company—'

'So's the dole office,' put in Jay. Toby belted out a laugh.

'But it can't go on indefinitely,' said Isobel. 'We need some income.'

'What about running children's parties?' Cara heard herself pipe up. 'People will pay good money to have someone take the kids off their hands.'

'Are you kidding?' Toby pulled a face. 'We're supposed to be a left-wing theatre collective, not a bunch of clowns.'

Isobel patted Cara's skirt kindly. 'It's a great idea, darling, but very much a last resort.' She stood up, slipping her violet-painted toes back into her shoes. 'I vote we do another push to get bookings, and if we still don't have any luck, we'll do a free performance in the city centre to attract publicity.' No actual vote followed – they no longer bothered pretending they were a cooperative – but there was a general murmur of agreement, and with that, they wandered back into the house to embark on yet another run-through.

The afternoon rehearsal seemed to go on forever, but Isobel finally sent the others home and the two women were alone again. Cara cooked a mediocre spaghetti bolognese, distracted by carnal thoughts of Jay, who was whiling away the time in the local pub with a pint and a packet of crisps. Was his head as full of her? she wondered.

'I'm not sure the others really get Purple Blaze,' said Isobel, dousing her meal with extra salt and pepper. 'Toby's more interested in politics than theatre and Jay's the opposite – he'd play Dick Whittington's cat if someone offered it. Not that he'd be any good at it. He doesn't have the talent, or the passion.' *His passion is for me*, replied Cara, but only inside her head.

Isobel reached forward, taking Cara's hand in hers and stroking it fondly. 'If I didn't have you, I don't know what I'd do.' She looked at her thoughtfully, as if waiting for the appropriate reply.

'Me too,' muttered Cara finally. Something felt wrong, but she couldn't work out what. Isobel must have felt it too, because she let go of her then, and stood up to run the tap for a glass of water.

'Is everything okay?' she asked.

'Yes, why wouldn't it be?' Cara bit her lip, relieved that Isobel had her back towards her. She glanced up at the kitchen clock. Two hours to go before her rendezvous with Jay. Two hours of lying and pretending to her dearest friend. Why couldn't she just come out with it? Maybe Isobel would be pleased that after her pathetic attempts at university, she'd finally landed a proper boyfriend. It would be neat if Isobel could get together with Toby and make a foursome. The two of them had so much in common, and they were both attractive. A thought occurred to her. What if Isobel was already secretly seeing Toby? That would be so ironic.

They went upstairs at a quarter to eleven. Isobel gave her the usual good-night hug on the landing, kissing her on the cheek, her lips grazing the outer edge of Cara's mouth.

'Nighty-night, darling. Sweet dreams,' she said.

Cara sat on her bed, listening out for Isobel in the bathroom. The loo was flushed, the taps were turned on, then off, and finally the water gurgled through the plughole. Isobel padded up to the attic room and Cara heard the brass rings on the curtains rattle against the pole as they were drawn across. A few more footsteps, a couple of creaks, then all was silent.

Now she had to wait for ten minutes or so. Cara knew from the time they shared a bedroom that Isobel usually dropped off as soon as her head hit the pillow. This ability had annoyed Cara, who tended to lie awake for ages, fighting off drifting, sinking feelings, as if frightened she would never wake again. But now she was pleased, because it meant she could leave the house unnoticed.

Carrying her pumps, she tiptoed down the stairs and escaped through the door of the conservatory. It was pitch black outside and she could only just make out the stepping-stone path that led to the gate in the back fence. She put on her shoes and made her way across the garden, the skirt of her dress catching on the thorns of a rambling rose that had been trained over the wooden arch. The gate wasn't padlocked, but the bolt was stiff and made a loud clang as she drew it back. She glanced back anxiously towards the house, but all seemed quiet. She lifted the gate off its hinges so that it didn't squeak, and swung it gently open.

'Jay?' she whispered. 'Are you there?'

He emerged immediately from behind a hawthorn tree, his face illuminated by the burning tip of his cigarette. The dim glow hollowed his eye sockets and cheeks, making him look almost ghostly. He took her hand and they walked silently around the path until they came to the old boathouse. There was a square of hard-standing there, which sloped down to the water's edge. Jay retrieved a blanket that he'd hidden round the side of the shed and laid it out as if preparing for a picnic. He pulled her towards him, pressing her shoulders downwards. She sank to her knees and he joined her, kissing her face and neck, removing her cardigan, slipping the thin straps of her dress from her shoulders and revealing her small pink breasts. She sighed as she leant backwards, twisting her legs round and letting him fall onto her like a stone.

He hadn't asked if she was on the pill (she wasn't) and had never even suggested using a condom. Why was she taking risks like this? Why didn't she care? The undergrowth stirred. Nobody else knows what we do, she thought. Only the night creatures. That's what I've become – Jay's night creature, asleep during the day and only properly alive in the dark. He began to thrust, crushing the base of her spine into the ground. Tomorrow there would be a bruise, but it didn't matter. All that mattered was this.

She opened her eyes to look upwards at the stars. Something in her peripheral vision moved and she turned her head to look. A black shape passed behind a tree.

'Somebody's there,' she whispered. 'Watching us.'

He laughed. 'No way.'

'I saw him!' She heard the sound of retreating footsteps along the path. 'Listen! He's running away.'

'So what? Let him look, I don't care. Makes it more exciting.'

'Stop it!' She pushed him off and he rolled onto his back, groaning. 'We've got to get out of here, now.' She clambered to her feet, grabbing her knickers and almost falling over as she tried to put them back on.

'But I haven't finished.' He spoke as if she was interrupting his meal.

'Well, I have. I want to go home.'

'You're pathetic,' he said, but he zipped up his flies and led her back round the path towards the house.

In the hostile silence, Cara listened to her thumping heart. She kept looking straight ahead, not wanting to think about who'd been lurking in the shadows, how much they might have seen. It made her feel dirty and cheap.

'Let's go to your room,' Jay said, as they arrived at the gate.

'We can't. She'll hear us.'

'Not if we're quiet.'

'No.'

'The conservatory, then, that's two floors below.'

She shook her head. 'I'm not in the mood any more.'

'Come on, Cara.' He raised his voice. 'You can't leave me high and dry like this! I'm still as hard as rock and it bloody hurts.'

His words stung her. 'That's all you care about, is it? Charming.'

'If you weren't so shit-scared of Isobel, we could do it in your bed. Anyone'd think she was your mum, the way you go on. No, no, actually it's worse than that; it's like you're married to her or something. Like she owns you.'

'Stop shouting,' she hissed. 'I'm going indoors now, let me go.'

She tried to release her arm, but he tightened his grip. 'Do you let her touch you up? Is that part of the deal?'

'What? No!'

'There must be some reason. Are you playing us off against each other?'

'Shut up!'

'Who do you prefer?' he snarled. 'Her or me, or don't you care?'

'Let me go, Jay, or I'll scream.'

'And wake her up?' He turned his head towards the house. 'Oops, too late.'

She looked up. The attic window was wide open and Isobel was standing there, her dark silhouette framed in light. Cara drew in a sharp breath, her throat tightening. 'Isobel!' she tried to shout, but it came out as a feeble squeak. Jay let her go and she ran into the house, tearing through the hallway and leaping up the stairs two at a time. 'Isobel! Isobel!'

She knocked loudly on the bedroom door, but Isobel didn't answer. She tried turning the handle, but something was jamming it from inside. A chair perhaps, wedged under.

'Isobel, please, let me in.' Still no reply. 'I want to explain…'

Several seconds of silence passed, then Cara thought she heard the sound of the window closing, the bed creaking as Isobel lay back down. There was a faint click and the sliver of light escaping from under the door went out like the last flicker of hope.

'You can't just go back to sleep.' Cara's voice was teary and desperate. 'Please! We need to talk.'

She would not leave, she decided; she would stay here until Isobel came out of the room. She sank to the floor and squeezed herself into the small gap between the top of the stairs and the door. Jay had gone home, thank God – at least she imagined he had. She coiled her body and lay there like a faithful, panting dog guarding its mistress, her nose and throat congested with tears. Minutes, maybe hours passed uncomfortably; soon all her joints felt locked and were starting to ache. She uncurled herself and sat with her back against the door. Her eyelids felt heavy and her head kept dropping to her chest. She didn't want to fall asleep, but if she did, at least Isobel couldn't leave the room without waking her up.

The next thing she knew, dawn had broken and the birds were singing. They were in strong voice this morning, as if there was much to celebrate, but Cara knew they were wrong. Utterly, totally wrong. Emotion flooded her body and she had to stuff her fist into her mouth to stop herself from screaming. She couldn't keep it all in any longer; she had to talk to Isobel. Now.

She crawled to her feet and knocked loudly several times. 'Isobel? Are you awake? It's me.' The silence was unbearable. She squeezed the handle, but it still wouldn't give. 'Isobel! Are you okay? If you don't answer, I'm going to have to kick the door in.'

She heard sounds of movement, the scraping of a chair, and then the handle spun free and the door opened a few inches. Isobel stood there, barefoot in a creased white cotton shift, strands of jet-black hair pasted across her forehead. Her eyes were puffy and red-rimmed from hours of crying.

'Please, just leave me alone.'

'But I need to explain…'

'No, you don't.' Isobel started to shut the door, but Cara leapt forward, barging her way into the room.

'Look, I know I've done wrong. I should have told you about me and Jay from the beginning – it was unfair to keep it a secret, after all you've done for me.'

Isobel looked at her askance. 'You think that's why I'm upset?'

'Well… er, yes. I…' Cara faltered. 'I mean, we've never had secrets from each other before.'

'Haven't we?' Isobel sat down heavily on the bed.

'What is it? I don't understand.'

'I've kept a secret from you for over three years. I thought you'd work it out, but you never did. You never even suspected.'

'What do you mean?'

'I'm in love with you, Cara. I've loved you from the very beginning. I knew you weren't naturally that way, so I didn't say anything. I didn't want to scare you off. I thought, in time, you'd understand how beautiful our friendship was, that things would develop and grow… and the fact that I was a woman wouldn't matter to you.' She paused to steady her voice. 'Why do you think I asked you to come and live with me here?'

Cara felt herself colour up. 'I don't know – to start Purple—'

'I couldn't give a toss about Purple Blaze. That was just an excuse. I was missing you so much, I thought I was going to die. I wanted to be with you again. I thought that once we were by ourselves, it would happen. I didn't invest all my inheritance so you could fuck the first bloke that came along.'

Cara flinched. 'I had no idea you felt like this,' she began, but Isobel shook her head dismissively.

'Not true. I've been thinking about it all night. If you had no idea, you'd have told me about Jay. Why else would you skulk around in the dark like a bitch on heat? You disgust me.'

The words stabbed at her like knives. Isobel thought her *disgusting*? 'I'm sorry,' she said stiffly. 'I never meant to hurt you. I've obviously made a huge mistake.'

'No, *I* made the mistake,' said Isobel. 'Now go, please.'

Cara hesitated; they couldn't end the conversation like this. 'I really care about you…'

'Stop making it worse and get out.'

She backed towards the door. 'What about the others? They'll be here soon…'

'Tell them to go home – tell them the whole thing's finished. And I never want to see Jay ever, ever again, okay?'

'And what about me?' said Cara. 'Do you want me to go too?'

'Yes… No… I don't know… Just leave me alone, please. I need to think.'

'Can I get you anything?'

Isobel shook her head and lay down on the bed, curling herself into a ball.

Cara went back to her room, shutting the door behind her. *Had* she always known that Isobel was in love with her? No, she thought, absolutely not. They had behaved like a couple, that was true; always together, not seeming to need other friends and not bothering with men. A few people at university had made probing remarks, but Cara had always been quick to put them right. They were just close friends, she'd insisted, but thinking back, Isobel had always kept uncharacteristically quiet on the subject. Cara sighed. How stupid and naive she'd been. This was the 1980s, for God's sake, not Victorian times. Several men on their course were openly gay and that hadn't troubled her one bit. She had nothing against lesbians; she just wasn't one of them, which was probably why she hadn't realised Isobel was attracted to her.

She paused her thoughts for a second, turning her head to gaze out of the window at the treetops. Was that entirely true?

Come on, admit it, she said to herself. There *had* been moments, hadn't there? Especially since they'd come to Darkwater Terrace. Like when Isobel jumped into her bed on Saturday mornings and started to play-fight, hitting her with the pillow and lifting her pyjama top to tickle her bare tummy. Or how she squeezed next to her on the tiny sofa every evening when there were plenty of other, more comfortable places to sit… And then there was their new ritual of the nighty-night kiss, started by Isobel. Cara touched her lips and remembered.

Yes, she'd sensed the longings but had chosen to ignore them. She felt bad because she couldn't love Isobel in the way she wanted to be loved, and yet she didn't want to lose the friendship. A guilty realisation sank into her. Isobel was right. She'd kept the fling with Jay a secret not out of daring and rebelliousness, but out of cowardice and selfishness. And now everything was spoilt.

CHAPTER EIGHTEEN

Me

Arlecchino's is a small private members' club in Soho, squashed between a Thai restaurant and a post-production studio. I must have passed the anonymous black door hundreds of times as it's only a few streets from my office, but I'm sure I've never noticed it before. It's as if it's appeared like magic, a pop-up – just for today, just for us. Normally, I'd be really excited to be invited to a place like this; I'd have told all the girls at work and taken pictures of my food. And later, I'd have rung Dad and regaled him with stories of celebs I'd spotted and how much shorter, or uglier, they looked in the flesh. But I daren't tell Dad I've made contact with Isobel Dalliday, or that she's watched the videotape and has been texting me ever since, desperate for us to meet up. My finger hovers over the entry button. To press or not to press? Once I pass through this door, there'll be no turning back.

I give my name to the unwelcoming voice at the other end and she buzzes me in. The narrow staircase wall is greasy with thousands of fingerprints – inhabitants, guests, customers. It feels, even smells like an old brothel. This is shabby-chic taken so far it's just shabby. At the top of the stairs is a small landing. The 'hostess' is perched behind an artistically chipped off-white desk, her platinum-blonde hair set in a victory roll, wearing a tight black dress with a white lace collar. So vintage. So very 'meedja'.

'Isobel's waiting for you in the Blue Room,' she says, without even looking at me. I scribble in the visitors' book, then follow her red-nailed finger to the back of the club.

The Blue Room is painted a purplish-grey like a cold dawn. Uneven dark floorboards, sofas draped with silken throws and velvet cushions that look like unmade beds, gloomy fringed lampshades and original shutters at the narrow windows. Everything's deliberately threadbare and tawdry, as if the whores have never left. There are several clubs like this in Soho; I've been in one or two, tagging along to meetings with clients. They're film sets, luxuriously distressed, the props carefully chosen, supporting artists all in place. Men in Harry Potter glasses and slim black shirts huddle boyishly around iPads; immaculate women in fitted dresses and everlasting lipstick are being charmingly ruthless to anyone who will listen, while everyone sitting on their own is pretending to be super-busy with their smartphone.

Isobel is by the window, sitting in a winged armchair: fraying fabric in thick grey and black stripes, its stuffing theatrically bulging out. She's rapid-reading what looks like a script, swilling a large glass of red in one hand. I study her from across the room. She's curled up to one side with her legs crossed, a pencil tucked behind her ear, which she's taking out now to scrawl something in the margin. She turns over the page, then another. Her natural rhythm quick, almost irritable, as if the rest of the world can't keep up. I hesitate, one foot poised to turn on its heel, but it's too late, she's already spotted me.

'Don't stand there like a lady-in-waiting,' she says, beckoning.

We're shown to a table in the corner of the dining room and sit down opposite each other. The tension between us zings, but we don't say anything. The waiter whisks up my linen napkin and deposits it gracefully on my lap, repeating the same action with Isobel before handing us the menus and retiring to the shadows.

'Well…' she says. Her skin is paper-white, tinged pink with lunchtime alcohol, and her blue eyes are sparkling like cheap jewels. 'Isn't this absolutely amazing?'

'This place? Yeah, it is kind of—'

'No, darling!' she laughs. 'I mean, the two of us, finding each other after all this time. I can't tell you how happy I feel.'

'Oh… right…'

'I know the menu like the back of my hand. To start, you must have the butternut squash ravioli. It's divine.' She calls the waiter over and orders for the two of us, identical starters and mains, with a bottle of very expensive-sounding wine 'to celebrate'.

'That video is… well, extraordinary,' she says. 'And I mean absolutely extraordinary. The first time I watched it, shivers went right through my spine. I couldn't sleep all night for thinking about it.' She lets out a trembling sigh and then leans forward across the table, so close that I can see her pores, clogged with deathly pale face powder. With the jet-black hair and scarlet lips, she looks more like a forgotten bride of Dracula than a forties movie star, which I imagine was the original intention.

'Tell me,' she says. 'What was your first reaction? I mean, did it bring back any memories?'

I shake my head. 'No. Not at all. But then, I was only four.'

'Hmm… That doesn't surprise me.' The waiter pours our wine and Isobel takes a generous glug. 'Children usually forget their past lives once they reach five or six. That's normal.'

It doesn't sound normal to me, but Isobel leaves no space for my opinion, embarking on a mini lecture about reincarnation, as if it factually exists, like cancer or heart disease – or death itself, for that matter. I drink my wine and let her talk. Not all of us reincarnate, apparently; it only happens when there's 'unfinished business'. I assume by that she doesn't mean incomplete kitchen extensions or not reaching your weight-loss target. She tells me that, despite being 'very drawn' to Buddhism, she doesn't subscribe to the karmic interpretation – disabled people, for example, being punished for wrongdoings in former lives. She thinks that's cruel and utterly ludicrous. Her jury's out on whether people ever reincarnate as domestic pets and believes it probably only happens occasionally, in exceptional circumstances. But the notion of dead people's spirits floating out of their bodies and wandering around the ether looking for new, unsuspecting hosts appears to make perfect sense. She's talking a load of crap and yet I seem unable – unwilling even – to contradict her. I just sit there, listening and nodding. To my shame, I even interject the odd agreeing noise. Isobel Dalliday is enchanting me. I find her warm, funny and extremely entertaining. And I mustn't forget, she's paying for lunch.

The food arrives – two butternut squash ravioli swimming in herby cream sauce. We eat a few forkfuls in welcome silence. The cream slides down my throat and plops into the pool of wine lying at the bottom of my stomach.

'So what do the police make of the tape?' Isobel wipes sauce from the corners of her mouth with her finger and then licks it clean. 'I don't suppose they're taking it seriously. They are such plods. The very least they should have done is put you through a past life regression.'

'Er… what's that?'

'You're put under deep hypnosis and taken back to your previous lives.'

'Oh,' I say, thinking, *You've got to be kidding.* No way would I ever agree to that.

We carry on eating and the waiter seizes the opportunity to leap in and top up our glasses. Isobel's pink cheeks are looking clownish, but she orders another bottle. This woman really knows how to put the booze away. I realise I'm going to be too pissed to go back to work this afternoon and am wondering what convincing excuse I could make when Isobel breaks into my thoughts.

'So… this investigation. Do they have any new leads?'

I shrug. 'Not that I know of. Eliot – that's my ex, you know, who's working on the case – he won't tell me. He's being very professional.'

'How boring of him.'

'They're trying to track Becca down. If they could get her to admit she was mistaken about Cara speaking to her, it could help massively.'

'Yes, absolutely,' Isobel says. 'Her evidence wrecked the entire prosecution case.'

'I think Jay got to her before the trial and made her change her evidence.'

'I can't think how. He was in prison, on remand. Anyway, they didn't know each other. Your mother was just a stranger passing by.'

I sigh. 'Maybe the shock of finding the body brought on a psychotic episode.'

Isobel puts down her fork with a dramatic ring, splashing sauce onto the crisp white tablecloth. 'No, do you know what I think it was? Oh. My. God. That's it! That's it! Yes, it all fits, doesn't it?' The people on the next table look up irritably, but she doesn't notice, or is too drunk to care. 'Cara was dead, but her departing spirit spoke to Becca. She helped Cara's soul enter the spirit world, creating a kind of surrogate maternal bond. When people die, they often call out for their mother, you know. So it's completely understandable that when Becca became a mother herself, Cara's restless, troubled soul wanted to be with her again. That's why she chose to reincarnate in you!'

I stare at her, not knowing how to respond, watching as a large emotional tear runs down her cheek, making a dark channel of mascara in her thick face powder. I should have stopped this ages ago, should have told her what I really thought. Now it's gone too far and I'm stuck in this pit of ridiculous madness.

She grips my arm tightly. 'I'm feeling so emotional, I feel like I could burst.' She starts to pant heavily. 'Oh God, it's as if a huge weight has lifted off me. For years I've felt so angry with your mother, I blamed her for the acquittal, but now I see… It wasn't her fault. She was simply telling the truth!' *The truth?* Now we really are getting into difficult territory.

'As *she* saw it, yes,' I reply, cautiously. 'But she was very ill, much worse than anyone realised…' I tail off pathetically. But it doesn't matter because Isobel isn't listening.

'Excuse me for a minute, will you?' She flings down her napkin and rises unsteadily to her feet, then staggers off to the toilets, presumably to have a good cathartic weep. I stare down at the tablecloth while the waiter leaps in to clear our plates. I'm a complete idiot. I've gone and made things worse.

Perhaps I should leave. Now. While I've got the chance. I bend down, pick up my bag and scrape back my chair. The waiter, who's now brushing invisible crumbs off the tablecloth with a silver brush, catches my eye briefly and we exchange a small conspiratorial smile. I realise that he's been eavesdropping, or at least observing our body language. God knows what he must be thinking. I hesitate. The woman's upset. I shouldn't abandon her. On the other hand, this is all getting so weird. How can somebody as intelligent and successful as Isobel Dalliday believe this stuff? I'm still wondering what to do when I see her walking towards me, looking a little green around the gills, her freshly painted vermilion lips set in an I'm-absolutely-fine-thank-you grin. I let my bag drop to the floor, defeated.

Our main course arrives – a slab of 55-day hung sirloin served with a couple of chargrilled baby carrots and a beige smear of celeriac puree. As I cut into the meat, blood spurts into some crushed new potatoes and I feel a bit queasy. Isobel, make-up repaired and breathing just about under control, starts to tell me about the original investigation; the trauma Cara's family went through and how angry they were when Jay was acquitted.

'Well, unfortunately, my mother's... er...' I grapple for the most neutral word, 'her *experience* confused the jury and the judge didn't exactly help...' I realise that Isobel is staring past me, a look of complete panic on her face. 'What's wrong?' I ask.

'Alice is here. Shit. My PA must have told her, stupid cow. Oh fuckity-fuckity-fuck.' She waves breezily. 'Darling! Over here!' I turn round to see a glamorous woman, verging on the tarty-looking, hovering by the doorway. She nods, then starts to walk towards us, her high heels clipping the floorboards.

'She doesn't know about you yet,' Isobel hisses quickly. 'Let me do the talking.'

Alice reaches our table and pauses to take in the cosy scene. Immediately I understand how this looks. 'You didn't say you were meeting anyone,' she says through tight bronze lips.

'I didn't know myself,' Isobel says, the lie slipping easily off her tongue. 'It was just a last-minute thing.'

But Alice doesn't seem to be buying it. 'My voice record fin-ished early...' She stares accusingly at our half-eaten food. 'I was going to buy you lunch.'

'Why didn't you text? Then we'd have waited.'

'I wanted it to be a surprise,' Alice pouts.

'Oh, darling, how sweet of you. Now I feel terrible. ' Isobel gestures to the waiter to bring another chair and a third wine glass.

This is embarrassing. I offer up an apologetic smile, but Alice doesn't react. She's stick-thin, her clavicle bones sticking out of her chest like two drawer knobs, and I sense many hours in the gym, pounding the step machine. Her long hair, professionally streaked in shades of brown and gold, is puffed up and back-combed, Julia Roberts style. I know exactly how it will feel to the touch – brittle and slightly sticky, like over-spun candyfloss.

Alice notices me staring. 'I don't know you, do I? Are you an actress?'

Isobel quickly butts in. 'No, no, it's nothing like that. Please sit down, darling…' She pats the newly arrived chair and Alice perches stiffly on the edge. We make an extremely uncomfortable triangle.

'I want you to meet Meredith Banks,' announces Isobel. Adding more gently, 'She's Rebecca Banks's daughter… You remember Rebecca Banks?'

Alice's eyes flick at me like a reptile who's just seen a threat in its peripheral vision. 'Of course I do, I'm not stupid.' She glares at Isobel for a few long seconds, absorbing the information. Then she says, 'A last-minute thing, eh? Like hell.'

'Now you mustn't be cross, darling,' Isobel soothes. 'I wanted to surprise you too.' She pours Alice a large glass of wine. 'You might need this… I've got something absolutely amazing to tell you about Cara.'

CHAPTER NINETEEN

Jay

Two weeks off sick in the middle of term is not to be sniffed at, he thinks as he makes a mug of strong tea and takes it back to bed. He sets the pillow against the headboard and sits upright with outstretched legs, tucking the duvet tightly across his chest, invalid style, leaving one arm free for putting mug to mouth. Being sick in the head is a lot more fun than being physically ill, he decides, briefly remembering the bout of flu he had in November: four miserable days lying in his pit with nobody to bring him so much as a Lemsip. The GP was suitably convinced by his symptoms – headaches, sleepless nights, sudden bursts of anger, paranoia, feelings of hopelessness… He wasn't lying; he's been like this for years, just never thought of it as a mental illness. Still not sure about it. Although it's okay these days to say you're depressed. Almost cool. All these celebrities coming out with their bipolar disorders and obsessive-compulsive whatsits… No wonder the suicide rate is up.

He drains the mug and rests it on his bedside table, then snuggles down further, pulling the duvet up to beneath his chin. He should have gone to the doctor years ago. Now he's got three free sessions of CBT on the NHS (which he won't bother with) and two weeks of lounging about on full pay while some poor bugger has to cover his lessons. He draws a mental picture of his timetable. Normally at this time, he'd be teaching acting techniques to the Level 2s – the same old stuff he's taught for years. He gets the students to create a character and give it a backstory, then he puts that character in a particular situation and everyone improvises. Acting, in his view, is simple. You play the given circumstances. Just like in real life.

Imagine you're a man in his early fifties, never married, no kids, living in a tiny flat in north London. You hate your job. You have a few acquaintances, but no real friends. You've only ever fallen in love once, a very long time ago, but it didn't work out. You haven't had sex for over ten years and you've almost forgotten what it feels like to be touched. In contrast, the woman responsible for ruining your life has become a massive success. She's written a book about theatre directing and is doing a personal signing at the Piccadilly Waterstones next week. How does your character feel about this? What do they do?

Jay leans back and thinks about his plans for the event to come. He won't make a mistake this time; he'll queue overnight on the pavement if that's what it takes to see her. He wriggles his toes excitedly, like a small boy looking forward to a football match. Plans a few moves in his head. Runs a lap of victory, proudly holding his prize. Let battle commence…

He snoozes for a bit, lost in strange, intricate dreams whose plots vanish the second he wakes. Feeling faint with hunger, he reluctantly gets up and dresses without showering, putting on the same sweaty clothes he wore yesterday and the day before. A pair of faded brown cords and a striped rugby-type shirt with a misbehaving collar. He pauses to study himself in the mirror: lank greying hair, puffy shadows beneath his eyes; his facial muscles, once so taut across his cheekbones now dragging downwards in a permanent scowl of disappointment. Maybe I *am* mentally ill, he thinks. I certainly look the part.

It's nearly midday when his doorbell rings. He doesn't register it at first, not used to having callers or receiving parcels, and it takes two more rings before he realises it's for him. Even then he hesitates before picking up the entryphone.

'Who is it?'

'Detective Sergeant Eliot Myles from Heartlands Police. Can I have a word, please?'

Jay feels his pulse quicken immediately. Heartlands Police. That can only mean one thing. 'I'm off sick,' he says, managing a bit of a cough.

'I know, I heard. I'm sorry to disturb you, but we do need to talk.' The chap sounds young and posh, with no trace of a Brummie accent. Only beginners are that polite.

'Top floor, flat C.' Jay presses the buzzer.

He quickly tidies the lounge, stacking the empty mugs and beer cans by the sink, stuffing papers and magazines under the sofa. Suddenly remembering, he runs into the hallway and shuts the door to the box room. Doesn't want anyone snooping around in there... Oh no.

'Thanks so much for seeing me,' says the detective. 'I really appreciate it.' He offers his card, self-consciously glancing at his printed name before handing it over. A new boy, Jay thinks, probably just promoted. He's surprised to see he's black – well, mixed race, actually, but he probably calls himself black. A box ticker. Although he's hardly off a council estate.

Jay nods and steps back. 'You'd better come in,' he says, walking into the lounge. He points at the low, uncomfortable sofa and the young man sits, sinking awkwardly. He's clutching a brown leather satchel, scuffed and worn at the edges. Either he's had it since he was a boy, or he paid hundreds of pounds for it in Portobello Road. Jay guesses the former. There's a definite whiff of public school about the detective, years of expensive education, Oxbridge perhaps. The product of privilege and overachievement, the type of person Jay used to want to put up against a

wall and shoot, though these days he'd probably donate a kidney
to teach someone like that.

'So what's this about?'

DS Myles opens the satchel and takes out a large notepad and
pen. 'As you probably know, unsolved murder cases are reviewed
every twenty-four months. For many years that's been routine,
but recent advances in the recovery of DNA material has made
those reviews more meaningful and indeed fruitful. Operation
Honeysuckle is—'

'Jesus Christ, do you people never give up?' Jay barks. 'I was
acquitted.'

'Yes, I know.' The boy fixes his gaze on Jay's face.

'So I'm a witness now, not a suspect, is that what you're
saying?'

'The jury decided you were innocent and I'm working on the
basis that they made the correct decision.'

Bullshit, thinks Jay, but he doesn't say anything. He has to
hand it to the guy: he's smart. Treating your enemy respectfully
can be very disarming. He watches as the detective takes a white
padded envelope out of the satchel and puts it on the coffee table. *Fuck*, he thinks.

'We're collecting voluntary DNA samples from everyone that
had access to 31 Darkwater Terrace. For elimination purposes,
that's all.'

'So you say…' Jay folds his arms in a huff.

'You've already admitted that you were at the house on the
day of the murder, so having DNA evidence of your presence
won't incriminate you. Your profile will only be analysed in connection with this particular case; it won't go on the national database.' DS Myles dips back into his satchel and takes out a pair
of disposable gloves. 'I can do it now, it won't take long.'

'Hmm… What if I refuse?'

'That's your right. Like I said, it's a voluntary sample.'

'So you can't make me.'

'No. Not unless I arrest you on suspicion of a recordable offence.'

The detective examines his notes, pretending to be looking for something, not saying a word. He doesn't need to speak; the implications are obvious. If Jay refuses to give a sample, it makes him look guilty. But he daren't risk it. If they're determined to stitch him up, why make it easy for them?

DS Myles rests his pen. 'I don't blame you for not cooperating,' he says. 'But it won't stop the process. Motive and opportunity are important, but these days scientific evidence is king. People are being caught for crimes they thought they'd long got away with.'

'I didn't kill her,' Jay says after a long silence. 'They put me in the frame; they were gunning for me from the start. I never had a chance. If Becca hadn't spoken up, I don't know what would have happened. Maybe I'd still be in prison. Maybe I'd have hanged myself or had my throat cut.' He's welling up, voice trembling. Memories of those months on remand flash through his brain. The beatings. The weeks of isolation, fearing for his own safety. After he was acquitted, it was almost worse: anonymous death threats, malicious phone calls, old friends spitting on him in the street. When a flaming petrol-soaked cloth was stuffed through the letter box and almost burnt the house down, he had to admit defeat. The police did nothing to protect him, didn't lift a finger to find out who'd nearly killed his mother. She was rehoused on the other side of the city and he was advised – no, instructed – to get out of town. If he didn't, he would have to face the consequences. And now, thirty years on, the police have decided he was innocent after all, have they? Just want to eliminate him from their enquiries? Like fuck they do. He's not stupid. He may have moved to London, but he's kept abreast of developments at Heartlands. He knows Brian Durley is the big boss now and would like to tidy this case up once and for all.

DS Myles, Durley's twenty-first-century replacement, hasn't even looked up. He's writing energetically on his pad, like a diligent student taking notes in a lecture. Jay breathes heavily, screwing his fists into tight, angry balls.

'I swear I didn't kill her, okay? You're wasting your time here. If you think you're going to be the hero, the one to break me down, get me to confess after all these years, give Cara's family closure, yadda-yadda, then you can go fuck yourself!' He bangs his fist on the coffee table. An electricity bill lying on top of a stack of magazines falls off and glides gracefully to the floor.

The detective barely flinches. 'Did you know Rebecca Banks then?' he says.

'No,' Jay replies quickly, wondering if his face is turning red. 'Why are you asking?'

'Because you called her Becca. A few moments ago, you said' – he looks down at his notes – ' "If Becca hadn't spoken up".'

'So? That's her name, isn't it?' Thinking, *fuck, fuck…*

'It's what her friends called her, yes. Not Rebecca, or Becky, or Becs. Becca.'

'That's probably what was said at the trial, I don't know,' he mutters. 'Does it matter?'

'No. I just wondered, that's all.' The boy is studying him carefully, using all his detective training, no doubt. Looking for tells.

Jay stands up. 'So is that it? Only I'm not feeling too great. I'm off work with stress.'

DS Myles picks up the DNA kit. 'Sure you don't want to help us?'

'What, help you fit me up for a crime I didn't commit? No thanks.'

The detective puts the kit back into his schoolboy satchel and buckles the straps. Then he stands up and walks towards the door. He puts his hand on the doorknob and turns around.

'And you definitely didn't know Rebecca Banks.' Jay shakes his head slowly. 'Well, thanks for your time. I'll see myself out.'

It seems to take forever for DS Myles to descend the stairs. Jay holds his breath until he hears the front door slam shut, then lets it out in an angry groan.

CHAPTER TWENTY

Me

Isobel Dalliday is my new best friend. Although she seems to think I'm her *old* best friend. Her oldest and bestest, in fact. I'm not sure how this has happened – well, I know it was me that sought her out and told her about the videotape, so in that respect I've only myself to blame. What I mean is, how have I let this latest madness happen? And why do I now feel powerless to stop it?

I give my name to the girl at the desk and take a seat on the brown leather sofa. I've never been to a private clinic for anything before, and as a committed Labour voter (apart from that brief defection to the Lib Dems in 2010) it feels like a class betrayal. I look around at the characterless white furniture, the neutral rug, the water-torture feature tinkling in the softly illuminated alcove, the photos of calm seascapes and hazy sunsets. Pan pipes are playing gently through the speakers and the atmosphere is so peaceful and pleased with itself that I feel an urge to swear loudly or trash the place.

The girls at work think I'm at the dentist – no way could I tell them I was having past life regression; I'd be less embarrassed to admit I was having liposuction or laser hair removal. The ridiculousness of being here literally makes me guffaw – the sound just bursts out of my mouth and I have to turn it into a cough. The receptionist asks me if I'd like a drink of water. She's wearing white scrubs, jet-black hair scraped off her heavily made-up face into a viciously tight ponytail, dragging her eyes upwards and making her look slightly oriental. Her body could have been created by an animator – tiny waist, oversized pointy boobs and pouty collagen lips; perks of the job no doubt.

I get a text. It's from Isobel – who else? She's '*Nearly here*', followed by six kisses. I wish she wasn't coming, but she's organised this *and* she's paying for it, so I couldn't really say no. She's aware that she's not allowed to sit in on the session, but she thinks I might need some support. I can't imagine what she thinks is going to happen; it's only hypnotherapy, not like I'm having an operation. And we're in Harley Street.

Yes, who would have thought you could have past life regression somewhere as reputable as Harley Street? I guess they'll take anyone as long as they can afford the rent. I'm handed a tiny paper cone of icy water and sit there clutching it, studying the framed diplomas on the walls attesting to qualifications from educational institutions I've never heard of. It strikes me as ironic that hypnotherapist Emily Backhouse, fully trained in Neuro-linguistic Programming, Cognitive Behavioural Therapy, Emotional Freedom Technique, Eye Movement Desensitisation and Reprocessing, Inner Child Work, Soul Retrieval and Spiritual Healing, shares her clinic with a cosmetic surgeon. Aren't they rivals – the good and bad angels? I was taught to believe it's what's on the inside that counts.

Another text from Isobel: '*Moments away xx*'. Only two kisses this time; she must be running at full speed. She texts me every day. Sweet, innocent messages, saying she's thinking of me, sending me her love. Sometimes she phones on her way home, tramping down the hill from the tube. Tells me funny stories about hopeless publicity officers, impossible producers and spoilt, misbehaving actors – some of them famous. 'I know you'd never betray me,' she says, 'but promise you won't breathe it to a living soul.'

I haven't told anyone, alive or dead. Mainly because I'm embarrassed. It's like I'm having an affair with an older married woman. And although Isobel keeps insisting that Alice is 'absolutely thrilled' about our cosy little triangle, and is desperate for me to come over for supper very, very soon, I'm not sure I believe it. For example, Isobel invited me to the launch of her new book, then withdrew the invitation, saying it would be as boring as hell and not to bother coming. I detected some marital foot-putting-down. Not that I blame Alice. It *is* a bit worrying when your wife believes some girl in her twenties is the reincarnation of the love of her life.

I shouldn't be going along with it, but I've quickly learnt that once Isobel gets an idea in her head, she's like a dog with a bone. She thinks the regression will liberate me, that it will unblock channels in my psyche (or something like that) and that only by facing the traumas of my past life will I be able to deal with my present unresolved issues. I told her that I don't really have any issues, unless you count a crap job, a £30,000 student loan debt and not having had sex for months, which made her shake her head sagely, as if to say that proved it. She says I use humour to deflect, because I'm uncomfortable with talking about my feelings – which is not surprising, in her view, because I was largely brought up by a man. But all is not lost, apparently. Isobel believes the tape emerged for a reason, which is a more palatable way of saying that it happened by magic. She is convinced that Cara's angelic spirit has been watching over me, waiting for the right time to reappear in my life and guide me on my spiritual journey.

Such a load of rubbish. But I knew Isobel wasn't going to give up unless I agreed to the regression. It won't work. No way is it going to work. Hopefully, once it's over, she'll stop banging on about it. I let out a long, audible sigh, which the receptionist takes for impatience. I shouldn't be so mean. Isobel is actually a lovely, warm, generous human being and I know she's only trying to help. But if anyone has unresolved issues, it's her.

The receptionist apologises and says that Emily Backhouse is running late with her current client. Isobel's moments have turned into minutes, and I'm thinking that if I'm not called in soon, I'll lose my nerve and go to Oxford Street for a spot of retail therapy instead. I need some new boots. I put down the copy of *Vogue* and give myself a silent talking-to. It's just a hypnosis session, for God's sake; people have them all the time for smoking or phobias. In a couple of hours it will all be over and done with, like having a tooth out. Come to think of it, I'd probably rather have a tooth out.

'Sorry, darling, I misremembered the door number and went to the wrong end of the street,' says Isobel, sweeping breathlessly into reception. She plants a sweaty kiss on my cheek. 'I thought you'd have gone in by now.'

'Running late,' I tell her.

She pulls at her coat as if discarding a straitjacket and plonks herself down next to me, squeezing my hand. 'How are you feeling? Nervous?'

'Not really.'

'You'll be fine,' she reassures me. 'I'm told she's the best there is. Apparently she regressed Diana, although she refuses to confirm it.' And look what happened to her, I think.

'Um, Miss Banks? Emily's ready for you now.' The receptionist flicks her switch of glossy black hair in the direction of the stairs.

Isobel squeezes my hand again, her eyes shining with excitement. 'Best of luck, darling,' she says, as if I'm a child about to sit a test.

The consulting room is very simple and non-medical, a bit tatty compared to front-of-house. 'Lovely to meet you,' Emily says, holding out her hand. She's not what I was expecting: in her late sixties, soft and motherly-looking, with large round features and a glossy silver-grey bob. A dark pink jumper over a white shirt and a full grey skirt. No wild hair or flowing scarves or large hooped earrings, which, actually, is a relief.

I move towards the couch but she redirects me to the upright chair next to the desk. 'Let's have a chat first.' I sit down and Emily looks into my eyes, tunnelling into me, as if she's already retrieving my soul. 'I've had a chat with your friend Isobel and watched the tape,' she says.

'Really?' I feel myself stiffen. 'How come?'

'She sent me a copy; I assumed she had your permission.'

I shrug. This feels to me like it's compromising the experiment.

Emily takes my silence as approval. 'I must say, I feel very honoured to be allowed to share in such a special experience.'

'So you think it's genuine?'

She puts her head on one side, considering. 'Well, it wasn't a spontaneous event; you were being asked to recall things you'd said before, and you needed prompting, so… hard to know for sure. But it's difficult to coach a child that young, so, on balance, I'd say it was genuine, yes. A great number of children come out with memories of past lives, but very few are listened to, particularly in Western culture. Most people can't accept reincarnation. But I've been doing this for many years, and I *know*.'

'Well… if I'm honest, I'm a bit sceptical.'

Emily smiles. 'I don't have a problem with that. In many ways, it's a better attitude to have. It means you won't force it. A lot of my clients are desperate to discover their past lives and try too hard.'

'I'm not sure you'll even manage to get me under,' I say, aware that I'm starting to sound a little aggressive.

'Some people are more susceptible than others,' she agrees, smiling. 'But don't worry, there's nothing to be scared of; your emotional safety and well-being is my number one concern. You'll remain in control the entire time. You're not asleep, you're fully aware that you're under hypnosis, and if you want to stop, you can do so instantly. You'll remember everything that you say, but the session will be recorded so you can listen to it at home. And Isobel has asked for a copy, is that okay?' I nod, feeling more and more helpless. 'When we finish, you'll feel incredibly relaxed. And your body temperature will have dropped, but don't worry, I'll make sure you keep warm. Any questions?'

'No, I'd just like to get on with it.'

She settles me on the reclining couch and puts a grey blanket over my legs; clips a small microphone to my shirt and fiddles with the recording equipment for a few moments, then goes to her laptop and taps at the keys. I'm told to close my eyes and to take deep, slow breaths, which I do. Emily assures me that I'll be put under hypnosis very slowly – she's not going to rush me straight to my past life. No, we're going to find a safe place first, somewhere I can return to if the feelings get too much to handle. I immediately think of a physical location – under the duvet, behind the curtains – but she means a memory of a time when I felt happy.

Happy times… There must be plenty to choose from, surely. My first thought is of my childhood, me and Dad, and I try to picture us together – reading a bedtime story, collecting shells on the beach, struggling over my maths homework. Such things definitely happened, but I can't remember a specific place or time. A significant birthday, perhaps. My eighteenth? No, that was a disaster; I got extremely drunk and ended up in A & E. A university experience then… I try to conjure something up but my mind has gone blank. There's only one more place to try. A happy memory of me and Eliot; there must be hundreds. What about when we moved into the flat above the greengrocer's? But the happy thought is roughly pushed away by the sad one that he no longer cares about me, that he hasn't called once since we fell out.

I'm starting to stress; the slow, deep breaths have turned quick and shallow. I *knew* I wouldn't be able to do this. But then Emily pulls her chair across and sits at my side. She starts talking in her low, unhurried voice, counting me down…

And miraculously, we find the safe place without too much trouble, settling on the garden in the house where I spent most of my childhood, the old house I can't go back to any more, so it's comforting to visit it in my imagination. I put myself on the swing and an old song starts to play in my head: *the green grass grew all around all around.* That's what I can see: the lawn stretching away from me, green grass apart from the patch of dusty bare earth beneath my feet, and above me solid blue sky, like the underside of a lid. I'm telling Emily I'm ten years old; it's the school summer holidays. Dad's sorting out the garage and I'm reading. One hand holding the book, the other holding on to the swing chain, rocking gently back and forth, back and forth, using my foot as a brake. Emily lets me swing: she lets the sun warm the back of my neck and the breeze cool my legs. Then she starts talking about doors.

There are five doors in the garden, each leading to one of my past lives. Because I haven't just got one, she explains; that wouldn't make any sense at all. There are hundreds, maybe thousands to choose from. It's up to me which door I walk through today – she tells me I'm totally in control. If one of them leads to Cara, I'll sense it, and if I feel ready, that's where I'll go. My limbs feel heavy. I sink further into the couch, my hands flopping at my sides. And I say – in a flat, neutral voice I barely recognise and yet know is mine – that I *am* ready. I choose the middle door.

CHAPTER TWENTY-ONE

File 20140504. Banks, Meredith

Emily: How are you feeling?

Meredith: Fine.

E: Good. Where are you? Can you describe it?

M: Er… I'm looking at the sea. Standing on a cliff, looking out. I know this place, I've been here before.

E: Who are you…? (Pause) What do you look like?

M: Don't know. I… er… I can't see myself…

E: Look down at your feet. Can you see what you're wearing on your feet?

M: Er… yes. Sandals… pink sandals with straps.

E: What else are you wearing? Try to describe your clothes.

M: A dress… no, shorts, red shorts, I can see my knees. And a yellow T-shirt. My mother's calling out to me, telling me not to go too near the edge…

E: Can you hear her? What's she saying?

M: *For heaven's sake, come away, you'll fall…* But I'm not going to fall. I'm going to fly. I want to step off, into the air. Swoop about the sky like a seagull. (Laughs) Mum's coming to get me now, grabbing my hand, pulling me back. She's cross.

E: Do you know what your name is?

M: I'm not sure…

E: Perhaps your mother's calling to you. Is she saying your name?

M: I don't know… Cara… I think I'm Cara…

E   Do you know how old you are at this moment?

M: No… Young.

E: Do you know where you are? The name of the place?

M: Um… it's just sea and cliffs. We're on holiday.

(Pause)

M: West Bay. Is there a place called West Bay?

E: Yes, in Dorset.

(Long pause)

E: Are you happy to leave West Bay now?

M: Yes, I think so.

(Long pause)

E: Good. So now I'm going to take you forward in your life… Is that all right with you?

M: Yes. I'll try…

E: Any time you want to stop, you just tell me, remember?

M: It's okay.

E: I'm going to count down from five, and when I get to one, you're going to be grown up and at—

M: I can't.

E: Just relax. Listen to your breathing. Everything's fine. If you don't want to go on, we won't.

(Pause)

M: No, it's okay. I'm okay.

E: Very well. You're still Cara, but we're moving forward in time. You're no longer a child, you're grown up and you're at university. Five, four, three, two, one. (Pause) Can you see yourself?

M: I think so. I'm walking through campus. Faculty buildings on both sides. Grass. People sitting on the grass, chatting, lying down. Must be the summer term.

E: Are you with anyone?

M: I don't know. Don't think so.

E: Look around – can you see any friends?

M: I'm with someone. My best friend, I think. A woman.

E: Do you know her name?

M: No… I don't know. I'm not sure.

E: Describe her to me.

M: Actually, I think this is my university. I think this is one of my memories. Sorry, I've… I've made a mistake, it's confusing.

E: That's fine, it happens sometimes. Okay, let's take you away from that. Let's go back to Cara. I want you to think about Cara again and I'm going to take you forward to the end of her life, her final moments on earth. Is that okay? I'm going to count you down from five and then we'll be there.

M: Okay, I'll try.

E: No rush. Just concentrate on your breathing… And then five, four, three, two, one… Can you tell me where you are now?

M: No. Sorry.

E: Try looking down at your feet again.

M: I can't. I… I can't see anything.

E: Where are you? Describe the place.

M: Can't see. It's dark. Can't see a thing.

E: Are you inside or—

M: Out. It's pitch black. (Pause) I'm scared.

E: It's night-time, yes? Why are you out in the darkness? Do you know?

M: Got to get away. Got to hide. I feel dizzy, my whole body's throbbing.

E: Where are you?

M: In the garden… Got to get away… I can't breathe, I'm shaking… My dress is wet, sticking to me… It's blood. I'm bleeding… Blood everywhere. I can't stop it… Got to open the gate… My hands are shaking, I can't breathe… Everything hurts, my head's spinning…

E: Try to stay calm. Tell me where you are now.

M: I'm at the pool, on the path, bare feet, the stones hurt. Everything's hurting. Deep, burning pain… I want to run but my legs won't let me. It's so dark, I don't know where I'm going …

E: Who did this to you?

M: Got to hide, got to get away… So much pain, so much blood… can't walk…

E: Who is it? Do you know them?

M: I'm trapped, can't escape… I'm falling… The ground's coming up to meet me… I hear footsteps. Breathing… They're coming after me.

E: Who? Who's coming after you?

M: No, no, leave me alone! Please go… (Screams)

E: Three, two, one… It's over, Meredith, you've left that place. You're back in the garden, in the old house. Reading a book and swinging gently on the swing. Your father's in the garage, sorting things out. Everything's fine. You're safe. Totally safe.

CHAPTER TWENTY-TWO

Cara
June 1984

Isobel imprisoned herself in her room for the next three days, only emerging to use the bathroom when she was sure nobody else was around. Cara brought her titbits of food – toasted teacakes, chocolate digestives, luxurious ice cream – and laid them on a tray outside her door. Sometimes the food stayed there for hours, melting in the heat and attracting flies, but she persisted. Nobody was going to accuse her of letting her friend starve to death.

Downstairs, Cara spent her time wandering from room to room, trailing her fingers through the dust that was accumulating on the antique furniture, browsing through old hardbacks with tiny, unreadable writing, and constantly listening for signs of life above. She only left the house to go to the corner shop, throwing supplies into her basket and running home as fast as she could, imagining all kinds of horrors that might greet her. It was as if she'd left a newborn baby alone in the house. This situation couldn't go on forever, she told herself. Eventually Isobel would have to come down and face her.

But then what would happen? Would she have to go home to her parents, back to temping and sending off hopeless applications? Purple Blaze was finished, that much was clear; there was no chance of resurrecting it now. Toby (who'd been very understanding, bless him) had gone back to Kent, and Jay had been banned from the house. They'd had a few whispered phone calls over the past few days, during which he'd apologised and begged her to meet him at the pool as before. At the moment, Cara was refusing. Not because she blamed him, or didn't want to see him – if anything, she wanted him more than ever – but she needed to put her friend first. Isobel seemed to be having a nervous breakdown and Cara felt the least she could do was be on hand to nurse her through it. She'd thought about calling the doctor, but felt embarrassed about explaining. Isobel was unlikely to do anything stupid, but Cara had cleared out the bathroom cabinet just in case. She was surprised at how spectacularly Isobel had collapsed under pressure – she'd always thought of her as strong and confident, a real fighter. But so many things were turning out to be not as she'd thought, she was starting to wonder if she knew Isobel at all.

In the end, it seemed to be the unusually warm weather that forced her out of her attic room. It was day four, mid-morning, and Cara was sitting in the conservatory with the door and windows thrown wide open, reading an ancient copy of *Great Expectations* from a leather-bound set of the complete works. She was so immersed in the story that she didn't hear Isobel coming down the stairs.

'I'm going to London,' she announced from the kitchen doorway.

Cara looked up, shutting the book guiltily. There were dark shadows beneath Isobel's eyes, but she was dressed smartly and looked as if she'd just washed her hair.

'What do you mean? For a break?'

'No, for good. I can't stay here, can I?' Isobel looked around, as if the place revolted her.

'I'm the one that should leave,' Cara said, her heart sinking as she uttered the words. 'I mean, this is your house.'

'It's never really felt like it, and anyway, it's all been spoilt. I'm going to sell it and share the money with Mum and Uncle Will.'

'Right… I see. Well, you've obviously been doing a lot of thinking…'

Isobel nodded. 'You can stay here until you get sorted. I'm not in a rush.' She was wobbling, as if slightly drunk. 'I'll be setting up a new company. With a different name, obviously.'

'Oh…' Cara said.

'I'll let you know my new address and phone number,' Isobel went on, stiffly. 'In case you ever need to get in touch.' *But not so I can visit*, thought Cara. She couldn't bear it – they'd never spoken to each other in this way before, not even on the first day they'd met, when they'd been total strangers. 'And while you're here, if you get a chance to do something about the garden… otherwise it's going to run away with itself.'

'No problem. I don't really know what I'm doing, but…'

'Thanks.' Isobel paused, as if expecting Cara to say something. There were a thousand things she wanted to say, but no words came. 'Right… better go, or I'll miss my coach.'

Isobel walked back into the hallway and picked up two large suitcases. Cara was so stunned she didn't follow her to protest, or even say a proper goodbye. Later, she was cross with herself for letting Isobel leave so easily. If she'd forced her to have a proper talk about what had happened and why it had gone so wrong, maybe they'd have been able to make up. Then again, maybe she'd wanted her to go; maybe these complicated, churned-up feelings were actually relief.

The first thing she did was call Jay. His mother answered, shouting out, 'Christopher! There's a girl on the phone for you!' So *that* was his real name – he'd refused to tell her before. No need for secrets now, she thought. He came over straight away, letting himself in with the key he was supposed to have returned.

'This is a stroke of luck,' he said. 'I'd have put money on her chucking you out.'

'What's in there?' Cara asked, pointing to his rucksack, although she knew full well.

'My stuff. Save keep going back to Mum's every time I need clean clothes. That's okay, isn't it?' Before she could answer, he flung it down on the floor and gave her a long, insistent kiss. They went immediately to bed and spent the next couple of hours having noisy, vigorous sex – Cara felt it was a release of tension more than an expression of love, and although she enjoyed it, she still couldn't fully relax. She kept listening out for the front door opening, or footsteps on the stairs, afraid that Isobel had suddenly changed her mind and come back.

'She's not that stupid,' said Jay. 'She'll know I'm here.'

'Then why make it easy for us? Why let us use her house?' Cara sat up and reached for her T-shirt. They'd missed lunch and she was feeling hungry. 'I suppose she doesn't love me any more so has nothing to feel jealous of.'

Jay laughed at that. 'Isobel, not jealous? That's a laugh. All this *you can stay here as long as you like* stuff is just an act. She wants you to think she's still in control, 'cos that's the one thing Isobel can't bear not to have. She wants control over everything and everyone. Especially you.'

Cara frowned. 'She didn't control me.'

'Are you kidding? She was so clever at it, you didn't even realise. You were her little pet.'

'I wasn't!'

'Yes you were, but not any more.' He ruffled her hair and kissed the tip of her nose. 'You're going to be *my* little pet instead.'

It was a month before Cara heard from Isobel. She didn't ring, but sent a letter, scrawled in purple ink and signed without a kiss.

Dear Cara,

Just wanted to let you know that I've moved into a bedsit just around the back of the Tricycle Theatre in Kilburn and am having a great time. There's loads more happening down here, it's so much livelier than Birmingham. I've started doing some improv workshops and have already made some brilliant new friends. And I've finally come out, which is a huge relief. I've even met a girl – it's very early days, but so far it's going extremely well. She is stunningly beautiful and an incredibly talented actress and seems really keen on me, which is amazing!

So, weirdly, this letter is to thank you. If you hadn't betrayed me, I'd still be in grotty old Birmingham, hacking away at Purple Blaze and getting nowhere. I've realised that the show we were working on was a pile of crap and a waste of my inheritance money. Luckily, I've still got several thousand left so I can pay the rent here and don't have to get a bar job or anything. So at the moment, life is pretty sweet and I'm really, really happy!

I'll let you know when I need you to move out. I'm still going to sell, but right now I'm too busy doing more interesting stuff like falling in love!!

On that subject, are you still with Jay or have you come to your senses and ditched him? I really feel you are making a big mistake there – you probably think I'm only saying that because I'm jealous, but I'm definitely not. You'll be pleased to hear that I'm completely over you – in fact, since meeting Alice I've realised that my feelings for you weren't as strong as I thought!

Please look after my house.

Will be in touch,

Isobel.

'What a prize bitch,' said Jay, when he read it. 'I bet half of it's not even true.' They were lying on a tablecloth in the garden. Cara still hadn't managed to cut the grass and it was nearly a foot high. The flower beds were suffocating from weeds, and white-flowered bindweed was choking the roses that trailed over the wooden arch. She'd been feeling bad about it – and the lack of housework indoors – but Isobel's letter had instantly wiped her guilt away.

'It's like she hates me.' She picked several daisies and began to make a chain, digging her fingernail into their stalks to make slits.

'*You'll be pleased to hear that I'm completely over you.*' Jay mimicked Isobel's posh voice. 'Yeah, right… Too many exclamation marks. When someone keeps telling you how happy they are, you always know the opposite's true.'

Cara smiled. 'So if I asked if you were happy right now, what would you say?'

He pretended to think about it. 'Hmm, I'd say I was so depressed I wanted to top myself.'

'Excellent!' She leant over and gave him a long kiss.

Later, when Jay popped out for some cans of beer, Cara read the letter again. The spitefulness of Isobel's tone still shocked her. It wasn't like her to brag about having lots of money, or to rubbish other people's work. Their show *hadn't* been crap; it had been good. Not that she and Jay were carrying on with it. They'd discussed the possibility of asking Toby to come back and doing it as a three-hander, but neither of them could really be bothered. It wasn't as if they had any bookings to fulfil. They were both still signing on, and although they were skint most of the time, they were managing.

Cara tore off Isobel's address and burnt the rest of the letter in the kitchen sink. Turning on the tap, she washed the black embers down the plughole. Isobel could go to hell.

A few mornings later, at about eight o'clock, she woke to find Jay wasn't lying next to her. This was unusual. They'd got into the habit of going to bed in the early hours and not getting up till midday. She sat up and called out his name, but there was no reply. She checked in the bathroom, then downstairs. She looked in the garden, then went out the front and looked along the street, but he wasn't there either. Panic rose in her throat. Had he left her? What had she done wrong?

Bertha the Bedford had disappeared too, presumably with Jay driving her. A local garage had resprayed the van purple months earlier in anticipation of their summer tour, but it had sat outside the house ever since as a monument to their failure. Cara wasn't even sure Jay had a driving licence – he'd recently confessed that he'd failed his test twice. But he must be driving Bertha; there was no other explanation. She went back inside, worrying that he might be stopped by the police. He was up to something, she knew that much.

It was when she drew back the sitting-room curtains that she realised what that something was. The little velvet armchair had gone, and the door of the half-moon display cabinet was wide open. Cara tried to remember what had been inside – a silver tea set, a porcelain shepherdess, maybe some coloured glass… It was like that game they used to play at children's parties, when you had to remember the objects on a tray. She'd never been any good at it and was no better now. But things were definitely missing; there were clues everywhere: indentations on the carpet where the feet of something had stood, dust-free shapes on the surface of the mantelpiece and bright squares of wallpaper that had once been covered with paintings.

Jay had got up early and burgled his own house. Except it wasn't his own house, was it? It was Isobel's, and all these valuable antiques belonged to her. Cara felt sick with distress. She'd been angry with Isobel too, but this was going way too far. So much was missing, he must have filled Bertha to the brim.

He returned early in the afternoon, parking badly with the wheels half on the pavement. Cara, who'd been looking out of the window for the past hour, came running out of the house to meet him.

'What the hell have you been doing?' she said.

Jay climbed out, sliding the van door shut. He had a huge smug grin on his face. 'Redistributing Isobel's wealth,' he said, taking a wad of notes from his back trouser pocket. 'There's nearly four hundred quid here! Four hundred fucking quid.'

'You sold all the stuff?'

'Of course I bloody sold it. What did you think, I took it to the dump? I drove out to Henley-in-Arden; the place is bunged with antique shops. I put on a snobby voice and told them my great-aunt Fanny had died, leaving me her heirlooms. Nobody turned a hair.'

Cara put her hands to her mouth. 'Oh my God…'

'Genius or what? Come on, let's go and get some booze. Time to celebrate!'

Cara shook her head. 'You shouldn't have done it, Jay. It's stealing.'

'Oh, stop being such a wet blanket. There's enough money here to last us a month at least. We can buy a load of dope and have takeaways every night!'

CHAPTER TWENTY-THREE

Me

The cold is lodged deep within me; my organs are frozen solid, toes like stones in my socks. I emerge from the consulting room, teeth chattering, and Isobel, who's been waiting for nearly two hours, leaps to her feet, scooping me up. She helps me on with my coat, but the tips of my fingers have gone waxy and she has to do up my buttons.

'Here, takes these,' she says, passing me a pair of gloves she's found in her bag. They are made of beautiful soft black leather, as thin as skin. We walk down the two flights of stairs and step into the street below. I'm too shocked to speak, and, to be fair, she doesn't ask me any questions, just grips my sleeve and shepherds me across the road when the lights change. I am a lost lamb, chilled in the snow. Take me back to the warmth and light, I think. Take me home before my system shuts down.

Thank God for John Lewis. It welcomes us like a kind grand-parent, bright and shiny, full of useful things. I slip through the door under Isobel's arm and we weave around the girls on the make-up counters, shaking our heads as a camp guy tries to squirt perfume on our wrists. Smooth, quiet escalators take us to the coffee shop on the fourth floor. Isobel buys me an enormous mug of hot chocolate and we find a table by the window, away from the chatty mums and tired shoppers.

I scatter brown sugar over the frothy top and watch the granules dissolve and sink, wishing I was small enough to jump into the warm, velvety bath. I clutch the mug with both hands, the heat seeping into my numb fingertips. God, I must have been so deeply under…

A very weird thing, hypnosis. You're awake and yet not awake, in control and yet not in control, a kind of waking dream, like watching a film in your head, only you're the one holding the camera. I can remember every single image I saw and every word I said. How true it felt, how *emotional* it was. At the time, I really thought I was Cara, living her final moments on the earth. But now? Sitting in this café with Isobel, surrounded by people fiddling with their phones or chatting to each other, the ease of the experience starts to worry me. Did I genuinely recall an actual past life, or was this all cleverly engineered by Emily Backhouse? She wanted me to be Cara, and hey presto, I was her; went straight there, no messing about with other past lives, no Egyptian princesses trying to butt in, no victims of the French Revolution about to face the guillotine, nobody else gagging to tell their story or claim their rights to my soul. Neat work. Worth every penny.

'How are you now?' says Isobel, looking at me with a disconcerting fondness. 'Warming up?'

I nod, still gripping the mug. 'She said my body temperature would drop, but I didn't know I was going to end up cryogenic.'

'So…' Isobel begins after a few moments of silence. 'What happened?'

'It was terrifying,' I reply, slurping at the hot chocolate. 'Like the worst nightmare I've ever had.'

'Oh, darling, I'm so sorry. Are you furious with me?'

'No, don't be silly.'

'So it worked, then? You regressed to when you were Cara?'

Hmm… That's a very good question, one that I'm not sure I can answer. 'I don't know. I've a horrible feeling I just made it all up. Not consciously,' I add. 'Not on purpose.'

'No, of course not, you'd never do that.'

'I could hear myself saying all these things, as if I was Cara, and yet I also knew I was still me. It was… incredibly intense. And so frightening. It really felt like someone wanted to kill me.'

'You're so brave.'

'No, no, I'm not. Because it wasn't *real*. It was like acting out a story.' She frowns at me, but I persist. 'I know too much about Cara, particularly how she died. I've even visited the scene of the crime. And Emily Backhouse knew too, because you'd sent her the footage.' I give her a gently reprimanding look and she holds her hands up.

'Sorry, I thought it would help.'

I shrug. 'I guess it depends what you're trying to prove.'

Isobel looks upwards, as if she can see my words hanging in the air.

'I just have to ask one thing,' she says finally, 'then I'll shut up about it and let you rest in—'

'I didn't see the killer, if that's what you were going to say.'

'Oh… well, I thought you probably wouldn't. Too traumatic,' she says, trying to sound relieved rather than disappointed. 'But even if you had, it wouldn't make any difference. It's inadmissible evidence.'

I look away, catching my reflection in the window, a head-and-shoulders portrait layered against the cityscape. We're a long way up and I suddenly feel dislocated from the rest of my body, as if I'm floating in the air. I start to impose Cara's features on my face. My eyes become a little rounder, my nose a little less snub. My hair shines blonder and falls straighter. She stares back at me through the glass, her expression tired and bewildered. I shudder and turn away. *Don't want to play this stupid game.* I want to be myself again.

'I don't feel great,' I tell Isobel. 'I need to go home.'

She summons a glossy black BMW with cream leather seats – a luxurious cocoon that plays a soundtrack of beautiful classical music as it glides through the dirty, crowded streets. Hot air circulates and my limbs start to thaw at last. By the time we arrive at my grim little terraced house, I'm so comfortable the driver has to drag me out of the car. I stand on the pavement, blinking at my surroundings, and he shakes his head disapprovingly as I drift unsteadily in the general direction of my front door.

Lizzie and Fay are at work, so I have the place to myself. I call the office and tell my boss I've had a bad reaction to the dental anaesthetic. And although it's a lie, that's kind of how it feels. Like I've been drugged and the chemicals are still swirling around my system. The house is cold – no heating on during the day – and my body temperature starts to drop again, so I fill a hot-water bottle and climb into bed with all my clothes on, my dressing gown laid on top of the duvet as an extra layer.

I must have fallen asleep – deeply, too – because it's halfway through the afternoon when my phone rings. It's Isobel. I was supposed to text her when I got home and forgot. She's been worrying about me, she says, so much so that she could hardly concentrate on her rehearsal. *As if that's my fault.* She tells me that Emily has pinged through the audio recording, copying her in. 'I haven't had a chance to play it yet,' she says, 'I'm going to do it at home, later. Would you like to come over, then the three of us can listen to it together?'

I can't imagine that being Alice's idea of an evening's entertainment. 'Er… I'm not really up to it at the moment,' I say. 'I might not even listen to it at all.'

'No? But I thought you'd want—'

'I can remember every single word, every sight and sound. It's all still going round and round in my head,' I tell her, nearly adding, *it feels like it's in control of me.*

'No problem. I completely understand. In your own time, darling, your own time.'

I dream I'm Cara. This time I'm with Isobel and we're walking across campus, arm in arm. We're students, except I'm young and Isobel's the age she is now. I'm telling her to let go and walk ahead without me – I don't want to be seen with an older woman; people will think she's my mother. But she just grips me more tightly, snuggling her face into my shoulder. It's my fault, she says, for dying so young. I tell her I'm not dead, but she sighs and says, *Sorry, my darling, but it's true.* I start to feel angry. I wrench myself free and run away across the grass, and she runs after me, calling out for me to stop. She wants to explain, she says. To apologise. She didn't mean to hurt me. *Too late*, I shout. *You're too late. Please, just go away!* When I wake up, my face is wet and I've dribbled all over the pillow.

There's no choice but to return to work the following day, but it's impossible to concentrate. I stare at my screen and let all my calls go straight to voicemail. The girls know something's wrong and that it's nothing to do with dental treatment. They exchange perturbed looks when they think I'm not looking, then Amy pops out and comes back with a huge frothy caramel latte, plonking it on my desk. It's a bribe. She gives me one of those *come on, you can tell me* smiles.

'Is it a man?' she whispers hopefully. They've been nagging me for ages to sign up to online dating. I tell her it's nothing to do with a man, more of a family matter, and that I can't talk about it.

'Oh.' Amy peers into my face, looking for clues as she tries to work out what kind of family matter it might be. I thank her for the latte and turn back to the mass of unread emails. Defeated, she goes back to her desk, quietly sighing and raising her eyebrows at the others, as if to say, *I did my best.*

My eyes are red with tiredness and I rub them with my fists. I hardly slept last night, mainly because I'd slept in the day, but also because every time I felt myself dropping off, I pulled myself back from the edge. I'm scared of my unconscious, of the new tricks it might play on me. I want facts. Facts and rational thought. But I'm still in a trance state, my edges blurred, identity flexible. I haven't listened to the recording yet, but it's already playing in my head.

The only checkable fact is the mention of West Bay. That came out of my head from nowhere. But just because it happens to be the name of a real place – in Dorset, Emily Backhouse said– it doesn't necessarily prove anything.

I google for images of West Bay and a load of little photos come up – seaside scenes, expanses of blue sea and tiny figures dotted on the beach. One picture stands out, and I click on it until it fills my screen. My heart jolts and I clasp my hands over my mouth. I know this place. Sandstone cliffs, huge and incongruous in an otherwise gentle landscape, looking as if they've been dropped from the sky rather than pushed up from the earth; golden yellow and pitted like a monstrous honeycomb. The turmeric colour of the sand is so familiar it brings tears to my eyes. I can feel my brain doing millions of calculations, trying to match the image on the screen with an identical one stored deep within me. But if this is a memory, who does it belong to – me or Cara? Surely it's got to belong to me.

I try to construct the scenario. West Bay, Dorset. When? I must have been little, because Becca was with us – so three or four at the most. A seaside holiday on the Jurassic Coast. Perhaps Dad went fishing or fossil-hunting while she took me for a walk on the clifftop. Or perhaps Becca took me away on her own. Whatever, it was just the two of us. We went for a walk, I ran on ahead, and the next thing she knew my toes were poking over the edge. Maybe she dragged me back and saved my life. That could easily be a traumatic childhood experience that I buried deep in my subconscious. Let a hypnotherapist dig around in awkward places and that kind of thing is bound to resurface.

Unfortunately, the only way to check out this theory is to ask Dad. He may not know about the incident, but he'll remember West Bay. I pick up my phone and start to key in the number, then stop. Our relationship is recovering, but very slowly. If I ask him anything about Becca, he'll get angry and we'll be back to where we were. I can't risk that, not at the moment.

There's an alternative option. I could ask Isobel if West Bay was a place Cara went to as a child. If she doesn't know herself, maybe she could ask Cara's parents, if she's still in touch with them, that is. But what if the family *did* go there? What if Cara's mother can remember the incident, right down to the red shorts and pink plastic sandals? What then? I can't risk that either.

The internal phone line buzzes. 'I've got a Detective Sergeant Myles here,' says Nikki from reception, her voice quivering like a fruit jelly. 'Says he wants to talk to you.' This is all I need. *What's Eliot doing here? He's supposed to be in Birmingham.* I stare into my desk.

Nikki sighs. 'Hello-o? Do I send him up or are you going to come down?'

'Er… tell him I'll be down in five minutes.'

Why didn't he call me on my mobile? Why come in person? It must be something important. Maybe there's news about Becca and he wants to tell me face to face. Shit. I don't feel ready for this.

'Will you cover for me?' I ask Amy. 'Got to pop out for a bit.'

She looks at me suspiciously. 'What's going on, Meri?'

'Eliot's here, wants to see me.'

She shakes her head as if to say, *So it* is *man trouble*. I leave her to draw her own mistaken conclusions, picking up my blue linen jacket and stopping off at the loos. I refresh my lipstick and add extra concealer to the grey shadows beneath my eyes, frowning at my reflection in the long mirror on the back of the door. This cream shirt isn't my favourite; it's too long and baggy – makes my legs look like a pair of matchsticks. But there's nothing I can do about that. And so what? We're not going on a date. He hasn't come to apologise, he's come to give me bad news – I know it. I step into the lift, feeling my gut rise to my throat as we hit the ground floor.

Eliot extracts himself from a lime-green tub chair and stands up. I move towards him and we hesitate, not sure whether to embrace or kiss on the cheeks.

'How's it going?' he says.

'Fine.' I scan his face for clues, but his expression is neutral. 'You?'

'Yeah, good.'

Pause. 'So, where do you want to go?'

He chooses a nearby noodle bar where we used to meet sometimes after work to share a large carton of something spicy before he dragged me off to the theatre. It's lunchtime-noisy – orders shouted over the clatter of woks, clanging tills, chatter in the queues, chrome chairs scraping on shiny floor tiles; a contemporary soundscape that could be entitled 'Bouncing off Hard Surfaces'. We squeeze into a gap at the long counter by the window and climb onto a pair of high stools.

'Sorry about last time,' he says. 'I was feeling stressed and you took me by surprise.'

'You shouldn't have said those things, El.'

'And you shouldn't have looked at those photos.'

'I was angry.'

'So was I. Look... can we just forget it?'

'Yeah, fine,' I reply, poking around my bowl as if searching for something more interesting. 'So, how's the investigation going? Or aren't you allowed to tell me?'

'Incredibly slowly,' he says, not rising to the bait. 'The team's full of second-rate pen-pushers, nine-to-fivers. There's no sense of urgency. I sent everything off to the labs and now I'm just waiting and waiting. Obviously a thirty-year-old case isn't going to take priority over active investigations, but honestly, it's a joke.'

'Well, Durley did say he wanted to give the team a kick up the bum.'

'I should never have taken the secondment,' he goes on. 'I don't fit in – they think I'm only on the High Potential Development Scheme because I'm mixed race. And – get this – the latest goss is that I'm Durley's gay lover.' I almost spit out my lunch. 'Yeah, I know,' he agrees.

So this is why he's come to see me, to make me feel bad for asking him to help in the first place, for sending him into boring, homophobic exile where nobody appreciates his talents.

'Oh, well... at least it's only for six months.' He stirs his noodles gloomily.

'So, what about...' I hesitate, trying to find the right phrase, 'the other lines of investigation?'

'Hopeless. Christopher Jay – did I tell you, he's a lecturer at Archway FE College? – I went to see him. He gave me the creeps… refused to give me a voluntary DNA sample. Bastard…'

'Can't you force him?'

'Only if I arrest him, and I can't do that without reasonable grounds.'

'But everyone knows he did it.'

'Yeah, but he was acquitted, so for a retrial I need "compelling new evidence". Unidentified DNA on the body, blood traces…I just need *something*.' He pauses to eat a couple of mouthfuls. 'If your mother was prepared to admit her mistake, that would help.'

The sick feeling floods back. Now we've come to the nub of it. 'Have you found her, then?'

He shakes his head, chewing. 'I spoke to your dad on the phone. It was an incredibly awkward conversation, like getting blood out of a stone. But basically he said he had no idea where Becca had gone.'

'He thinks she killed herself. I already told you that.'

I play with my chopsticks, tracing swirls through the leftover chilli sauce, wondering whether to tell him I've made friends with Isobel. He'll go apeshit. And if he finds out I've had a past life regression, he'll never speak to me again. It seems a shame to start another argument when we've only just got over the last one.

'My DC's been following up with relatives,' says Eliot, breaking the loaded silence. 'Your aunt said there was a big family falling-out when Becca was a teenager. They completely lost touch with her. Unfortunately, both your grandparents are now dead – did you know that?'

I feel as if I've suddenly been dropped from a great height. 'No, I didn't even know I had an aunt!'

'But you *must*…'

'Well, I didn't. What's her name?'

'Sorry, I don't know, I'll have to ask my DC. I'm really sorry, I didn't realise, I thought you would have…' He looks at me with those huge, tender brown eyes. 'Are you okay? You've gone all pale.'

I wipe my hands and add the napkin to our pile of debris. 'Yeah, I'm fine,' I say. 'Bit surprised about Auntie Whatsername, but I guess that's par for the course. I never had anything to do with my maternal grandparents, so it's a bit pointless to feel upset about them being dead. No other relatives I should know about? Uncles? Cousins?' I attempt an ironic laugh.

'It's okay, Meri, you're allowed to be upset. This kind of thing is tough.' He looks away from me briefly and I imagine him thinking about his own family – mother, father, brother, sister, aunts and uncles, first and second cousins, all four grandparents still alive. Everyone successful in their chosen field, partnered up, well off, no major health problems, comfortable with their liberal multiculturalism. Not smug either, just genuinely lovely people. I was part of it for four years, wrapped in their genial embrace: big Christmas parties, summer barbecues, three generations happily holidaying together every year on the Pembroke coast. I missed it when we split up and I had to go back to just me and Dad. But now there are all these other people out there that I'm connected to. Blood relations. Strangers…

'Do *you* think Becca's dead?'

He turns back to me. 'There were no DNA matches with unidentified bodies.' A wave of relief whooshes over me. 'But that doesn't mean…' He pauses.

'It doesn't mean she's not dead.'

'No. And something that Jay said… I probably shouldn't be telling you this, but I thought you ought to know…' He pauses again, unsure.

'Well, what?'

'He called her Becca.' I look at him blankly. 'Like he knew her. I checked, and they both said at the trial that they'd never seen each other before. I read the entire trial transcript to see if anyone referred to her as Becca, and they didn't. Not once. It slipped out by mistake – I saw him cursing himself.'

'So you think they were in it together?' My heart clenches.

'Possibly. I don't know.' He stares out of the window, as if the answer might run into the road. 'If it wasn't for your dad's statement, I'd be smelling a rat. But he completely backed Becca up about that night. They both claimed they had a bedtime row; she went out for a walk, found the body. I asked Graeme if there was anything in his original statement he wanted to change, but he insisted there wasn't. Then again, you said yourself you thought he was hiding something…'

'He wouldn't lie to the police.'

'No, I know… He picks up his can of Coke and drains it with a noisy slurp. 'Jay knew Becca, I'm sure of it. I've got this nagging feeling it's important, but I haven't worked out how it fits together yet.' He pauses, crushing the can with one hand. 'I thought you were being a bit melodramatic at first, but now I think you could be right.'

'About what?'

'Becca's disappearance. It's looking more and more suspicious. Maybe Jay *did* need to silence her. '

'Arrest him!' I say immediately. 'Arrest him and then you can take his DNA.'

'How many more times, Meri . . . There's no evidence. I need compelling new evidence.'

I pick up my bag. 'Okay. I'll find some.'

'Meri!' he calls as I swing towards the doors. 'You mustn't get involved – come back!'

But it's too late. I've gone.

CHAPTER TWENTY-FOUR

Jay

He shaves slowly and carefully, making sure not to cut himself, then brushes his thinning, grey hair towards the back of his scalp, exposing his ever-enlarging forehead. His shirt – dark green linen, selected for its casual artiness – is already waiting for him, washed and ironed by his own fair hand and hanging on the door handle of his wardrobe. He puts it on and buttons it up, not as far as his neck and not so low that it shows his vest. The sight of himself in the mirror, however, is not appealing. He wishes he looked more confident.

To be honest, he's shitting himself with nerves. But he's going to do it; he's promised himself. And it's more important than ever now that the case is being reviewed again. Who knows how long he's got? Okay, so he refused to give them his DNA, but that won't stop them – they'll trump up some other charges against him and he'll be forced to give a sample. They'll pretend to find traces under Cara's fingernails, or semen stains on her dress, or maybe there *will* be traces and they'll claim they're from the night of the murder. This time there'll be no Becca to save him. No, he has to face facts. Freedom could be snatched from him at any moment. This could be his last chance.

He takes the tube to Green Park and arrives at Waterstones with time to spare. He wanders around the ground floor, idly picking up books, then makes his way to the top floor, climbing the stairs with heavy, trembling legs, his heart beating fast. Ten minutes to kick-off. About twenty fans are already mingling by the ubiquitous drinks table, and a slim young woman in a little black dress is handing out plastic cups of wine.

'White or red?' she asks as he approaches.

'Red,' he says, adding, 'please.'

She pours him a desultory half-cup and he has to hold himself back from swigging it down in one mouthful. He looks anxiously around, but there's no sign of Isobel. Presumably she's going to sweep up the stairs and make a grand entrance. A couple of solitary people have bagged their seats and are studying their freshly purchased copies of Isobel's book. The rest are hovering by the drinks table, plastic cups in hand, talking in loud, authoritative voices punctuated with bursts of jolly laughter. Jay takes up position a few feet away and leans lightly against a bookshelf. He feels, as ever, an outsider. Everyone looks so fucking smug. God, he'd like to finish off the lot of them.

He chooses a seat in the back row and takes out his phone. There's an email from Isatu, confirming his return to work on Monday, and he's starting to reply when he hears a buzz of activity behind him. He briefly swivels round to look, and yes, Isobel has arrived, accompanied by some PR chap in a blue stripy shirt and her wife-cum-henchman, the dreadful Alice Anderson. No surprise that Alice is here; they are never seen apart. Jay has almost as many photos of Alice as he has of Isobel, although usually he cuts around her and puts her in the bin. She's an actress – not a very good one, but Isobel casts her whenever there's a suitable part, and sometimes when there isn't. Either love is blind, he thinks, or Alice has some strange power over her partner. He has a vague memory of her accompanying Isobel to the trial, but she looks so different now, it might have been somebody else.

He keeps his head down while the rest of the attendees take their seats. 'Thank you all so much for coming tonight,' says the PR chap. 'What a lot of you!' Isobel beams at everyone appreciatively. 'Marvellous. I'm going to start by asking Isobel a few questions, then she's going to read a short extract from the book, and then it's your turn. So without further ado…'

Jay slides his back down the seat so as to disappear behind the large man in front of him and takes abstemious sips of his wine. He finds the sound of Isobel's voice excruciating. She uses the same public-schoolgirl expressions that drove him crazy thirty years ago – 'Oh, absolutely!' and 'Honestly, darling!' and 'Terrific!' – and it's pulling him unwillingly back to those times in Darkwater Terrace, rehearsing their post-apocalyptic play in the upstairs front room, with Isobel bossing everyone about and Cara sitting there like a faithful puppy, agreeing with every stupid word she said.

'I absolutely thrive on collaboration,' she's telling Mr PR now. Jay nearly huffs out loud. Collaboration? She never knew the meaning of the word. It was Isobel's house so it was *her* theatre company and *her* show. Jay would have accepted that if she hadn't tried to pretend they were all on equal terms.

He hadn't joined Purple Blaze deliberately to cause trouble. He'd arrived with a song in his heart, thrilled that he'd finally got his first acting job – even though nobody was being paid and they had to sign on. Isobel had impressed him at first, although he found her upper-class accent a bit intimidating. He'd liked her energy. She'd certainly talked a good game, denouncing Thatcher and cheering on the *Rainbow Warrior*, leaving her Labour Party card ostentatiously on the kitchen table, mainly as a hint to him, he thought, the only non-member. He'd realised after a short while that it wasn't his acting talent that had got him the job, but his working-class credentials: his single mum and his council estate address. That was what ignited it – first humiliation, then anger and finally burning hatred. He did what he did purely to hurt Isobel, but he never dreamt she'd react so violently, or that she'd try to make him take the blame. How naive he'd been, thinking he could take on such a formidable enemy.

Isobel reads a few pages aloud while Jay sits there with his eyes closed, not listening, spasmodically visiting scenes from the past. It's like a useless leg he drags after him: painful and encumbering, but he can't imagine ever being rid of it. He has a sudden image of Isobel standing in the witness box at the trial, telling all those lies in her posh voice about how he regularly beat Cara up, how she'd seen the bruises, how Cara had said she was afraid for her life. He told them she was lying, but nobody believed him, not even his own counsel. Lies. Lies. Lies.

And if there's a retrial, she'll do the same again. She'll be believed all the more now because of who she is. Isobel won't care if he ends his days in solitary confinement. He hasn't got a successful career to ruin or loved ones to miss him. He glances across at Alice, sitting to one side, in a no-man's-land between the stage and the audience, bathing in the reflected glory, an adoring gaze fixed on her partner's face. Nobody will campaign for his release, or even visit him in prison. On the contrary. Isobel, Cara's family, that young detective, that old bastard Brian Durley – they'll convince the rest of the world that justice has finally been done and he'll be left to rot. But he won't go quietly. If there's one thing he's learnt from thirty years of living with injustice, it's that attack is the best form of defence.

The reading finally draws to an end and, predictably, there's no time for questions from the audience. Jay feels his heart pumping again, his nerves taking hold.

'I'm sure you'd all like me to thank Isobel on your behalf for giving us such a fascinating insight into her career,' booms the

PR guy before leading a round of applause. Jay doesn't clap, realising to his satisfaction that he's got through the whole event without listening to a word she's said. 'Isobel has very kindly agreed to sign copies of her book, which we are able to offer – for tonight only – at a fantastic ten per cent discount.' The attendees get to their feet, murmuring enthusiastically to each other. A few beat a hasty retreat, but most of them form a compliant queue, credit cards at the ready.

His mouth feels dry. He scouts around, more in hope than expectation, for the drinks table, but everything has been cleared away and the girl who was serving the wine is now selling Isobel's books. Jay joins the signing queue; there are five or six people in front of him. He stands there, knees weakening, pulse racing, feeling sick. Isobel is sitting just a few feet away, but her voice sounds as if it's coming from the other end of a long tunnel.

'Thank you *so* much,' she croons, adding her swirling autograph in purple ink. '*Do* hope you enjoy it.'

He gently pats his inside pocket. The knife is still there, wrapped in a piece of butterfly-patterned kitchen towel, for safety's sake. He didn't have to buy it specially; just found it lurking in the kitchen drawer. And it's virtually unused, so it should be sharp. He imagines thrusting it into Isobel's chest, the squelch of flesh, the blade crunching on bone, blood spurting over her wretched books.

Just one person in front of him now, who tells Isobel he's always been a huge admirer of her work. Isobel asks for his name and writes a message on the title page.

'Oh thank you, thank you,' says the man. 'I'm an actor, you see, and I'd love to work with you—'

The PR guy, who has been hovering, leaps to the rescue. 'Who's next?' he shouts.

'I am.' Jay stands in front of the table.

Isobel lifts her pen in anticipation, and then stops. 'Where's your book?'

He locks his knees and tries not to sway. 'Don't you recognise me?' There's a brief time delay, then Isobel's face drops.

'*You?* What the fuck are you doing here?' she hisses.

'It's a public event. You can't stop me.'

Isobel looks frantically towards her PR man, but he's still trying to deal with the annoying actor. She stands up. 'Sorry, everyone, but I've got to leave now. Train to catch!' There are cries of disappointment as she throws her pen in her bag and hoists it over her shoulder. She calls out to Alice, who rushes over.

'What's wrong?'

Isobel cocks her head in his direction. 'Jay's here,' she says quietly.

Alice freezes momentarily, then whispers, 'Okay. Let me handle this.' She turns towards him, fixing him with her most withering look. 'Just go. Now. Or you'll be sorry.'

'Why? What are you going to do?' he counters. 'Shall we fight for her honour? Lipsticks at dawn?'

Alice rounds on him. 'You're pathetic, Jay, you know that?' She takes out her phone and starts to dial.

'No, don't call the police,' says Isobel quickly.

'I'm not. I'm calling a car.'

Jay leaps forward and knocks the phone out of Alice's hands. 'Isobel Dalliday is a murderer!'

'What's going on?' says the PR man. He calls out to the girl in the tight black dress, 'Don't just sit there. Get Security. Now!' The girl runs off like a frightened goose, flapping her arms and tripping in her high-heeled shoes. Everyone else is still in audience mode, observing the drama curiously and definitely not in the mood for any participation. Jay sees Alice glance down at her phone and he immediately sticks his foot on it.

'What is it you want, Jay?' asks Isobel, peering out from behind Alice's back.

He opens his mouth, but his throat is closing up and he can hardly breathe, let alone speak. Everything he was going to say has suddenly evaporated from his brain. He tries to grasp the sentences but they're lost, fragmented into short, nonsensical phrases or random words. He reaches for the knife, but his fingers are as thick and useless as raw sausages. Can't seem to find it… Impossible… It was there a second ago… Nothing is making sense. His head is spinning; he thinks he's going to faint.

Two security guards are running towards the scene. Alice points and they grab him by his armpits. He gets one last look at Isobel – her face paler than ever, eyes open wide – and goes to spit at her, but there's no saliva in his mouth. The guards frogmarch him down the stairs. He doesn't protest, doesn't struggle. His legs buckle and he floats down between them, flight after flight, his toes skimming the floor.

'Piss off or we'll call the police,' says one of them, pushing him out of the main door.

Jay drops to the pavement, bashing his kneecaps. As he collapses onto his side, the knife falls out of his pocket and unrolls from the kitchen towel. It lies there, taunting him. He stays still for a few moments, his legs drawn to his chest, catching his breath, waiting for the dizziness to go. Then he snatches up the knife and tucks it away before standing up slowly, gasping with pain as he puts his weight down.

He staggers to the shop window and leans on the glass. People stare as they walk past, some sympathetically and others with looks of grand disdain. How quickly you can look like a down-and-out, he thinks. He straightens himself up and hobbles away, stopping to rest in an office doorway. The pain in his knees is agonising; no way will he cope on the tube. He looks back towards Waterstones, just as Alice and Isobel emerge, flanked by the security guards. Jay retreats into the shadow of the doorway, holding his breath. Moments later, a smart grey car draws up and Alice and Isobel get in. As it drives towards him, Jay turns his face to the large wooden doors, hoping they won't see him as they pass. Then he staggers to the kerb and hails a taxi.

CHAPTER TWENTY-FIVE

Me

There are nine people in the UK named Christopher Jay on Facebook, twenty-five on LinkedIn and 140 on the electoral roll, but none of the profiles seem to fit – wrong age, wrong location, wrong nationality. Then I remember Eliot telling me he works at an FE college. Archway. Northeast London. Sure enough, his details are on the college website. Christopher Jay, Tutor, Department of Performing Arts. Gotcha.

It's definitely the same person I've seen in the press photos from the trial. Same narrow eyes, same gaunt cheeks. His features have been dragged downwards with age, but the expression, or lack of it, hasn't changed one bit. All these years he's had his freedom, doing the things that people do. Earning a living, enjoying the company of friends, travelling, falling in love, fathering children, striving for happiness… Who knows? Whatever he's achieved, it's more than Cara or Becca ever got a chance to do.

I study his cold, blank face, imagining that he's in a police cell and I'm questioning him. *So, Christopher, tell me what it's like to have two deaths on your conscience. Do you wake up every morning hating yourself, wondering why God has let you survive so long? Or does the guilt go in and out like the tide? Talk to me, Christopher – let me get inside your head. Give me a life in the day of…* He stares back, defiant and grim-lipped. But he won't be able to avoid me when I meet him in the flesh.

I told Eliot I would bring him compelling new evidence, and I will. DNA is the obvious thing. I imagine following Christopher Jay into Costa and stealing his empty coffee cup. Or standing behind him on the bus and deftly plucking a hair from his head. Detectives are always doing that kind of thing on television, but I bet it's far more difficult in real life. Maybe I could make him so angry he'd threaten me and I'd call the police. He'd be arrested for assault and they'd have his DNA. Sorted. But it's a risky enterprise. I have to remember that this is a man who's already killed once, very possibly twice.

A confession is what we need. To be honest, I can't see the police ever solving this case without it. But if a murderer's got away with it for over thirty years, they're not going to spill the beans just because somebody asks them a direct question. Unless they've had some kind of religious conversion, and that's unlikely. But if I could get him to open up, make him feel like I'm on his side, like I understand… He's already made one slip; perhaps I could get him to make another.

I should make a secret recording of our meeting, in case he says something incriminating and backtracks later. I fetch my phone and do a test. It works fine, although not so well when I put the phone in my bag. It needs to be on the table, near to Jay. That would be okay, I think; people put their phones on the table all the time. This assumes that we'll be somewhere with a table, however, and I can't guarantee that. Jay might well refuse to see me; he might not even be there.

It's too late to book a day off work, so I call in sick, hating myself for all this repeated lying. I *am* sick, I tell myself as I get dressed: smart but not too smart, black jeans and a grey top, my hair pulled into a scrunchie, natural make-up, flat shoes in case I want to run away. I swing my laptop bag over my shoulder, shut the front door and walk purposefully towards the tube station. I don't know what I'm doing, but I'm doing it for her.

Archway College is huge and security seems tight. A row of shiny chrome turnstiles stretch across the airy foyer and two tall men in dark trousers and thick navy jumpers are sitting at the reception desk, one of them arguing with a girl who's forgotten to bring her ID and the other – labelled *Saf* – eating sandwiches from a Tupperware box.

'Can I help?' he asks, with his mouth full.

I try to sound casual and friendly. 'Yeah, I hope so. I'm looking for Christopher Jay, he's a tutor in Performing Arts.'

Saf looks up at his colleague. 'He's off sick, isn't he?'

'Nah, he's back. Saw him this morning.'

'Oh, right.' He looks up at the neon clock. 'He'll be in the pub, I expect – just across the street.' He makes a drinking gesture with his hand.

'Oh, great, thanks.'

'Friend of yours?' He looks at me doubtfully. I don't reply.

The Star and Garter is a large barn of a pub, red patterned carpets, shiny polished wooden tables and leather-topped stools. Hits from the nineties are playing at full volume, like somebody's trying to get a party going and failing. A few regulars are lolling against the bar; a married-looking couple are studying the All-Day 2-for-1 Menu. I have to walk right down to the end, where the toilets are, before I see Jay. He's sitting by himself in a gloomy booth, a half-drunk pint of Guinness and an unopened packet of peanuts before him, reading the *Metro*. He has no idea that I'm staring at him. I wrinkle my nose at the faint whiff of piss coming from the gents'.

I go back to the bar and ask for a Beck's. As soon as the barman reaches for the bottle, I regret my choice. A soft drink would have been more sensible and would have done just as well as a prop. He takes off the lid and the beer froths. I turn and look into the shadows, Jay's solitary figure bent over the table. My knees start to knock with fear.

You're here now. You've got to go through with it.

I walk back to the dark recesses of the saloon and put my beer down on the table opposite Jay. 'Mind if I sit here?' My voice is feverish. I sound like someone else, someone I don't know.

He looks up from the newspaper and frowns. 'Why? Not like there's nowhere else.' He gestures at the expanse of free tables. I smile weakly and sit down, reaching into my bag and taking out my phone. It's already set to record.

'Well? What is it? What do you want?'

I take the laptop bag off my shoulder. My hands are shaking so much I can barely open the zip. He stares at me as I take out the laptop and put it on the table, flipping open the lid and pressing the start button.

'I don't do surveys,' he says. 'Or opinion polls.'

'I want to show you something. It won't take long. You might have already seen it.'

His expression is half curious, half couldn't-care-less. 'Do I know you? Are you an ex-student?'

I meet his gaze. This is the moment. *Tell him. Tell him.* 'I'm Becca's daughter. Rebecca Banks. Remember her?'

He looks shocked for a second, then peers into my face, shadowy in the pub gloom. 'Becca,' he says, the word escaping from his mouth in a whisper. He looks around, as if expecting to see more people behind me – other ghosts from his past perhaps. 'God… You look a lot like her.'

'So I've been told.'

'How did you know where to find me? Did that detective tell you?'

'No,' I reply quickly. 'I just did a search – it wasn't difficult.' I open Media Player and click on the file named 'Me'. 'I'm going to show you a video that was made when I was four years old.'

'Sorry, but what's this about?'

I turn the laptop around so he can see the screen. He picks up his pint and takes a gulp, quickly licking the foam off his top lip. Does he know what's coming? He puts the glass down and hides his hands beneath the table. I picture his fingers writhing nervously, his palms sweating.

Leaning across, I press play. He stares at the screen, listening but not really comprehending. 'What's this got to do with me?' he says after a few moments.

'You'll see.' I train my eyes on his features, watching every blink, every twitch, looking for signs – of what exactly, I don't know. Recognition? Guilt? I try to imagine how he must have looked thirty years ago: taut skin, hair dark and thick, thin-framed, sharp-boned…

Suddenly he pulls back as if something's just hit him in the gut. I can't see the screen from where I'm sitting, but I know he must have got to the bit where Becca walks into frame. He's transfixed now, his eyes darting across the screen, mouth open for more air. Shocked. Like all this is new to him, like he's watching it for the first time. Or is he only pretending to watch it for the first time? I don't know, I can't read him. When we get to the important bit, where I mention his name, he gasps loudly and slams down the lid.

'What the fuck is this? Some kind of joke?'

'I found it at my father's house a couple of months ago.'

'And you showed it to the police, right?' I shrug. 'So *that's* why...' He takes several deep breaths. 'They can't take this seriously, they can't. It's absurd. I mean, it's... it's... nonsense. Why did she say that? Why?'

'I don't know.'

'I've got to talk to her. Where is she?' He flings his arm out towards me, grabbing my wrist.

'You're hurting ...' I wrench my hand free and pull the laptop back.

His eyes are bulging and his face has broken out in a sweat. 'Please. Give me her number.'

'I don't have it. I don't know where she is.' I slide the laptop back into its case. He looks at me disbelievingly. 'Sorry, you'll have to ask the police. They're looking for her; they might know.'

'Jesus Christ...' He lifts up his glass, his hand trembling violently, and takes a large swig, slamming it back on the table so hard I think it's going to break. 'I'm not going to prison for this, no way, no fucking way. They've got nothing else on me, it's her word against mine. There's no evidence. This... this shit' – he points accusingly at the laptop case – 'doesn't mean a thing, it'd never stand up in court.'

'I never said it would,' I reply coolly. 'But it does raise a few questions. Understandably, the police want to talk to her, but they can't find her. She's missing.'

'Missing?' He narrows his eyes. 'What do you mean, missing?'

'Nobody's seen her for twenty-five years. But I think you already know that. You've been lying to me, pretending you want her number... talking about her in the present tense to mislead me.'

The penny drops. 'What are you getting at?'

'The police know you already knew each other.' He shakes his head vehemently. 'They think she lied for you.'

'Not true. Absolutely not true.'

'And years later, when she told you she was going to tell the police the truth, you flipped.'

'This is crazy. I'm not listening to this crap.'

'You're the one who went crazy. You killed her in a fit of anger, just like you killed Cara.'

He leans over and grabs my shoulder. 'Who the fuck do you think you are? I could have you done for harassment. And that detective – I'll have him too, for persecuting an innocent witness.'

'Let go of me now, or I'll be the one calling the police.' He pulls his hand away and tucks it under the other arm. His whole body is jerking in tiny spasms of tension. 'You're not an innocent witness,' I say. 'You're the prime suspect. The police are re-testing everything for DNA. They're going to find something, I promise, and, when they do, you'll be charged again, and this time there's no way you're going to get away with it.'

'Fuck off.'

I look him straight in the eye. 'To be honest, it's not looking good. You've probably only got a few days at the most before they come back and arrest you.'

He stands up suddenly, banging the table with his legs. His beer glass shakes and my bottle slides a few centimetres across the polished surface. 'I said, fuck off!'

I watch him limp off in the direction of the exit. He doesn't look back once, but when he gets near the door he stumbles and has to hold on to the bar to steady himself. He walks out and the door slams behind him.

I pick up the Beck's and drink it down in one go.

CHAPTER TWENTY-SIX

Jay

He feels the anger rising within him, like a swollen, surging river. Stinking, filthy liquid is swirling around the pit of his stomach, threatening to vomit itself out of his mouth, to burst through his veins, explode from his ears. It's a furious demon, a vile monster, but he has to contain it, keep it at bay. Pile up the sandbags. Shift the valuables upstairs. I *will* control it, he thinks, as he stands twitching at the edge of the pavement, breathing hard through his nostrils. Cars and trucks pass nose to tail, tormenting him, driving just that bit too fast for him to weave a path in between. He's so wired he could risk it – just step into the road and make a beeline for the other side. If he's struck down, so what? Better to be killed now than go to prison. He will *not* go to prison – not for Cara, not for Becca. Whatever happens, he will *not* go.

He turns his head slowly from left to right and back again, waiting for a gap. Something – it must be the anger – is pressing down heavily on his brain; there's a sharp pain behind his eyes and his vision has narrowed. It's like looking out from a lift as the doors slowly close, his world disappearing. He feels himself dropping, descending into hell.

The cars come to a brief halt to let a large articulated lorry swing around the corner, and Jay crosses – somehow – in its wake. He dodges in and out of small groups of students dotted around the college steps and walks into the foyer, pushing through a turnstile. When he arrives at Studio One, a couple of students are already there, waiting. He unlocks the door and turns on the fluorescent lights. The pain behind his eyes sharpens to a point.

He drags a grey plastic chair away from the wall and sits down. He tries not to think about what's just happened, but the images on the tape keep playing on his inner screen. The little girl stabbing the air, Becca looking a ghost of herself, so thin and haggard, so desperate and afraid. He'd barely recognised her. Questions tumble over each other as they speed through his brain. Why is Becca trying to frame him? Why do something as bizarre as force a little child to act out a murder? It's sick. Disgusting. And who's the 'bad man' she keeps talking about? Is that supposed to be *him*? Did somebody put her up to this?

He starts to smell the rancid traces of Isobel. Not satisfied with killing Cara and wrecking his life, she's turned on poor, innocent Becca. The evil bitch. Jay grips the edges of his seat until his knuckles go white. He should have killed Isobel while he had the chance. If Becca's daughter is right and the police have got him in their sights, he hasn't got much time. It's now or never. Proper justice has to be done.

There's a loud burst of laughter. Jay looks up, bewildered. He'd almost forgotten where he was, hadn't noticed the rest of the students coming in, or heard their chatter. There must be about twenty of them now, suddenly appeared from nowhere. As usual, they're ignoring him, behaving like he doesn't exist. The atmosphere is more animated than usual; there's electricity in the air. The tension is tangible. Or maybe it's just him. His heart is pounding and sweat is seeping through his pores. How can he teach a lesson in this state? He should leave now, sneak out while nobody's looking. Go and find Isobel. Get it over and done with before it's too late.

But then a couple of lads walk in. Mo B, the techno-geek, and Devonte Lennox, a good-looking black kid, the best actor in the class.

'She's taking the fucking piss,' Dev says as they walk past him to the back of the studio, sliding their backs down the black-painted wall, crouching on their haunches, holding themselves up by the strength of their thighs. They carry on muttering under their breath and he catches Santianna's name.

Something's going on downstairs. Maybe she's planning an attack, Jay thinks. Another fucking bitch out to get him. He hears noise and looks towards the door. She's coming, and she won't be alone. Her over-loud voice bounces off the walls of the narrow corridor, the march of clumpy high heels like a bass drum keeping the beat. Santianna and her junk-fed, hyped-up army are coming to get him. In five seconds they'll walk into the room, and who knows what will happen. He's bubbling over like a boiling pot, can't contain it much longer. If she steps over the line, just by an inch…

But it's Devonte Lennox who makes the first move. He stands up and walks towards Santianna and her posse – three girls and two lads – as they swagger in. Mo B stays crouching against the wall, eyes fixed on the screen of his phone, keeping well out of it.

'What the fuck are you on, fam?' Devonte raises his arm and flicks his hand in Santianna's face. She blinks at him with her thick false lashes. 'Think man's gonna sit on my fuckin' arse all day waitin' for you? We're supposed to be fuckin' rehearsin'. You might not give a fuck, yeah, but I ain't gonna be going up on stage looking like a dickhead, you get me? Not like every other man in here!'

'Are you mad!?' She pushes Dev in the chest. 'Who the fuck do you think you're chatting to? Get the fuck away from me, I swear down – you need to get the fuck away!'

'I beg you push me again.' Devonte advances on her, face up close. 'Watch what happens to you if you push me again, watch what I do – watch.'

'Take it easy, man,' says Mo B, still sitting with his back to the wall. 'Bitch in't worth it.'

Santianna lunges at Dev, her long, spiky pink fingernails reaching for his cheek; scratches him so hard she draws a thin line of blood. He cries out involuntarily, backing away for a second or two. There's a brief moment of silence, a freeze frame, then it's like somebody's fast-forwarded and restarted the action several minutes further on, because suddenly everything is noise and chaos and everyone's involved, except Mo B, who stays where he is and holds up his phone to start filming.

Santianna is shouting, 'Look what happens when you get rude to me. I told you, don't get fuckin' rude to me, fam!' Two of the girls grab hold of her and she wrestles to get free, turning her rage on them. 'Don't hold me back! Oh my daiz, don't fuckin' hold me back!'

Devonte Lennox wipes the blood off his face with his sleeve. 'You wanna step to me, yeah? You sure you wanna do dat?' The others start joining in, incoherent phrases firing from their mouths against Santianna, or in support of her; it's impossible to know who is on whose side as they jostle around the room like out-of-control dodgem cars, shouting and bumping into each other.

Jay stares at the swirl of bodies, the kaleidoscope of faces. He blinks, disorientated. Was that Isobel he saw just then? Her jet-black hair, her swipe of red lipstick? A flash of her purple sleeve? He rises from his chair and staggers towards the chaos. There she is again! He saw her. She's somewhere in this crowd. He turns in a circle, peering through the forest of bodies; he glimpses her face again as it slips behind Santianna; grabs at her shadow as it dissolves behind Devonte.

Isobel in the witness box, lying through her teeth. Isobel on the steps of the court, head back, mouth open, screaming at him as he was jostled by reporters. Isobel's face on posters and book jackets. Isobel in magazines, her smile always mocking him. Isobel the puppet master, Isobel the murderer. He knows she's here somewhere, hiding in the crowd. She won't get away from him this time. He reaches into his inside pocket. The knife is still there from the other night, warm against his chest. A surge of power shoots up his arm as he whips it out and swivels the blade, letting it catch the light. *Now let's see who's boss.*

'Fuck! Teacher man's got a shank!'

'What the fuck's he doin'?'

Jay walks towards Santianna, except she's not Santianna any more; her features are morphing and blurring and now it's Isobel standing before him, hands on hips, red mouth agape, her defiant stare taunting him. He's found her at last.

'Put it down, man!'

'Get back, Santi! Man's gonna cut you.'

'Nah, he's a pussy. He won't use it.'

He lifts the blade and lunges at her. There's a dull squelching noise. A red circle forms around the blade, which sticks in her chest, just beneath her large fleshy boobs. He lets go of the handle and steps back. He's dimly aware of heavy breathing, a falling movement, a thud; dark shapes gathering around a body. Stillness. Silence.

He releases his breath and turns away, walks out of the studio and down the white-walled corridor, reaches reception and swipes himself through the barrier. He feels light-headed, floating on air. Nobody shouts out his name, nobody runs after him. Nobody stops him at the front doors. He looks back for a moment at the empty foyer. Why is nobody stopping him? Why are there no sirens or alarms?

Maybe it didn't happen. Maybe it was just a beautiful fantasy. He limps down the steps and disappears quietly into the afternoon crowd.

CHAPTER TWENTY-SEVEN

Me

I'm woken by the sound of my phone, its insistent ring coming from somewhere in the bedclothes. My arms flail about, patting the mattress, feeling under the pillow, but by the time I find it – for some strange reason nestling at my feet – it's too late. A missed call from Eliot. Shit. What if Jay has made a complaint? No way am I up to defending myself right now. Groaning, I pull back the duvet and swing my legs around the side of the bed. I'm still fully dressed, my clothes sweaty and creased, my eyes sticky with melted mascara. How long was I asleep? I glance at the alarm clock. It says ten to seven, and for a few seconds I can't work out whether it's morning or evening. I get up and lift the edge of the curtain. It's dark outside and I can smell cooking, fried onions and meat. Evening then. The day is a dog running around in the distance, not wanting to return to my side. I call it in and the memories start to lick at me.

I remember Christopher Jay on the other side of the table, his eyes blinking, his pint of Guinness shaking in his hand. Was that the flicker of guilt that I was hoping to see? It looked more like terror to me. I remember him shouting abuse at me and storming out. What did I do afterwards? I scan my memory. That's right. I drank four bottles of Beck's on an empty stomach and wandered off down the Holloway Road. Came home and went to bed with a raging headache. Now I'm starving hungry. No wonder those smells are driving me crazy.

I take off the day's used clothes and nip across the landing to the bathroom. I can hear pots and pans clattering downstairs, music playing. Which of my housemates is cooking? Fay or Lizzie? My bet's on the former. We don't cook for each other as a rule – we tried, but it became too complicated. Fay's always out doing exercise classes, or Spanish, or celebrating one of her countless friends' birthdays, and Lizzie's hardly here at all.

My face is gritty with make-up. As I wash it off, I think of Eliot. I miss living with him. With someone, anyway. I liked being part of a couple; it felt grown-up. If Eliot wasn't on duty we'd always eat together, and if I was on my own I'd cook for us both and he'd put a plate in the microwave when he came home. Since we split up, I've gone back to a student kind of existence. I don't plan any more and I've fallen out of love with domesticity. There's no enjoyment in cooking just for yourself, so why bother when you can live off Nando's and chocolate? I examine my tired, blotchy skin. No wonder I'm getting spots again, like a teenager.

Back in my room, I put on jogging bottoms and a sweatshirt, then venture downstairs. As I predicted, it's Fay doing the cooking. She tells me her Pilates class was cancelled so she's making a big pot of chilli con carne – later tonight, her freezer drawer will be full of neat plastic boxes, labelled with days of the week.

'Did you hear about that girl getting stabbed by her drama teacher? It's massive on Twitter,' she says as I go to the fridge, hoping against hope that some of the food inside it will belong to me. There's an egg past its use-by date that Fay smugly assures me is mine. I look hungrily at the saucepan and tell her how good it smells, but she doesn't take the hint. 'It's actually on YouTube, like the whole thing,' she carries on, stirring and tasting from the tip of her wooden spoon. 'You can see blood and everything. It's gross. Why film it? Like why didn't they just call the police? Some people are sick.'

I consider the egg briefly – dare I risk it? Boiled, poached or fried? One egg is not enough for scrambled. I can't decide, so I shut the fridge door and make for the bread bin instead. There's a hard heel from a loaf that I have a vague memory of buying a few days ago. I ate a few slices over the weekend – toasted and variously topped with baked beans, cheese and strawberry jam, some of which I stole from Lizzie's cupboard.

Fay tries again. 'Terrifying, eh?'

'What?'

'That stabbing. I mean, like you hear of it the other way round, but a teacher killing a student?' Her laptop is open on the kitchen table and she goes over to it, tapping away with her polished nails. 'It happened today, after lunch. Unbelievable. The police are asking for calm, like what do they expect? The killer's still out there, duh! They should have found him by now. That is so typical.'

'Give them a chance.' I hear myself defending the police, like I always used to.

'It says here there's a vigil going on outside the college.'

'Where? What college?'

'Er ... somewhere in north London.' She scrolls down the page. 'Archway.'

It can't be, can it? Please let it just be a coincidence.

'I've... er... got some work to do.' It's the lamest excuse – I never bring work home – but Fay's not listening anyway.

I run up the stairs and into my room, slamming the door. My phone lies hot and silent on my pillow. Is that what Eliot was calling about? Did he leave a message? I grab the phone and quickly dial into my voicemail.

'Hi, me here. Christopher Jay's gone crazy and killed a student. I can't tell you any more, just google "Archway stabbing". Don't try to call me back, I'm on my way to London. It's difficult to speak. I'll try and call you later, depends what happens. Sorry… Hope you're okay.'

He has no idea how not okay I am.

I think I'm going to be sick. I slide off the bed onto all fours, then cautiously stand up. The room is spinning. The bathroom's only next door, but it seems a mile away as I stagger there, falling on my knees in front of the toilet. The faint smell of urine mixed with disinfectant makes me heave, but when I try to vomit nothing comes up. I lean my forehead on the plastic seat and wait. But I'm not going to be sick, because I haven't eaten anything. I drag myself to my feet and stumble back to my room, collapsing on the bed again. I should tell him what happened. It's the very least I owe him and better he finds out from me. Always own up, that's what Dad taught me. Own up and the punishment won't be as bad. Eliot said not to call back, but… My finger hovers over the screen as I try to work out what to say. Sorry would be a good start, but it seems so inadequate. I rehearse the words in my head, hearing his reply. He'll be absolutely furious, I know he will; he'll tell me I'm out of control, he'll hit the roof.

Got to think. Think hard. Be logical. How will the police know it was me at the pub? I didn't give my name to anyone. I paid for my beer in cash. The only person who knows is Jay and he's done a bunk. So basically nobody else knows, and they're unlikely to find out. But if I tell Eliot, he'll be obliged to tell his boss and I'll be interviewed. Some difficult questions will be asked and he could get into big trouble – especially if they find out that he told me where to find Jay. He could be suspended. Sacked. I don't want that. Which means that telling him is the very last thing I should do. For his sake.

My heart rate is starting to slow down; the singing in my head has stopped. I'm okay. I can deal with this. I've got to keep calm and get things in proportion. I wasn't to know Jay was going to go off his head like that. It's not my fault.

The phone rings, making me start. It's Isobel.

'Hi,' I squeak.

'Have you heard?' Her voice is vibrating; it sounds as if she's running down the street. 'Have you heard what he's done? You must have, it's all over the news.'

'Yes. Unbelievable.'

'No, one thing it's *not* is unbelievable. Oh, that poor girl! Her poor family!' She stops and I hear the bleeps of a pedestrian crossing. Then she starts again, her words jumping about like beans in a sack. 'Can you imagine what they're going through? It's brought it all flooding back. It's like living through the whole thing all over again.'

'Yes… must be awful for you.'

'I'm so cross with myself. If I'd called the police this would never have happened,' she wails.

'What do you mean?'

'He turned up to my book launch last week and made a scene. I thought he was just drunk, I didn't want a fuss… Oh God, we have to prepare ourselves. The media are going to have a field day with this. It's all going to come out. My connection with Cara, Jay's wrongful acquittal. Everything!'

Everything and more. Will the police be blamed for failing to make a watertight case? Will the judge be denounced for confusing the jury? I doubt it. It will be the fault of the crazy witness. The madwoman who heard voices in her head. Eliot put the videotape on the police network. What if it's leaked and ends up on YouTube, the next thing that comes up after the student murder? I'm going to look like a freak.

'Meredith?' Isobel says sharply. 'Are you all right?'

'Yes… sorry…'

'Now, listen. Take my advice and don't talk to anyone about this – friends, people at work…' She pauses and I hear a key turning, a door opening and shutting. 'I'm afraid my celebrity status will only make it worse. I've already been on to my agent and she's going to do what she can, but once the press find out… well, you know how they twist things.'

She's right, and she doesn't know the half of it. If anyone finds out I was with Jay moments before …

'Isobel – please, can we talk?'

'What is it, darling?'

I take a long, deep breath. And then I tell her.

CHAPTER TWENTY-EIGHT

Cara
July 1984

What was she going to do? Whatever way she looked at it, the situation was a ghastly mess and there was no easy way out of it. Jay had stolen valuable items, and because she hadn't stopped him, or gone to the police, or at the very least told Isobel, everyone would assume she was guilty too. And she *was* guilty, in a way, because she'd not only kept quiet, she'd knowingly lived off the proceeds.

She couldn't understand how it had happened, and all within such a short space of time. Cara Jane Travers the criminal. Where was the world's biggest goody-goody, the swotty teenager who'd not had one detention in her entire school career? Where was the responsible adult who'd never had a parking fine or even been on a protest march? Would the judge take this into account when sentencing? she wondered. Because she and Jay were going to be found out eventually, she was convinced of it. The idea of prison terrified her. How would she deal with her parents' shame? She would rather kill herself.

Since the DIY burglary, the relationship with Jay had unsurprisingly soured. He was still living at Darkwater Terrace, still lounging around the house all day smoking joints and drinking vodka; still sharing her bed and having sex with her every night. Cara had started faking her orgasms so it would be over quicker, and Jay, who was usually stoned up to the eyeballs, hadn't noticed. Or he *had* noticed and didn't care. He kept telling her he loved her, but she no longer believed him. If you love someone, you don't do something you know will upset them, she told herself. You don't implicate them in a crime.

Jay had gone to sign on this morning, then he was going to buy some dope. For once, she had some time to herself. Cara sat on the bed with her legs crossed and considered her options. She longed to confide in someone, but she couldn't trust her university friends because they all knew Isobel, and she'd lost touch with the girls from school. Telling Mum and Dad was obviously out of the question. She wanted to finish with Jay but was scared that he'd refuse to go. What if he turned violent? It was like being trapped in a lift with the oxygen running out.

She stood up and went to the window. She stared down at the garden, which was fast turning into an urban jungle, the grass so tall that you could no longer see the stepping-stone path. At the bottom was the gate that led to the pool and further round the path was the old boathouse. She thought back to those first times with Jay, the small of her back pushed against the ground as he thrust, oblivious that he was hurting her. Her hand went to the place, the bruise long disappeared. Jay wasn't a sensitive lover, but he wasn't an animal either. He was just a man.

She went back to bed.

'Cara?' Jay's voice lifted her head from the pillow. 'Cara? Where are you?' His feet thumped up the stairs. 'What are you doing up here?' he said, coming into the room. 'I thought you'd be outside. It's sweltering out there. Eighty-three degrees they said on the radio.'

'I wasn't feeling very well,' she lied, turning away from him.

He sat down on the bed and reached across to feel her forehead. 'Wow, you're burning up. I'll get you a cold flannel.'

'No. Don't want one.'

'You sure?' He looked disappointed. 'My mum swears by them.'

'I just need to rest.' What she really needed was a pee and some lunch, but not as much as she needed him to go.

'Okay.' He took a small plastic bag out of his pocket and dangled it over her face. 'Grass. I blew the last of our dosh on it, but I've a feeling we won't regret it.' He opened the bag and took a long, indulgent sniff. 'Yup. Epic.'

Cara closed her eyes and bit down on her tongue. It was not *their* dosh. And how on earth had he got through four hundred quid in the last two weeks? He would steal more stuff, she knew it. But next time she would stop him.

Over the next few days, the atmosphere between them deteriorated. Jay noticed it, although at first he put it down to the strong weed, which he said sometimes made him feel paranoid. Was it the heat? he wondered. She still loved him, didn't she? He even asked her if she was pregnant, as if the possibility had only just occurred to him.

'No, I'm not,' she replied, tersely. 'Although I should be.'

'What do you mean, *should* be?' He gave her an odd look.

'Well, we've been doing it virtually every day for the past three months without protection.'

'*Have* we?'

Yes, she thought. I've been utterly stupid. I don't want a baby, and I don't want an abortion, so why haven't I sorted myself out?

'I'm sorry,' he said, looking sheepish. 'I thought you were on the pill.'

'No. You *assumed* I was on the pill.'

'Jesus…' He shook his head disbelievingly. 'All this time? Why didn't you tell me?'

'You didn't ask.' She'd been punishing him. As if *he* was the one who would suffer if she conceived! Her thinking was all upside down. Mad. And she was supposed to be an educated, liberated woman. A feminist, God help her…

Jay was upset. He went straight to the chemist's and came back with a pregnancy test and a large box of condoms, determined to cover both bases. The test was negative, which made her feel relieved and slightly worried. That night she feigned the traditional headache and lay at the edge of the bed, saying she was too hot to be touched.

The air was heavy with heat, without even the hint of a breeze. Jay took the duvet out of its cover and threw it on the floor. A fly had got into the room and was buzzing around in a tizzy, unable to find its way out. Cara tried to sleep, but her mind plagued her with uncomfortable questions. Should she finish with Jay? Should she tell the police? Why hadn't she got pregnant? Was she infertile? Was it her punishment for treating Isobel so badly? She *had* treated Isobel badly, she understood that now.

She turned to face Jay's naked back. He was sleeping in the foetal position, snoring very gently, the duvet cover crumpled around his waist. She tried to imagine her dear friend lying in his place. Would it have been so hard to love her in the way she'd wanted? They were all human beings, after all…

When she woke, it was half-six and the room was flooded with fresh sunlight. Her heart started to race when she realised Jay wasn't there. How had she missed him? She went straight to the empty rehearsal room and looked out of the window. Bertha's back was open and Jay was dragging an old seaman's chest down the front path. Cara threw on yesterday's clothes and ran down the stairs, hurtling through the open door.

'Stop it! Stop it!' she shouted.

Jay let go of the leather handle and straightened up. 'Don't shout, you'll wake everyone up.'

'I'm not letting you do this. Enough! What have you taken?' She marched past him and looked into the van. Her eyes quickly took in a marble washstand, two upright chairs, a brass coal bucket, several large pictures draped in blankets, a hat stand, an enormous mirror...

'You've got to put it back. All it of it! Now!'

'Don't worry,' Jay said soothingly. 'She won't find out.'

'She will when she comes back.'

'She won't, though. Too many bad memories, right?' He glanced back at the house, as if it could overhear. 'I've worked it all out. When she says she wants to sell, you offer to help. Find the estate agent, do the viewings and stuff, then when it's sold you get some clearance company to take away the contents. She won't even care and she'll still make a shitload of money.' He picked up the wooden chest and shoved it onto the van.

Cara took a sharp inward breath. 'Put it all back or I'll call the police.'

'Weren't you listening?'

'I mean it.'

He looked at her contemptuously. 'You wouldn't dare.'

'Wouldn't I?' She turned around and strode back inside, feeling more powerful and more determined with every step. Jay followed her into the hallway, telling her to calm down. Cara picked up the phone and started to dial, but he knocked the receiver out of her hand, pinning her to the side of the stairs. She struggled against him, kicking with her feet. 'Let me go, you bastard!'

'You're not thinking straight.' His mouth was only an inch from her face. 'If you dob me in, I'll take you down with me. Is that what you want? A prison sentence?'

'I can't do this any more!' she wailed. 'Can't live like this. It's all wrong!'

'You're pathetic.' He let go of her and she slid to the floor.

He grabbed a couple of random items – a plant-pot stand and an umbrella holder – and left the house. A minute later Cara heard the sound of Bertha's clapped-out diesel engine pulling away. At least she'd stopped him taking more stuff, she thought, uncurling herself and standing up. She put the phone back and went into the kitchen, turning on the tap and letting it run cold before she filled a glass. She took it into the garden and sat on the conservatory step, letting the cool water soothe the back of her throat. Enough was enough. When he came back, she decided, she would tell him the relationship was over and that he'd have to move out immediately. If he refused, she would call the police. Or maybe Isobel. Yes, better to call Isobel. It was her house; let her decide what to do.

'You cannot be serious!' he said when she told him, reminding her fleetingly of John McEnroe. If he hadn't been in such an agitated state – charging around the room like a caged animal, growling and pulling at his hair – she would have said so and tried to lighten the argument. It was mid-afternoon and the hot sunshine was streaming in through the floor-to-ceiling windows; it was like a bloody sauna in there and she was sweating. A bedraggled bunch of flowers was lying on the coffee table next to an unopened bottle of cava – Jay had brought them home as a peace offering, but she'd not even let him begin to apologise. It was way too late for that.

'I *am* serious,' she replied instead, keeping her voice calm and her tone cold. She'd been practising all day, as if it was an audition piece. 'I've packed your rucksack. If you could give me the keys to the house and Bertha—'

'You can't do this. I won't let you.'

'Jay, stop pacing around, for God's sake, and calm down!'

'I'm not going,' he said, thumping his fist on the back wall. 'You can't make me.'

'You're only here because I invited you,' she said, remembering that he'd actually invited himself. 'In fact, you're actually banned, remember? Isobel said—'

Jay rounded on her. 'I see, been speaking to that bitch, have you? *Oh Isobel, I'm so sorry, it wasn't my fault, Jay made me do it.*' He jumped into a vicious mockery of Isobel's accent. '*Oh darling, how positively dreadful, you must get rid of him at once!*' He shook Cara by the shoulders. 'Did she tell you to dump me? Did she?'

'No.'

'She must have – you'd never have the guts to do it by yourself.'

'This isn't helping,' she said. Calm, cold, decisive.

He released his hands and lunged for the bottle of cava, flinging it against the back wall. Pieces of wet glass flew everywhere and foamy bubbles dribbled down the pine panelling. 'How about that?' he shouted. 'Did that help?' He flung himself into the bamboo armchair and sobbed into the cushion like an angry, hurt child.

She edged slowly forward, trying to avoid the broken glass. 'Jay… please… It doesn't have to end like this.'

'Fuck off, bitch,' he muttered from behind his fingers.

That was it. Cara straightened to her full height. 'Your rucksack's in the front room. Please take it and go. Now. Or I *will* contact the police and tell them what you've done.'

He sat up, pointing with a trembling, jabbing finger. 'You'll pay for this, you know that? Somehow I'm going to make you pay.' She didn't reply, just kept her eyes on him as he left the room. The front door clicked open and slammed shut. She held her breath for a few seconds, then let out a long, exhausted sigh. Jay was gone and it was over.

It was only hours later, after she'd cleared up the mess and put the poor flowers in water, that she realised he hadn't left his key.

CHAPTER TWENTY-NINE

Me

'What's happening? Have they caught the bastard?' asks Amy, peering over my shoulder at the computer screen.

I start guiltily. 'Not yet.' I click off the news feed and return to the blog I'm supposed to be writing about effective content marketing. But it's impossible to concentrate and two minutes later I'm back on the news again, fixated. Live-at-the-scene journalist Sally French has been standing outside Archway College all morning, ready to bring us developments, but all that's playing is a montage of shots on a loop – students weeping high-octane tears, sobbing into each other's hair and laying flowers on the pavement, close-ups of notes attached to teddies, cross-fades of plastic windmills spinning in the breeze.

I thought I'd feel better if I came to work. 'Say nothing, do nothing, just act normal,' was Isobel's advice, but it's not working. Everyone in the office is talking about the murder, and although they think it's outrageous that someone could film a real stabbing and put it on YouTube, they've all watched it. They're speculating in that gossipy, salacious way people do about why it happened – I've done it myself in the past so I can't blame them – but it's making me feel physically sick.

'It's not your fault,' Isobel said last night, but I know she was shocked when I told her. 'He killed the girl, not you. Hold on to that fact.'

I click back to the news site. Every few minutes we are shown the same photo of Santianna Makepeace, angelic and big-busted in a white jumper embroidered with a silver sequinned rose. The journalist, chirpy in a bright yellow raincoat, keeps reminding us about the poetic irony of her surname. Now it's the turn of the college principal, who looks as if he's been up all night, to give his 'our hearts go out to the victim's family' speech. He clams up when he's asked if the college knew that Christopher Jay had anger-management issues. Apparently he'd only just gone back to work after two weeks off following a bad row with the victim – somebody leaked that helpful information via social media in the middle of the night. In the absence of the murderer himself, everyone is looking to cast the scapegoat. 'Was this a tragedy that could have been avoided?' Sally French says rhetorically to camera, pulling her collar up against the rain.

Yes, Sally, it could have been avoided. If Jay hadn't been passed fit, he wouldn't have been at the college and I wouldn't have found him so easily. How was I to know he was mentally ill? *Hold on to that fact.*

Now we've switched to the local police station and another journalist is telling us that a 'massive manhunt' is under way – parks, wasteland and derelict buildings within a wide radius are being searched by teams of specially trained armed officers. There have been numerous reported sightings from as far away as Devon and Newcastle, which detectives are following up, although we are told that he's probably somewhere close by. The SIO is interviewed and says that a man answering Christopher Jay's description bought a new set of clothes from a charity shop on the Camden Road and soon they'll release an updated e-fit. She urges the public to be alert, but not to confront the suspect as he could be dangerous.

I take out my earphones and sigh loudly. Why on earth did *I* confront him? How stupid was that?

'You okay, Meri?' asks Amy from her desk. She's been giving me strange looks all morning, even commented on the dark shadows beneath my eyes. 'Is it a migraine?'

As much as I'd like an excuse to go home, I can't keep lying to my friends. 'No, just tired, that's all. Not sleeping too well.'

'You should try meditation,' she says, and proceeds to tell me about this course she's thinking of doing – not *actually* doing – on mindfulness. I try to listen but my eyes keep returning to the laptop screen. They're showing a photo of Christopher Jay now – the one that's on the college website – and I remember the picture of him that was used during the trial. How long will it be, I wonder, before the media make the connection?

Amy insists that we get some fresh air, so we buy sandwiches and sit heroically on a bench in Soho Square, where we're pestered by fat pigeons and emaciated drug addicts. The sun may be shining but summer it isn't, and before long I've lost the sensation in my fingertips. I know she wants me to open up, and part of me is tempted, but I know I mustn't. 'Tell nobody,' Isobel said. 'In times like this, you can't trust a living soul.'

Amy removes her second sandwich from its packet. 'Are you still feeling depressed over Eliot? Perhaps you should go back to the doctor, get some more happy pills.'

'I'm fine,' I retort, shooing away a group of sparrows waiting eagerly for crumbs.

She chews on her crayfish and rocket and then says, 'You sure? Only you've been acting a bit weird lately. Don't be afraid to ask for help. We don't want you ending up in hospital with a bag on your head.' She laughs, and I join in her unwittingly tactless joke, as if the idea is unthinkable. Amy doesn't know about Becca or the dodgy genes she passed on. She doesn't know there's a 12 per cent chance that I will become schizophrenic. I must banish these absurd ideas and start taking preventative measures instead.

I must take comfort in the laws of probability – the 88 per cent chance that I *won't* end up with nets in the stairwell and plastic windows, a woman knitting at the end of my bed. Thinking about it positively, those are pretty good odds.

We finish our sandwiches in silence. The grass is patchy and tired of waiting for new growth. I look up at the thin blue sky – clouds like tufts of wool caught on invisible hedges – and try to imagine a future in which all this is over and life is ordinary again. I shiver. It's too early in the year for picnics; my toes are cold and the tip of my nose feels like an ice cube. Amy, sensing that I've had enough, holds out the brown paper carrier bag and I drop my waste in.

'Are you absolutely, positively sure you're okay, Meri?'

'Just some family stuff going on, that's all,' I say. Vague, but true.

She looks unconvinced. 'Well, you know where I am if you need to talk.'

We go back to the office and I take up my usual position in front of my computer screen. I rewrite the opening paragraph of my blog – not making it any better or worse, just different – and then make everyone in my section a cup of tea. I even attempt a bit of idle chit-chat as I hand round the mugs. Preventative measures. The saner I act, the saner I'll be. I just wish the internet would go down so I can't check for the latest news on Christopher Jay every five minutes. But the afternoon reports are simply reruns of the morning, and eventually I get bored. I finish the blog and post it on the company's website, then make an excuse for leaving early and go home.

The evening passes slowly. Fay and Lizzie are chatting in the kitchen over a bottle of wine. They offer me a glass but I tell

them I've got a headache and go up to my room. I lie on my
bed, fiddling with my phone and watching the news feed. I'm
addicted to it, even though it's making me feel worse with every
minute. Floral tributes have been arriving all day and the pavement is overflowing. Right now, there's a candlelit vigil outside
the college – several hundred people have turned up and a Bap-
tist choir is singing hymns. Rather beautifully, too. So far, all is
peaceful, but there is an increased police presence in the area and
dark warnings on Twitter. #Santianna is full of complaints about
the lack of justice for young black victims, and we're told that if
the police don't find Jay soon it could be the Tottenham riots all
over again.

I exchange a few texts with Isobel, who's banking on Jay killing himself because 'that's what they usually do'. It's supposed to
be comforting, but it just makes me panic. If he dies, his secrets
will die with him and I'll never know what happened to Becca.

How's the manhunt progressing? I wonder. The word makes
me think of cavemen in animal skins, brandishing spears. Maybe
the police have some leads but aren't divulging them to the public. I think about calling Eliot – he might know what's really
going on – but I don't trust myself not to blurt out the truth. I
haven't responded to the message he left yesterday, which he'll
think is odd, but not so odd that he's called again. Maybe he's
just too busy. Dad hasn't been in touch either, which is less surprising. He must have heard about the murder but obviously
doesn't want to talk about it; probably thinks it's nothing to do
with us. I wish.

I crawl into bed and lie in the darkness, trying to put the
house of my mind in order – a place for everything and everything in its place. Only then, I think, will I be able to sleep. But
the task is impossible. The past-life regression session won't leave
my brain. Christopher Jay, Isobel, Cara, Becca – alive, dead or

somewhere in-between – take it in turns to wreck my efforts, demanding my attention like spoilt children. Their faces zoom forward, jostling for centre stage, then recede and linger in the background, muttering half-phrases that play over and over again in my brain like bits of annoying pop songs. They won't let me go, tugging at my sleeve, grabbing my hand, trying to pull me in and give me a part in their drama. But I'm not interested; I don't want to know who did what or when and why and how. I'm the innocent bystander, the four-year-old with wispy golden hair, sitting on a plastic chair. All I want is an ice lolly, a strawberry one. I'm Meredith Banks and I live in the here and now. Meredith Banks, do you all understand? Go away and leave me be. I cry out for my father, but he doesn't come. He's busy in the garden, burning the past.

I wake before the alarm goes off. No idea how much sleep I managed in the end; a couple of hours perhaps. I feel worn out, but there's nothing I can do about that right now. Got to get up and face the day. I shower and dress, put on my make-up, eat a bowl of cereal, walk to the tube, stand for the whole journey and arrive at the office ten minutes early. Amazing what you can do when you try. Act normal, I tell myself, as I take the lift to the second floor. Act normal.

But it's so hard. Everyone in the office is still talking about the murder. There's a protest march planned for 11 a.m., I'm told, starting at the college and processing down the main road to the police station. Santianna Makepeace's mother has made an appeal for calm, but according to Twitter, the local community is on a knife-edge. It's an unfortunate metaphor. Thousands are expected to join the protest and reinforcements are being brought in from other boroughs. If the police behave as if they're expecting trouble, does it make it more or less likely? Discuss. Why haven't they caught Christopher Jay yet – is it laziness, incompetence or both? Now my colleagues are swapping 'chilling' memories of the Tottenham riots, by which they mean evenings glued to their laptops watching young men with scarves over their faces hurl beer bottles at policemen, and people running out of shops with tellies like it was the January sales. Those awful 'other' people, destroying their own communities to provide real-life entertainment for the rest of us. I can't stand the way they talk about it, as if it was the latest episode of *Hollyoaks*. If I was really acting normally I'd be right in there, saying my piece, but not today. Today I'm keeping my head down, saying nothing and pretending to be absorbed in my work.

The internal line rings. I pick up and say, 'Hi, Meredith here,' in the brightest tone I can manage. It's the receptionist, her voice wet with excitement, telling me that Detective Sergeant Myles is here again, insisting that he talks to me. I suddenly feel exhausted, my bones heavy, muscles weak. It takes an enormous effort just to stand up, and as I walk out of our section to the lift, my knees almost give way beneath me.

Eliot's right there, standing in front of the lifts on the ground floor, waiting for me. He doesn't say hello, or give the customary peck, just pulls me roughly to one side and whispers, 'Is there somewhere private we can talk?'

'Why? What's up? Can't we just go to the pub?' I bluff, but he shakes his head. 'Okay. I'll see what I can do.'

I enquire at the front desk and am told the Burgundy Suite is free for the next fifteen minutes. Eliot says that should be enough. Enough for what? Is he planning to torture me? We get into the lift, standing in awkward silence as we ascend to the third floor. I look at our reflections in the large mirror that takes up most of the back wall and remember the skip of happiness I used to feel when I caught sight of us in a shop window – small and tall, white and brown, physical opposites and yet somehow the perfect pair. And then the happiness twists and we look like two strangers vaguely annoyed with each other.

Eliot glances doubtfully at the glass cube plonked in the middle of the room, surrounded by busy workstations. 'This is the Burgundy Suite? Bit of a goldfish bowl,' he says, and, on cue, a few people turn away from their screens to look at us curiously. The room has already been prepared for a meeting – cups and saucers, large flasks of coffee and tea, a plate of chocolate biscuits, a bowl of fruit. I tear off a banana, peel back the skin and take a large bite.

'Breakfast,' I tell him, taking a seat. *Act normal.*

Eliot sits down opposite me, clasping his hands together as if in prayer, chewing at his thumbs. Thinking.

'You went to see Christopher Jay, didn't you?' The last bite of banana sticks to the roof of my mouth. 'The security guy mentioned that somebody asked for him at reception, and the barman in the Star and Garter remembers you too. Said the two of you were arguing.'

'What makes you think it was me?' I say, swallowing.

'Let's not play games. You're there, clear as day, on the CCTV footage. That was about half an hour before he stabbed Santianna Makepeace.'

'Does anyone else know?'

'*I* know, Meri,' he replies quickly. '*I* know. I should have said something to my boss yesterday but I bottled it. I was awake all night trying to decide what to do. I even tried to kid myself that I was wrong, that it wasn't you at all, just someone who looked identical to you. I so wanted to be wrong.'

'I'm sorry.'

His brown eyes are blazing at me. 'You should've told me straight up. You've put me in an impossible position.' He shifts angrily in his seat, like he's trying to stop himself from punching me in the face.

'You're working on the murder case then?'

'Yes. I interviewed Jay, so my name came up on HOLMES. They called me down to help with background and profiling.'

'Sorry, I didn't realise.'

'That's no excuse. You should have contacted the police anyway.'

'I didn't think it was relevant.'

'Oh, don't give me that bullshit. Why did you go and see him? What did you say to him?'

'I showed him the tape.'

'You did *what*?'

'I wasn't to know he was going to walk straight back into class and do that! I didn't kill her, it wasn't my fault!'

'I'm not saying it was!'

Our raised voices bounce off the glass, making the guys at the nearest desks look up.

'Look,' I say more quietly. 'Nobody else has to know, do they?'

'They already do. I went in this morning and told my boss I'd suddenly had a feeling it could possibly be you. Not sure she bought it, but she let me come and pick you up.'

'Pick me up? You mean, you're *arresting* me?'

'No, no, we just need to ask you a few questions.'

'About what?'

'Oh, Meri,' he sighs. 'Don't you understand? This is a murder enquiry. You're involved.'

DCI Paula Abrahams shows me into what's called the family room – a small rectangular space with a brown leather sofa, office armchair, and a wooden blind at the narrow window. A bowl of dusty potpourri, its aroma long departed, sits on the cheap coffee table.

'Thanks for coming in,' she says, gesturing me to the sofa. Her tone is terse, almost sarcastic. I watch her settle herself in the armchair, resting a pad on her slim knees, clicking her pen into action.

'Can Eliot sit in on this?'

'Detective Sergeant Myles? No, I'm sorry, he can't.' She looks up at me. 'Can I start with your full name and date of birth?'

'Meredith Louise Banks. Eleventh of the second, eighty-six.'

She writes it down, then adjusts her body to sit up straighter. 'I'm speaking to you as a witness in connection with the murder of Santianna Makepeace, which took place on Monday the 14th of April. In our discussion, I'm hoping to establish the nature of your relationship with Christopher Jay and what happened between you in the Star and Garter pub, shortly before the murder took place. Do you understand?'

'Yes.'

'Why did you go to Archway College?'

'I wanted to talk to Christopher Jay.'

'Was this a planned meeting? I mean, was he expecting you?'

'No.'

'So what did you want to talk to him about?'

'I… er…' What am I going to say? She looks at me steadily, waiting for my reply. 'I wanted to ask him about my mother. She… she was a witness at the trial – I mean, the Cara Travers trial – and she's a missing person.'

'Yes, DS Myles explained. So what was it you asked Jay about your mother?'

'I just wanted to see how he'd react when I mentioned her name.'

'What else did you say to him?'

'I can't remember exactly.' I feel myself going red and hot. She fixes her stare. I'm not going to get away with such a feeble answer, I can tell.

'Did you reveal any details about the investigation? Things DS Myles might have told you, or let slip?'

'No. Eliot's got nothing to do with this. He wouldn't talk to me about the case; that's the main reason I wanted to talk to Jay. I was pissed off, I wanted to do something for myself.'

'I see.' She writes something down. 'So you weren't satisfied with how the investigation was going.'

'No, it wasn't that. I just… It's what happened to my mother that interests me.'

'When you went to see him, how would you describe Christopher Jay's mood?'

'Jumpy, aggressive. He was obviously nervous about the Cara Travers case being reopened—'

'It's never been closed,' she corrects. 'It's being reviewed.'

God, I really don't like this woman, and I can tell she really doesn't like me.

'Okay, sorry. I'm not a detective.'

'Too right you're not.'

'I didn't make him kill that girl.'

'I never said you did.'

'So why am I feeling like you think I'm to blame?' I fold my arms across my chest.

Abrahams rests her pen on her notepad and puts her head on one side, studying me with an air of disappointment. 'I'm surprised, given your…' she pauses to add another pinch of sarcasm, 'your *involvement* in the Cara Travers case review, and your *friendship* with Detective Sergeant Myles, not to mention the enormous amount of press coverage and numerous police appeals for witnesses, that you didn't come forward of your own accord.'

'I didn't think it was relevant.'

She sighs irritably. 'When did you tell DS Myles you'd been to see Jay?'

'I didn't.'

'Hmm…'

'That's the truth. Eliot didn't know, I swear.'

'How did you know where to find Jay?'

'I googled him.'

She makes a loud tutting noise. 'I really hope you're not lying to me, for both your sakes.'

The door opens and a young mop-haired detective pops his head round. 'Can I have a word, boss?'

'Is it urgent?' He nods. Abrahams apologises and leaves the room. I sit there for – I don't know how long – five or ten minutes. I drum my fingers on the arm of the sofa. Our chat's over now; surely I'm free to go. I sigh loudly. This is all so unnecessary, such a waste of their time. It's got nothing to do with the murder of this poor student and it's not going to help them find Jay. I'm cross with Eliot for telling Abrahams; they never would have found me otherwise and all it's done is cause a load of trouble for both me and him. I've started rehearsing a speech to Eliot in my head when Abrahams opens the door and comes back in.

'You've been lying, haven't you, Meredith?' she says, standing over me, looking at me so sharply I could cut myself on her edges.

'No. Not at all!'

'DS Myles asked for a sample of your DNA and you agreed to it going on the national database, is that right?'

'Yes. I was told there might be a match with an unidentified… with my mother.'

'Well, the results have come through and there *is* a match.' She raises her eyebrows and holds them there dramatically.

My heart pulls up short and then starts pounding again, faster than before. *Becca. They've found Becca.* Images swirl in my brain. I see a body being pulled from a river, her corpse lying on a slab. I see her face, but it's my face. I'm looking down at myself and I'm dead. I see a cardboard coffin being lowered into a mass grave. Everything's spinning; my body's swaying. I grasp uselessly at the sofa cushion, trying to hold on. *They've found Becca.*

DCI Abrahams is just standing there, observing me, gauging my reaction; doesn't seem to care that I'm struggling to take in the news, doesn't offer me a glass of water for the shock. She's looking at me like I'm nothing, a dirty mark on her white blouse, a piece of gum stuck to her shoe, like she hates me.

'We know who you are, Meredith,' she says. 'And we know why you didn't come forward.'

I gaze up at her wide-eyed.

'You're Christopher Jay's daughter.'

CHAPTER THIRTY

Me

'That's impossible. It's ridiculous.' I stare at DCI Abrahams's grim expression, as if waiting for her face to crack. 'This is a joke, right? A sick joke.'

'Putting on an act won't help,' says Abrahams impatiently. 'A team's already on the way to search your house.'

'You can't be serious. Christopher Jay is not my father! There must have been some mistake. Contamination of evidence. Mixed-up samples…'

'His DNA was all over the murder scene – there's no possibility of a mistake. I need to examine your mobile. Where is it, in your bag?' She takes my phone and hands it to her assistant.

'It's not true. Please tell me it's not true.' I press my hands against the sides of my head and rock from side to side, trying to shake her voice out of my ears. *She's lying. I'm not going to listen to her. I know who my father is. I am not the daughter of a killer.* My head starts to spin, my vision closing in from the edges.

'Meredith – what are you doing? Sit up!'

'I think I'm going to f—' My eyes close and the world turns black.

'Meri? Are you okay?' Eliot's voice. He's sitting on the edge of the sofa. 'This is a dreadful shock for her,' he says. 'You've got to give her some time.'

'We don't have any time,' a female voice replies; Abrahams, I think. 'If she knows something—'

'She doesn't. Can you call the duty doctor?'

'I'm sure that's not necessary.'

'She needs checking over.'

The duty doctor arrives. He smells musty but his voice is kind. He takes me by the shoulders and tries to pull me up. I've gone floppy and he has to hold me to stop me falling to one side. I'm a doll, a soft toy; my bones have disintegrated and my insides are mush. I bend my head, making my hair fall forward so they can't see my face. He takes my pulse and checks my blood pressure; it's on the low side, but he says it's no cause for concern. He makes me open my eyes and shines a torch in them till I blink. Satisfied I'm not going to die in police custody, he asks Abrahams if she's going to make an arrest. She says not yet, she's waiting for news. I lie down again and close my eyes, listening to the conversation going on over my head.

'You can see how she is, there's no way she knew,' Eliot's saying. 'She went to see Jay because she thinks he killed her mother. The last thing she'd do is protect him.'

'She didn't come forward,' replies Abrahams. 'Doesn't that strike you as suspicious?'

'Yeah, I can see that, but… look, I know her really well, we're friends.' *Friends? Is that all he's prepared to admit to?* 'I promise you, she's told you the truth. We both have.'

She, she, she. As if I'm not here.

Abrahams gets a call and by the tone of her voice I can tell she's disappointed. They've broken into the house, and guess what, Christopher Jay wasn't hiding under my bed.

'I *told* you you were wasting your time,' says Eliot.

'Have they checked the loft, cellar, garden shed?' continues Abrahams. 'Any signs that he might have been staying…? Okay, well as long as you're sure.' She ends the call abruptly and turns to me. 'Meredith,' she says, 'sit up, please. I need to talk to you.'

'Can't you see she's not up to it right now?' Eliot crouches down next to me. The tenderness of his touch is familiar and I start to cry.

'DS Myles, return to your desk, please,' says Abrahams sharply. 'And stay there until you're sent for. I haven't finished with you yet.'

But he ignores her. 'Is there someone I should call, Meri? Graeme?'

'No, not Dad,' I croak. 'Please, you mustn't tell him. El – promise me.'

'DS Myles, you're skating on extremely thin ice here.'

'I'll call you later,' he whispers, standing up. He walks out of the room, not bothering to shut the door.

Abrahams questions me for the next hour or so and then I have to go through it all over again while one of her lackeys laboriously writes it down in his childish handwriting. Statement made and signed, I'm finally allowed to call a taxi, although Abrahams insists on keeping my phone for forensic examination, meaning she still doesn't believe me, even though it's completely obvious to anyone but a moron that I've told the truth. I think she's just doing it to be a bitch and make me suffer for not coming forward.

I sit in the cab, numbly looking out of the window, my eyes wandering through the crowds of shoppers, workers, tourists. I know nothing about these strangers yet I envy them. They look content with who they are and where they're going. I can't place myself among them. I feel like the victim of a life-changing accident, the cause pinned down to one brief moment that replays constantly in your head. A slip, a fall, a second of inattention, a decision so slight that at the time it didn't even feel like a decision: to cross the road, overtake a car, climb a ladder; to reach into a cardboard box marked *Baby clothes* ...

As we chug painfully through the traffic, I try to do the maths. I was born eighteen months after Cara was murdered. Becca could have been having an affair with Jay from the moment he arrived at Darkwater Terrace, or even before that. Or she might only have met him during the trial. I wonder whether Jay knew about me. I don't think so. There was no sign of it in his face when we met, though that doesn't mean anything. People lie so easily.

And what about Dad? My dear, dear father – he'll always be my father, no matter what the science says. I stare out of the taxi window, the scene blurring with tears. Is this what he's been trying to protect me from? If he finds out I know I'm not his biological daughter, it'll break his heart. And if he *doesn't* know already and I tell him, it'll break his heart anyway. Which means that now I must lie too.

I wish the detective hadn't confiscated my phone – I want to talk to Isobel. Then I remember she gave me her business card. I fish it out of my bag and give her address to the taxi driver. He makes a big swooping circle in the street, setting off in the opposite direction. We head west towards Belsize Park, veering off down side streets littered with cars, the cab swerving around speed bumps and slamming on the brakes as schoolchildren wander across the road.

Alice answers the door. She stares at my tear-stained face so disapprovingly I retreat a couple of steps. 'Isobel's working,' she says.

'Sorry, it's an emergency.'

'Really? You'd better come in then.' She opens the door just wide enough for me to pass through and shouts up. 'Izzy! Your friend Meredith's here.'

Isobel rushes down the stairs and sees the expression on my face. 'Oh God, darling, you look like you've been in a fight. What on earth's happened?'

She pushes past Alice and envelops me. It seems to unblock something and I start crying again. Alice stands behind her, studying my face, her lips drawn in a thin line. Isobel ushers me into the front room and plants me on the sofa, sitting next to me and clasping my hands with both of hers.

'She's in shock. Needs something strong. Darling, would you mind?'

'I think we could all do with a drink, don't you?' says Alice, slouching off to the kitchen.

'So what happened?' says Isobel. 'Did they find out you'd been to see Jay?' I nod. 'Oh shit. Why didn't you keep quiet about it? I bet they gave you a hard time. They've no right to, you know; you can lodge a complaint.'

Alice comes back with a bottle of Scotch and three crystal tumblers. She pours me a shot, which I gulp down, the peaty bitterness of it scorching my throat.

'Did you know all along? That he's my father?'

Isobel starts. 'Sorry?'

'Christopher Jay is my biological father.' The words taste like bile in my mouth. 'They tested my DNA.'

Alice lets out a low whistle and Isobel clasps her hands to her face. 'But... but... oh my God... Oh, you poor darling.' She looks down at the pattern on her shirt, thinking for a few seconds, and then adds, 'How ghastly. Of all the people...'

'I still can't really believe it.'

Isobel lets out a heavy sigh. 'What a bastard... Christopher Jay has ruined so many lives.'

'But now they've got him. This proves Rebecca Banks lied for him. Bang goes his alibi.' Alice raises her glass. 'Cheers!' She downs the whisky and smacks her lips.

Isobel gives her a warning frown. 'Darling, please... this is not something to celebrate. Think of poor Meredith, what's she been through.'

'It's okay,' I say, staring miserably into my tumbler. 'I've got to face facts. If Becca knew Jay before the murder, there's a good chance she was involved in some way.'

'I'd say it was the final piece of the jigsaw.' Alice sits on the edge of the sofa, stretching her free arm across Isobel's shoulders. 'I always thought it was weird, the key witness just happening to be walking around Darkwater Pool in the dead of night. Would you go somewhere so creepy if you needed fresh air? God knows why the police ever believed her.'

'They should have worked out that Becca and Jay were connected,' agrees Isobel. 'But it was par for the course with that lot, I'm afraid. Utterly hopeless. How Brian Durley ever made it to chief constable…'

Alice swirls the ice thoughtfully around her glass. 'Jay must have gone to see Rebecca straight after he killed Cara. He probably threatened to tell her husband about the affair unless she helped out.'

I look up sharply. 'No, that's not possible. My father was at home that evening. He and Becca had had a row.'

'That's what he said in court, but—'

'It's all starting to make sense,' interrupts Isobel, suddenly animated. 'Becca confessed about the affair and what Jay had made her do. She was in big trouble, but your father forgave her and lied to protect her.'

'He'd never lie about something that serious. He hates lies.' I feel myself bristling. They don't know him; nobody knows him like I do. 'My father's a good man,' I say. 'A really good man.'

'Exactly,' says Isobel, warming to her theme. 'He was frightened about what would happen to Becca if she went to prison. He lied because there was no other choice, because he loved her. He probably thought Jay would be convicted anyway, so it wouldn't matter. It wasn't his fault it all went wrong at the trial.'

'But now that the truth's coming out,' says Alice, 'he might have to answer some awkward questions.'

'Don't say that. Please don't! I can't bear it.' Tears start to well up behind my eyes and I cover my face with my hands.

'You poor thing,' soothes Isobel. 'I can't imagine how bad you must feel. Everywhere you look it's a fucking awful mess. Still, I'm glad you came to us for help. You shouldn't be on your own at a time like this. You must stay for a few days and let us look after you.'

I'm not sure that's a good idea, but what are the alternatives? I don't want to go back to the house and face Fay, and I'm not ready to see Dad. I don't want to involve any other friends and I've completely screwed up with Eliot. There's nowhere else to go.

'That's really kind,' I say, through wet fingers, 'but... I don't want to impose.'

'You're not imposing.' Isobel strokes my hair. 'We insist, don't we, Alice?'

It's late. I lie on my back, legs straight, arms at my sides, the alcohol paralysing me, limb by limb. The bed is vast; sheets cold and icy. It's as if Isobel has shrunk me and put me to sleep in her doll's house. My eyes swivel from left to right. The room is square and sparsely furnished, Nordic style. Shiny grey curtains hang motionless like polished concrete and unframed mono-chrome seascapes float off the white walls. The bedstead is paint-ed in cool eau de Nil with a matching chest of drawers – the wood smells new, as if it's just come from the forest. I'm drunk and dehydrated with crying, but I like it here. I like the feeling of surrender.

Dad made me a doll's house once, from a kit. He assembled it secretly while I was asleep and gave it to me for my ninth birthday, decorated, furnished and fully inhabited. It hadn't occurred to him that I would have liked that job; that saving my pocket money and going to the shop to choose the dolls and all the lovely miniature items was the whole point of the toy. He'd thought of everything: tables and chairs, beds, sofas, a bathroom suite, the baby's crib – right down to tiny plates of eggs and bacon. He'd painted the outside girlie pink, with white shutters at the windows, and each room had different wallpaper made from patterned gift-wrap, the floors carpeted with brown felt. You could turn all the lights on with one switch, and when I went to bed at night I'd leave them on and watch the house from my own giant bed. It comforted me to see the light bulbs twinkling extravagantly in the dark, the dolls safely tucked up in their beds, dreaming of tomorrow's breakfast. I liked to imagine I was one of them – small and wooden, with peg feet, yellow woollen plaits and a painted smile. I used to lie stiff and straight, just as I am now, pretending I was in the doll's house, part of its ready-made family – Mummy, Daddy, brother, sister, and the baby that would never grow out of his crib.

I sink into a sudden sleep and wake – I don't know how much later – with a thudding head and a dry mouth. I ease myself up, blinking as my eyes adjust to the solid darkness around me. A pair of shoes sits neatly on the pale carpet. Dark trousers and a shirt are draped over the chair like a misshapen ghost. *My* clothes, by the look of them, although I have no memory of taking them off. Time seems to have stopped, or has it moved forward without me, leaving me stranded? There's no clock in this room. Is it still the middle of the night, or is dawn breaking? I listen for birdsong, traffic, voices and footsteps in the street, but there's nothing. A canopy of silence hangs over the bed. The room feels sterilised and sealed, as if I'm in an airtight capsule floating through space. I could stay like this forever, I think. How good would it

feel to drift aimlessly around the universe? Doing nothing, talking to no one…

In the distance, a telephone rings. I hear Isobel's voice. And
then I remember why I'm here. And who I am.

CHAPTER THIRTY-ONE

Me

There's a gentle knock on my door. 'Meredith?' Isobel enters before I can answer. She's fully dressed and carrying a mug of tea, which she puts on the bedside cabinet. She goes to the window and pulls the curtain cord. The drapes part theatrically, revealing a bright blue sky and the tops of blossomy trees. It's so perfect it looks false, like a painted backdrop she's ordered specially to cheer me up. Sunlight swoops across the room and I have to shield my eyes with my arm.

'Did you manage to sleep?' she asks.

'I think so.' I sit up, drawing my knees to my chest and pulling the duvet up to my chin, suddenly aware of my nakedness.

'You're not going to believe this.' Isobel stands at the foot of the bed, her lips pursed with worry.

'They've caught Jay?'

'Not yet, I'm afraid. I've just had a call from your ex.'

'Eliot? You didn't tell him I was staying here, did you?'

She pulls her silky dressing gown tightly across her chest. 'Yes. Why? Shouldn't I?'

'It's just that… I hadn't told him. Oh shit…' As if things aren't bad enough.

'So that's why he sounded so surprised,' Isobel says, sitting on the edge of the bed. 'I'm sorry, darling, you should have warned me – I didn't know we were a dark secret.'

'I bet he was furious.'

'He didn't sound furious, just shocked. Started interrogating me about how and when we'd met. He's very worried about you, sends you his lurve. I told him I was letting you rest but he could call you here later. That's okay, isn't it?'

I nod. 'Suppose so.'

She rattles on. 'Anyway, the *Mirror* has made the link to Cara's murder and now everyone's going to want to know why Jay wasn't convicted. The shit's going to hit the fan big-time – which is what the police deserve, so I'm not sorry. I expect I'll be dragged into it…' She sighs. 'Anyway, Heartlands and the Met are coordinating their media response, God help us. They want to make sure we're all singing off the same hymn sheet. In other words, they're warning me not to sell my story to the highest bidder.' She huffs. 'As if I'd ever betray Cara's memory like that.'

'What about me? Do the press know who I am? Do they know I went to see Jay?'

'No, and your boy says they're trying to keep it that way. But if there's a leak…' She frowns. 'Honestly, darling, I'd keep your head down if I were you. Stay here with us, at least until Jay's caught.' She kisses me lightly on the cheek and asks me what I'd like for breakfast.

Eliot calls me on Isobel's landline just before lunch. I'm up and dressed, ensconced in a tartan armchair by the window, large pottery mug of coffee in hand. Isobel has gone to meet her agent to 'discuss tactics' and Alice is learning lines upstairs; at least that was the excuse she gave. I know she doesn't want me here and I'd leave if I had anywhere else to go.

'How are you?' he asks, and then, before I have a chance to reply, 'Why didn't you tell me you'd got in touch with Isobel Dalliday?'

'You know why.' Because I didn't want a conversation like this.

'I couldn't believe it.' I can hear noises in the background: people talking, the dull rhythm of a train. 'She made it sound like you were best friends.'

'Yeah, well, she's been really lovely to me—'

'I don't understand what you're playing at,' he interrupts, his tone growing more and more peevish. 'I told you not to get involved, but, as always, you knew better. I know things were moving slowly – that's what cold cases are like; it's just as frustrating for me – but you can't crash around like you're part of the investigation team. You've seen how disastrous it can be.'

I feel my body stiffen. 'I didn't make him kill that girl.'

His voice lowers to a whisper. 'If the press find out that you're Christopher Jay's daughter—'

'I'm not his daughter!'

'Biologically you are, and that's all they're interested in. If they find out you went to see him – that your mother got him acquitted – I swear you'll have to change your name and leave the country.'

'I didn't mean any of this to happen, you know that. I was only trying to find out what happened to Becca.' I sniff up angry tears. 'I wish I'd never found that fucking tape.'

'I know, I know how devastating this is.' He lets out a long, troubled sigh. 'I'm really worried about you, Meri, it's like… like you're…' He hesitates, knowing what dangerous territory he's just entered.

'Like I'm going mad? Having a nervous breakdown? Jesus, you sound just like my dad.'

'You're under incredible stress and you need help.'

'Isobel's helping me.'

'I mean professional help.' He means doctors. A diagnosis. Medication. Synapses in my brain connect and suddenly I'm the one in the hospital, in the little plastic booth, pillows stacked behind my back, forcing me to sit up. I'm staring at the bare walls and the scratched plastic windows, and at the end of my bed a woman is knitting and watching, knitting and watching. What chance have I got? The love child of a schizophrenic and a psychotic murderer.

'Please let's not fall out again, El. Can't we just talk? You could come here.'

'I've been formally instructed not to contact you; we shouldn't even be having this conversation.' His voice is cold and full of pain.

'But why?'

'For fuck's sake, Meri, why do you think? Because I'm in deep shit for telling you where Jay worked. Durley had to step in to prevent a formal reprimand. He's made a deal with Abrahams. I go back to Operation Honeysuckle and she forgets I was ever on the case. So much for my brilliant career as a murder detective.'

He's silent for a few seconds, punishing me. I think of everything we were, everything we've shared; I walk through the museum of our life together, looking at pictures, picking up objects – ah yes, we did this, and then we did that, and wasn't that funny and do you remember when?... We're in the past tense now, boxed up and archived.

'I'm sorry,' I say. It sounds so inadequate. Eliot replies but I can't hear him properly beneath the chatter of strangers, and I know he won't speak up; he hates people shouting down their phones on the train.

'El? Are you still there?' The line goes dead. I've lost him somewhere in the Chilterns. He doesn't try to call back and nor do I. It feels like the end of more than just a phone call.

Isobel arrives home just after six and finds me lying on top of the bed, half asleep. She tells me off when she discovers I haven't eaten since breakfast.

'Didn't Alice make you lunch?' *No, Alice didn't. She kept out of my way all morning and only went downstairs once she'd heard me go back to my room.*

'I didn't want any,' I say, which isn't true, I'm actually starving, but there's no point in causing more trouble. I can't help that Alice is pissed off by my presence; I just wish she had the good manners to hide it. Isobel doesn't seem to have noticed, unless she's pretending in the hope that Alice will eventually stop sulking and get on side.

'You have to eat to keep up your strength,' she says, and I think: strength for what? What's the next ordeal I'm going to be put through? Can't I just hide away and sleep? 'Tidy yourself up and then come down.' She hands me a fresh towel and points me in the direction of the bathroom. 'I'll make us all some supper.'

I splash water over my tired, blotchy face and drag my fingers through my hair. I haven't got so much as a hairbrush with me; I need to go back to the house and collect my make-up and some clothes. Except I don't know how long I'll be staying. I don't want to leave yet, don't want to face the hostile world outside. It feels safe here, even though the stick insect keeps giving me the evil eye. Isobel's the one in charge, and if she wants me here, there's not much Alice can do about it.

Isobel is guzzling wine and chopping vegetables, immediately dropping her knife when she sees me. 'Red?' She reaches for the bottle.

'Thanks,' I say, at the same time thinking I shouldn't drink on an empty stomach. The wine tastes strong and fruity. It makes me feel slightly sick, but I take another gulp and sit in the tartan armchair again, like a cat that's found its favourite place. The light is fading. In the garden, the artfully arranged flowerpots – bushy herbs, lavender and dark velvety tulips – disappear as my reflection sharpens against the darkness. Isobel tells me that the piece in the *Mirror* wasn't 'too bad' – it didn't mention her or Becca – but the other papers will start digging around now…

'It's just a matter of time,' she says gloomily. 'And you can imagine the reaction on Twitter – everyone getting on their soapboxes. Loads of people horrified that Jay was allowed to teach when he'd been previously tried for murder, others reminding us that he was acquitted in a court of law… Honestly, it's been going on all day. I so wanted to join in with a few facts about police incompetence, but I didn't dare.'

I look suspiciously through the window, as if our enemies are hiding in the shadows of the garden, waiting to leap out. Journalists in pale raincoats and trilbies, brandishing notebooks.

'At least yesterday's protest march went off peacefully, thank God,' Isobel continues. 'Only one arrest, but now there's a massive police presence in the area. The stupidity of it is, it's diverting resources away from the manhunt.' She peels a large clove of garlic and chops it finely. 'If they don't find Jay by the weekend, it could turn very nasty. The community's desperate not to have a riot, but if troublemakers turn up from outside… well, I don't trust the police to be able to contain it.'

Alice comes in. 'Are we going to talk about this all night?' She gives me a hostile glance, as if I was the one rattling on, then kisses Isobel – rather pointedly – on the neck. 'What are you cooking?' Chicken and chorizo pasta is the reply. Alice takes her wine and goes upstairs, claiming she needs to check her lines for tomorrow's shoot.

'It's a teeny-tiny part, only two speeches,' Isobel explains in a whisper after she's gone, 'but at least it's something. Good for the self-esteem.'

I pull my legs under me, sinking further into the armchair. 'I don't think she wants me here.'

'Oh, don't take any notice of Alice. You must stay for as long as you like. It's unbearably horrible what you've been through these past few days. All that bastard's fault. If I came face to face with him right now, I swear I'd kill him.' She pauses with her knife raised, her face twisted with hate.

'Thank you, Isobel. You've been so kind to me, I don't know what I would have done if—'

'There's a connection between us,' she says, turning round to face me. 'I can't explain it. You feel it too, I know you do.' She moves closer to me. 'We're already close friends, despite the age gap. That doesn't happen in an instant; it builds up over many years. That's what makes me think we've known each other in a past life, in *many* past lives. As friends, or sisters, perhaps even as lovers. They say people meet again and again, but not always in the same relationship, or the same sex.' She drains her glass, the wine lingering wet on her lips. 'That's what's happening when you meet someone for the first time but get this feeling you've known them all your life. It's instant. That's how it felt with Cara, how it feels with you. A sort of psychic love at first sight.'

'But you're married to Alice,' I say, trying to bring her back down to earth.

'Yes, and I wish she understood.'

I look up at the ceiling and picture Alice in the room above, rehearsing her part as an excuse to get away. 'She hates me.'

'Nonsense,' says Isobel airily.

She carries on cooking and I watch her deftly chop and fry and stir. Neither of us feels the need to fill the silence with conversation, and I start to feel the tension in my neck untwisting. Maybe it's just the alcohol, or maybe there really is a special connection between us. I feel *something*, that's for sure, although I can't put it into words, can't give it a name. She… comforts me. No, that's not quite it. She… she just understands me, I suppose.

She accepts me. But is that because she thinks she's got her beloved Cara back? I don't want to be Cara. I just want to be me… whoever that is. I just want to be me.

Isobel looks at me thoughtfully, standing up and pressing her hands into the small of her back. 'I've just had a brilliant idea. You need a break. We've got a little cottage in Cornwall, right by the sea, miles from anywhere. Honestly, it's really beautiful. We can go there tomorrow, as soon as Alice gets back from her shoot. We'll stay for the weekend, help you settle in, and then you can stay as long as you like, come back when you're ready. It's incredibly relaxing down there, good for the soul. You can go for walks, read, cook… The freezer's jammed full; you won't even have to go to the shops.'

I look up. 'I don't know. I've already had quite a few days off work.'

She shakes her head. 'You're not up to going back at the moment. Please come to Cornwall. Take next week off; I'm sure your boss will understand, and who cares if he doesn't? Honestly, darling, it'll do you the world of good.'

I guess she's right. I need to get out of London. I can't think properly here, my mind's so clogged up. But if I can spend some time alone in a beautiful cottage, walking by the sea, breathing the fresh air, no TV, no internet, nobody to get at me…

'Well… yes,' I hear myself saying. 'As long as Alice is cool about it.'

Isobel tosses her head. 'Leave her to me. She'll be fine.'

But Alice is not fine. When the subject is broached later over dinner, she glues her lips together and stares at the wall. Isobel affects not to notice, launching into the story of how they stumbled upon Samphire Cottage five years ago while walking on the clifftops near Bude. It was virtually derelict and they've had it lovingly restored, using local materials and craftsmen. *Coast* magazine did a feature on it, and she makes me get up from the table to look at the article, which they've had framed and put in the downstairs loo.

Alice still hasn't said a word. Her eyes fixed downwards on her plate, she continues to pick at her food and is catching up with Isobel on the wine consumption, the small veins on her cheeks flushing pink.

This is not good, I think. I have to step in here. 'It's incredibly kind of you both,' I say, 'but maybe it would be better if I went home.'

'Only to pick up some things,' says Isobel. 'Then we'll drive straight down.'

Alice gets up and starts clearing the plates. 'Stop bullying her,' she says finally. 'Let her do what she wants.'

Isobel looks up, her eyes shining with childlike innocence beneath her short black fringe. 'I'm not bullying her.'

'Yes, you are.' Alice empties the remains into a small brown compost bin. 'You do it with everyone. You're behaving as if Meredith's your best friend, but the fact is, she's a total stranger.'

'I'm sorry, this is my fault. I think I'd better go.' I stand up and my chair scrapes violently on the terracotta floor tiles.

'No, no, you mustn't!' Isobel shoves me back into my seat. 'It's not your fault, not at all!' She scrambles towards Alice, who's wiping the cast-iron skillet, and touches her arm. Alice shoves her off with her elbow; she looks so angry, I half expect her to swing the pan at her partner's head.

'Don't be so hard on me, darling,' begs Isobel. 'You know what I'm like when it comes to anything to do with Cara. I feel so bad, I only want a chance to make up for the past.'

Alice turns round and glares at me. 'Over thirty years I've had to put up with this. Can you imagine? I guessed it would take a while for her to get over it, a few years even, but this is insane.' She grips the back of the dining chair. 'You'd think she'd have moved on by now, that we wouldn't have to celebrate Cara's birthday every year with her favourite fucking chocolate cake, and walk around with a fucking long face on the anniversary of her fucking death.'

'Stop it, you're embarrassing Meredith!'

'You'd think she'd have got tired of thanking Cara in the acknowledgements of every fucking book she writes and—'

'I always thank you too,' Isobel protests.

'And generally shoving her name in my face at every fucking opportunity, like I should be okay with this, like I should love Cara just as much as she does. Why the fuck should I? I never even knew her.'

I stand up again and back away, my body hitting the wall. I feel a painting swing on its hook behind me. I have to go. Where did I put my bag?

'Please, please don't be like this,' says Isobel. 'You've always been so supportive.'

'I have limits, Izzy, and you've gone way beyond. Meredith is *not* the reincarnation of Cara. You're fucking insane!'

'No, I'm not, you can't say that. You've got to have an open mind. There's a deep connection between us. We both felt it instantly.'

'Oh yeah, I bet you did.' Alice slams down a cooking dish and storms off upstairs.

'Sorry about that,' says Isobel after a few moments. She lights a cigarette, throws open the patio doors and stands with one foot in the garden while she smokes, drawing the nicotine into the bottom of her lungs and exhaling noisily.

I spot my bag nestling at the foot of the tartan armchair and start to creep forward, but just then Isobel steps back into the room, throwing her cigarette stub in the bin.

'Please don't go,' she says.

'No, really, I think I should.' I pick up the bag and hug it to my chest.

'You can't leave at this time of night. I won't let you. We all need to sober up. I'll make some coffee.' She goes to the kettle and starts filling it.

'Honestly, I'd rather go.'

'No!' She turns to me, lowering her voice. 'Alice is jealous, but she'll get over it. I'll talk her round and by tomorrow I promise you she'll be absolutely fine.'

'No, she won't, it's too awkward.'

'Meredith, believe me, I know how to handle Alice.' She takes the bag off me and smiles.

CHAPTER THIRTY-TWO

Cara
August 1984

She was doing okay, all things considered. Keeping busy was the main thing and, luckily, there was a lot to do. Once Jay had gone and she was by herself in the house, she realised just how filthy the place had become. They'd never once used the vacuum cleaner and she didn't even know if there were any cleaning materials or where they were kept. The stair carpet was edged with grey fluff, the toilet bowl stank, there was mould along the side of the bath, the windows were almost opaque with dirt, the kitchen was thick with grease and everything she picked up seemed to be covered in hair. It was worse than when she'd been a student, and that was saying something. She would clean one room at a time, starting at the top and working downwards.

For the next two days, she hoovered and dusted and scrubbed, defiant against the heat. She didn't go to the police. Jay was right in that respect; she didn't have the guts. And anyway, the person she should confess to first was Isobel. And confess she would, but not until she'd got the house back into some order.

She paused from washing the kitchen floor, and sat back on her heels. Bananarama's hit 'Cruel Summer' sang out of the radio – too right, she thought. The heatwave was showing no signs of abating. Sweat was running from her neck into her cleavage and her armpits felt sticky. At least the quarry tiles were looking cleaner, no longer covered in a film of grime. She looked down at the gritty black water in the bucket and shuddered. How could they have let it get so bad?

The garden was worse; she had no idea how to tackle that. It needed a team of professionals with proper equipment, but her dole money wouldn't run to it. How shameful, she thought, to have let it get into such a state. By rights, Jay should come and help her, but she wasn't going to ask. She hadn't seen him since the split, but she'd had a few creepy phone calls she guessed were from him – either the phone would ring twice then stop, or she'd pick it up and hear someone breathing. Once the doorbell rang, but when she went to answer, nobody was there. It could have been kids, but somehow she knew it had been Jay. He'd left a few things at the house – clothes, toiletries, music tapes – and she guessed he wanted them back. Perhaps she should put them in a bin liner and stick them on the front doorstep.

What worried her most was that he still had his key. She bolted the front door every night before she went to bed, but it didn't make her feel any safer. The locks needed changing, but she couldn't afford to have it done. She suspected he was watching the house; just had this strange feeling that he was close by, as if some ancient part of her brain could subliminally detect his scent. When it got dark, she turned off the lights and stared through the window, waiting for him to emerge from the shadows or pop up from behind the parked cars. Then she decided he wouldn't risk entering at the front of the house; he'd come in via the path around the pool and get in through the garden. The summer foliage was out and he would be completely hidden from the road. And the bottom gate wasn't padlocked; all he had to do was reach over to draw back the bolt. At night she lay with her ears pricked for the creak of the hinges, his footsteps coming up the path, glass breaking in the conservatory…

The daytime was problematic too. What if Jay let himself in while she was out? He might steal more things, or lie in wait for her to come back. She'd made an emergency dash to the corner shop three days ago, and brought some basics, but they wouldn't last forever. Then there was signing on, she couldn't miss that. And she'd have to go to the post office to collect her dole money. The situation was becoming impossible.

Cara finished off the kitchen floor, moving backwards with the mop until she reached the doorway that led into the conservatory. She left the tiles to dry, collapsing in a bamboo armchair and putting her legs up on the coffee table. The cleaning was finished, at last, obviously not up to her mother's impossible standards, but good enough to salve her guilty conscience. Just the garden to go, then. She puffed out a long sigh. The longer she left it, the worse it would get. Help was what she needed. Someone with muscles.

Toby! She leapt from her chair, sliding over the wet kitchen floor and running into the dining room (she no longer called it the office). His details would be on his application. Cara opened the old filing cabinet and took out a thick folder labelled 'Auditions'. There he was. She gazed at his black-and-white 10x8, at the kind eyes and the easy, open smile. She liked Toby. He was far more handsome than Jay, who always looked as if he was either sickening for an illness or just recovering from one. She went back to the folder and found Jay's application too – the short, handwritten CV littered with spelling mistakes, and his tiny, overexposed head shot from a photo booth. Isobel had liked the look of him because he was 'real'. Hmm… he'd turned out to be a bit too real for Cara's liking. She ripped up Jay's application and threw it in the bin, then reached for the phone.

'Hi! Is that you, Toby? Cara here… Yes, it's me… I'm fine, thanks… Well, actually that's a lie…' And she broke down in tears.

He took the coach that evening, arriving at Darkwater Terrace at about 11 p.m. As Cara ran downstairs to answer the doorbell, she was suddenly reminded of her own arrival, eight long months ago; how her heart had jolted as she'd stepped over the threshold, like a bride about to embark on a wonderful new life.

'Sorry I'm so late,' said Toby, as she opened the door.

'Don't be silly, it's fine.' She threw her arms around him and they embraced, illuminated by the light in the hallway. 'I'm so glad you've come,' she whispered, glancing over his shoulder into the street. She gasped. Had she just seen someone slipping behind the van parked opposite the house? She'd only glimpsed him for a second, but she thought she recognised Jay's slim build and the hunched shape of his bomber jacket.

She withdrew. 'Quickly, come inside,' she said. Toby stepped in and she shut the front door behind him. 'I think I saw Jay out there.'

'Really? You sure?'

'There was a shadowy figure, in dark clothes… It couldn't be anyone else.'

'I'll go and check.' He made to turn round, but she grabbed his arm.

'No, don't. I don't want a fight.'

'I'll just have a word…'

'No, please don't. Leave it. Come and have a beer. I've only got one left, but we can share it.'

The next morning, Toby was up early. He went to the corner shop and came back with milk, fresh bread and a packet of bacon. He fried the rashers, dipping the bread slices in the fat before assembling thick, delicious sandwiches. They took them into the garden and ate them standing up, discussing how best to attack the weed-infested flower beds and the lawn that had become a wild-flower meadow. Toby found a scythe in the shed, but it was too blunt and rusty to deal with the grass, so he searched the Yellow Pages and found a place that hired out electric strimmers. Cara gave him the keys to Bertha and he went to collect it while she dug at the hard, dry earth and pulled out all the obvious-looking weeds. They worked hard, only stopping briefly for lunch. The weather was punishingly hot and the back of Cara's neck burnt in the sun.

At the end of the day, they stopped to admire their work. The stepping-stone path had reappeared and one of the flower beds was looking almost normal.

'I'll go over it with the strimmer again tomorrow,' Toby said. 'Then it should be short enough for the lawnmower.'

'It's fantastic, thank you so much. I couldn't have done it without you.'

'No problem.' He stretched out his weary limbs. 'I'm starving. Shall we go for a curry?'

They went to the Indian on Redborne High Street – it wasn't the best curry house in Birmingham, but it was cheap and, most importantly, close by. Cara felt nervous leaving the house unguarded.

'If it *was* him outside last night, he'll know I'm here,' Toby reassured her. 'He won't try anything, I promise.'

'But what about when you leave?' She prodded an onion bhaji with her fork. It had been cooked for too long and the batter was rock hard.

'I think you should leave too,' Toby replied. 'For your own safety.'

'But I've got nowhere to go.' Cara pushed her plate away. 'I've wrecked everything and hurt the person I care most about in the whole world.' Her eyes were smarting with tears.

Toby reached across the table and took her hand. 'Ask her to come back.'

'It's too late. She hates me.'

'No, she doesn't, she loves you.'

'Not any more; she's got a girlfriend now. Apparently it's serious.'

He shook his head. 'No, it's too early to be serious, but I didn't mean in *that* way.' Cara felt herself blush. 'Oh… I see. Are you saying what I think you're saying?'

She nodded and looked down, not wanting to meet his eyes. The realisation had dawned on her gradually, since she'd got rid of Jay and allowed her emotions to breathe freely again. She'd pushed the idea aside at first, telling herself that she was missing Isobel's company, nothing more. But since she'd been in solitary confinement, she'd had time to put her own internal house in order. As she scrubbed and swept, she'd gone back over the past and remembered how happy she'd been with Isobel, how well they'd got on from the very first moment they'd met, how beautifully their personalities complemented each other. She had never doubted Isobel's love and she wanted that joyful sense of security back. As each day passed, she had ached for Isobel more and more, knowing this was too sharp a pain to feel for just a friend. Letting her go had been a colossal mistake.

'You've got to be sure,' Toby said gently. 'If you *do* love her – you know, like properly – you mustn't mess her around. It would be too cruel.'

The waiter intervened then, taking their plates away, and Toby ordered two more Cobras.

'I don't know what I feel exactly,' Cara said, when they were alone again. 'It's really confusing. But I *do* know that Isobel's the most important person in my life. Is that what being in love means?'

'Write to her,' said Toby. 'Put it all down, then she can decide what she wants to do.'

* * *

Cara composed the letter that night, emptying her emotions onto the page and begging for forgiveness. She told Isobel she'd got rid of Jay, but not about the thefts – it would be easier to explain face to face, she decided. Instead, she focused on Jay's anger at being dumped and how frightened she was of him. As she confessed her shortcomings, she began to see the situation through Isobel's eyes. She had been a silly fool and Isobel had been right all along. The tears poured down her cheeks as she wrote that she missed Isobel desperately and longed for the old times. She begged her friend to come back so they could start afresh, on a new, open and honest basis. She finished with a flourish: *I love you with all my heart and will never let you down again.*

A bit melodramatic, she thought, rereading it next morning; the sort of thing Isobel would write, rather than her, but that was probably a good thing. She wouldn't get Isobel back with bland, non-committal statements – it would require guts and blood.

'I've done it,' she told Toby. 'I've just put it in the postbox.' It was early morning but the air was already stiff with heat. He was lying face-down on Isobel's bed in his boxer shorts, smelling of stale alcohol and sleep.

'What? Oh… yeah…' He slowly turned onto his back. 'You didn't hang about then.'

'No.' She smiled at him proudly, waiting for his congratulations.

'Well… that's good… great. Fingers crossed, eh?'

She nodded.

They spent the day in the garden again, clearing more flower beds, mowing the lawn, disentangling the bindweed from the rose arch and piling all the cuttings in a heap by the bottom gate. Toby added some bits of timber he'd found in the shed, and when evening fell they lit the bonfire.

'I've got to go back tonight,' he said, putting his arm around her shoulders as they stared at the flames. 'Will you be okay by yourself?'

'Yes,' she answered. 'I'll be fine.'

He left her to watch the fire burn out. As darkness fell, she felt a deep catharsis. Everything had been cleansed and purified. The house, the garden, but most important of all, herself. She was ready for a new future. All she needed now was Isobel.

Isobel's reply came by return, a few lines scrawled in purple ink on the back of a picture postcard. The image was of a Pre-Raphaelite painting, *The Beloved* by Dante Gabriel Rossetti, and when she saw it, Cara sank onto the hallway floor and cried. Isobel loved this painting – she'd had a poster-sized version of it on the wall above her bed at university.

> *Dearest Cara,*
>
> *I can't tell you how wonderful it was to get your letter, even though your news has really worried me. Change the locks and try to keep calm. Coming to see you on Saturday. We'll work it out, my darling. Promise.*
>
> *Love you always,*
>
> *Isobel xx*

Cara stood the postcard on the mantelpiece and smiled. Just forty-eight hours to wait and then everything would be all right.

CHAPTER THIRTY-THREE

Me

The traffic thickens like gravy as we approach Bristol, cars backing up on the slip roads, their tail lights shimmering in the sloppy darkness. Isobel is leaning right forward, her face scrunched in concentration, breasts touching the steering wheel, trying to get closer to the windscreen, as if this will somehow improve her vision. The rain has reduced to an irritating drizzle; every time a lorry thunders past, it decorates the screen in opaque brown streaks. The wiper blades are squeaking and it feels like they're scraping against my brain. I wipe the thoughts away and for a second my head is clear, but then they come straight back at me. Again I wipe, and again they return. Back and forth we go in rhythm, until all I can see is mud.

Isobel switches on the radio to catch the evening news. What they're calling 'the Archway student killing' has already been demoted to third in the running order. A disembodied female voice announces that the body of a man in his fifties was found this morning hanging from a tree in a south London park. He hasn't yet been formally identified, but it's pretty obvious it's Christopher Jay.

'Thank God. It's over,' says Isobel, turning the radio off.

It's not over for me, though.

Christopher Jay. As far as I know, I only met him once, that day in the pub, but there may have been other times, when I was a baby. *My father.* Not my father in any meaningful sense, but his death still pulls at me, like a child tugging mistakenly at my skirt. How can I feel the loss of someone I never wanted or needed, never knew I even had? I realise now that I was hoping they'd find him alive, imagining – foolishly – that I'd get some answers. That they'd put him in a locked interview room and torture him until he broke and told them what happened to Becca. But then again, I'm so angry with her for cheating on Dad, I hardly care any more.

'We'll have to stop for petrol soon,' says Isobel, her voice breaking out of the darkness.

I turn my head from the window. 'Okay. I'm sure you could do with a break anyway.'

'True. And we can get something to eat.'

We leave Bristol's dotted outskirts behind and enter a dark, featureless landscape that reminds me of a computer game. I hate motorways at night: the cold winking lights, the cars speeding past with invisible drivers, the persistent idea that the world has lost its third dimension and actions have no consequences. Sometimes I get this terrifying urge, even from the passenger seat, to prove my theory. I want to grab the wheel and veer off into black nothingness.

'I pity her,' says Isobel. She signals to pass a lorry and the indicator tick-ticks, beating out the pause as I wait for her to elaborate. 'Alice. I pity her, having to put up with Cara. It's always been a bit of a threesome.'

'When somebody's murdered like that, it must be impossible to forget.'

'I don't want to forget,' Isobel replies sharply. 'That would be a betrayal of the woman I loved.'

'But you love Alice too. And she's the one who's stayed with you all these years.'

'I know… but sometimes I wish I'd never…' She pulls back into the nearside lane and I briefly imagine the car continuing its trajectory, ploughing through the metal barrier and into the undergrowth. 'Don't get me wrong, Alice means the world to me, but she isn't easy, you know? The number of friends I don't see any more because she's fallen out with them…' She tut-tuts, more cross with herself than with Alice, perhaps. 'She absolutely forbade me to take you to Cornwall. Well, for once I stood up to her.'

'Oh… I did wonder.'

'Bad of me, wasn't it?' She nibbles at her lip. 'I've never done that before. She'll go crazy when she gets home and realises we've gone.'

'That makes me feel awful. I don't want to be the cause of a bust-up.'

'She caused it, not you. She was out of order last night, saying all those horrible things about Cara.'

Isobel drives on, eyes fixed manically on the road ahead as if averting her gaze would mean certain death. The rain is falling faster now and she puts the wipers on at double speed. I study her profile: a break in the line of her nose that's not noticeable from the front, her eyes set slightly too far back in the hollow of her skull, the wrinkles around her mouth erased by the darkness. Hard to read somebody's expression if you can only see the side of their face, but I sense she's upset and trying to hide it. Whatever she says, she loves Alice and this is hurting. I face front and concentrate on the fuzzy red tail lights of the car ahead, which are wandering slightly within the lane, as if the driver is tired. Isobel lets out a deep, weary sigh. She's about to tell me something, whether I want to hear it or not. The car has become a confessional box and I'm the priest. *Forgive me, Meredith, for I have sinned.*

'She was such a little mouse when I met her,' she begins, keeping her eyes on the road. 'Cara, I mean. I can see her now on the first day of our course, sitting all prim and proper in the departmental corridor, beige raincoat buttoned up to the chin, hair scraped back into a neat ponytail, and those dowdy brown court shoes. She looked about forty-five, not eighteen – talk about a fish out of water.' She laughs fondly. 'She didn't try to talk to anyone and nobody was bothering to talk to her – I don't think they'd even noticed her. But I saw immediately that there was something special about her. I don't know what it was exactly. An innocence.'

I'm not sure I want to hear any more about Cara. 'Did you see the sign?' I say. 'Services in one mile.'

'We became best friends, inseparable,' Isobel continues, on a roll now. 'I don't think it was physical attraction on my part, not immediately anyway, but there was an instant connection. Cara became my project, far more important than anything I did on the course.' She steals a glance at the expression on my face. 'I know that sounds awful, but it wasn't. She wanted me to help her. She knew she needed to loosen up, throw off all those suburban inhibitions and get away from those awful, repressive parents. She was desperate to find her true self. I persuaded her to move out of university halls and in with me. We were together the whole three years, never had a cross word. I transformed her and she blossomed. I blossomed with her. We were twin souls.'

She takes the next exit, slamming on the brakes as we approach the little roundabout at the end of the slip road and parking in a disabled bay outside the service station entrance. There are very few other cars around and the over-illuminated building looks cold and empty. She turns off the engine and rests her forehead briefly on the steering wheel. The windscreen instantly fills up with large, bulbous water drops, and now that we've stopped, I can hear the rain pounding the sunroof.

'I knew Cara didn't love me in the way I loved her,' she carries on, 'but I was prepared to be patient. That was the main reason I started Purple Blaze, so we could carry on living and working together. I did it all for her. I thought, in time, she'd understand. Then Jay came along. He hated me right from the start, just because I had money and spoke in a posh accent. He tried to turn Cara against me, and like an idiot I fell for it. I completely overreacted. If I'd just kept my cool, it would have fizzled out. But I loved her so much, I couldn't help being jealous. It felt like an attack. A betrayal. After all I'd done for her…'

The rain's slashing at our sides, drumming above us. We could be in a submarine, deep underwater; we could have sunk into another time, another space.

'I should have fought for her, you know,' Isobel continues, 'but I was such a coward – I just ran away. I fled to London and left them to it. In *my* house! The inevitable happened – Cara quickly grew sick of Jay and told him it was over. He wouldn't have it, started threatening her, beating her up. That's when she knew she was in trouble. She sent me this wonderful letter saying she'd realised she was in love with me after all. I was so happy, yet utterly confused. I was really enjoying living in London, and I'd met Alice – we'd only been together a couple of months, but it was incredibly intense. I was sure I'd completely got over Cara, but when I received that letter…' She laughs quietly. 'I couldn't work out what or who I wanted; I thought I was going to go mad. In the end, I decided to go back to Birmingham and talk to Cara face to face. But Alice said that if I went, it would be over between us. So I stayed in London. I should have gone, I could have saved her.'

'You don't know that,' I mumble.

'I do. I let her down. Cara was my best friend and when she really needed me I wasn't there. I betrayed her.'

'I'm sure she wouldn't have seen it that way.'

'No?' She lets out a small gasp. 'Oh, darling, I can't tell you how much it means to hear you say that. Because you know, don't you? You know what Cara felt.'

'No, I don't mean that. I'm just saying—'

She leans across and hugs me so tightly I feel my ribs compressing. 'Everything's going to be all right now,' she whispers, her lips grazing my neck. 'Jay is dead and you've come back to me. My darling, darling Cara…'

A cold wave of dread rushes through me, as I realise this trip is a terrible mistake.

A big dose of normality is what's needed here. I gently steer Isobel into the service station and order two large coffees and two portions of beer-battered cod, chunky chips and mushy peas from the hot food counter. The place is very quiet and there are plenty of empty tables, but she seems to have trouble deciding where to sit. She hovers at my side, following my every movement with adoring eyes. The food and drink seem to revive her a little, but she keeps smiling at me between mouthfuls, the sort of conspiratorial smile that lovers exchange in public places, except I'm not smiling back. I shovel the food into my mouth, even though I'm feeling sick, and try to engage her in chit-chat. How's the production going? I ask. Fine, she says, adding that she's worried she might have cast the wrong actor for Mr Rochester. I tell her I can't remember if I've ever read *Jane Eyre*; maybe when I was a teenager. I ask her to remind me of the plot, and she obliges, all the time gazing at me as if I'm the most precious, most desirable being in the whole world. But at least she doesn't call me Cara again.

She says she needs a cigarette before we drive on, and wanders out, standing under the entrance canopy to avoid the rain. I stay at the table, trying to think of a way to get out of this mess. I can't just do a bunk. I don't know where I am, other than in the middle of nowhere. Even if I could find my way to the nearest railway station, there won't be any trains to London at this time of night. Isobel's not going to let me go without a struggle and I don't want a nasty scene while she's driving – being thrown onto the roadside in the dead of night, miles from anywhere, would be horrible, and potentially dangerous. So I'm stuck with her for now. I'll stay at the cottage with her tonight and then leave in the morning. As long as she doesn't try to seduce me… The thought makes me squirm. It could be so embarrassing, utterly humiliating for her. Perhaps I'll have to lock the door to stop her coming into my room.

She's still standing in the entrance, head tilted back as she blows smoke into the canopy roof. She plays emotionally vulnerable but inside she has nerves of steel. Was this her plan all along? I wonder. Inviting Alice, knowing full well she'd refuse to come, then skipping off without her? Poor Alice, no wonder she's jealous – I'd be the same. Maybe I'm not the first Cara; maybe there have been others: young women with similar looks and shy, impressionable personalities, actresses desperate for work who can't believe their luck when they're chosen by the great Isobel Dalliday. And now she thinks she's got the real deal. Cara reincarnated, finally reunited with her beloved Isobel. And I thought *I* was the one going mad…

The rain raps impatiently at the windows and Isobel pops back into the foyer, waving at me. I rise and zip up my jacket. No time for psychological analysis; let's just get to the cottage in one piece. There's nothing I can do about it tonight, but tomorrow I'll talk to her properly.

'Not far to go now,' she says brightly, unlocking the car door. 'I'll light a fire when we get in; the place will soon warm up.'

'Great,' I say. She pats my thigh and I try not to flinch.

* * *

We left the motorway some time ago, and now Isobel is confi-
dently negotiating the bends as if she drives these lanes every day
of the week. There are hardly any other cars on the road, so she
keeps the lights on full beam. The rain has finally stopped but
the hedgerows are still wet, glistening magically as we snake past.
My stomach is sinking with anxiety. I feel trapped in the car, but
I don't want to get out.

'This is it,' says Isobel ten minutes later, taking an unsign-
posted left turn down a muddy track. She drives on for several
hundred yards as the uneven path narrows and twists. The hedgerows are high and gangly, their branches scraping the car on both
sides. Wild grass is growing down the middle of the track like a
tatty pale ribbon and I think of it brushing the undercarriage as
we drive over it.

'I know you said it was remote, but…'

'Incredible, isn't it? Like Sleeping Beauty's castle – we ought
to trim it back a bit, but we love the privacy. Nobody bothers
us, not even the postman. I collect our mail from the post office
in the village. There isn't even a landline. I can't tell you how
relaxing it is, being able to leave the outside world behind.' She
laughs, pleased with herself. I've never felt less relaxed in my life.

The track finally opens out into a courtyard, and the cottage
– white-painted stone with dark window frames – is suddenly
caught in the headlights, frozen like a startled deer. I get the bags
out of the boot, and as I slam the door the sound echoes like a
gunshot. Isobel turns the engine off and we're plunged into silence
and darkness. We both pause for a few seconds, absorbing it.

She takes out a jangling set of keys, her fingers feeling for the
right one, then unlocks the door, switching on the hallway light.
Nothing happens. 'Bugger,' she says, 'the fuse has tripped again.'

She gropes around for a torch that she claims they keep on the hall table, but it doesn't appear to be there. 'That'll be Alice,' she complains. 'She keeps forgetting to put it back.'

I peer into the gloom. 'Where's the fuse box?'

'In the utility room. The kitchen's ahead and it's just off there, above the washing machine… I'll light some candles,' Isobel calls after me. 'We'll have it cosy in no time.'

I walk blindly down the narrow corridor, arms outstretched in front, wishing I had my torch app and cursing the police for having confiscated my phone. It's completely dark, not a chink of light coming from anywhere. I try not to think about mice. As I enter the kitchen a cold draught hits me. I continue to the utility room and feel for the cold, hard shape of the washing machine, put my hands on the top and heave myself onto it, knocking a plastic bottle of something over as I scramble up. The fuse box is above the shelf, its main switch in the 'off' position. I push it back up and the tiny space is suddenly flooded with light.

'It's okay! I've done it!' I call out, although it's obvious. Isobel doesn't reply. She's flitting about lighting fragrant candles, no doubt. I walk back through the kitchen and into the hallway, turning on the lights as I go. 'Isobel?' The door to what must be the sitting room is open, but it's still dark inside. 'Where are you?' I glance up the stairs. Maybe she's gone to the loo. I shrug to myself and make for the sitting room, feeling for the light switch by the door. I turn it on and walk in.

Isobel is standing there, wild-eyed and trembling, a knife held to her throat. And behind her, his free arm clasped tightly around her waist, is Christopher Jay.

CHAPTER THIRTY-FOUR

Me

'Get down! Lie flat on the floor, hands behind your back, and don't fucking move! If you run, I'll slit her throat.' His eyes bore into my skull. 'You know I mean it.' I fall to my knees and lie face down. 'Hands behind your back, I said.'

'Please don't hurt us,' I plead into the rug.

'No talking!'

Jay drags Isobel to a chair and picks up a length of rope. Pushing her down, he yanks her arms behind her and ties them at the wrists, then does the same with her ankles. She cries out in pain as he pulls the rope tight.

He looks down at me. 'Stay still, or she'll get it.'

I peer out of the corner of my eye, watching him as he goes back to the sofa and picks up more rope, luggage straps, strips of ripped-up towel. He's well prepared. Isobel and I stare at each other across the room. Her eyes are bulging with fear, the whites large like a cartoon character.

'Where's Alice in fucking Wonderland, then? On her way?' Isobel frantically shakes her head. 'Didn't realise I knew the location of your little love-nest, did you? Those property websites are so useful. I must say, it makes a great hideaway. So remote.' He ties my wrists and ankles behind my back, then grabs me under the armpits and yanks me up, pushing me over to another chair. 'I knew you'd come here sooner or later. All I had to do was wait.'

He forces me into the seat and uses the luggage straps to tie me to the frame.

'She's got nothing to do with this. Please let her go!' cries Isobel.

'Shut the fuck up.'

He picks up our bags, shaking them out onto the coffee table. He empties our purses, putting the cash and Isobel's car keys in his pocket.

'No phone?' I shake my head. He removes the SIM from Isobel's mobile and leaves the room. A few seconds later, I hear the downstairs loo flush. Isobel starts to mewl, like a small trapped animal.

So how come the bastard's alive? That's what I want to know. He's supposed to be lying on a slab in the pathologist's lab, having his chest ripped open, the contents of his stomach analysed, his evil brain weighed. He's supposed to be dead. It was on the news, for God's sake. How can the police have got it so wrong? Putting us all off guard. I hate them, almost more than this monster who's biologically my father.

Jay comes back into the room with a black bin liner. He stops and studies me for a few moments. Whatever it was he was going to say, he's decided against it. Fine. I don't want him to talk to me anyway, I can do without the self-justifying explanations. I feel strong, even though I'm tied up and at his mercy. It's Isobel he wants, not me. I'm just an unlucky bystander. *He won't kill you*, I tell myself. *He won't kill you.*

He shakes the bin liner, letting it billow out, and Isobel shudders, as if she thinks Jay's going to chop her into pieces and put her inside. He starts flinging ornaments, candlesticks, pictures, seashells, bits of driftwood, books, board games, cushions – all Isobel and Alice's personal stuff – into the bag. Stripping the room of its character. Why? What's he doing?

I stare hard at him, waiting for our genes to signal to each other, for something deep inside to stop him in his tracks. If I'm really his daughter, there must be some kind of connection there. I once read about an adopted girl who saw a stranger on the beach and instantly knew she was her mother. But when Jay and I met, we felt no connection at all. I still don't feel it, and yet science insists this deeply angry, murderous and possibly insane man *made* me. We come from the same tribe; we are natural allies, not enemies. I drill into his face, searching for a feature that we might share. The shape of our eyes or nostrils or ear lobes, the turn of our chin, our hairline, our skin tone, the thickness of our eyebrows… But there's nothing I recognise. I am all my mother's child.

The bin liner is becoming heavy and bulky; the corner of a metal photo frame is poking through the plastic and it clips Isobel's leg as he walks past. She flinches dramatically and Jay lets out a sarcastic laugh.

'If you think *that* hurts…' he says. Isobel bows her head, defeated.

He's moving the furniture now, rolling up the woollen rug and dragging the dining table into the centre of the room. It screeches across the flagstones, setting my teeth on edge. He draws the heavy velvet curtains. Then he takes a dining chair and places it behind the table, transforming it into a giant desk.

'Right. Time to get started.'

I watch him straighten up, tuck in his shirt, smooth his hair, bend at the knees a couple of times and balance his posture. A sort of limbering-up procedure; he's an actor standing in the wings, preparing to make his entrance onto the stage. Then I realise. I know why he's emptied the room and rearranged the furniture. The dining table isn't a desk, it's a judge's bench. This is a trial, and Isobel's in the dock.

Jay walks into the centre of the room and clears his throat. 'Isobel Dalliday, you are charged with the murder of Cara Jane Travers. How do you plead?'

CHAPTER THIRTY-FIVE

Jay

After all those years of dreaming and planning, the moment has finally arrived and it feels incredible. Waves of power surge through his veins, pumping up his muscles. There can be no stopping him now. He has her under his control and justice *will* be done.

'Please, I'm begging you,' Isobel says. 'Please let us go!'

'Silence!' He lets his voice echo around the makeshift courtroom. 'The defendant must only answer "guilty" or "not guilty".'

'Let's just talk it through like adults. This is rid—' He slaps her hard across the face, stinging his palm, and she cries out. 'Okay, I'm sorry... I'm sorry. Whatever you... you go ahead. I'm sorry.'

'We'll start again,' he hisses, slipping briefly out of character. 'And this time, you'll do as I fucking well tell you.'

He takes a breath, taking himself back in time. He looks around at the denuded room and tries to transpose Court Number One on its features. Remembers the cheap blue suit his mother had bought and given him to wear. The white shirt, straight out of its packet, the crease lines bisecting his chest as a butcher might mark up meat – his body ready to be hung, drawn and quartered. They brought him up the narrow staircase to the dock, where he stood while the charge was read out.

It had taken four months to bring the case to trial, four nightmare months he'd had to spend in Winson Green, on remand.

He'd already resolved to find a way to top himself if they found him guilty – even his brief seemed pretty convinced that they would. 'If you change your plea, the judge will take it into consideration when sentencing,' she'd advised the day before, and when Jay had thumped the table and repeated that he hadn't done it and what use was a defence lawyer if they didn't believe their client, she'd simply shrugged and tidied her papers.

The prosecutor put forward the case and the plot sounded so logical and so convincing that, for a moment, even Jay wondered if he'd killed Cara in a psychotic rage, and buried it deep in his subconscious. Nobody was interested in his opinion, or his theories. To him, Isobel was the obvious suspect, but it was never mentioned that she'd been in love with Cara, a love – crucially – that had been unrequited. Everyone believed Isobel's version of events, when there were no marks or bruises on Cara's body to support it. Even Toby turned against him, said Jay had been lurking around outside the house, that Cara was terrified to go out because she thought he was going to attack her. All fabricated to divert attention from Isobel and put him in the frame.

He glances across at his prisoner – her cheek smarting red from his slap – and takes a few seconds to enjoy her terror. When she took the witness stand all those years ago, she looked calm and poised. Wore purple, of course, with black stockings and a pillbox hat trimmed with a black net veil. 'Forget Cara's parents,' that veil said. '*I*, the one and only Isobel Dalliday, am the chief mourner here.' It was a bold disguise, he thought – hiding in plain sight. She lifted the veil from her face and looked directly at the jury, as if to say, 'Out of everyone here, I'm the one you can trust the most.' Cocky bitch.

She's not looking cocky today. Far from it. She looks scared and defeated, and old. Seeing her like this seems to give him strength, as if all her energy has magically transferred to his body.

He steps back, straightening to his full height again, closing his eyes as he conjures up his costume. He digs his thumbs into the sides of his chest, imagining the sharp edges of a black barrister's gown. Dark suit, white silk cravat, forbidding grey wig. Queen's Counsel for the prosecution. A searing intelligence, a sharp wit. Feared by the guilty, admired by his peers. He looks around, nodding as Isobel's sobs subside and the courtroom falls silent.

He clears his throat. 'Isobel Dalliday, I must ask you once again. How do you plead?'

Isobel hesitates, and Jay, sidestepping for a moment into the role of judge, barks at her, 'The court is waiting, Miss Dalliday.'

'Not… guilty,' she stammers.

Jay raises his eyebrows theatrically. 'I see. So you want a full trial. You want to go through every little detail. That's brave of you, Miss Dalliday. Very brave, considering.'

Becca's daughter (what *is* her name?), who's been staring at him defiantly all this time, starts to struggle in her chair. He walks up to her and lifts a reprimanding finger. Their eyes meet. She looks so much like her mother, it makes the centre of his heart soften. He won't harm the girl, not unless he has to. For Becca's sake. He tugs on his imaginary gown and swings away to face Isobel again.

'Miss Dalliday, you must have thanked your lucky stars the day Christopher Jay was charged,' he says. 'Mr Jay was a sitting duck. The jealous boyfriend who wouldn't take no for an answer, who smoked pot and stole antiques to fund his habit. All you had to do was embroider your evidence, make up a few stories, give him a motive and the character assassination was complete. Did the police help you? Did DC Brian Durley make a few suggestions?'

'No… Jay, please…'

'Yes, I think he probably did. Because they had no concrete evidence against Mr Jay. It was pure supposition.' He moves closer to Isobel, shoving his face in hers. 'Christopher Jay had an alibi – and I mean a proper, honest alibi, not one cooked up with a lesbian lover girl… Ah yes, you're blushing and looking away.' He grabs her by the chin and forces her to meet his gaze. 'But we're getting ahead of ourselves, Miss Dalliday. I want to back-track a little, to the beginning. We must set the story straight.'

He takes a deep, dramatic breath and fills his lungs, as if pre-paring to dive. This is what he should have said in his defence thirty years ago, but his brief advised him against it. 'Miss Dal-liday isn't on trial here,' she'd reminded him, 'you are. Your job is to convince the jury of your innocence, not her guilt.'

'I used Cara,' he says, abandoning the barrister persona. 'I ad-mit that, and it was wrong. She didn't deserve what happened to her. She was a sweet girl, but too bland for me; if I'm honest, she didn't excite me much. I mean, no bloke's going to turn down a bit of sex if it's on offer, but there was never that spark, you know? I got with Cara to spite you. You thought you owned her, like you owned the house, the van, the company, the show…'

'I didn't own her – we were best—'

'Shut up!' He lurches forward and slaps her again, harder this time. 'It's not your turn to speak yet.' He turns away and stands with his back to the women, placing his fingers on his temples. Got to refocus, put himself back into the role. Needs to remem-ber his lines. He's been preparing this speech for years and he doesn't want to miss out a single word.

'Gina – remember her? – she got wise to you straight off; that's why you gave her the sack. Toby knew what you were about too. We all hated you. Me the most, though. All that creative energy pouring forth like an erupting volcano, so bloody tiring. And the fake generosity, pretending you couldn't care less about money when you were actually buying us, to make us dependent on you. It was how you kept control.' Isobel opens her mouth to protest, then decides against it.

Jay carries on, getting into his stride. 'I didn't like Cara much either at first; she was your little sidekick, afraid to express an opinion in case it didn't agree with yours. She did her best to be your clone, but it was never a very convincing performance. If you scraped away at the surface, you saw a different person. Quite dull really. Not my type. But *you* were madly in love with her. And why? Because you made her in your image and you were madly in love with yourself. Your vanity was your weak spot… That was where I could strike.

'Cara was desperate to keep our thing a secret. I pretended I was too, but it was always my plan that you'd find out. I wanted you to catch us at it, but she was scared, refused to have sex in her room with you sleeping right above, so I took her down to the pool. That night, when we had the row, I deliberately shouted so it would wake you up. And… well, you know what happened next.

'I couldn't believe how easily you caved in. You went totally to pieces, packed your bags and left us to it. But it didn't make me happy; it made me angry. There was my mum, living in a grotty council house with mould growing up the walls, and you had so much money you could just take off to London and rent somewhere else. How fucking decadent was that? That house meant nothing to you; you thought you could just come back when you felt like it and it would all still be there. That's why I started selling the antiques, to teach you a lesson. Some of the stuff was really valuable, much more than poor Cara realised. We kept a bit of the cash, but most of it I gave to my mum. Cara was getting in a right old state over it, terrified of what you'd do when you came back. She finished with me and chucked me out. I was okay about it. I'd done what I'd set out to do – done a pretty brilliant job, in fact.'

Isobel is staring into her lap, large tears rolling down her bedraggled face, and Becca's girl is looking from one to the other of them. She knows I'm telling the truth, he thinks. She knows it.

He turns back to Isobel. 'That Saturday afternoon, the day she died, I went round to the house to pick up the last of my stuff and leave the key. Cara was in a different sort of mood. She told me she'd realised she loved you after all; she was expecting you later that evening for a big romantic reunion. She showed me the postcard you'd sent her. Some Pre-Raphaelite picture, remember?' Isobel nods slightly. 'Yet it never turned up in the exhibits. Did DC Durley magic it away, or did you destroy it?' He allows himself a small, gloating smile. 'That's how I worked out it was you, see. So, what happened when you got to Darkwater Terrace? Did you make a pass? Did silly little Cara get cold feet? Maybe you saw all the antiques had gone and hit the roof. I don't know, but there was a fight and you stabbed her. Then you let her run down to the pool and bleed to death.'

He glares at Isobel. Her mouth parts, and when she speaks her voice is soft and wavering.

'Oh, Jay…' she says, sighing. 'Have you lied for so long that you believe this fantasy yourself? You can't rewrite the story and make us magically swap places – you famous and successful, me in prison serving a life sentence. You did a wicked thing and you weren't properly punished. Imagine how that's made me feel all these years. It could have eaten away at me, but I turned it into a positive. Everything I've done, all my successes, has been for her sake. Cara's death has inspired my life.'

'That's bullshit. Fucking bullshit!' His body is tensing with anger, every muscle clenched as tight as his fists. 'Do you have any idea how I've suffered because of you?' he shouts. 'Any idea what it's like when strangers spit on you in the street and old friends refuse to answer your calls? When you're no longer welcome at Christmas, when your mother dies and you pay for the coffin and the sausage rolls at the pub afterwards, and nobody in the family so much as says they're sorry for your loss? I may have been acquitted, but I've served a life sentence!'

He sweeps his gaze around to take in Becca's girl. She's looking at him with pity in her eyes, silent tears pouring down her cheeks. He knows she believes him, just as his mother believed him all those years ago. He didn't plan for her to be here, but it's fitting, in a theatrical kind of way.

He walks slowly back behind the table, trying to get into character, searching for the stern, authoritative voice of the judge.

'Ladies and gentlemen of the jury,' he says to Becca's daughter, 'you've heard the evidence. Is Isobel Dalliday guilty or not guilty? You decide.'

CHAPTER THIRTY-SIX

Me

I look from one to the other. This is absurd. Impossible. He can't make me do this.

'Come on, play the game,' says Jay. 'Imagine you're in Court Number One.' He embraces the room with a sweep of his arm, summoning up the grandeur. 'After weeks of evidence, it's the final day of the trial – the moment we've all been waiting for. Everyone's assembled – barristers, clerks, detectives… Cara's family in the public gallery, clutching each other, perched on the edge of their seats.' He looks upwards, conjuring them forth. Then he swings his head back to Isobel. 'Here's the defendant in the witness box… Just look at her, trembling like a rabbit. Playing the part so well.'

He adjusts his invisible wig and twitches his gown. 'The scene is set. We've waited six hours for the jury to return with the verdict, and now they're back. The atmosphere is electric – the journalists' pencils are poised. Cara's family can hardly breathe. The judge enters and takes her seat. All eyes are on the jury. Everyone's waiting to hear those words – guilty or not guilty. The tension in the room is as tight as a drawn bow.' He takes an excited breath and turns to me. 'This is your big moment.'

The seconds pass. Silence looms over us like a dark cloud. I know what he *wants* me to say, but I can't say it… Because it can't be true. Isobel loved Cara, she's spent her whole life mourning her death. And yet… why would Jay go to these extraordinary lengths if he was guilty himself? Unless he's insane and has blocked it out, his mind warped and twisted with jealousy. Maybe he's been innocent all along and this is his final chance to take revenge on the woman who got away with murder and ruined his life.

One of them is lying to me. But who?

'Come on!' Jay stands in front of me, gripping my shoulders with his stubby fingers. 'Is she guilty or what?'

I'm just an innocent bystander here, in the wrong place at the wrong time. If I pronounce Isobel guilty, I'm handing out a death sentence. Because he *will* kill her – his eyes are staring like a madman, his whole body itching with desire. Nothing I say is going to stop him. But if I insist she's innocent, that puts my life in danger too.

I can't let him kill Isobel. I have to stop him, have to act smarter than I've ever done in my life. Somehow I have to get us both out of here alive. *Think, Meri, think.*

Jay looms over me. 'I'm warning you…'

'Okay, I'll play the game,' I say as steadily as I can, trying to keep my eyes from flickering towards the knife that Jay has left on the sofa.

'Good. That's better,' he says, stepping back.

'Yes, let's make it like it should have been thirty years ago. Isobel Dalliday on trial for the murder of her best friend… You're right, Jay. It's about time justice was done. For Cara's sake, for her family. Because that's what's really important, isn't it? That after all this time, and all this pain, all this suffering, finally everyone's going to know the truth.'

'I don't need a fucking speech,' Jay says. 'Just give your verdict.'

'I know, I'm going to, but I can't do it like this.' I gesture with my head at the straps tying me to the chair. 'That's not how it's done in a real court, is it? The jury can't make a proper decision if they're tied up like a prisoner. I need to be free, I need to be able to stand… Don't you see? If you don't release me, it won't be right, you won't be able to trust what I say.'

Isobel lets out a small cry of hope. *Please don't say anything*, I think. *Don't spoil it.* I keep my gaze fixed on Jay, my heart pounding so strongly I can almost hear it.

'Fair enough,' he says grudgingly, 'but one false move and you'll both get it.' He goes behind me, crouching down and unfastening the luggage straps, then he picks up the knife and saws away at the bonds around my ankles and wrists. I try to keep still, but the urge to break free and attack him is growing stronger by the second. *Got to stay calm, make him believe I'm on his side. Then, when he's off guard…*

He walks back behind the table and stands there imperiously, raising his voice as he addresses the room. 'Will the foreman of the jury please rise and deliver her verdict.'

I bring my sore wrists to my sides, pushing down on the seat as I heave myself slowly to my feet. My knees have turned to jelly; I can hardly support my weight. But I mustn't let him see that I'm scared. I lean the backs of my legs against the chair and lift my head. Slowly I start to open my mouth, still unsure of what's going to come out.

Guilty or not guilty? I don't know what to say.

A rumbling noise pierces the silence. We all hear it, simultaneously catching our breath and looking towards the drawn curtains. The sound is coming from outside, growing louder as it gets closer. Unmistakable now. Tyres on gravel, the slam of a car door. Somebody's here. Somebody's come to save us!

Jay's eyes dart from side to side and our gazes meet for a fraction of a second as we both think the same thought. Who is it? The police? No. It can't be the police; they don't know we're here. Footsteps are approaching. A key's turning in the lock.

'Alice!' gasps Isobel.

'Fuck!' Jay picks up the knife and edges his way to the door of the room, pushing it closed and hiding behind it. 'Don't move!' he hisses at me. 'Nobody say a word!' I hold my breath, my heart beating out of my chest.

Alice's thin heels clip the slate flooring as she walks down the hall. 'Isobel? Where are you? Isobel?' She flings the door open and marches in – then stops. Her bag falls to the floor as she brings her hand to her open mouth, making a statue of surprise.

'Run!' I scream. 'Run!'

But Alice hesitates, and at that moment Jay springs out from behind the door, grabbing her from behind and holding the knife against her throat. She starts to pant, her eyes alight with fear.

'Don't move, or I'll slice you to ribbons.'

'Okay, okay...'

He nods at me. 'You – sit back down. Hands in the air, where I can see them.' He jerks Alice's arm up behind her back until she squeals, pushing her into the centre of the room.

I lower myself gently onto the seat, my mind racing with possibilities. I'm not tied up. Could I leap forward and jump on him from here? There's two of us; we could wrestle him to the floor. But he has a knife. What if we fail? What if he goes mad and attacks us? We could all end up hurt. And Isobel is vulnerable; she can't escape. But we've got to do something, we've got to *try*. Timing is everything. I try to signal to Alice with my eyes, begging for her support, but she's staring at Isobel, her expression a mixture of terror and fury.

'Please, Jay, please don't harm Alice,' says Isobel. 'This has nothing to do with her, it's between you and me. Let her go. Let them both go. We'll sort this out, just the two of us.'

'Shut up! I'm warning you, bitch, one more word out of you and lover girl...' He hisses in Alice's ear. 'You've come just at the right time. Your darling wife's on trial for murder and we're about to hear the verdict.' He flicks his eyes towards me. 'You. Becca's girl. Say it. Now.'

My mouth has gone dry. Even if I knew what to say, nothing would come out of it. I swallow hard, digging with my tongue for saliva. I can't put the moment off any longer. I have to make a decision…

'Guilty,' says Isobel. 'I'm guilty.'

CHAPTER THIRTY-SEVEN

Me

Isobel's voice is strangely strong and calm. Alice and I gasp out loud. Jay swings his head to face her and for a split second loses his balance.

'No, Izzy,' whispers Alice. 'Don't do this.'

Jay tightens his grip again. 'Shut up and let her talk!'

Isobel draws herself up. 'Let Alice go and I'll tell you what happened.' Her voice is growing stronger with every word. 'I'll write it down in a confession and you can show it to the police.'

'She didn't do it,' Alice croaks, as Jay presses the blade on her throat. 'She's lying to save me. Saying what you want to hear. She didn't kill her – she was with me that night.'

'That's not true and she knows it,' says Isobel. 'Alice lied for me. I told her I was worried because I didn't have an alibi, so she told the police we were together, but it wasn't true – we'd had an almighty row; we'd split up. So I went to Birmingham and—'

'Stop it! Stop it, Izzy!' says Alice, writhing in Jay's grasp. 'She's lying, Jay, I know she's lying. Izzy – tell the truth or he's going to kill all of us.'

Jay drags the blade lightly across the surface of Alice's neck, drawing a thin streak of blood. Isobel screws up her eyes. 'Well?' he says. 'Did you or didn't you kill Cara?'

'She didn't, she didn't!' cries Alice, her eyes darting towards me. 'It was that little bitch's mother – Rebecca Banks!'

'Becca? That's a new one.'

'It's true! The police know now that it wasn't you, they told me – I came here to give Isobel the news.'

'*Really?* Is that so? How interesting.' A low chuckle rumbles in his chest. 'Well, well, well, what a shocking twist. To think that after all these years it was dear, sweet Becca. What do you make of that, Isobel?'

'It… it makes s-sense,' she stutters. 'She was sick in the head, violent…'

'Yeah, see what you mean…' Jay jabs a look at me. 'Did you know your mother was a murderer?' I shake my head.

What is he playing at? No way can he possibly believe Becca killed Cara. Alice is mad if she thinks this is going to save Isobel. It's too late. The woman's already confessed.

Jay presses his head against the side of Alice's face. 'So tell us all about it. We're gagging to know how we got it so wrong.'

'Well… um, it was that tape she made – they worked it out from that.'

'Who worked it out? Not Chief Constable Durley, surely; he's too thick. The youngster, was it? DS Myles?' I flinch at the sound of his name.

'Yes, that's right.'

'Doesn't surprise me. He's good, isn't he? Sharp as the blade of my knife.' He presses down again on Alice's neck and she lets out a tiny gasp.

'Don't hurt her, please,' cries Isobel. 'You know the truth, now let her go.'

'But we've only just begun,' says Jay. 'I want to hear all the details. The how, the when, the why. I want the full trial. Surely you want to know too, Isobel? After all, Becca killed the only woman you ever really loved. Isn't that right, Alice?'

'If you say so.'

'Oh, I do say so. Poor Alice, you never could compete, could you? No matter how hard you tried, Isobel still didn't love you as much as she loved Cara. Wouldn't even let you play the leads in her shows. But this is your chance to win her heart! Make her see you're not just a washed-up old has-been and show her just what a terrific little actress you really are.'

Alice winces. 'Just tell me what you want me to do.'

'Play the barrister. Make the case against Becca, and if you convince me that she killed Cara, I'll let Isobel go. How's that for a deal? Then you two can ride off into the sunset and live happily ever after... Go on, the stage is yours.'

Her face fills with panic. 'I can't... I don't...'

'What's the problem? You're supposed to be a fucking actress, aren't you?' Jay barks. 'Act it out! Come on, this is Courtroom Number One. You're Queen's Counsel for the prosecution in your fancy wig and gown. Don't turn it down, love, it's the best part you've had in years.'

'But... I don't know...'

'Do as he says, darling,' says Isobel gently. 'Do it for me. Tell them what Becca did.' Her voice is quivering with hope. But there's no chance Jay will let Isobel escape – not now she's confessed. Can't she see that he's just jerking her around? He wants to torment her, prolong her suffering. Finally Christopher Jay is in charge of the show, and he's going to make the most of it.

Jay tuts. 'If you're not interested, just say.'

'I can't... can't do it with you holding me like this.'

He thinks about it for a second, then releases her and steps back.

'Don't forget, I'm right behind you,' he whispers menacingly. 'Now get on with it. Give us the performance of your life.'

I sneak a look across the room to Alice's bag, lying in the doorway where she dropped it. A small can of hairspray has rolled out onto the floor. Jay's wrapped up in his absurd melodrama; he's forgotten all about me. If I could run forward, grab the can and spray it in his face, then knee him in the balls… It's got to be worth a try. Making sure his eyes are fixed on Alice, I slide myself quietly off my chair and slowly stand up.

Alice clears her throat. 'Yes… well… Rebecca Ba—'

'Not like that!' shouts Jay. 'Start again and do it properly! Ladies and gentlemen of the jury…'

I take a small step forward.

'Sorry, yes, ladies and gentlemen of the jury… Rebecca Banks was having an affair with you– I mean, with Christopher Jay– um, at the same time as he was seeing Cara. Cara Travers. Yes, and Becca was madly jealous because she loved Jay and wanted him all to herself.'

'And? What happened that night? Come on, use your imagination. Act your heart out or I'll slit Isobel's throat and have done with it.'

Another step.

'Okay, okay… yes… It was about ten o'clock on the night of the murder. Rebecca Banks went to 31 Darkwater Terrace and knocked on the door. Cara opened it and her face fell.'

'Go on,' says Jay. 'Let's have some detail.'

And another. Like Grandmother's Footsteps.

'There she was, in her pretty yellow dress covered with roses, her long hair down like a princess. All excited and eager…'

'That's more like it. And what did Becca say?'

I'm getting nearer.

' "I'm a friend of Isobel, we need to talk. Can I come in?" '

'Hang on,' says Jay, holding up his hand. 'Becca wasn't a friend of Isobel's. Are you taking the piss? Get it right!'

Alice swallows. 'Sorry. A friend of *Jay*, I mean. Yes, Cara let this stranger in, even offered her a glass of wine.'

Almost close enough now. Another small step.

Jay prods her in the back with the tip of the knife. 'Enough scene-setting. Cara's standing there in her yellow dress, looking as pretty as a picture – what happened next?'

Suddenly a trigger goes off somewhere deep in the recesses of my brain and I let out a gasp. Jay hears it and turns to me. 'What is it?'

Fuck. 'Nothing... nothing. I was just... listening.'

'What are you doing standing up? Get back! Go on, right back! Sit in your chair and don't move, or I'll tie you up again.' He waves the knife at me and I shuffle all the way back to the starting line, cursing myself.

'This is getting boring,' he says, turning his attention back to Alice. 'Let's get to the climax. Come on, little Miss Actress, show us what you're made of. Who knows, when all this is over, Isobel might even give you a starring role in her next production.'

Alice clears her throat again. 'Well... Cara and Becca started talking about... about Jay, and the conversation soon turned nasty. Cara got upset, hysterical. She said she loved Jay and she refused to give him up. They'd be together forever, she said.' Her voice is shaking with emotion. 'She told Becca to get out. There was a horrible, ugly fight, and before Becca knew it, she had a knife in her hand and... she stabbed Cara in the stomach.'

Jay claps his free hand against his thigh. 'Very entertaining, well done. What do you say, Isobel? Not quite BAFTA material, but better than you thought, eh?' His voice suddenly hardens. 'It's all complete crap, of course. Do you think I'm stupid? No way did Becca kill Cara – your case is full of holes. One: they didn't know each other, never even met. Two: Cara and I were finished and she didn't want anything more to do with me. As for my affair with Becca... I didn't get together with her until after the trial.'

Alice turns around to face him. 'Well, that's what the police told me,' she blusters. 'They've got DNA proof too, they've worked it all out. It gets you off the hook, so if I were you I'd just go along—'

'You're lying to me.'

'I'm not, I promise,' she pleads, 'on Isobel's life! Please, please, you've got to believe me, Isobel didn't kill Cara!'

But Jay's right. Alice *is* lying. The yellow floral dress – I saw it in the scene-of-crime photos at Eliot's flat. Crumpled above her knees, stained darkly with her blood. Only the jury would have been shown those photos. Apart from the police, the only other person who knew what Cara was wearing that night was her killer. Becca didn't kill Cara. She wasn't the stranger at the door, the 'friend of Isobel'. It was—

I catch a sharp intake of breath and my hands shoot up to my face. I know. I know! And I can't hold the truth in any longer. The words shoot out of my mouth and fly across the room like missiles. 'It was you, wasn't it, Alice?'

She swings back to me. 'What?'

'You were supposed to be lying, but you accidentally told the truth.'

'That's ridiculous!' Her eyes dart from side to side and she spins round to Jay, hopping like an animal trapped on all sides. 'She's just covering up for her crazy mother.' She's trying to sound dismissive, but there's a telltale tremor in her voice.

I stand up and take a step closer. 'All these years, the police have been looking in the wrong place, at the wrong relationship. The centre of the love triangle wasn't Cara, it was Isobel. And who loves Isobel more than anyone? You! You went to Birmingham to tell Cara to back off, but she refused. There was a fight, just like you said. You stabbed her and left her to die at Darkwater Pool.'

'I've never even been to Darkwater.' Alice turns again and directs an appealing look towards Isobel.

'Really?' I say. 'You mentioned the other night how creepy it was.'

'Everyone knows that! Don't listen to her, Izzy.'

'What happened next? After you killed her? You didn't panic, did you? Just put the knife in your bag, took the postcard and caught the early train back to London. You even had the nerve to offer to give Isobel an alibi for the night.'

'Stop it, you stupid little bitch! You're going to get us all killed.'

'You see, only the murderer would know what dress Cara was wearing…'

'I made that up – for dramatic effect.'

'But you were right. Cara *was* wearing that dress. You remember the one, don't you, Isobel?'

'Yes,' she whispers, 'it was my favourite. She must have put it on to please me… Oh Alice… Alice… All these years we've been together, sharing our lives, sharing our bed. And all that time it was you – *you* killed my darling Cara…'

'Your darling Cara?' mocks Alice, spitting out the words. 'She never loved you, not like I do. She would have hurt you, she would have broken your heart. I couldn't let her do that. I had to stop her, Izzy. I did it for you, to protect you. I did it for *us*.'

There's a long pause – long enough to rewind thirty years and fast-forward back to the present. And then the universe changes. It happens so quickly, I don't really see it, but suddenly Jay has leapt on Alice, grabbing her from behind and driving the knife down into her stomach, heaving it out again and holding it triumphantly in the air, its blade thick with her blood. He lets her go, staggering back as she falls to her knees, groaning and clutching the hole in her gut. Isobel starts to hyperventilate, screwing up her eyes as if expecting to be next. But

Jay drops the knife, then walks unsteadily into the hallway and out of the front door.

What have I done?

There's blood everywhere. Everywhere. I lurch forward and turn Alice onto her side, pulling her knees up. Her mouth is open in an expression of astonishment and her limbs are twitching.

I rush over to her bag, pick it up by its bottom and tip out the rest of its contents. Mascara tubes, a lipstick, pens, a spiky comb, mirror, purse, car keys spill noisily onto the slate tiles. Picking up her phone, I dial 999, my trembling fingers sweaty on the screen. But there's no signal. Of course there's no fucking signal, this place is too remote. Jesus Christ, why didn't they have a landline installed? I tuck the phone into my jeans pocket.

Alice has gone quiet. Her skin is as pale as paper and her eyes have rolled into the top of her head. The blood, black on the granite floor, is sticky beneath my feet. I bend down and pick up the knife, then go to Isobel and start hacking away at her bonds.

'Listen, Isobel. I need you to drive until you get a signal. Jay took your keys, so take Alice's car. I'm going to stay here and look after her.' I pull off the ropes and remove the strips of towelling from her legs, but she doesn't move. 'Please Isobel, it'll be quicker if you go, I can't drive. If we don't get an ambulance, Alice is going to die.'

'Too late.' Her voice sounds strange and distant.

'No, if you hurry, you can save her.'

'She let Cara bleed to death.'

'Don't think about that now. Listen to me!' I shake her by the shoulders. 'If you're not up to driving, you'd better stay. I'll go on foot. You find some towels and press down on Alice's wound. Keep pressing as hard as you can till the ambulance arrives. Promise me you'll do that? Isobel?' She doesn't respond – just looks straight through me like I'm made of glass. 'Isobel, please don't let her die. I'll be back as soon as I can.'

I step outside the cottage into sudden darkness. It's the middle of the night and the sky is jet black, studded with millions of stars. The rain has stopped and I can hear the endless roar of the sea nearby, underscoring the silence. There are no security lamps and tonight's thin rim of a moon is hardly giving off any light. Does Alice's phone have a torch? I swipe into her apps, finding it and shooting the bar up to maximum. Even then, it's almost impossible to see where I'm going. I inch my way forward, shining a dim path over the gravel, looking for the start of the track we drove down to get here. But it's pitch black and I'm feeling disorientated. There seem to be two paths here, but I don't which one leads back to the road.

'Help!' I shout. 'Ambulance! Police!' My call echoes uselessly through the darkness. If I could just get a signal on the phone… I run around the back of the house, through the wet, uncut grass of what must be a garden, holding the phone up and twisting it around, praying for it to leap into action. As I move further away from the cottage, a single bar appears; it flickers for a brief joyous moment then fades to nothing. But it's hopeful. Maybe I'll get a better signal nearer the sea.

I find a gate at the bottom of the garden and step onto a deeply furrowed farmer's field, uneven and muddy. My torch passes over something green growing in straight lines, and I find the edge, where there's more room to walk. After a few unsteady paces, I stop and hold the phone up to the sky, squinting in the darkness to see the signal. The single bar appears again and my heart leaps with hope, but as I walk on I trip over a jagged stone. I stagger forward, trying to save myself, and the phone flies out of my grasp. I land badly, scraping my elbows and knees. Now I can't see a fucking thing…

I scrabble around blindly, feeling for the handset among the clumps of mud and grass and stones. It's got to be here somewhere! At last I see the glow of the torch and pick it up. I turn it over and swipe in all directions. Is it broken? *Please don't let it be broken.* Suddenly it comes back to life, a web of fractured light sparkling across the smashed screen. I hold it up and squint at the tiny icons along the top. Just one bar of signal again. It's not enough. I've got to keep going forward…

I get to my feet and stumble on. The field gives way to a stony path, dotted with patches of spiky gorse. I hold the phone as high as I can. The night cold is creeping under my skin, the salty wind whipping around my face. Ahead of me is the sea, its deep rumbling voice growing louder and more menacing as I walk towards it.

The bar of signal appears again. Then a second. *Thank God.* With a trembling finger, I start to dial…

CHAPTER THIRTY-EIGHT

Jay

He stands at the edge of the cliff and lets the cold spray lick his face, lets the relentless ocean reverberate in his head. Below, the frothy waves glisten white in the darkness. Above, the black sky twinkles with fairy lights. So this is where it ends, he thinks. In a strange place. On a starry night, miles from home…

There are things that need to be said at a time like this, but there's nobody to say them to. But then so much of his life has been an internal monologue. Words, actions, impulses, decisions – good and bad – line up now to be counted. His biggest regret? Not being satisfied with the acquittal. Holding on to his anger and refusing to let it go. The worst thing he did in his fifty-odd years? Taking the life of young Santianna Makepeace. Nothing else even comes close.

His chest heaves and he blinks back tears. Poor kid… She was a pain in the arse, but she didn't deserve that. Her mother will never understand that when he took out the knife, it wasn't her daughter standing there, mocking him – challenging him to be a man. A red mist had risen, blurring his vision, muddling his senses. He can't remember how the knife got from his pocket and into her chest, can't remember the feeling of stabbing her. How will he plead? Diminished responsibility, perhaps. The best he can hope for is Broadmoor, detained at Her Majesty's pleasure. No thanks. He won't risk it. Then there's the kidnapping, the execution of Alice… He can't face another trial. Better to end it here, purely and simply. Save everyone the bother.

He steps a little closer to the edge and allows himself to blow gently with the wind. At least his mother died before she could witness the complete fuck-up of his life. *Jesus Christ… It could have all turned out so differently.* He probably wouldn't have been as successful as Isobel, but he might have earned a modest living as an actor. It wouldn't have taken much to make Mr Nellis, his old teacher, proud. He might have married and had a family – he would have liked that. But no, he preferred to keep company with all the negative emotions – anger and jealousy and hate – and he allowed them to control him. He knew he was innocent, but that wasn't enough. Not when everyone else thought he was guilty. Not when the real killer was still out there, leading the life he'd dreamed of for himself.

Except Isobel wasn't the real killer after all; it was Alice. She's confessed. Jay draws in a deep breath. He can still barely be-lieve it. All those years of plotting revenge and he was aiming at the wrong target. Maybe that was why nothing he did ever worked. He couldn't touch Isobel because she was innocent too. How Alice must have secretly laughed at the two of them, each convinced that the other had got away with murder. What fools they'd both been – Isobel even more than him, when you think about it. Jay permits a weary smile to cross his face.

He doesn't regret stabbing Alice; he hopes she's dead. For the first time in his life, he acted decisively and spontaneously. Lis-tened to his gut. Prison is far too good for her; no length of sen-tence could compensate for the damage she's caused – to Cara, to him, to Isobel…

But enough of them. He wants his last moments to be posi-tive. He wants to die thinking about the only woman he ever truly loved. When he jumps off the edge, he wants to see Becca's face shining out of the darkness; he wants to feel her full breasts pressing against his chest as he hangs in the air for the briefest of moments, then plummets like a boulder towards the rocks.

Sweet, kind, gentle Becca... She was older than him, a married woman, and he'd felt like a child when he was with her. He'd loved her, as in *really, really* loved her. She'd believed him and believed *in* him. She said that from the first moment she saw him in the defendant's box she knew he was innocent, so when the prosecution barrister gave her a hard time over her story, she stood her ground. And after she'd given evidence, she came back to court every day and sat on her own in the public gallery, despite the death stares from Isobel and Cara's family; sat there sending him constant telepathic messages of support. He'd felt them beaming down on him like rays of sunshine, warming his soul. If it hadn't been for Becca, he would have served twenty years or more. She had saved his life.

Becca sought him out after the trial, said she felt sorry for him – if he needed someone to talk to, she was there. There was a strange wildness in her eyes that attracted him. The second time they met – in a pub on Redborne High Street – she dragged him down an alleyway and lifted her skirt, unzipping his flies and pulling him into her, entwining her legs like snakes around his waist. He hadn't had sex for months and the hit it gave him blew his head off. After that, she rang him several times every day, made feverish, passionate calls from phone boxes in the middle of the night, begging him to meet her. He found her intoxicating. For the first time he felt he was having a relationship with a real woman. She wouldn't allow him into her house and refused to go to his place, so they had to have sex outside in the dark and freezing cold – in the long grass, behind bushes, against a tree. The riskier the location, the more it turned them on, and he spent his days in suspended animation, only feeling alive when they were moving together as one flesh.

In their quieter moments, she told him desperately sad stories about her life – thrown out by her parents, bullied by the other teachers at work, badly treated by her husband, rejected by her friends. She said he was the only person in the world she could trust, that fate had brought them together and they would never be apart. He told her he felt the same. They clung to each other like a mast in a storm. Even at the time, he knew she was a bit crazy, but he didn't care. After his time on remand and the terrifying trial, crazy had become a way of life.

Then suddenly, after just a few months, she ended it. Told him she'd made a terrible mistake; that she didn't love him after all and was going back to her husband. He didn't believe her, begged her to change her mind, but she was resolute. Cruel, even. She wasn't the Becca he knew and loved and he couldn't understand what he'd done wrong. After that, he really had no reason to stay in Birmingham. Went home to his mum's, packed a suitcase and caught the coach to London. He never saw or heard from her again, but in the last thirty years she'd never been far from his thoughts.

'Jay? Is that you?' A female voice comes out of the darkness. It sounds like Becca and, for a moment, he thinks he's hearing her in his head. Then she speaks again. 'Jay?'

He turns around slowly, staring into the nothingness.

'Who's that?'

'Me. Meredith.' She steps closer, her face illuminated by an object she's holding. She looks so much like Becca that if it weren't for her quick, shallow breathing, he could believe he'd conjured Becca's ghost.

'Go away, please,' he says. 'I need to do this alone.' But she doesn't move.

'I had to come out this far to get a signal,' she says. 'Then I saw you and...' She pauses. 'The police are on their way, and an ambulance. But I think it's too late for Alice.'

'Good,' he replies gruffly. There's a longer pause, punctuated by the roaring ocean, the slap of water against rock. 'Now, please go.'

'There's something I want to tell you first,' she says, her voice wavering with emotion. 'It's hard for me to say it, and I don't know if it will change your mind, but...' She hesitates. He can sense her summoning up the courage. Is she going to tell him that she feels sorry for him? That's she's on his side? That she understands his pain and suffering and wants to make it better? Like any of that matters any more.

Clashing sirens ring in the distance. His time is running out. If he doesn't do it now, the police will arrest him and he'll lose his chance. He shuffles his feet forward, balancing on his heels, feeling the air beneath the tips of his toes.

'Alice told the truth about one thing,' Meredith says. 'The police *do* know about your relationship with Becca. They tested my DNA, you see...'

But he can't understand what she's saying. The sirens are getting louder, skewering into his brain. He puts his hands over his ears, shutting out the noise. He has to take control. Act now. Why won't she go away and leave him in peace?

Instead, she steps nearer to him, reaching out – she looks like an angel, bearing a glowing beacon to lead him out of the darkness. But it's too late for redemption. He holds his arms out like wings and leans into the wind.

'Jay, please listen to me...'

As he steps forward, he hears her voice riding the air.

'You're my father.'

CHAPTER THIRTY-NINE

Me

I've been here four days so far. The hospital discharged me with a few cuts and bruises, and after I'd given the police my statement, Dad drove me back to Suffolk. We haven't agreed the length of my stay, but I know he'd like to keep hold of me for a while. He's making a huge fuss of me. It was the same when I was a child. He never moaned when I had a cold and he had to take the day off. He'd cook my favourite meals to encourage me to eat, and he'd read me stories till his throat was hoarse. We've taken to playing Scrabble every afternoon – a grown-up alternative.

So here I am, installed in the spare bedroom, although sometimes it feels as if I'm back in my room in the old house. My dressing table is sitting in the corner, I'm sleeping in the same white metal-framed bed, and he's hung my old curtains at the window. They're too big for this little cottage with its low ceilings, and when I wake up and see the sunlight streaming through the familiar striped fabric, it disorientates me for a few seconds. I'm at home, yet not at home. And it reminds me that I don't really have a proper home any more, not in the sense of having a refuge. A safe place. But strangely, it doesn't bother me.

I can't go back to the house share. It never really worked, and anyway, the media have been sniffing around, trying to get my side of the story. At the moment they think I'm just the 'other hostage victim', but if the news that I'm Jay's biological daughter gets out, I'm in big trouble. Eliot's promised me that won't happen, but you can't always trust the police not to leak information. And if the story *does* break, I need to be here to look after Dad.

I'll have to go back to London eventually, but only to pack up my stuff and move out. Right now, I'm strangely unencumbered by possessions. Surprising what you can manage without when you have to. There's something liberating about it, makes me feel light-headed. All I needed was a change of clothes. Dad went to the big Tesco and bought me some jogging bottoms, a jumper and a pack of white T-shirts, none of which fit properly, but it doesn't matter. I'm not going anywhere at the moment. Just sitting in the conservatory, watching Dad dig the garden. Don't want to speak to my friends or the girls at work. Don't want to go out, not even for a walk. I'm having nightmares, screaming and waking up drenched in sweat, which I guess was predictable. I can't help feeling that it was my fault – telling Jay that Alice was the killer; but another part of me feels she deserved to die. It's all very confusing. The doctor signed me off for a month and says I'm going to need counselling to help me get through the next few months.

I sit in the armchair by the window and count the toll on my fingers. Jay's dead. Alice is dead. Isobel has had a full-scale nervous breakdown and has booked herself into the Priory. Eliot has solved his first murder case and Durley's got his retirement present. So everything else is tying itself into a big, satisfying bow. I'm the only one with loose ends. The one with the secret.

Downstairs, Dad is making lunch. Radio Five Live is on – he likes it for the sport. It's a happy, comforting, normal sound. Clinking pots, the boiling kettle, radio commentary interspersed with well-worn jingles… Do I really want to disrupt all that with a piece of information that seems increasingly irrelevant? He is my father in every meaningful definition of the word. Any other label is purely biological and I've never been keen on science. Give me uncertainty any time. Give me speculation, intuition, gut instinct, wild leaps of the imagination. Give me human error.

Maybe Dad already knows my true parentage. It's certainly possible. And it makes him even more of a hero if he does, because he knowingly brought up another man's child. My dear old dad, with his paunch, his balding head, his glasses, his heart disease... Does he need his heroism recognised? I don't think so. Let virtue be its own reward. And what if he *doesn't* know who I am biologically? The news could devastate him. No, I'm not going to take that risk. Because it doesn't matter. It really, truly doesn't matter. He may not be my father, but he'll always be my dad.

And with that decision firmly made – at least for the time being – I come downstairs. I sit down and he puts a plate of baked beans and cheese on toast in front of me – the cheese has been generously applied and gooey chunks of it are melting deliciously into the tomato sauce. One of my favourite snacks when I was little, and it touches me that he still remembers.

'I've been doing a bit of research,' he says, sitting down and starting to eat. 'Train times and fares and all that.' I look up him curiously. 'I know you're not fit enough to go back to work at the moment, but when you do... Well, I reckon you could commute from here. It's expensive, I know, but I wouldn't take any money off you for your keep. All in all, it would even out.'

'You mean, live here permanently?'

'Yes. At least till you've got your confidence back.'

My response is immediate. 'That's a really generous offer, Dad, and you know I've enjoyed spending time with you, but...' His face immediately falls as I pause, embarrassed, not knowing how to end my sentence. It's true that I don't want to go back to the house share, but the thought of retreating to sleepy Suffolk and spending several hours a day sitting on a crowded commuter train to do a job I don't even care about feels like an admission of defeat. If nothing else, this experience has made me realise that I can do better than that. I can take control. And then a thought forms and the words flow into my head, and suddenly I know exactly what I want to do. I lean across the table and take his hand.

'Actually, I've been thinking about making some changes. Big changes. I'd like to take some time out, do some travelling, you know, "discover myself"… I never did that. I was going to go to Australia, remember, and then I met Eliot…'

Dad frowns at the mention of his name. 'You're nearly thirty, Meri. It's time you grew up and settled down.'

I lower my eyes. Maybe I won't grow up, I think, until you stop being so protective. *Maybe I won't grow up until I find out what happened to my mother.* I don't know how to explain it to him, but I feel as if I'm tied to an endlessly long cord. I keep thinking of Becca in the far distance, patiently holding on to the other end; waiting for me to tug her back into the light.

'I'm sorry, Dad, but I don't think I'll ever feel settled until I know what happened to Becca… There's this gap, this emptiness… I can't describe it any other way. Whether she's alive or dead, I just need to know.'

'Okay,' he says, his tone suddenly decisive. 'Okay.' He pushes back his chair and stands up. 'Just promise you won't be angry with me.'

'Sorry? Angry for what?'

'Promise! I was trying to do what was best for you. That's all I've ever tried to do. My best. So you have to promise.'

'Yes, yes,' I say, not at all sure that I mean it. What the hell is he on about? I follow him up the stairs, watching as he hooks a pole onto the handle of the loft hatch. The door opens and a wooden ladder swings down.

'Steady it for me,' he orders. I rest my foot on the bottom rung as he climbs into the black void. My heart is starting to race, and I think back to all those months ago, when I sat in the attic sorting through my baby clothes. What other secrets lay hidden there? What important treasures did I miss?

A few moments later Dad emerges, a small shoebox wedged beneath his arm. He climbs down and hands it to me. We go back downstairs and sit in the lounge, side by side on the sofa. I untie the string and remove the lid. Inside are photos. They are old-fashioned-looking, small and square with glossy surfaces. Some of them feature Becca on her own, some are with Dad, some are of the two of us, and a few are threesomes – Mummy, Daddy and Meri. Holiday shots, mostly, taken on beaches, on a boat out at sea, on a pier. One shows me and Becca huddled together, smiling and shivering, on a picnic rug. Behind us are tall yellow sandstone cliffs. I turn the photograph over and it says *West Bay, July 1989*. As if I needed confirmation.

'I'm not angry,' I whisper. 'I understand.'

'Wait. There's something else,' he says anxiously. 'At the bottom. Underneath the photos.'

I delve down and take out an envelope; it's addressed to me in the same generous, looped handwriting that's on the video-tape. Inside is a birthday card. On the cover is a drawing of two jolly rabbits, one sitting on a stool playing a guitar, the other, a lady rabbit, dressed in a flamenco dress and fluttering a fan. *Feliz Cumpleaños* it says in dancing pink letters. My hands start to shake as I open it and read the message. *Happy birthday to my beautiful little Meri. I'm sorry I can't be with you on your special day, but I'm thinking of you now and always. I love you. Mummy xxx*

I gulp down a tear. 'When did she send this?'

'The first year after she left.'

'Is it the only one?'

'I don't know. There could well have been more, but we moved, remember? She didn't put her address anywhere so I couldn't get in touch.' His expression is pained, as if flinching from some invisible strike.

Angry words form in my head. Couldn't you have tried to track her down? She must have had friends. Somebody she kept in touch with. When my birthday came round, couldn't you have checked with the owners of the old house and asked them to forward any mail? But I don't say any of those things, because I made a promise.

'I'm sorry,' he says, cutting into my silence. 'I thought hearing from her would upset you. We were doing so well without her, I didn't want to rock the boat. And then the years went by and... I thought it best not to mention it.' He attempts a small forgive-me smile. 'At least I kept it, eh?'

I look back at the envelope. The postmark is smudged and faded, but I can just about make out the word *Sevilla*.

'It was a very long time ago,' Dad says. 'There's no guarantee she's still in Spain. Or whether she stayed well. You mustn't get your hopes up.'

'I know...' I hold the birthday card to my chest, cradling it like a beloved doll. 'But if I'm going to go travelling, it's as good a place as any to start.'

EPILOGUE

Becca

The water from the tap runs clear and Becca holds her fingers under the stream for a few moments, enjoying the cold on her skin. Leaning against the sink, she stares at the view through the small window – a rectangle like an oil painting. The forest, the mountains, the sun rising in the lavender-coloured sky. They've been living here for twelve years and it still takes her breath away. All this space, and just for them.

She likes to get up early and wander around the house, feeling the surfaces – cool stone walls, rough wooden furniture, the whiskery woven rug… She likes to stand on the front step and gaze at the still, dusty street, breathing in the village while everyone else is still in bed. She can't hear a single unnatural sound. There are no shop shutters being raised, no trucks delivering crates of beer to the bars; no shops or bars at all. And the narrow single track leading from the road up to the village has fallen into such disrepair that you can't get so much as a moped up it. That's what she likes most of all. The isolation. The timelessness. It's worth the sacrifices.

She pulls on a jumper and slips her feet into her flip-flops, walking up the narrow cobbled street to the small square, with the dry fountain in the centre and the empty horse troughs. She sits on the cool stone and leans back, lifting her face to the sun. Yes, twelve years they've been here now, she and Luis, living *la vida*, the life, some would say, although people have no idea how tough it is up here. Before that they were in Seville. Luis was a struggling artist and she taught English as a foreign language to people heading off to the country she'd escaped from.

They'd heard about the abandoned villages in the Sierra, small communities of people trying to live in a different way. They'd wanted to take themselves out of the system. Becca smiles to herself. Now they couldn't get back into it if they tried. But it's worked out well enough. They survive. Just. Feeding themselves from vegetables they grow on a patch of land behind the deconsecrated church. Luis does casual labouring when he can get it – general repairs, a bit of plumbing, painting and decorating.

It feels about eight o'clock. She goes back to the house and wakes Luis. He's got a small job in Aracena today and he's got to catch a bus from the main road, which is a good forty minutes' walk away, all uphill. She's agreed to go with him, otherwise he worries that she doesn't leave the village often enough. He thinks it's bad for her spirits. She still has her low days, when she struggles to get out of bed, but meditation helps to keep the dark memories at bay and she's no longer on the brain-numbing medication. She doesn't drink alcohol or smoke weed; she takes long walks in the mountains and follows a vegan diet. Most importantly, she's in a loving, supportive relationship. If she didn't have Luis, it would be a lot harder to keep away from the edge. She knows she's one of the lucky ones…

The bus drops them off just before the Plaza Alta and Becca kisses Luis goodbye, wishing him a nice day at the office – their little joke. She passes a newsagent's kiosk. There are a few English papers on the stand, some as much as a couple of weeks old. She doesn't usually bother even to look at the headlines, but today she feels strangely drawn and chooses the *Mirror*, lifting it gently from its stand and unfolding it to look at the front page. The headline declares that there has been a 'Day of Reckoning'. There's a fuzzy mug shot of an older man, staring with dead eyes. Somehow he looks familiar. She skims through the first paragraph – Darkwater, Cara Travers, Christopher Jay… *Hostia*, she swears under her breath. That's who it is.

She turns to the double-page spread inside – more photos, more text. Her knees start to dissolve and the newspaper shakes violently in her hands. The *kioskero* asks if she's okay, but she can't speak. A small photo of a smiling young woman stares out at her. She doesn't understand; this is a picture of *her*, isn't it? Taken years ago. But no, it's not her, just someone who looks almost identical. But how can this be? Nothing's making sense and the paper is shaking so much she can't read the words. Just one leaps off the page, as if illuminated: Meredith. The past rears up and knocks her over.

She told the truth at the trial, as far as she understood it. Cara had definitely spoken to her; she was sure she hadn't imagined it. But years later, when the voices started – confusing her thoughts, telling her lies – she began to wonder. Had Cara's voice been in her head? There had been signs at the time that she was losing her hold on reality, but she'd been afraid to admit it.

That summer, her behaviour had become secretive and weird. She'd become obsessed with Darkwater Pool, couldn't keep away from the place. She felt as if someone, something was pulling her there and she couldn't stop it. She'd had night terrors for years and was frightened of sleeping; kept leaving her bed and ending up at Darkwater, not knowing how she'd got there. Sometimes she forgot to dress and went in her pyjamas. She'd stare for hours at the deep, murky water, returning to the house at dawn, her arms covered in bramble scratches, her feet black with dirt. Graeme found out what she was doing and thought she was suicidal. He tried to keep her locked in at night, but she always found a way to escape.

She never told him about the couple, though. She would creep up and hide behind the trees, holding her breath as she watched them humping and grunting and tearing at each other's hair. At the time, she had no idea it was Cara and Jay. They didn't seem like humans. Or even wild animals. They were unearthly beings – water sprites, wood demons, creatures of the night. Darkwater Pool belonged to them and she was an intruder, but she couldn't stop watching them, couldn't stop going to see if they were there. They haunted her imagination, day and night. She heard their moans and cries behind every door, smelt their sweaty passion on her hands. Their dark, shadowy forms lurked in the corners of her vision, beckoning her to join them.

That night in August, the night of the murder, her urge to go to Darkwater was stronger than it had ever been. She couldn't bear to be locked indoors in the suffocating heat, and even contemplated jumping out of the window. Graeme had woken up and caught her rummaging in the bedside cabinet for the deadlock keys to the front door. He lost his temper, told her she was a danger to herself and that he couldn't deal with her any more. She ran out of the house and through the streets, her desire deepening with every step. She wanted to lose herself in the pool's sinister darkness, wanted to disappear into its shadows. She shudders now as she remembers taking the narrow, overgrown path, creeping as quietly as she could until she got to the boathouse. She had been expecting – hoping – to see the couple fucking, but when she got there, it was just the girl. Lying on the ground in a pool of her own blood.

The memory of finding Cara wouldn't leave her; it seemed to intensify rather than fade, complicating itself with new details that emerged gradually, like a film coming into focus. As the months passed, she kept finding herself back at Darkwater Pool – standing in that very spot in the middle of the night, reliving the moment over and over again until she collapsed, exhausted and sobbing, to the ground. It was a kind of emotional self-harm and she felt compelled to keep doing it. By the time it came to the trial, the memory was at its darkest, an elaborate patchwork of fact and fiction. She couldn't separate the good pieces from the bad, so she gave it to the court whole, in its most recent incarnation. She doesn't know to this day whether Cara was still alive and spoke to her. But at the moment she took the witness stand, that was the only version of the story she knew.

Did Graeme secretly believe she'd killed Cara? He certainly had his doubts. He didn't tell the police about her nightly wanderings or her obsession with Darkwater Pool. He said they'd had a row about something domestic and she'd stormed out – he covered for her, just in case. After the murder, things changed between them. Graeme seemed wary of her. Sometimes he'd gaze at her for ages and she'd see the wondering in his eyes. He no longer really trusted her. It made her angry and she wanted to make him pay.

The affair with Jay was an accident waiting to happen. They were two damaged human beings in need of love, and she felt propelled towards him by powerful, unknown forces. The sexual chemistry between them was so strong, it transformed her into a woman she couldn't recognise. Now *she* was the night creature rutting with Jay in the dark. It was a crazy, wicked, dangerous, wild, strangely beautiful time. But when she found out she was pregnant, reality hit home. She felt dirty and stupid and ashamed and ended the affair immediately.

Graeme was besotted with Meri – so gentle and endlessly patient. When Becca gave up breastfeeding, he took over the night feeds with a bottle, even though he was the one with the day job. She'd lie in bed, half asleep, listening to him as he paced the bedroom with the child in his arms. 'Who's Daddy's little girl? Best in all the world,' he'd sing to a soft, made-up tune. It wasn't hard for Meri to believe that Daddy loved her more – bathing her every evening, making up funny stories, deftly combing out the knots in her hair. Becca was too ill to compete. 'First you have to learn to love yourself' – that was what the psychotherapist told her, putting the child in a hopeless, endless queue. But she *did* love Meri. She has always loved her – in a deep, sad, silent way.

They struggled on for a few years. Meri was a toddler now, but the postnatal depression hadn't gone away and the Prozac just made her feel tired. She'd never been free of the murder memories, but now they attacked her with a new viciousness. Images of Cara dominated her night terrors, which were so violent and frightening she couldn't bear to close her eyes. She started going to the pool again in the middle of the night, searching for wood demons. She refused to eat anything but fruit because she thought Graeme was poisoning her. Sometimes when she looked in the mirror, she only saw half her face.

Then the voices started telling her she wasn't Meri's real mother. And Meri wasn't Meri, she was Cara. A dead woman come back to life. It was all so confusing. She tried to talk to Meri about it, but the little girl didn't understand – she said things to please her, then got upset and said they weren't true. Becca didn't know who was really who; everyone seemed to be tormenting her. The voices kept on and on, shouting in her head day and night. *Cara wants Meri to tell the truth*, they said. They wouldn't stop until she told the police. One voice frightened her the most.

She called him the bad man, but she knew he was the Devil. He made her fill little Meri's mind with violence, forcing her to act out her own death. He made her make that tape.

The doctor gave her yet more drugs, but nothing worked and her life was spinning out of control. Everyone seemed to agree that she was a danger both to herself and her daughter. She decided they were right, so one night she went to Darkwater Pool. In her confused and shattered mind it was where the trouble had started and where it had to end. She couldn't fight the pool any more; she would let it claim her. She sat down beside the old boathouse, in the spot where Cara had died, and took forty-eight paracetamol tablets washed down with a party-sized bottle of Coke. By the time she'd managed to swallow them all, a pale dawn was breaking over the water. When Graeme woke up next to an empty pillow, he knew where to find her. It was *his* turn to find the body, *his* turn to run to the phone box and dial 999. But this time, it was not too late.

She's back there now, in the hospital, sitting on her bed in that little orange cubicle, waiting for Graeme and Meri to arrive. She can see it all so clearly: the large, lifeless room devoid of ornament, stinking of pine disinfectant and overcooked food. She can hear the click of knitting needles, their constant rhythm drilling into her brain. Her guard is sitting on a low stool at the end of the bed. Becca wants to grab the wool and tie it into a noose. For her own neck, not the knitter's, although that wouldn't be such a bad idea either. There's nothing else to kill herself with here; they won't even let you have a proper knife and fork.

Graeme carries Meri into the ward and Becca tries to raise her arm in a vague wave. He spots her then and comes over, lowering himself onto a brown plastic chair and resting Meri on his lap. He doesn't so much as give her a peck on the cheek to say hello.

Meri is staring at the knitter, fascinated by the quick click of her needles, the twitching ball of fluffy white wool, like the tail of a rabbit. 'Meri,' Becca says, patting the bed. 'Come and sit next to me.' But the child behaves as if she hasn't heard, doesn't even look at her mother, just carries on staring at the other woman, her little blonde head nodding in rhythm. *Click-click-click-click*.

'Come and sit with Mummy,' Becca tries again, but Meri turns away from her, burying her face in her father's shirt.

'She doesn't want to,' he says. 'She's scared of you.'

'I don't see why.'

Graeme starts whispering something in Meri's ear. Secrets he doesn't want his wife to hear. Meri nods and puts her arms around his neck.

'We're leaving. We won't come again,' he says. 'It doesn't do any of us any good.'

'No. You're probably right.'

'She was doing fine until today. Hadn't even asked about you.'

Becca finds that hard to believe. How long has she been in here? She's lost track of time. A week, perhaps. Maybe two.

Graeme leans forward. 'I'm sorry, Becca,' he whispers, 'but we can't go on like this. Meredith needs stability, she needs parents she can rely on, who'll look after her, be role models. She can't come home every day from school not knowing whether she's going to find her mother dead or alive. You can't do that to her, I won't let you.' He draws Meri into him, holding her even more tightly.

'Yes, I understand,' Becca says, the tears welling up behind her eyes.

'I'm not sure you *do* understand. You're nowhere near ready to leave yet, but you need to know that when that time comes...' He takes a deep breath. 'I'm sorry, but you can't come home to us.'

'But… but I need to be there for Meri. She's my daughter.'

'My daughter too.'

'No, she's not.' The words just fall out of her mouth, before she's had a second to think. The big secret she's been holding inside her, like a wild, wriggling thing, has finally broken free. He looks at her, uncomprehending. 'I had an affair,' she says. 'I'm almost certain the child is his.'

He puts his hands over Meri's ears. 'Stop it, stop it. This is what I mean, this is the damage you do.'

'I'm not making it up. When I told you I was pregnant, you were really surprised, remember? Because we hardly ever had sex.' A glimmer of anxiety crosses his face. 'Meri's father is Christopher Jay.'

'What? That's impossible.'

'We got together after the trial.'

He shakes his head. 'That's the most preposterous thing I've ever heard in my life.' He takes Meri by the waist and plants her on her feet. 'Come along, love, time to go.'

But Becca hasn't finished yet. The wild, wriggling secret has been released and is running around the room; she's powerless to stop it. 'He needed someone to turn to and I needed someone too. It was…' she searches for the right word, 'good. For a while. Exciting. But I wasn't really in love with him.' She pauses. 'He doesn't know, by the way.'

'You're lying,' Graeme says, hurriedly putting on Meri's jacket, pushing his fingers into the ends of the sleeves to pull out her hands. 'I know you can't help it – it's the illness, the voices, the fantasies – I understand.' He looks up, his eyes full of tears. 'I'm sorry, Becca. I tried. I really tried…'

'Believe what you like, but it's true.'

'You think I wouldn't know my own flesh and blood?' Graeme picks her daughter up and carries her out of the ward. The last glimpse Becca has is of Meri's blonde hair draped over his shoulder, her spindly legs wrapped round his waist.

They don't visit again. The doctors try yet another drug and this one seems to work. Over the next few months, the voices fade and the nightmare visions subside. Her therapist teaches her strategies for dealing with the memories of Darkwater, and most of the time she succeeds in keeping them at bay. When she looks in the mirror, she sees a whole human being she almost recognises. She puts on half a stone, goes to yoga sessions, does a pottery class and makes an ashtray, even though she doesn't smoke. There are real signs of improvement and the doctors are delighted, especially because she's achieved it on her own, without any help.

The first time she's allowed a day pass, she takes the bus home. She hasn't told Graeme she's coming and she's hoping he'll be out, because she wants it to be a surprise. Saturday is usually supermarket day and there's no reason why he'll have changed the routine. Becca can't wait to see the look on his face when he realises how much she's changed.

She finds the key under the flowerpot, letting herself in quietly. But she feels disorientated. This isn't how she remembers it. The big armchair has been swapped with the sofa so it's nearer the television, and the dining table has been shoved against the wall. She walks into the kitchen. The surfaces are bare, everything tidied away in the cupboards, not how she arranges things at all. This feels wrong. It's as if they've moved without her knowing and a different family lives here now. But she makes herself a mug of tea all the same and goes back into the lounge, standing by the window and looking out at the garden. There's a small child's swing in the centre of the lawn. That's new, isn't it? She stares at it, puzzled. She doesn't think it was there before, but maybe it was. Meri had been asking for a swing, she remembers that, but Graeme had said she'd have to wait for her birthday. Unless Meri's birthday has been and gone. What month is it, then? Becca starts to cry. Tears drip into her mug – she tries a sip, but the tea is undrinkable.

When she woke up this morning, she thought she was just going out for the day, but now she knows she doesn't want to go back. She has to do something different, go somewhere new. Start again. She rinses out the mug and leaves it on the drainer. It's important that he knows she's been here today.

She goes upstairs to the bedroom, unsurprised to find no trace of her there either – the stack of books next to her side of the bed, her jewellery box and make-up bag on the dressing table, they've all been tidied away. She crosses the room and opens her wardrobe. At least her blouses and dresses are still hanging there, and her underwear is still stuffed higgledy-piggledy in the drawers. She drags a suitcase out from under the bed and starts filling it with clothes. She needs to work quickly now, before Graeme returns from the supermarket. If he finds her here there'll be another horrible scene and he'll take her back to the hospital. Must get away as far away as possible – another country, it almost doesn't matter where.

Her passport is stored under P for personal in Graeme's concertina file of documents – mortgage statements, electricity bills, receipts and instruction booklets. She pauses briefly to look at Meri's birth certificate. *FATHER: Name and surname – Graeme John Banks.* Tears prick at her eyes. What chance would she have of getting custody? Zero. One day, she thinks, when I'm well again, I'll return to England and fight him in the courts. Even if I could kidnap her and take her with me, it would be the wrong thing to do. Got to get myself well first, then I'll get back in touch. The thought of being without her daughter makes her heart swell and crack, but she knows there's no other choice. Meri's better off with Graeme for now, but one day. One day...

A chequebook won't be of any use abroad, she realises; what she needs is some cash. Graeme keeps a wad for emergencies in a secret compartment at the back of his desk – it's an antique reproduction with a dark green leather top, edged in gilt. The key is in an old margarine tub in the top drawer, hiding among stubby pencils, erasers, drawing pins and paper clips. She pulls the desk away from the wall and unlocks the little box. There's over two hundred quid there, but that won't be enough. She goes back to the concertina file and finds her building society passbook. Just under six hundred pounds; that should do it. The local Halifax is open on Saturday morning; if she hurries, she should just get there in time.

She leaves the concertina file out and doesn't push the desk back against the wall. She wants to leave clues behind that show she was in control and thinking clearly. Suicidal people don't pack suitcases and withdraw their savings. They don't take their passports and they certainly don't wash up their dirty mugs. More eloquent than a note, she decides. And anyway, there's not enough time to write down everything she wants to say, even if she could find the right words.

She puts the passbook in her handbag and wheels the suitcase to the front door, pausing for a second to look back at the place that once felt like home.

It's a short bus ride to New Street station in the city centre, and then a train to Birmingham airport. Strangers rush back and forth, not noticing her. There are millions of people in the world, she thinks, and I'm just one of them. There's no reason that I can't start again and make it work this time.

She stares at the departures board. Paris. Stockholm. Munich. Vienna. None of the destinations seem real. It's a game, she tells herself: buy a ticket for the first available plane, no matter where it's going…

It's going to Madrid.

Becca opens her eyes as she's lifted off the pavement. The *kioskero* takes her to the bar opposite and orders a large brandy and a glass of water, talking to her rapidly in his local accent: '*Qué te pasa, señora? Qué te pasa?*' But she can't tell him what's just happened, because she doesn't know. The past and the present are weaving in and out of each other, knotting up her brain, and she's lost all sense of time and place. The *kioskero* picks up the newspaper and tries to puzzle things out from the photos, but it makes about as much sense to him as it does to her. He puts it back on the table. She thanks him for his kindness and he says, '*De nada,*' and goes back to his stall.

Becca sits there for several minutes, taking a sip of brandy followed by a sip of water until her heart rate starts to slow. The newspaper headline stares out at her. Whose day of reckoning was it? she wonders. She spreads the pages out, takes a deep breath and starts to read.

AUTHOR LETTER

Well, I guess this means you made it to the end! Thank you so much for reading *Lie to Me*; I hope you were caught up in the story and enjoyed exploring its themes and characters.

For me, the whole point of writing is to engage with readers. In the past, writers never knew what their readers really thought, but now we can communicate directly, which is great news. I'd love to know what you enjoyed most about the book, which characters particularly appealed to you, and how gripping you found the plot. So if you can manage to find the time to post a short, constructive review, that would be fantastic. Thank you.

Lie to Me is my first foray into the world of crime fiction. It's been a very exciting and interesting journey and I've learnt masses from the experience, which I'm now putting into my next book. It's a twisting psychological thriller, and hopefully you'll want to read that too.

You can easily get in touch with me on my Facebook or Goodreads page, via Twitter or through my website. I'm always happy to hear from thriller fans, as well as other writers working in my genre. If you'd like to keep up to date with my latest releases, just sign up at the link below. Your email address will never be shared and you can unsubscribe at any time.

www.bookouture.com/jess-ryder/

Thanks again for reading *Lie to Me* – it really does makes all the hard work worthwhile. I look forward to hearing from you!

Jess Ryder

@ JessRyderauthor

jessryder.co.uk

@JessRyderAuthor

ACKNOWLEDGMENTS

Special thanks to the following:

Andy Trotter and Jayme Johnson, who gamely answered all my questions about detective work. Any errors are entirely of my own making.

My fantastic family, in particular my mother Brenda Page, who assisted with the research, and my son Harry, who has a keen eye for storytelling and helped with some 'translation'.

My discerning thriller-reading friends Wendy Cartwright, Mary Cutler, Karen Drury, Fiona Eldridge and Christine Glover. Your comments were always valuable.

Very importantly, to my dynamic and perceptive literary agent, Rowan Lawton at Furniss Lawton; my rigorous and insightful editor Jessie Botterill, and of course, Lydia Vassar-Smith, who first commissioned the book.

And finally, to my husband, David. You know why.